SOUTH SEA ADVENTURE

The giant squid, trapped in the blazing heat, began to thrash about violently. Its tentacles flailed the rocks and their sharp teeth made deep scratches in the coral.

Suddenly with a mighty heave it lurched forward six feet and at the same time flung out one of its long tentacles. Roger fled to safety. Hal, trying to escape, stumbled and fell.

At once the great arm slipped around his waist. It tightened upon him. He could feel the teeth biting into him through his palm-cloth shirt.

VOLCANO ADVENTURE

The darkness was turning from black to grey. Day was coming. Presently there was enough light to see by and they could turn off their torches.

And what a dreary waste they saw! Great black blocks of lava, streams of ashes, not a tree, not a bush, not a blade of grass. The moon itself could not be any more bare and bald. This was a place where nothing dared to grow and it seemed as if man himself had no right to be here.

SOUTH SEA & VOLCANO
ADVENTURES

Willard Price

**Illustrated from drawings by
Pat Marriott**

RED FOX

SOUTH SEA & VOLCANO ADVENTURES
A RED FOX BOOK ISBN: 978 0 099 48774 6

Published in Great Britain by Red Fox,
an imprint of Random House Children's Publishers UK

South Sea Adventure first published in Great Britain by Jonathan Cape Ltd, 1952
First Red Fox edition 1993
Copyright © Willard Price, 1952

Volcano Adventure first published in Great Britain by Jonathan Cape Ltd, 1956
First Red Fox edition 1993
Copyright © Willard Price, 1956

This Red Fox edition 2005

11

Red Fox Books are published by Random House Children's Publishers UK
61–63 Uxbridge Road, London W5 5SA,
a division of The Random House Group Ltd,
Addresses for companies within The Random House Group Limited can be found at:
www.randomhouse.co.uk/offices.htm

THE RANDOM HOUSE GROUP Limited Reg. No. 954009
www.**randomhousechildrens**.co.uk

A CIP catalogue record for this book is available from the British Library.

Typeset in Bembo by Palimpsest Book Production Limited,
Polmont, Stirlingshire

The Random House Group Limited supports The Forest Stewardship
Council® (FSC®), the leading international forest-certification organisation.
Our books carrying the FSC label are printed on FSC®-certified paper.
FSC is the only forest-certification scheme supported by the leading
environmental organisations, including Greenpeace. Our
paper procurement policy can be found at
www.randomhouse.co.uk/environment

Printed and bound in Great Britain by Clays Ltd, St Ives plc

SOUTH SEA
ADVENTURE

Contents

Contents

Illustrations

For Ken

1

Bring Them Back Alive

John Hunt put down the phone. He sat for a moment, thinking, tapping his pencil nervously on his desk.

The roar of lions, scream of hyenas, cough of jaguars, came in the open window – sounds strange to hear within an hour's journey of New York. They were nothing new to the man at the desk. He was an animal collector. It was his business to bring them back alive from the ends of the earth, keep them in his animal farm until called for, then sell them to zoos, menageries, circuses, motion-picture companies – anyone who might have use for any sort of wild creature from an African elephant to a titmouse.

But he had never had so strange a request as the one that had just come over the phone.

"Hal!" he called. "Come in – and bring Roger with you."

When his sons entered, they found him studying a wall map of the Pacific. He turned to them.

"Well, boys," he said as casually as if he were merely proposing an afternoon's picnic, "how soon can you take off for the South Seas?"

"Dad, you don't mean it!" exploded fourteen-year-old Roger.

His big brother, Hal, with the calm of a young man about to enter the university, managed to suppress his excitement. Hal was not going to let a little thing like the South Seas make him act like a juvenile.

After all, wasn't he an experienced animal man? He and his kid brother had just come back from an animal hunt in the Amazon jungle – a story already told in the book *Amazon Adventure*. They had brought home living specimens of the jaguar, ant bear, vampire bat, anaconda, boa-constrictor, sloth, and tapir. Surely their father could not have in mind any creature of the South Seas that

2

would be stranger or more difficult to capture than these.

John Hunt looked at his sons proudly. Roger was still too young and too full of mischief to make a first-rate animal man; but Hal was a steady fellow. He was larger and stronger than his father. Leaving him in charge of an expedition in the Amazon wilds had been a risky experiment – but it had paid off. He could be trusted now with a bigger job.

"You know I promised you a trip to the South Seas if you made a success of the Amazon project. I didn't expect it would come so soon. But I've just had an urgent call – from Henry Bassin. You've heard his name."

"He made a fortune in steel," remembered Hal. "What does he want with animals?"

"He's building a private aquarium on his estate. He says he wants the strangest things from the Seven Seas. He has one big pool reserved for – what do you think?"

"Sea lions," said Hal contemptuously.

"No. A giant octopus."

Hal forgot his poise. "Not one of those monsters thirty feet across! How could we ever get it? He's asking the impossible."

"But that's not all," went on his father, consulting a pad on which he had pencilled his notes. "He wants a tiger shark, a flying gurnard, a grampus, a sea lizard, a dugong, a conger-eel, one of those huge clams that are fond of catching divers between their jaws, a manta or sea bat . . ."

"Why, they grow big enough to sink a boat," said Hal in dismay. "How . . ."

"A sea centipede," continued Hunt, "a sawfish, and a swordfish, and a giant squid . . . yes," he added, enjoying the startled expression on Hal's face, "the squid that grows tentacles up to forty feet long, has suction cups as big as plates, and an eye fifteen inches across . . . the one that has earned for itself the pleasant name of 'nightmare of the Pacific'."

"But how would we ever get such big specimens home?"

"You'll charter a schooner with tanks big enough for two or three such specimens at a time. These can be transferred to freighters and shipped home."

"Oh, boy!" Roger began to dance. "We'll sail our own schooner?"

"Nothing elaborate," warned his father. "No yacht. Just a fishing boat. You'll fly from here to San Francisco, get a boat there, and take on a crew. Then get to work. Of course Bassin's job is only part of it. You'll collect other specimens, large and small, that are in demand by public aquariums. Perhaps I'll send you more assignments as you go along. It depends on your performance. You've been wanting to skip a year of school because you're both too young for your classes. That may be a good idea. I'll try to give you more education in a year than you could get in a classroom. There are jobs in Japan, Alaska, Africa, waiting to be done. Whether you get to do them depends upon you."

He looked wistfully out the window.

"I wish I could go with you – but there's too much here to attend to. Besides," he sighed, "I'm afraid I'm getting too old for that sort of rough-and-tumble."

The eagerness of the boys as contrasted with the weariness of the older man showed that it was exactly the idea of rough-and-tumble that appealed to them.

"How soon can we get off?" asked Hal.

"Just as soon as you can pack and get seats in a plane. By the way – before you leave, drop around to see Professor Stuyvesant. He asked me to let him know next time I sent anybody down Pacific way. He has a project out there that he wants somebody to look in on. Something to do with pearls."

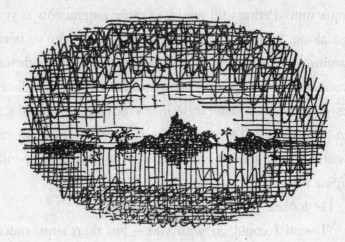

2
The Danger of Knowing Too Much

"Close the door," said the professor. "We must not be overheard."

Hal closed the door and resumed his seat beside Roger at the scientist's desk. Professor Stuyvesant glanced about the room as if he feared that even the walls might have ears. They had – but all the ears were deaf. The famous zoologist was surrounded by friends he could trust not to listen and not to talk. Some were stuffed and some were pickled, but they were all alike in one way – they were all thoroughly dead. Auks, penguins, terns, moonfish, peacock fish, sea bass, tuna, mullet, hermit crabs, jellyfish, puffers, porpoises, and porcupine fish stood in rows on shelves that lined the walls from floor to ceiling.

Dr. Richard Stuyvesant was a world authority on sea life. He conducted an advanced course in the university and was executive secretary of the National Oceanographic Institute. He knew the oceans. He knew fish. His research in the employ of great commercial fishing interests of America, England, and Norway had brought him such rewards that he had been able to buy this big gloomy old mansion and convert it into a great laboratory. In nearly every room there were tanks and a fish-breeding experiment of one sort or another was going on.

The grey-haired professor lowered his head so that he could peer at his visitors sharply through the upper part of his trifocals.

"Your father tells me that you are making an expedition to the Pacific," he said, and smiled. "You seem rather young for such a responsibility."

"But we have had some experience," said Hal, and outlined briefly the expedition to the Amazon.

"Well," reflected the scientist, "I have known your father for many years and have the utmost confidence in him –

and so must have confidence in you too. I must say at the start that this matter is highly confidential. And rather dangerous too. You see, there's a valuable secret involved. Twice my life has been threatened if I did not divulge this secret. Three times this room has been entered by unknown persons at night and my files ransacked. They didn't find what they wanted – because it's not written down. It's no place but here," and he tapped his forehead.

"To do the errand I have in mind," went on the professor, "you will have to know this secret. But if you know it, you are likely to be annoyed as I have been by the person or persons who are trying to steal this information. Perhaps you would rather not run this risk?" He looked inquiringly at Hal.

"Tell us more about the project," Hal suggested.

The professor fished a map out of a drawer and opened it on the desk. Roger felt electric sparks move along his spine. Was this a pirate chart of buried treasure of the sort he had read about in tales of roving swashbucklers and Spanish galleons?

But then he saw it was only a National Geographic map of the western Pacific from Hawaii to Formosa. It was a big map and spattered with myriads of islands never shown on smaller maps.

Hawaii, Tahiti, Samoa, Fiji, were familiar names. But the professor's pencil circled an area littered with islands bearing such names as Ponape, Truk, Yap, Olol, Losap, Pakin, Pingelap, and many others as peculiar.

"This is the blind spot of the Pacific," said the professor. "There are twenty-five hundred nearly unknown islands in this area. For thirty years they constituted the Japanese mandate and Japan jealously kept foreign ships out of these seas. During World War II a few, a very few, of these islands were the scene of fighting but most of them were bypassed by Allied ships on their way to Japan. Now all the islands of what was the Japanese mandate are a trusteeship placed by the United Nations under control of the United States – and on some of the islands you will find American naval stations. The boys of the navy have a pretty lonesome time out there. It's almost like a lost world.

"Now, the good thing about this lost world so far as you and I are concerned, is that it is the best place in the Pacific to collect marine specimens and it also happens to be the scene of my pearl farm."

"Pearls!" exclaimed Roger under his breath.

Dr Stuyvesant put the point of his pencil on the island named Ponape. "North of this island – I won't say just how far – there is a small uninhabited atoll. It is too small

9

to show on this map and since it is quite off the paths of ocean travel, it does not even appear on nautical charts. I have chosen to call it Pearl Lagoon. I am conducting an experiment in that lagoon.

"The most beautiful pearls in the world are produced in the Persian Gulf. Five years ago I collected twenty thousand Persian Gulf oysters and transported them under natural conditions of habitat to my Pearl Lagoon. I brought also large quantities of the organisms that are the customary food of these oysters. I am trying to reproduce the Persian Gulf in Pearl Lagoon and I hope to show that it is possible to raise pearls in the American Trusteeship, as well as in adjacent British waters, equal to the finest to be found anywhere.

"It is time to see how my experiment is working out. I can't go myself, and I can't afford to send someone for that purpose alone. But perhaps in the course of your other duties you could stop by at Pearl Lagoon and get me some specimens from my oyster beds. Of course I'll take care of any expense involved in this side trip."

"It sounds like a mighty interesting assignment," said Hal. "Naturally we'd have to know the exact location of Pearl Lagoon."

"Exactly. And that is the secret." He glanced about. Then he leaned forward and fixed Hal with his penetrating gaze.

10

"Do you have a curious feeling that we are being overheard?"

"Not particularly," smiled Hal.

The professor smiled back and shrugged his shoulders. "I'm probably just imagining things. It's all this trouble – threatening letters – intruders at night. And yet I wouldn't be at all surprised if there were a dictograph planted somewhere in this room, and someone listening at the other end of the wire. I've searched, but couldn't find a thing.

"But I'm sure that all I have told you so far is already known to my enemies. And what I'm about to tell you now they won't hear."

He tore a slip of paper from a pad and wrote on it: N. Lat. 11.34. E. Long. 158.12.

He pushed the paper before the boys.

"This is the first time these figures have been written down and I hope the last time. I suggest that you commit them to memory. They are the bearings of Pearl Lagoon. You must never write them down and never speak them to anyone."

The boys concentrated on the task of memorizing the bearings – North Latitude 11 degrees 34 minutes, East Longitude 158 degrees 12 minutes.

When the professor was satisfied that the lesson had

been learned he turned over the slip and drew an irregular outline. "The lagoon," he said. "This direction is north. The oyster bed is here," and he placed the point of his pencil on a cove in the north-east corner of the lagoon.

Again he paused to let this information take root in the boys' minds.

Then he struck a match and burned the paper to a crisp. He placed the charred remains between his palms and rubbed them until there was nothing left but fine ash.

As the boys came out of the house to regain their father's car in which they had made the trip to the city, Hal noticed a man come hurriedly from the next house. The man's face could not be seen and there was nothing noticeable about him except the slight hunch of his back. He got into a black sedan.

Hal would not have noticed these details if he had not been keyed up by the curious interview of the last half-hour with its air of secrecy and suspicion.

He drove out to the animal farm. As he entered the home driveway he saw a black sedan go by and continue down the highway.

Hal felt a sudden impulse to give chase. He began to whirl his car about.

"Hey, what's the idea?" Roger protested.

Hal laughed, straightened out, and drove on to the house. He told himself that he was letting his imagination run away with him. Why should he suppose that the car he had just seen was the same as the one he had noticed in town? The world was full of black sedans.

And yet, suppose someone had seen them go into the scientist's house and come out again. Suppose he had even heard their conversation. Suppose the professor's enemy was now their enemy too. Suppose that by following them to the Hunt Animal Farm he now knew where they lived and that their name was Hunt. What would his next move be?

"Suppose I quit supposing," said Hal severely to himself and tried to dismiss the subject from his mind.

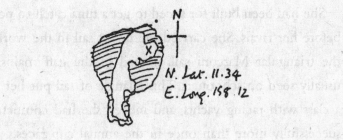

N. Lat. 11.34
E. Long. 158.12

3
The Downhill Run

"How she scoons!" cried Roger as the fishing schooner, *Lively Lady*, sped out of San Francisco Bay between the pillars of Golden Gate Bridge and into the Pacific on the first lap of her "downhill run" to the South Seas.

For Roger recalled the story that someone had exclaimed, "How she scoons!" when the first craft of this sort put to sea. The owner had replied, "A scooner let her be." And from that time on this type of vessel was known as a scooner or schooner, from the old verb scoon, meaning to skip or skim.

And certainly the ship the boys had chartered seemed to skip and skim now as she flew wing-and-wing before the wind.

She had been built for speed to get a tuna catch to port before her rivals. She carried the fastest sail in the world, the triangular Marconi sail, instead of the gaff mainsail usually seen on schooners. This triangle of sail put her in a class with racing yachts, and indeed she had competed successfully more than once in the annual cup races.

But she was different in other ways from the ordinary

schooner. Between the two masts, in place of the usual foresail, she carried two staysails, while forward of the foremast billowed a giant jib.

There was an auxiliary engine but it was only to help the ship through narrow passages when the wind failed. Given a fair wind, her sails could push her along at twice the speed that could be wrung out of her engine. Right now she was doing seventeen knots with ease.

Hal and Roger strode the deck with mighty pride. Temporarily at least she was their ship although the money with which they had chartered her came from John Hunt and his wealthy client and she still carried her real owner on board, Captain Ike Flint.

He served as skipper, for the boys as yet knew too little about sailing to handle a sixty-foot ship. The skipper's crew consisted of two brawny young seamen, one of them a rough, hard-bitten character nicknamed Crab who refused to be bothered with a real name, and the other a handsome brown giant named Omo, a native of the South Sea isle of Raiatea. He had come to San Francisco as a hand on a trading ship, had been bewildered by the rush of American life, and was now well content to be heading back toward the Polynesian islands.

Captain Ike and his men would sleep in a snug cabin

under the forward deck. Hal and Roger would occupy a still snugger cabin aft. Space had been stolen from it to afford more room for the huge specimen tanks that had been installed amidships. These filled the hold between the two cabins.

It was not possible to use one giant tank for all specimens, for the big creatures would devour the little ones. They must be kept separate. And that meant many tanks, large and small. These various aquariums were covered with removable lids. Even when these covers were battened down air was admitted to each tank by a valve in the lid so devised that while it would allow air to go in it would not permit water to come out even in the roughest weather.

In a tiny galley was a Primus stove and a stock of food. A storeroom was stuffed with supplies including equipment needed for gathering specimens, seines, gill nets, tow nets, scoop nets, poles and lines, and harpoons.

High on the crosstress of the mainmast was a platform that would serve as a crow's-nest where a lookout might sit and watch the sea for game.

Out ahead of the ship on the tip of her bowsprit was a pulpit – the sort in which a fisherman stands, harpoon in hand, watching for swordfish. It was thrilling to stand here with nothing but the sky above and the rushing sea beneath.

From this point you could look straight down into water still undisturbed by the ship. If anything interesting came along you were in a position to get a preview of it.

And who could tell what discoveries the two young explorers might make? The professor had said, "Probably more than half of the living things of the Pacific are still unknown to science".

This enormous ocean, eleven thousand miles across at its widest part, averaging three miles deep and at some points six times as deep as the Grand Canyon, sprinkled with tens of thousands of islands of which only three thousand have yet been named — what secrets it must still hold locked in its mighty deeps.

Captain Ike stood at the wheel. His small blue eyes, as sharp as the eyes of a fox, peered out of a brown leather face at the wavering needle of the compass in the binnacle before him. He held the ship to a course south-west by west.

"With luck," he said, "we could slide downhill all the way to Ponape."

"Why do they call this the downhill run?" asked Hal.

"Because we're in the path of the trades. That doesn't mean much to a steamer but it's everything to a sailing ship. With the trade winds behind us we'll make fast time.

17

O' course here in the horse latitudes they're a bit temperamental, but when we get past Hawaii they ought to be mighty steady – barring accidents."

"What accidents?"

"Hurricanes. They can spoil the best of plans."

"Is this the season for them?"

"It is. But no telling. We might be lucky. Anyway," and he gave Hal a sharp glance, "what you're after is worth the trouble."

Hal was suddenly suspicious. Was the captain fishing for information? Or did he already know more than he was supposed to know? He had been told only that they were after marine specimens. No mention had been made of pearls.

Hal turned away and walked the deck. The buoyant exhilaration he had felt as the ship raced before the wind was dulled by worry.

He had almost ceased to think of the menace that had threatened the expedition before it left home. There had been no sign that anyone had shadowed them at the airfield or on the plane or during the days in San Francisco. When they sailed out into the great freedom of the Pacific he felt that all evil plots had been left behind and that there was nothing ahead but delightful adventure.

Now he wondered about Captain Ike. He wondered about the rough fellow named Crab. He wondered about Omo – being from the South Seas, might he not have picked up some information about the professor's experiment?

"What's eating you?" demanded Roger, noting his brother's worried look.

Hal laughed. He wouldn't worry Roger with his ill-founded fears. "Just wondering if we were going to have a change in the weather. See that cloud?"

"It looks as if it means business," said Roger, looking up at the black cloud passing above. Presently a few drops fell.

"Rain!" exclaimed Hal. "That means a bath to me. Here goes to get off some of that sweaty dirt I put on in the city."

He dashed down into the cabin and came up a few moments later stripped naked, with a cake of soap in his hand.

As the raindrops wet his skin he vigorously soaped himself all over until he was covered with a white lather from head to foot. He waited for the rain to increase in volume and wash him clean.

Instead, the rain ceased abruptly. The black cloud passed over and not another drop was squeezed out of it. Hal stood like a pillar of soap, waiting patiently, and considerably embarrassed under the gaze of the captain and the crew. He consoled himself with the thought that there were no ladies on board and none within dozens of miles.

But his mischievous younger brother, much amused, had a sudden flash of inspiration. He went down to the storeroom and opened the slop chest. He had already seen a woman's dress and hat in this chest and when he had asked about them the captain had explained that his wife sometimes accompanied him on his voyages.

Roger hastily slipped the dress on over his shirt and slacks. It was big enough for a couple of boys his size. The hat was fortunately very large and droopy, effectively concealing most of his face.

Hal knew that Captain Flint's wife often went along but it had been distinctly understood that this time she would stay home. So he was completely stunned when he saw a female figure rise from the cabin companionway and step out on deck.

He looked for a place of hiding and made a move to get behind the mainmast. At the same moment the lady saw him and the sight was too much for her delicate sensibilities. She screamed to high heaven and fell face downward on the deck.

The poor soul, she had fainted! She might even have killed herself striking her head on the deck. Hal forgot his embarrassment. He ran to her aid, soapsuds flying. He lifted the limp form. He pushed back the big hat and looked into the face of Roger who burst into a mighty guffaw in which he was joined by the captain and Crab.

Laughing always made Roger weak. Hal took advantage of that weakness. He draped his impish brother over his soapy knee and administered a sound spanking.

Roger quit laughing. Hal might have known that that was a sign of more mischief. Only a low rail stood between the deck and the sea. Roger pretended not to have a muscle in his body. But his drooping hands were close to Hal's foot.

Suddenly he clutched the foot, reared up, and heaved his brother into the ocean.

"Enough of that nonsense," bawled the captain as he threw the wheel hard over and smartly brought the ship about. He crawled up on the starboard tack, close-hauled, to where Hal, now quite unsoaped, lazily splashed in the water. As the ship bore up to him, Hal reached for the bobstay that held the bowsprit to the stem, and clambered aboard.

His skin tingled with the shock of the cold water.

"Thanks a million, Roger," he said. "That was grand."

He went down and dressed. The fun with Roger and the cold bath that had ended it had restored his high spirits. If there was any menace waiting at the end of the downhill run he felt he would be a match for it.

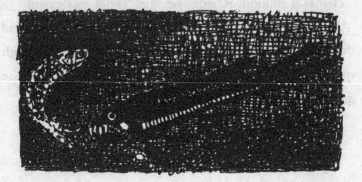

4

Mysteries of the Deep

It was night on deck and there was no lantern near enough to read by. And yet Hal was reading.

His only light was a fish!

Swimming about the small tank between the two boys, it threw out a stronger glow than that of a forty-watt bulb.

"Do you find it in the manual?" asked Roger.

"Yes, here it is. A lantern fish. A good name for it!"

The fish had a row of lights along each side, like the lighted portholes of a steamer. Then there were other lights thickly sprinkled over the back. All these lights burned continuously. But most startling were the tail lights which flashed on and off.

Hal had just spent an hour out ahead of the ship on the tip end of the bowsprit. Standing in the pulpit and hanging onto the curved rail which half-surrounded it, he had watched the scudding sea a few feet below him. When he saw anything interesting, his hand net flashed down and up. It was in one of these strikes that he had caught the lantern fish.

"What do you suppose it wants with all those lights?" asked Roger.

"Well," explained Hal, "it's a deep-sea fish. It comes to the surface only at night. During the day it lives away down where it is always dark, night and day. So it needs lanterns to find its way about."

"But the sun can shine through water," objected Roger.

"The sunlight only goes down a thousand feet or so. Below that, if you did any deep-sea diving, you would need a lamp. On down to the bottom, a distance of a mile to six miles, there is total darkness — or would be if the fish didn't carry lanterns."

"But what's the idea of those flashing tail lights?"

"Probably to blind enemies. Just as you would be blinded if I flashed an electric torch in your eyes. When I turned it off you wouldn't be able to see me and I could escape."

25

"Pretty smart fish," marvelled Roger.

Every day a net was towed behind the ship. Sometimes it was a surface net, sometimes a deep-sea trawl which collected specimens from a depth of a quarter-mile or more.

These denizens of the deep Hal had put together in a small aquarium.

"Let's put the lantern fish in with his friends," suggested Roger.

Hal scooped it up with a small net and transferred it to the deep-sea tank.

Immediately there was wild commotion. The lantern fish was pursued by a slightly larger fish which was also sprinkled with lights. Even its fins were illuminated. From its chin dangled brilliantly lighted whiskers.

"Its name is star-eater," said Hal.

"It sure looks as if it had eaten plenty of stars," said Roger, following the movements of the star-spangled fish, "and it will eat some more if it can get that lantern fish."

Suddenly the lantern fish flashed its blinding tail light. The confused star-eater stopped and its quarry escaped to hide in a far corner of the tank.

Some of the fish gave out a green light, some yellow, some red. One carried what looked like a small electric bulb suspended in front of its face.

But one had no lights. Hal found its description in his manual. It was blind, therefore it could not use lights to see where it was going. Instead, it was like a blind man walking down the street and tapping with his cane ahead of him. Only in this case there were about twenty canes – long feelers that spread out in every direction like reaching fingers. With these the fish could avoid bumping into unpleasant neighbours, and find its food.

But some of the specimens were not in the manual. Hal wrote descriptions of these and made careful drawings. Perhaps they were new to science. He was their discoverer. Some of them might be named after him.

It seemed a little absurd to Hal and Roger that they should be finding things unknown to the scientists.

"But it could be," said Hal. "Last year the Smithsonian Institution made a study of fish near the Bikini atoll. Of four hundred and eighty-one species studied, seventy-nine were new. That's one out of every six. If the same proportion holds here, one out of every six kinds of fish in that tank has never been named or described or had its picture taken until tonight."

Wham! Something hit the lower staysail just over Hal's head, then fell to the deck. Wham! Wham! Two more.

"Flying-fish!" cried Hal. The tank of luminous fish cast

27

a glow on the staysail. Flying-fish, attracted by the light, were flying on board.

"I'll be catcher!" said Roger, and planted himself in front of the sail. This was as good as baseball. A dark object came hurtling toward him. He caught it neatly and passed it to Omo who had come to gather up the fish. They would be served at breakfast. Flying-fish make fine eating.

Roger caught another, and another. Then a larger object came speeding toward him. It missed his hands and struck him a terrific thump in the stomach. It was as if he had been hit with a sledgehammer. He doubled up, dropped to the deck, and lay still. Hal hastily covered the luminous tank so that no more visitors would be attracted. He leaned over Roger who was beginning to mutter weakly, "What hit me?"

Planted against Roger's stomach Hal found something that felt like a large rock covered with razor-sharp ridges. He played his torch on it and saw a fish that looked something like a knight in full armour.

"It's a flying gurnard!" he said. "You might have been killed." He remembered stories of sailors at the wheel who had been hit between the eyes by these flying cannonballs and knocked senseless. The knifelike scales had cut through Roger's shirt and drawn blood.

Hal put the flying gurnard into a tank by itself and

treated his brother's wounds. When the boy was able to stand they both went to inspect the new catch.

Hal was delighted. "Mr Bassin will be tickled to get this," he said. "It's a circus all by itself. It can swim, it can fly, and it can even walk. Look at it now."

Sure enough the gurnard was walking about on the bottom of the tank. Two of its fins served as legs. It strolled for a while, then broke into a sudden trot. It ran to a bit of seaweed, turned it over using its fin as a hand, plucked a morsel out from under it, and popped it into its mouth.

Roger laughed, holding his hand over his sore stomach. "What a performer! Mr Bassin will love it. Until it jumps out of the pool and hits the big chief in the pit of the stomach." He patted his bruised midriff. "Not that I wish the gentleman any harm but – I'd like to be there when it happens."

5
The Giant Sea Bat

"Bats!" cried Roger the next morning from his perch in the crow's-nest. "I see bats as big as barn doors."

That sounded silly even to Roger. Bats don't swim. And bats are never as big as barn doors. And yet these were certainly that big and they were swimming along the surface, their great black wings rising and falling.

Roger was official announcer. He spent much of every day in the crow's-nest, watching the sea. His sharp eyes had spotted many interesting specimens. When he saw anything he would call out and the ship would change course if necessary to come up with it. If it proved to be something that Hal wanted, an effort would be made to net it and add it to the collection.

The captain put the wheel over a spoke or two and headed for the school of black, flapping monsters. Hal came tumbling up from below with a pair of binoculars. He could not believe what he saw through them.

"What are they?" he asked Captain Ike.

"Sea bats. Some call 'em devilfish."

It came back to Hal that this was one of the specimens

his father's important client especially wanted. It was a manta, a giant ray.

How could they hope to capture one? And would the biggest tank be big enough to hold it?

The mantas were going around in circles, evidently pursuing small fish. As the *Lively Lady* came nearer, all on board could plainly see what went on. They fixed their attention especially on one monster close by. It was turning in a tight circle, one wing above the water and the other wing under. It was fully twenty feet across from wing-tip to wing-tip. It was about eighteen feet long from mouth to tail.

It was chasing a school of mullet.

On each side of its mouth was a great flat flipper or arm. These arms spread out, gathered in fish, and shovelled them into the monster's mouth.

And what a mouth! It was four feet wide, big enough to swallow two men at one gulp.

But Hal knew that the giant ray was not a man-eater. It preferred fish.

It was extremely dangerous just the same. It had been known to leap in the air and bring its two-ton weight down upon a small boat, smashing the boat to kindling wood and killing its occupants. Its whiplike tail could cut like a knife. Sometimes instead of falling upon a boat the giant ray would come up beneath it, lifting it clear out of the water and then upsetting it. It might then thrash about among the swimmers, killing or maiming them.

It had no fear of man. Perhaps it was too stupid to fear him, perhaps it was too confident of its own great strength. It would sometimes accompany a boat for miles, swimming under it and around it and leaping over it. If the boatmen beat it with their oars, it did not seem to mind. The blows did not disturb it any more than a tap on the ribs would hurt a man.

Once a man had fallen overboard into the great open mouth of the devilfish. The creature evidently didn't like the taste and disgustedly spat him out. The man was unhurt except for a bad scratching from the monster's lower teeth.

The captain brought the ship up into the wind and crawled slowly into the middle of the school. There the ship came to a standstill, sails flapping idly. On every side huge black wings were lifting and dropping. Mantas evidently liked company. They usually travelled in packs. Hal could count twenty-eight of them in this school.

Captain Ike grinned at Hal who looked the picture of bewilderment.

"Well, here we are. What do you want to do?"

"I want to get one of those things alive."

The captain snorted. "You'll never do that, son. We could get one of them dead, but not alive. We could harpoon one."

"That won't do," said Hal. Then he came out of his trance and began to issue orders. "Roger and Omo, go below and get the big net. Crab, launch the dinghy. Captain, keep her in stays – we'll be here for some time."

Captain Ike began to show real worry. "What are you up to?"

"Going to get in the way of that big fellow. We'll stretch the net between the dinghy and the ship so he'll run into it."

"You crazy fool . . ." began the captain, but Hal was not listening.

One lead of the heavy net was made fast to the capstan on the deck of the *Lively Lady*. The net was dropped into the dinghy and Hal, Roger, and Omo let themselves down into the small boat. They rowed away from the ship, letting out the net as they went.

When the net was all out the dinghy was about fifty feet from the ship. The lead of the net was made fast to the mooring bitts in the dinghy.

The circle that the big fellow was making should bring

him right into the net. Just what would happen then, nobody dared guess.

Around came the sea bat. He ignored the boat. He looked far larger and more terrifying than he had from the deck of the ship. The upper edge of the net projected from the water.

The devilfish seemed to sense that there was some obstruction ahead of him. But instead of slowing down or swimming to one side he came faster and faster until he was going like a speedboat.

Then he suddenly came clear of the water and soared through the air. He crossed ten feet above the net. He looked like a flying barn door carried away by a cyclone. He reminded Hal of a Northrop flying wing. Then he hit the water on the other side of the net with a sound like the report of a five-inch naval gun.

He came ploughing around again in another circle. His excitement seemed to be transferred to the other mantas and they began to leap out of the water, coming down again with terrific smacks. Some of them turned complete somersaults, their white bellies gleaming in the sun.

Curiosity was bringing them closer to the small boat.

"They're ganging up on us," cried Roger. Hal began to believe the captain was right. Only a crazy fool could

34

have put himself and two companions in the way of twenty-eight devilfish.

This time it was another manta that approached the net. Instead of leaping over it, it turned sharply away from it and toward the boat. Suddenly finding the boat in its way, it leaped into the air.

The boys were suddenly cut off from the sunshine by the flying cloud. Hal crouched low, fearing the terrible crushing smash of the monster's weight. Roger had a better idea and slipped under a thwart. Omo, belonging to a race that accepts life or death calmly, sat smiling. As the devilfish came down with a terrific crack on the other side of the boat only its razor tail failed to clear the boat and cut a deep gash in the gunwale.

Another manta was examining the boat with great interest. It gave it a crack with one of its powerful armlike fins. If it had struck hard enough it could have smashed the boat. As it was it splintered the top strake on the port side but fortunately the plank was above the waterline and no leak resulted. Then it circled the boat and ran into the net.

"We've got him!" cried Hal.

"If he doesn't back out," said Roger.

"I think they're just one-way fish. They can't back."

Certainly the manta was not attempting to go backward but was trying to bore its way straight through the obstruction. It managed to get one arm through, and then the other. It turned on edge and its tail slipped through the meshes. Once in, it did not come out easily since the tail was covered with sharp spikes that acted as fish-hooks.

"Row!" shouted Hal, and two pairs of oars and a paddle propelled the boat forward and in toward the ship. Thus the net began to close in on the giant ray.

But it was not one to surrender easily. It threshed about violently, churning the sea into whirlpools and sending up geysers of water that promptly soaked the three boatmen. The boat began to settle under the gallons of water that were splashed into it.

It was lucky that the line from the net had been made fast to the mooring bitt, for no man or men could have held it. The tugs on the line jerked the boat here and there, many times nearly upsetting it.

But now the boat was under the counter of the schooner. The captain was leaning over the rail, his eyes popping.

"Quick! Throw me the line."

Hal pulled the line free of the bitts and heaved it to the captain who caught it deftly and ran to make it fast to the capstan.

Now both ends of the net were secured to the capstan. The sea giant was in a pocket from which there was little chance of escape.

Crab was swinging out the cargo boom. It was hinged to the mainmast and from its seaward end hung a great hook. Hal meshed the hook in the net.

The schooner's engine began to whirr and the net with its writhing contents started upward.

A cheer broke from the boys in the dinghy. But they cheered too soon. In a convulsive struggle the manta flailed out with arms, wing ends, and tail. One of these flying appendages caught the boat amidships and stove it in as if it had been an eggshell.

The boys found themselves in the water and made all haste to swim clear of the churning devilfish. The captain threw out a line and Hal and Roger climbed on board.

They looked back to see that Omo had been struck by the monster's razor-edge tail and was lying in the water, stunned and bleeding. Sharks, instantly attracted by blood, were closing in on him.

Hal drew his knife and was about to leap back into the sea when the captain said, "Don't do it. You wouldn't have a chance," and Crab growled, "Let him sink. He's only a kanaka anyhow."

It was all Hal needed. Boiling with rage over Crab's callous words, he dived into the blood-tinged sea, not forgetting to take the end of the captain's line with him. This he looped around Omo's chest, meanwhile keeping up a lively splashing and making passes at inquisitive sharks with his knife.

Omo was hauled aboard. Hal fended off sharks until the line came again. Then he lost no time gaining the safety of the deck.

Omo came to life just enough to open one eye and say, "Thanks!" Then he closed his eye and submitted in silence while Hal dressed the painful wound.

"There goes a good dinghy," said Captain Ike ruefully, looking at the splinters floating about in the foam whipped up by the whirling mass of fury in the net. "Hoist away!" he cried, and up, up, went the struggling sea bat. Its teeth and spines cut the net in a dozen places. But the net was made of inch-thick hemp cables and enough of it held until the captive had been brought over the tank and lowered into it.

Hal was glad to see that the tank was just big enough to hold its huge guest. But the visitor did not like its new home and proceeded to splash all the water out of the tank. The pump was turned on and more water poured in. The crew struggled to get the lid on the tank for it seemed quite likely that the manta would leap clear out of its prison and thrash about the decks demolishing spars and rigging.

The lid or hatch was finally locked in place. Then all crowded around the glass porthole to get a look at the prize. It had given up the fight and lay quietly on the bottom of the tank like an immense black blanket. The net was still draped about it.

"How will we get the net out of there?" Roger wanted to know.

Hal had no taste for another bout with his unwilling guest. "We'll leave him in the net. That way, it will be possible to lift him out of there. We ought to make Honolulu in a couple of days now. We'll tranship him to a cargo steamer bound for home. Then we'll have the tank free in case we want to take on another big passenger."

"An octopus, maybe?" hoped Roger.

"Maybe. But in the meantime, Roger, you are appointed chef to Mr Manta. You've got to get enough fish to keep him full and happy."

"And no dinghy to fish from," mourned Roger. Then his eyes brightened. "I think I know how to catch enough fish for his majesty."

When night came, the fish began to pour on board. For Roger had adjusted a torch so that it threw a bright light on a sail and brought flying-fish by the dozen. When enough had accumulated to make a good meal, Roger and Omo gathered them and dumped them into the tank where they speedily disappeared down the mighty maw of the sea bat.

6
Coral Atoll

"No wonder they call it paradise!" exclaimed Hal as the *Lively Lady* rounded Diamond Head, sailed past the white beach of Waikiki where brown giants stood erect of flying surfboards, glided by lovely groves of palms and flowering trees, and dropped anchor in the harbour of Honolulu.

Hawaii was all the boys had dreamed it should be. But they could stay only long enough to have some tanks built and ship their prizes, including the giant manta, on the cargo steamer *Pacific Star*, bound for New York and London by way of Panama.

Omo did not want them to like Hawaii too much. The islands in the part of the Pacific he called home were quite different.

"Oh, this is all right," he said with a shrug of his brown shoulders, "but wait till you see the coral atolls!"

And so, having taken aboard a new dinghy in place of the one destroyed by the too-athletic sea bat, the *Lively Lady* proceeded on her way.

As the ship neared the countless isles and islets of the Marshall archipelago the sea swarmed with life. Dolphins and porpoises raced the schooner for miles, taking time off from the race to indulge in high jumps and broad jumps and play with each other like overgrown puppies. A big sperm whale accompanied the ship for a whole day.

On another day a whale shark, which is truly a shark but as big as a whale, took delight in bumping the ship with its frightfully ugly face. It looked as if its face had been bumped too often. It was twisted and lumpy and had a horrifying expression.

Captain Ike said the whale shark was harmless. But Roger dreamed about it that night. He woke in terror and turned on his torch, fully expecting to see the whale shark's dreadful face leering at him over the edge of his bunk.

At night the sea gleamed like a sheet of silver. Millions upon millions of plankton, tiny living organisms, glowed with phosphorescent light.

The nets, towed behind, captured many wonderful specimens. When the ship rode into a school of large fish a big trawl net was let down. By this means a bad-tempered conger-eel was captured, and later a swordfish.

But they had trouble with the swordfish. This creature's sword is as deadly as any ever used by the Knights of the Round Table. When the swordfish chooses to attack a boat it can sink it with one thrust of its sword.

The swordfish had not been in the tank for an hour before it pierced its prison wall with its blade and the water ran out. The pump had to be turned on to rid the hold of the water. The swordfish lay gasping on the bottom of the tank.

Prompt action was necessary to save the fish. The hole was hastily patched. But how to prevent the same thing happening again?

Roger came up with an idea.

"How about a boxing-glove?" The boys had brought along two pairs of boxing-gloves so that they might amuse themselves when life on board became too monotonous – if it ever did.

Roger slipped down to the cabin and brought back a glove. And a thimble!

Crab, standing by, was contemptuous.

"Do you think you're going to stop that brute with a boxing-glove and a thimble?"

The thimble was a big one, for a seaman's use. Hal caught the idea at once and gave his smart younger brother an admiring grin.

He put the solid steel thimble over the point of the sword, then drew the boxing-glove on over the thimble. With his knife he cut notches in the sword and laced the glove to the notches so firmly that it could not come off.

Then water was pumped into the tank. The swordfish slowly revived. He swam lazily about. Then he backed and made a rush at the side of the tank. The boxing-glove harmlessly thumped the wall and bounced off.

Time and again the four-hundred-pound fish threw his weight into a swift plunge only to have the blow cushioned by that mysterious bulbous thing on the end of his sword. Finally he gave up making a battering ram of himself and turned his attention to the meal of fresh fish that had been poured into his tank.

★ ★ ★

45

"Land!" called Omo from the masthead.

Captain Ike peered ahead. "It's land sure enough."

Hal and Roger strained their eyes but could see nothing that looked like land.

But they did see something very strange. Straight ahead just over the horizon was a brilliant green cloud. Perhaps it wouldn't be right to call it a cloud – it was more like a light, a luminous glow.

One might see a greenish tint in the sky at sunrise or sunset, but whoever saw green in the middle of the morning?

It burned with a wavering light as if it were made of flame or gas or rippling water. It seemed to dissolve and flow away and then come back as strong as ever.

"What in the world is it?" Hal asked Omo who had now descended to the deck and seemed much amused by Hal's bewilderment.

"It's the Bikini atoll," Omo replied. "Not that we can see the atoll, but we know it is there by that glow in the sky."

"What makes the glow?"

"Reflection from the lagoon. It has a floor of white sand and coral and is very shallow in some places – that makes the water appear a very light green – and it makes a mirage in the sky. You can see the mirage for half a day before you can see the island."

Late in the afternoon Bikini reared its palms above the horizon. As the ship drew nearer Hal and Roger drank in the beauty of the first coral atoll they had ever seen.

It was like a necklace of pearls laid out on the sea. It was a great circle of coral reef surrounding a lagoon. The waves roared white on the reef, but the lagoon inside was calm and glowed with an aquamarine light. It was like a lake set down in the middle of the ocean. The captain said the lagoon was large, some twenty miles across.

Tiny coral polyps had industriously built up this long reef. Seeds of palms and plants that had drifted across the ocean had washed up on the reef and sprouted in the decaying coral and sand. The result was that here and there along the reef an island had formed, a green lovely island contrasting sharply with the barren whiteness of the rest of the reef.

Some of these islands were little fellows, only about as long as the *Lively Lady*. Some were a mile long. But they were all very narrow. In every case only a few hundred yards separated the ocean shore from the shore of the lagoon.

At three points the reef was broken and it was possible to sail through into the lagoon. The *Lively Lady* headed for the south-eastern passage. The ship was sailing full before a strong wind and yawed dangerously as the following seas threw her stern this way and that. The tide poured in through the entrance like water through a funnel and savage conflicting currents thrashed the ship and sought to throw her upon the sharp coral. But Captain Ike knew his schooner and brought her in safely upon the quiet green mirror of the ocean lake. He hove-to and dropped anchor a cable's length from the gleaming white beach of a palm-covered islet.

Hal studied the captain's chart. The map showed twenty islands on the coral reef. The one close at hand was named Enyu. Others bore such names as Bikini, Aomoen, Namu, Rukoji, Enirikku, and – a real jaw-breaker – Vokororyuru.

In the north-east corner of the lagoon was a cross.

"What does the cross mean?" asked Hal.

"That's where the atom bomb tests were held."

"Aren't you afraid of radioactivity?"

"Not any more," said the captain. "Those explosions were set off in 1946. Of course they made everything radioactive – the soil, the coconuts, even the fish. But now scientists report the place safe for human beings – provided they don't stay too long."

"What happened to the natives who were here before the test?"

"There were one hundred and sixty-five of them living here. They and their King Juda were moved to Rongerik Island. It's a hundred and thirty miles east."

"Wasn't that pretty tough – being rooted out of their home islands?"

"Pretty tough," Captain Ike admitted. "They didn't like Rongerik. There were no fish there and few food plants. The king appealed to the U.S. Navy to save them from starvation. So they were moved again – to Ujelang Island."

"And they're still there?"

"Still there. But not very happy about it. Their old way of life has been ripped to pieces. The island is poor compared with these. The people have to depend upon the American Navy for food. They've lost their interest in life."

"Hard luck," sympathized Hal. "But I suppose there was nothing else that the navy could have done. The tests had to be made. Will there be any more tests here?"

"Hard to say. But now the main proving ground is

Eniwetok atoll. It's about two hundred miles farther west. We'll pass it."

"I suppose the natives were shipped out of there too?"

"One hundred and forty-seven of them." The captain's leather face crinkled in a smile around his sharp blue eyes. "Oh well," he said, "don't pay to get too sentimental about these kanakas. They've always been pushed around and I guess they always will be."

The dinghy was lowered and all went ashore. It was good to feel solid ground underfoot. The island was a lush and lovely garden. If the trees had been injured by the atomic bomb blast there was little sign of it left. Nature had triumphed in spite of the most devastating blow that man could strike.

It took only half an hour to walk around the island. It was uninhabited. As night came on the men sat around the small campfire and ate a picnic supper. Hal noticed that Omo had wandered away down the beach, perhaps to enjoy the stillness of the lagoon under the night sky. During these past days he had felt strangely drawn toward Omo. He admired his even disposition, his patience and cheerfulness, his skill in handling the schooner, and his quiet courage. He wondered what Omo was thinking now that he had come back to the sort of islands he loved.

50

He excused himself and wandered down the beach. He found Omo leaning against a coconut tree and looking out over the lagoon. Hal joined him. Omo seemed so wrapped up in his reverie that Hal did not speak.

Now the lagoon was black instead of green. It looked like a sheet of black glass. It reflected blue-white Vega, yellow Arcturus, fiery-red Antares. A thousand other pinpoints of light stabbed its surface. In a few hours it would reflect the Southern Cross, quite visible here although Bikini was a few degrees north of the equator.

There was no sound except the muffled roar of the surf on the outer edge of the reef. The islands across the lagoon were dark.

"I was here once long ago," said Omo. "People lived here then. It was a happy place. Now it is very sad."

"But it had to be," Hal replied. "I mean, the atom bomb tests and all that."

"I know, I know. I blame no one."

They sat down on the bank that shelved to the beach.

"Omo," said Hal, "how does it come that you speak English so well? I thought everybody down here spoke pidgin-English or – what do you call it? – bêche-de-mer."

Omo's white teeth gleamed in a smile. "I am glad you

51

like my English. I learned it from an American missionary lady. She was very good – she taught our people much. Some of our other visitors were not so kind."

Hal did not need to ask what he meant. The early European and American visitors to these waters had been more interested in copra and pearls than in kindness. They had given the natives their diseases, debauched them with their strong liquors, and slaughtered them with firearms. And was this cruelty a thing of the past? He remembered what Crab had said the other day: "Let him sink. He's only a kanaka anyhow." Had Omo heard him say it?

"Omo," Hal said, "I want you to do me a favour."

Omo turned toward him eagerly. "Anything in the world!"

"I have heard that your people have a custom of exchanging names. Two friends swap names as a sign that they are blood brothers and are ready to give their lives for each other. Would you be willing to swap names with me, Omo?"

Omo tried to answer, but choked with emotion. Hal caught the glint of starlight on a tear rolling down the brown man's cheek. Then Omo's powerful hand grasped his.

"It shall be so," said Omo. "In the depths of our hearts you shall be Omo and I shall be Hal. What we would do for ourselves we will do for each other."

7
Argument with an Octopus

Roger could never seem to get over the idea that this trip was a lark arranged for his special amusement.

His chief object in life was to have a good time. His brother could be as serious as he liked. But as for him, he was going to have some fun.

So, instead of hunting specimens along the reef the next morning, he stripped to his shorts and dived in for a cool swim.

This was the ocean side of the reef. The ocean was quiet this morning except for a lazy swell.

Hal saw his brother dive into the sea and smiled tolerantly. The kid was too young to work for long at a time. Let him enjoy himself.

Hal followed Omo, Crab, and the captain as they walked along the reef, peering over the edge. He saw a baby octopus in the shallows, then another, and another. Each was about as big as a plate. Omo picked up several of them, saying that he would cook them for lunch. In the islands, octopus tentacles were considered quite a choice titbit.

Roger was a powerful swimmer for his age. He was quite at home either on the surface or under water. Now he chose to swim straight down a couple of fathoms, keeping his eyes open and enjoying the marvellous coral formations.

A hole appeared in the reef wall and he swam through it into a cave. Sunlight striking a shelf of coral was reflected into the cave and filled it with a soft blue light. It was a place of bewildering beauty. Here the coral polyps had shown their skill as architects and the floor and walls were covered with fairy castles and palaces in blue, white, rose, and green coral.

But Roger was getting winded and could not stay to enjoy the scene. He was about to swim out and up when he noticed that the water did not extend to the top of the cave.

He rose until his head emerged. There was just room for his head between the surface of the water and the cavern roof.

A mischievous idea crept into his mind. What a joke it would be if he stayed here just long enough to get the folks a little worried.

He knew they had seen him dive in. If he didn't come up they would think he had drowned. They would have to dive in and hunt for him and it wasn't likely that they would happen upon this cave.

Perhaps they'd appreciate him more if they thought for a little while that he was dead.

He turned on his back and floated. He could breathe easily. The coral reef above him was so porous that it admitted plenty of air.

He could vaguely hear shouts above him and the splashing of divers into the sea. He lay quietly, chuckling to himself.

At the end of about ten minutes he filled his lungs with air and swam down and out of the cave. He did not come straight up but swam under water some twenty yards along the shore to where he knew some palm trees grew close to the edge.

Then he rose softly, slipped out of the water without a splash, and hid behind a palm.

The first thing he heard was Hal's agonized voice saying, "I don't know how I'll ever explain this to Father. I should have kept a closer eye on him."

Then Captain Ike: "Poor kid! Such a nice kid too. I'm all broken up, that's what I am," and he ended with what sounded very much like a snuffle.

Even crusty Crab had something nice to say. Omo,

panting from his last dive into the sea, fell back upon something the missionary lady had taught him. He tried to comfort Hal by reminding him that he would meet his brother in heaven.

Roger could not keep down a snort of glee. Then he stepped out from behind the palm tree, roaring with laughter.

He was still laughing and crying all at once when the captain, Crab, and Omo held him down while Hal administered a whale of a spanking.

"That'll hold you for a while, you crazy spalpeen," fumed his angry elder brother. He was left flat on the reef, sick with laughter, while his annoyed companions resumed their search for specimens.

"That'll teach you to hide behind trees," Hal flung back.

Roger stood up. "But you've got it all wrong," he chuckled. "I wasn't behind the tree — most of the time. Look. I'll prove it to you. Keep your eye on the tree."

And he dived again.

But Hal had had enough of his brother's pranks. Why should he keep his eye on the tree? Roger wouldn't come up behind the same tree — it would be another this time.

The idea of a submarine retreat never occurred to him. He went on after the others down the beach.

As Roger swam into the cave he caught a glimpse of

what looked like a huge snake stretched across the cave floor. One end of it disappeared into a black hole at the back of the cave.

When he had reached the surface and taken breath he looked down to study this strange creature more carefully. It was hard to see plainly because it took on the colour of its background. Where it lay on pink coral it was pink, and it was blue, white or black, according to what lay behind it.

Presently Roger made out another like it, and then two more. The ends of them all went up to the black hole.

And what was that at the hole? It was half in and half out, something almost as black as the hole. It was a bulbous baggy mass of no definite shape. In it were two eyes. They were small slanting eyes with a frightfully evil expression and they were looking straight at him.

A chill ran through him as he realized that here, lying doggo, waiting for a victim to come too close, concealing itself by taking on the colour of its surroundings like a chameleon, was a full-grown octopus!

He was horrified but not surprised. Where there were little fellows in the shallows it was only natural that there might be bigger ones in deeper water. But he hadn't expected to share the same cave with one.

Taking a deep breath – for he knew that it might have

to last him a long time if he tangled with this beast – he swam down toward the entrance with strong swift strokes. His head, arms, shoulders emerged into the blessed freedom of the ocean. Another stroke and he would be safe.

Something lightly slipped around his ankle. He was gently drawn back into the cave. He struggled to free himself. But the grip on his ankle was as firm as it was gentle.

Roger's hand went to his knife – or where his knife should be. But the knife and the belt to which it was attached were with the slacks he had stripped off and left on the reef above.

He seized the tentacle and tried to pull it away from his ankle. He could see that the tentacle was lined with two rows of suction cups. He got his ankle loose from the beast's vacuum grip – only to feel another tentacle go around his other leg, and another slide softly over his shoulder.

Now he yelled for help. Hal and the rest must be on the reef just above his head waiting for him to come up. They would hear him and come.

The yell used up most of his precious breath. If he did not get air in the next half-minute he would pass out. He fought to reach the top of the cave. Seizing the lumps of coral that projected from the wall he tried to pull himself up.

The Old Man of the Sea kept a heavy arm over his shoulder. Roger could not dislodge it. With all his might he thrust his shoulder forward, jamming the tentacle against some sharp coral.

A sound exactly like a human groan came from the octopus. It relaxed its grip on his shoulder and he was able to slide free. His legs were still held. But he managed to break water and draw breath.

Then he yelled – and how! He had never yelled as loud at any ball game.

"Hey, Hal! For the love o' Mike! Octopus! Hal! Hurry!"

He felt a sharp pang of remorse for the trick he had played upon his brother. Pretending he was in trouble, he had seriously worried his friends. Now that he was in real trouble – would they think he was just fooling again? The boy who had cried "Wolf" once too often . . . .

The octopus was tugging at his legs. He yelled again and put his heart into it.

"Hal! Honest! An octopus's got me!"

He just had time to gulp air before he was dragged again beneath the surface.

Now the great arms were closing in on him, around his shoulders, his chest, his stomach, his legs.

He remembered the boa-constrictor of his Amazon

adventure. But these tentacles were like eight boa-constrictors all attacking at once. They began tightening upon him, cramping his stomach, crowding his lungs, retarding his heartbeat. A little more of this terrific pressure and his heart must stop.

The light was partly shut off as someone or something came into the entrance to the cave. It must be Hal. Roger twisted about so that he could see. What he saw was the great head of a tiger shark. The scavenger of the sea had smelled the blood running from Roger's scratches made by the coral.

The unexpected visit had a remarkable effect upon the octopus. It at once loosened its grip on the boy's body. It turned an angry purple.

Its sac of a body swelled as it drew in water. The sac suddenly contracted and the octopus shot like a torpedo toward its enemy. It went through the water so fast that the eye could hardly follow it.

It was on the order of a jet plane or a rocket. The water suddenly expelled from the sac through a funnel propelled the beast forward at terrific speed, with the tentacles closed in and trailing behind. It was quite like a comet with a tail.

The eight mighty arms with their hundreds of suckers

slapped around the impudent fish who had dared hope to steal the octopus's dinner. Just outside the entrance to the cave was fought a battle royal. Roger could get only an occasional glimpse of thrashing fins and tightening tentacles. The visibility was made worse when the octopus emitted a great black cloud from its ink sac.

It would be suicide to venture out just now. Roger breathed and rested and hoped against hope that the two contenders might move far enough away so that he could escape.

He shouted again – but he no longer had confidence that his friends were near by.

Now he could see nothing but the black cloud. The two mortal enemies might be whirling inside it, or they might be gone.

He must take a chance. He drew breath and went down. Half-way to the cave entrance he twisted and rose again to the roof – for he had seen the Old Man of the Sea peering into the cave from the ink cloud.

It was alone. Evidently it had triumphed over its rival. Now it came in through the cave door, walking on its tentacles, pirouetting like a dancer or a gigantic spider.

It stepped along delicately, almost gracefully. It was like a cat stalking a mouse. Rainbow colours flitted over its body. Roger had learned in his talks with Captain Ike and Omo that this was a sign of great anger.

For the octopus was quite capable of emotions. It could be affectionate with its young and furious with enemies. It had a highly developed brain far finer than that of any fish, eyes that were similar to human eyes, and it was as cunning as a fox.

Roger could see the beast's mantle swelling. He yelled again, for he knew that the final struggle was now only a matter of seconds.

Then the mantle squeezed tight like the bulb of a squirt-gun. The octopus catapulted up through the water and whipped its arms around its dinner.

A boy with less fighting spirit than Roger would have given up now. He kept battling and, at the same time, trying to remember. What was it Omo had told him? A way the islanders sometimes used to conquer the terror of the deep. Something about a nerve centre between the eyes. If you could get at it, the beast could be paralysed.

He would win yet. He would not only beat this devil, he would take it alive. They wanted an octopus for the collection. Perhaps they would forgive the scare he had given them if he made good now.

He stayed with his head above water as long as

possible, clinging to the coral. Then the octopus with a terrific jerk pulled him under. But his lungs were full of air and his heart full of fight. Only he did not struggle this time against the enveloping arms. He saved his strength.

He was drawn closer to the two evil eyes. They were exactly like the small slanting eyes of an angry rhino such as one he had seen maim a foreman at his father's animal farm.

The monster's jaws, until now concealed under the mantle, opened to receive him. They were shaped like the beak of a parrot, but many times as large. They could smash a coconut or a robber crab at one crunch – so what chance would his head have?

And yet he let himself be drawn closer.

He pretended to be weaker than he was. The Old Man of the Sea would think that he had given up. The octopus did not clutch him so tightly now – it did not need to. This was going to be an easy victim after all. The tentacles drew the morsel closer.

He felt as if his lungs would burst. But he must stick it out a little longer. Where was that thing? – Omo had said it was just between the eyes. All the nerves of the body met there in a little ganglia about the size of a pea.

Yes, there it was – a little bump, like a wart or a pimple. He nerved himself. He looked straight into the hating eyes and could not help dreading that they would read his mind. He tried to relax his muscles and hang limp so that his sudden move, when he made it, would be unexpected.

With a sharp twist he lunged at the pealike protuberance and caught it firmly between his teeth. Then he bit – hard.

The monster groaned like a human being in great agony. It struggled weakly and clouded the water with ink. The suckers lost their vacuum control and the tentacles fell away from the boy's body.

The first thing Roger did was to come up to breathe – and just in time. He rested for a few moments. The octopus hung, inert, below him.

He hoped he had bitten just hard enough to paralyse the beast. Omo had said that an octopus could be killed in this way. When the creature did not move he began to worry.

He submerged now, gripped one tentacle of the octopus, and drew the limp giant out of the cave. Although it had a tremendous spread it was not heavy, having no bone structure except its beak. Roger rose to the surface with his quarry.

When his head came out into the sunlight he breathed a mighty sigh of thankfulness. The world had never looked so good. Perhaps Roger was several years older now than he had been half an hour before – older and wiser. He had a better perspective upon life and death.

He crawled out of the water. He saw the others far down the reef. He shouted and they turned to look. When they saw what he lifted out of the water they came running back.

"For heaven's sake!" exclaimed Hal. "What have you got there? The Old Man of the Sea himself! Is he dead?"

"I hope not," Roger said. "How can we get him to the ship?"

"Keep him in the water," warned Omo. "The sun will kill him. I'll get the dinghy – it's on the other side of the island."

While Omo went to bring the boat around, Roger recounted his adventure. Hal's face went pale and green by turns. Crab's eyes looked as if they would pop out of his ugly face.

"Well," remarked Captain Ike when Roger had finished, "you may have a bit o' mischief in you, but you've got some guts too."

Omo rowed up with the dinghy. "Just sit in the stern

and tow him," he advised Roger. "Keep him under water."

They rowed through the pass into the lagoon and to the ship's side. A line was slipped around the pulpy mass and it was drawn up and plopped into a tank without delay.

It was far too big for the tank if it chose to extend its arms. Each of those boa-constrictor tentacles was twelve feet long. "But he doesn't need to stretch his arms," Omo said. "He's used to living hunched up like a ball."

The monster was beginning to show signs of life. A light came into the eyes. Colours began to play across the body. The tentacles began to squirm.

The mantle swelled. Then the creature shot like a rocket across the tank, coming with a crash against the far wall. It shot in the other direction and encountered another wall. Finding itself a prisoner it began to dash about wildly using its four methods of locomotion – for the octopus can walk on its tentacles, slide along on its mouth, swim by waving its arms, or project itself by jet propulsion. It began to chew at its own arms.

"They do that," said Captain Ike. "Sometimes they eat their own arms off when they're caught. They're just so blamed mad they don't care what they do. Your man won't want an octopus with no arms."

But Omo already came, tugging the answer, an empty iron barrel. He lowered it into the tank. He laid it on its side, completely under water.

The octopus immediately rocketed into its dark interior and drew its tentacles in after it.

"On the sea bottom," said Omo, "they always like a black hole like that. He'll feel at home there."

8
Hurricane

Since dawn everyone on board had been cranky and nervous.

The *Lively Lady* had left Bikini and was once more sliding "downhill" on her way to Ponape. The wind was fair, the sea was normal, and there was no apparent reason for uneasiness.

But the air was hot, the breeze was no longer refreshing. It seemed to come out of a steam bath. Or it was like the close, thick air in the bilge of a ship.

It had no life in it. It nauseated you – it made you feel as if you would like to be rid of your breakfast.

And the sky, instead of being blue, was a sort of white-black.

Now, nothing can be white and black at the same time, yet that was the way of it. A sort of pallid darkness was filling the firmament and pressing down upon the ship and upon the spirits of those aboard her. The hour was twelve noon but you would have supposed it to be early dawn or late twilight.

Hal stood near the binnacle, sextant in hand, trying to

get a noon reading. Then with the *Nautical Almanac* he could compute the ship's position.

Hal had been studying navigation with a will. Not only was it a useful thing for anybody to know. But it was especially important for him – if he was to carry out the secret instructions of Professor Richard Stuyvesant.

A dozen times a day the figures he had never written down drummed in his mind – North Latitude 11° 34', East Longitude 158° 12' – the position of Pearl Lagoon.

There was a puzzle he had not yet solved. How was he to reach the island without disclosing the secret of its position? If the captain and Crab and Omo went along, all three would learn the location of the pearl atoll.

He thought he could trust Omo. He was not so sure of the captain and Crab. Could they be in with the gang that had threatened the professor and ransacked his files? Some remarks they had dropped made him suspicious.

Anyhow, he would feel safer if they did not accompany him and Roger to Pearl Lagoon. But he could never reach the island without the help of someone who understood navigation.

The answer was plain – he must understand it himself. He must learn to steer a vessel by sun, stars, and chronometer so he could bring it to that pinpoint in the sea, North Latitude 11° 34', East Longitude 158° 12'.

How he would get rid of the captain and Crab was a problem he had yet to figure out.

Captain Ike broke in on his thoughts.

"Having trouble?"

"Can't get the sun sharp," complained Hal.

Captain Ike looked up. A whitish glow had taken the place of the usually clear-cut sun. In the increasing darkness, the sky looked like the face of a ghost.

Captain Ike looked at the barometer. It usually stood well above thirty. Now it had dropped close to twenty-nine.

"Looks like we're in for a blow," said Captain Ike.

It seemed an odd statement to Hal because the wind, instead of getting stronger, was growing weaker. Now it came only in fitful puffs. The sails sagged and slatted. The booms swung idly. The wind had failed altogether.

"What's the matter with everything?" inquired Roger emerging from below where he had been resting from his bout with the octopus the day before. His body was covered with ring-shaped welts left by the beast's vacuum cups. "I can't seem to breathe."

It was as if a great blanket had been pressed down upon

the ship and its occupants, smothering them under its folds.

"Hurricane!" declared Captain Ike. Never was there anything less like a hurricane than this breathless calm. "Omo, make everything tight! Crab, sails down!" Crab stepped sluggishly toward the mainsail halyards. "Step lively!" cried the captain. "There's not a minute to lose." He with Hal and Roger tackled the jib and staysails.

The halyard of the upper staysail jammed in the block.

"Got to get up there and free it," panted the captain. He looked around for his crew. Omo and Crab were busy. He himself was a bit old and bulky to attempt the climb to the masthead. Roger was wobbly after yesterday's tussle.

Hal jumped to the ratlines and began to climb. Up past the lower crosstrees, past the crow's-nest, to the peak. He loosed the halyard and the staysail came rattling down.

Meanwhile things were happening on deck. Omo lashed down the hatches and the dinghy, braced the octopus's barrel with two by fours so that it would not roll, and saw to it that the lids of all tanks were made secure. Crab, who could be fast enough when he wished but took delight in being as slow as molasses when he was asked to be quick, reefed the mainsail and jib and took the staysail below. There he stopped in the storeroom to take a swig of his favourite liquor.

The captain started the engine. He began to bring the ship about to face whatever danger was coming. The thing to do was to heave-to with the ship's nose to the storm until it blew over.

The *Lively Lady* was lively with sails but took her time to respond to an engine. She was only half-way about when the thing came.

Hal at the masthead saw it coming. He could not get down before it would arrive. He managed to drop into the crow's-nest and there he crouched to meet it.

It was a wave that towered far above him, high though he was. A single gigantic wave with not a ripple to announce its coming and no billows to be seen in its train. Hal gazed up and into it. Its top was like an overhanging cliff. The green over-curl was edged with white foam. Untold tons of water hung between sea and sky ready to crash down upon the *Lively Lady*.

The ship, broadside on, began to climb the mountain. She listed to starboard until her masts were horizontal and Hal looked down from his perch not upon the deck but into the glassy sea.

Should he jump clear now? Nothing afloat could stand

this. The schooner was bound to roll bottom-side up. Then he might be tangled in the rigging and never get to the surface.

But something made him trust the *Lively Lady* and hang on. He flinched as the overhang descended upon him. He was struck a crushing, stunning blow. He could never have hung on in the face of it but he did not need to, for he was so jammed against the mast and the rail of the crow's-nest that he could not escape if he wanted to.

The falling sea knocked the wind out of his body. He breathed stinging salt water into his lungs. He felt his strength going. And yet the whole thing seemed unreal. How could he be drowned forty feet above deck?

Where was Roger? Had he been washed overboard? So this was a hurricane! He had never thought it would be like this. Would they ever come out of this wave?

Then the water slipped away from him with a dragging pull on his body. The mast seemed to be upright once more. He looked down to where the deck should be. There was nothing but a swirling surge of sea.

Then it washed away and the deck leaped into view. His eyes searched for Roger. There he was. His smart kid brother had lashed himself to the foremast. He looked more dead than alive, but he was still with the ship. The captain had flattened himself out on the floor of the cockpit. Omo had come through the deluge like a seal and was already busy trying to repair a damaged rudder.

Crab was nowhere to be seen.

Crab had never known a drink to take effect so fast. He had no sooner swallowed it than he was struck a terrific crack on the skull, hurled against the bulkhead, pelted with boxes, bales, crates, and cans and covered with flour from a burst bag. Half-buried by supplies, he lay on the wall, with his head on the ceiling. Then there was a roll and the ship's stores left him, only to come flying back the next instant, pummelling him black and blue.

He struggled through the welter of flying things to the door which had slammed shut. He could not open it. It was not locked. It was never locked. Yet with all his strength he couldn't budge it. There was a terrific roaring outside.

For the wind had come at last. It had sealed the door as securely as if it had been nailed. The room again lay on its side. Crab stood on the wall and battled with the door.

But things had stopped flying about. He was a fool to try to get out, Crab thought. He could rest here and let the others work. After all, they couldn't blame him for it wasn't his fault that the door was jammed. He stretched himself out on the wall.

During the interval between the great wave and the wind Hal had slipped to the deck. The ship lying broadside to the wind was on her beam ends. Her deck was steeper than the roof of a house. She did not roll. She seemed held there by a mighty hand. The water had been as smooth after the wave as before it, but it was beginning to kick up now under the gale.

The plucky little engine laboured to bring her about. As it gradually succeeded the deck levelled out. The great wave rolled away to leeward like a moving sky-scraper.

As the ship put her nose into the storm those on deck got the full force of the wind. It moved in on you like a solid wall. When Hal tried to face it it blew his eyes shut and crowded into his lungs until he thought he would burst with the pressure. He would have been swept away like a leaf if he had not taken the precaution of lashing himself to the mast. Now he squirmed around to get on the lee side of it.

He could believe the captain when he told him later that the wind force of the hurricane was twelve on the Beaufort scale. This was twice the force of the average strong gale which rarely registered above six.

A strange elation tingled through his veins. He had always wondered what a hurricane was like. Of course he had read about it – how it got its name from the devil Hurakan, the thunder-and-lightning god of the Indians of Central America; how the same thing was called a typhoon in the western Pacific after the Chinese word *taifung*, meaning great wind; how it went elsewhere by such names as chubasco, ciclon, huracan, torbellino, tormenta, tropical. But whatever you chose to call it, it was something to remember for a lifetime.

Behind the mast it was as hard to get air as it had been to avoid getting too much before the mast. The wind slid by in two currents, one on each side, with such speed that between them a vacuum was created. Water splashed up on the forecastle was at once atomized and blown aft as spray.

It was dangerous spray as Hal found when he experimentally put out his hand. The hand was flung back at him with terrific force. The fingers were bleeding where they had been stabbed by the shafts of spray. The arm felt as numb as if a bolt of electricity had gone through it. Hal estimated that the wind must be travelling at a good hundred and fifty miles an hour.

It did not take such a wind long to end the momentary calm after the passing of the big wave. The sea came alive with leaping hills of water. The ship, which had been on an even keel for a few moments, began to pitch wildly. It climbed the slopes with its nose in the air and plunged head first into the troughs.

Hal was glad of the mast and the lashings that held him to it. Roger was lashed to the other mast. Omo continued to skip about the dipping deck like a monkey, but Captain Ike lay wedged in the cockpit. His hand gripped the lower spokes of the wheel. There was still no sign of Crab. He ought to be on deck helping his crew-mate battle with flying gear and rigging.

In the meantime, all was not well with Crab. His dream of a quiet siesta while the storm raged was not working out. He had a few moments of peace to gloat over the jammed door that locked him away from his labours.

Then the sudden pitching of the ship in the wind-whipped sea began to play football with him. He was flung from the floor to the wall and from the wall to the floor. There was a bunk at one side of the room and he got into it. It threw him out. He got in again and was again tossed out amid a shower of cans. Everything loose seemed to come alive and to take delight in pelting him. It was like being inside the crazy house in an amusement park.

In a frenzy of fear he attacked the door. It was as solid

as a bulkhead. He backed off and ran, crashing it with his shoulder. Nothing happened except to his shoulder.

He tried to shield his head from the flying missiles. He beat upon the door with his fists and yelled blue murder – well knowing he could not be heard. He flung a heavy box against the door. But on the other side was the heavier hand of the wind. He was a prisoner in a torture chamber.

He began to repent of his sins. If he got out of this place alive he would never drink again, he would never try to get out of work, he would be a model of sweetness and light.

As if an angel had been waiting for just such resolutions the door against which he was leaning suddenly opened in a lull of the wind and he fell head over heels into the corridor. The door slammed shut again, leaving him in peace.

He promptly forgot his fine promises, braced himself between the bulkheads in a curled-up position and took a nap.

The wind had grown fitful. It came in gusts and gasps, then stopped altogether. The roar had been so great that Hal was deafened by the silence. The clouds of flying spray disappeared and the blue sky broke out.

"We're through it!" shouted Roger.

Hal was not so sure.

"That's only half of it," growled Captain Ike.

The wind of a hurricane goes around in a circle. It may move at a rate of anywhere from a hundred to two hundred miles an hour. But the entire revolving mass does not move forward much faster than twelve miles an hour.

At the centre of this merry-go-round is the "eye" of the hurricane, a quiet spot with little or no wind.

"We're in the centre," Captain Ike said. "Half an hour perhaps – then we'll catch it on the other side."

Hal and Roger unlashed themselves to go to Omo's assistance. The canvas had torn out of the gaskets. The running gear was a tangle of lines knotted by the wind. The dinghy was about to pull away.

The men gasped as they worked. The air was suffocatingly thin and hot.

It was hard to understand at first why the ship should roll and pitch worse than ever. The waves were much higher than in the path of the wind. Here they had no pressure of wind to keep them under control. They shot up in great spouts fifty, sixty feet high. It seemed as if mines or torpedoes must be exploding under the surface to send up such geysers.

Huge pointed lumps of water as big as houses raced about madly in all directions, crashed into each other, sent up fountains of spray, fell away in a hundred waterfalls.

The confusion was due to the fact that from every point of the compass winds were blowing in toward this centre of calm. And so the waves popped up helter-skelter and went wildly north, south, east, west, anywhere. It was anarchy, it was chaos.

But the *Lively Lady* took it. In such a sea a passenger ship or cargo steamer would have gone to Davy Jones's locker. But a small craft can often weather such treatment better than a large one.

One reason is that the wooden schooner is more buoyant than the steel steamship and rides the waves. Also a small craft can slide down one wave and climb another while the big ship lies across several waves and is attacked by all of them; and the parts of her hull that are not supported may buckle under the strain. The big ship resists the waves, the small craft goes with them.

So the *Lively Lady* shot heaven high and dropped into dark depths and flung herself this way and that so that it was hard to hang on – but she stayed on top.

Birds by the hundreds swept into the centre by the storm collected in the rigging. Noddies, boobies, and gulls slid about the deck and two big frigate birds settled in the dinghy. Thousands upon thousands of butterflies, moths, flies, bees, hornets, grasshoppers, were clustered on the masts and ratlines or buzzed about the faces of the men at work.

The ship had been headed north-east to keep her nose in the wind. Now the captain brought her around to south-west.

"What's that for?" Hal asked.

"When the wind comes again it'll be from the opposite quarter."

And then it came — with a bang. Its arrival was so abrupt that Roger and Hal were all but swept overboard. The roar of the wind struck like a clap of thunder. The stinging spray began to cut into faces and hands. The blue sky was gone and there was nothing but that ghostly darkness streaming past.

The waves were lower, not much higher than the masts now, but they were all going one way and seemed to have a deadly purpose.

It was soon plain that the hurricane's second act was going to be worse than the first. Both wind and wave were more violent than before. Birds and insects disappeared as if by magic. Rigging was being blown to bits. The sails escaped from their lashings and went up into the wind in rags and tatters. The boom broke loose and swung murderously back and forth across the deck.

There was too much to do for Hal and Roger to consider the luxury of lashing themselves to the masts. They helped Omo – and wondered about Crab.

The ship was wrenched as if by giant hands. There was a rending sound aft and the wheel went lifeless.

"The rudder!" cried Captain Ike. "It's gone!"

The ship's nose dropped away from the wind. She broached to and lay in the trough, rolling with a sickening wallow.

At every roll she took on tons of water that surged across the deck shoulder-deep and thundered down the companionway into the hold.

The captain already had the pumps working to clear the hold but water was coming on board too fast.

Crab's siesta came to a choking end. He woke to find himself under water, salt sea crowding down into his lungs. He got into action with remarkable speed, and struggled up to the deck, gasping and sputtering.

Nature evidently liked to play tricks with Crab. He had no sooner come on deck than a wave caught him and washed him over the rail.

"Man overboard!" shouted the captain.

The words were just out of his mouth when the backwash of the same wave that had carried Crab overboard carried him back and deposited him with a thump on the deck. The boys laughed to see the look of dumb surprise on his face.

"Get a grip on yourself," said the captain sharply, "or you'll be going over again."

But no one had time to pay much attention to Crab. The Wind that Kills, as the Polynesians call the hurricane, seemed determined to do away with the *Lively Lady*.

The ship lurched violently, there was a tearing, splitting sound, and the mainmast fell. Still bound to the ship by stays, ratlines, and halyards, it dragged in the sea, listing the deck heavily to port. A few moments later the foremast went down, smashing the dinghy as it fell.

This was no longer an adventure. It was a tragedy. The *Lively Lady* was no longer a ship, she was a wreck. And the lives of those on board could not have been insured for tuppence.

"Rig a sea anchor!" bawled the captain.

With the hold full of water, every wave now rolled clear over the ship. To add to the torment, rain began to fall, not in drops but in bucketsful. Unbelievable weights of water dropped like sledgehammers on the heads and shoulders of the seamen.

Hal could now believe what he had been told of hurricane rain. In a certain Philippine hurricane more rain fell in four days than the average rainfall for a whole year in the United States.

It was almost more comfortable under a wave than under the flailing of the rain.

But there was no moment for rest – if a sea anchor were not rigged quickly the ship was going to founder with all hands.

The boys swung the fallen foremast parallel with the mainmast. They lashed the two together. They made fast a stout cable to the masts and looped the other end over mooring bitts on the bow of the vessel.

Then they cut the stays and lines that held the masts to the ship. The masts slid off the deck into the sea.

Since the ship was carried along by the wind, while the masts, half-submerged, were not, the effect of the sea anchor was to bring the bow of the ship up into the wind. So it met the waves head-on and the danger of foundering was a little diminished.

Another hour the gallant little ship struggled to stay above the surface.

Then, as suddenly as it had come, the wind howled away. Men who had been braced against the wind found themselves unbalanced for lack of it. They had become used to lying on it as on a firm bed.

The blue sky appeared again. The sun blazed. The whirling wrack of the storm full of howling devils, and looking like a monstrous evil genie, bore off to the westward at about twelve knots.

For a time the sea, without the wind to hold it down, was worse than ever. Then it moderated and waves ceased to surge over the deck and pour into the hold. The pumps began to win. The ship rose.

Five exhausted men breathed a silent prayer of thanks.

Hal anxiously inspected the tanks. None of the lids had been dislodged and since he was always careful to keep the tanks full to the brim there had been no sloshing to injure the specimens. They seemed to have come through the experience better than their human friends.

"Do we abandon the masts?" Hal asked the captain.

"No. We'll tow 'em to Ponape. We can get them restepped there."

And so, with a roughly repaired rudder, her proud sails replaced by a chugging engine, her masts dragging behind her, the unlively lady limped on to Ponape.

9
Into the Lost World

Now they were in little-known seas. Even Captain Ike Flint had never been here before. They saw no ships, for the regular ship lanes lie far to the north and south.

Between the two world wars this part of the Pacific had been governed by the Japanese. They had jealously barred all ships but their own from its waters. Its 2,500 islands had no contact with the outside world except through Japan. Non-Japanese travellers visited them at risk of their lives.

And it was still a shutaway world in spite of the fact that it had been taken from Japan in World War II and was now governed by the United States as a trust under the United Nations.

Boys of the U.S. Navy stationed here felt as if they had been marooned on the moon. So it was with some excitement that they saw a strange craft enter the harbour of Ponape. They were going to have visitors!

Their excitement was shared by the visitors who were eager to step from the deck of the limping lady to the shores of the loveliest island they had yet seen.

"Isn't it a beauty!" exclaimed Hal, looking at the white reef, the blue lagoon inside it, and, inside that, the towering green skyscraper of an island. Its wildly picturesque mountains were dressed with groves of coconut palms, spreading mango trees, giant banyans, and hundreds of unknown varieties bearing brilliant flowers or heavy fruit. The old Spaniards were right – they had called this "the garden island".

And, unlike the low coral atolls, it evidently got plenty of rain. The high peaks invited storms. Even now around lofty Totolom peak there roared a black thunderstorm pierced with yellow shafts of lightning.

"Gosh!" said Roger, his eyes popping. "They talk about

91

Tahiti and Samoa and all that. Are they really any better than this?"

"Not near as fine," declared Captain Ike, who had seen them.

"Then why do we never hear about this – gee, I don't even know how to pronounce it . . ."

"Po-nah-PAY is the way they say it. You don't hear about it because mighty few people have ever been here."

"Look at Gibraltar!" cried Roger.

It did look like Gibraltar. But according to the chart it was the Rock of Chokach. It loomed 900 feet high over the harbour, its basaltic cliffs falling away so steeply as to defy climbers.

Through a gap in the reef the dismasted schooner put-putted her way into the harbour. The lagoon was sprinkled with fairy islands. Between two of them, charming Takatik and Langar, Captain Ike dropped anchor in ten fathoms. The chart indicated dangerous shallows near shore.

There were no craft in the harbour except fishing boats and a few naval A.K.s and L.S.T.s. There was one plane to be seen – a tired-looking Catalina.

From the town of Ponape which nestled on a point of the mainland a launch put out. It came alongside and a smart young naval officer climbed on board. He made himself known as Commander Tom Brady, Deputy Military Governor of Ponape.

"You evidently got a taste of the hurricane," he said.

"More than a taste," admitted Captain Ike. "Did you feel it here?"

"Luckily it slid by to the north of us. But one of our supply ships was in its path."

"What happened?"

"It went down – all five thousand tons of it. It's a miracle that this little eggshell came through on top."

Captain Ike proudly surveyed his battered schooner. "Pretty stout little ship! Is there a place here where we can get her repaired?"

"Right around in the shipyard."

"You'll want to see her papers," said Captain Ike, producing them. "And how about port charges?"

Commander Tom Brady laughed. "Don't worry about that. We don't have enough visitors to have to levy port charges. You're the first, outside of Navy, in six months. How long do you stay?"

"That's for Mr Hunt to say. He's the master of this expedition."

"Not long," Hal said. "While the captain is having the ship repaired I'd like to hire a motor-boat and make a little side trip – out to some of the small islands."

There was a moment's silence. Brady seemed to be waiting for more details. But Hal had no intention of disclosing the nature of his errand to Pearl Lagoon, especially in the presence of witnesses.

"Fine," said Brady, accepting the situation. "We'll get you a boat. But just now I know you'd all like to get ashore. Pile into the launch."

The captain, Roger, and Omo boarded the launch. Hal was about to follow them when the captain said, "Where's Crab?"

"I'll find him," said Hal, and went forward. Crab was not in the forecastle. Hal returned aft and went down to look in the storeroom. Crab was not there. A rustling attracted his attention and he opened the door to his and Roger's cabin.

There was Crab, rummaging through Hal's notebooks and papers.

"What are you doing here?" Hal asked sharply.

"Nothing. Nothing at all," Crab sullenly answered, and pushed past Hal out of the door and up the companionway. Hal followed him and they both dropped aboard the launch without another word.

But Hal was thinking hard. Crab must have been looking

for information about the pearl island. Evidently he was in with the plotters who had searched Professor Stuyvesant's papers and threatened his life. They had put him aboard the *Lively Lady* to get the information that they had failed to get.

There was no use making a scene over it. But Hal knew that whoever went with him to Pearl Lagoon, it would not be Crab, and when the *Lively Lady* sailed again Crab would not be a member of the crew.

The town of Ponape consisted mainly of Japanese stores and houses built by the Japanese during the thirty years they had held the island. In the outskirts were the thatch homes of native brown Ponapeans.

Brady led the way to a Japanese house on the edge of a bluff with a magnificent view across the harbour to the towering Rock of Chokach.

"This is yours for as long as you want it," he said. "Make yourselves at home."

It was pleasant to lie at full length on the clean, golden-yellow mats and look out over the blue lagoon dotted with green islets and the white sails of fishing boats, to the big rock backed by mountains thousands of feet high from whose cliffs tumbled silvery waterfalls.

"It's a sort of paradise," said Hal.

But a worm of anxiety crept into his pleasure when he noticed that his party was one man short. Crab had again disappeared. What was that rascal up to now?

10
The Pearl Trader

There was only one business street in the town and Crab
had no difficulty in finding the Post Exchange. He went
in and looked about as if he had an appointment to meet
someone here. A big man with a slight hunch in his back
came toward him.

He did not smile or offer to shake hands. He only said
gruffly:

"What took you so long? I saw your ship come in and
I've been waiting here for half an hour." He cast a
suspicious glance at the clerk. "Let's get out of here – go
some place where we can talk."

They went out into the street and turned at the next
corner into a quiet lane. It wound away toward the hills
between thatch huts set in lush gardens from which came
the perfume of jasmine, frangipani, cinnamon, and aloes.
Crab and his companion walked under a huge breadfruit
tree from which hung fruits almost as big as footballs.
They passed dozens of strange plants and trees – it was
like going through a botanical garden.

The people were as fine as the trees. The men were

more than six feet tall and powerful muscles rippled under their brown skins. Women wore white flowers in their hair. The babies were fat and cheerful. One of them sat in the road directly in the path of the big man. It laughed up at him.

He scooped it up with his foot and gave it a fling into the bushes, whereupon it broke into a loud wail.

Crab grew more and more nervous. It was evident that the man was in a bad temper. What Crab had to tell him would not make him any happier.

They came to a European-style house in a garden of orange and lemon trees, mangosteens, pomegranates, and peacock palms.

The man flung open the door and took Crab into a musty parlour. Two Ponapean servants promptly appeared – a woman who arranged the chairs and a man who asked in broken English whether master would like to have drinks.

"Get out of here!" roared the big man. "Get out, both of you!" He helped them with a push or two and slammed the door after them.

"Dirty scum!" he said savagely. "Curse their brown hides. If I was Uncle Sam I'd wipe 'em all clean off the island."

He motioned Crab to sit down and took a chair facing him. He drew it close and leaned forward until his eyes were not two feet from Crab's. His hunched back gave him the appearance of a crouching lion about to spring.

"All right, out with it!" he snapped. "Did you get the bearings?"

Crab could hardly breathe. He must stall for time. "It was a hard job you gave me. I did my best. I listened in on him and his kid brother too but they never said anything. I went through all their things . . ."

"Never mind all that. Did you get the location of the island?"

"Can't say that I did but . . ."

He got no further. A crashing blow from the big man's fist spun his head backward, overturned his chair, and left him in a half-conscious heap on the floor. He got up shakily, dabbing at his bleeding nose.

"You'll be sorry for that, Kaggs."

"You threaten me?" said the man called Kaggs, looming over Crab like a cliff about to fall upon his head. Looking down, Crab saw that the big man's hand held a revolver. He dropped back.

"I didn't mean anything, Mr Kaggs."

For which he got a clout on the head with the butt of

the gun. "Shut up! Don't use my name. I don't intend for anybody to know me here."

"Not know you? Why everybody knows you're the biggest pearl trader from Thursday Island to the Sulu Sea."

"Down there they know. Not up here. Nobody thinks pearls up here. And these navy kids – what do they know about the Pacific? Most of them are just fresh out of school."

"So if you aren't Merlin Kaggs – the crookedest pearl trader south of the equator – just who are you?"

The big man straightened slightly and nearly allowed a smile to take over his face. "I am, if you please, the Reverend Archibald Jones. I am a missionary of the Go-Ye-Forth Church of America. I have flown here from San Francisco bearing glad tidings to the heathen of these benighted islands."

Crab snorted. "How can you make anybody believe you're a missionary? You, with two murders and a spell in San Quentin to your credit!"

"You'd be surprised, my friend. Even the devil can quote Scripture to his purpose. You see, my old man was a clergyman. I went to Sunday-school until it came out of my ears. I can quote the Bible like nobody's business. Perhaps my quotes aren't always letter perfect, but who's going to know that? My folks even started to make a preacher out of me. And don't you believe I wouldn't have made a good one. In prison I supplied the pulpit when the Reverend wasn't able to make it. I did pretty well too. No complaints from the parishioners."

"But why the masquerade?" Crab inquired.

Kaggs' good humour disappeared. "You ought to know," he growled. "I suspected you'd flop on this job. So I had to be ready to take over."

"You mean you're going to play up to Hunt?"

"Sure. He's a good, God-fearing young man. He'll appreciate a gentleman of my qualities. I'll find a way to get what I want out of him. Don't forget that I know a lot already. I had the place wired. I heard every word he and Stuyvesant said to each other. Only trouble is, they were mum about the bearings. Then I followed his visitors when they went away. Out into the country, to the Hunt Animal Farm. That's how I learned their name was Hunt. From there on it was easy – just a job of follow-up. And if you'd done your part of it right we'd be in the clover now."

He slipped his revolver back into the shoulder holster under his coat and motioned Crab toward the door. "You can get along now. I've no more time to waste on you."

But Crab did not move. "Aren't you forgetting something?"

"Forgetting what?"

"To pay me."

Kaggs bristled. "Pay you – for what? You made a botch of it. For all I know you got Hunt suspicious. I ought to charge you – not pay you. Now get out of here before I break you in two." He made a lunge at Crab.

"I'll go," whined Crab, making for the door. Only when he had opened it and stood half-way out of it did he feel safe to say, "You'll be sorry. Don't forget I can spoil your little game. I'm going to see Hunt right now."

Kaggs' face darkened as his hand moved instinctively toward his gun. But it stopped half-way. Kaggs was thinking fast. Crab was right – he could spill the beans. Kaggs must stop him, but how? A killing in broad daylight wouldn't do. A hundred people would hear the shot. Even if he paid Crab something he couldn't be sure that the sneak would keep his mouth shut. No, there must be a better way.

His crafty face took on a look that was almost genial. "Come to think of it," he said, "guess I've been a little too hard on you. After all, you did your best. No man can do more. Okay, I'll play ball with you. And I'm going to start right now by treating you to drinks. Come with me."

Crab regarded this sudden change of heart with

suspicion, but the appeal of flowing liquor was too much for him.

He accompanied Kaggs. They returned to the main street, then branched off toward the bluff. Crab grew apprehensive for they seemed to be going straight toward the house occupied by the Hunt party.

But across the road from the house was a small liquor shop, and here Kaggs turned in.

He pushed through a group of Ponapean men resting under the trees after their early morning fishing and entered the door of the shop. A seedy-looking white man was behind the counter.

"Tony," said Kaggs, "here's a good friend of mine. Just arrived. I want to treat him to a drink. A lot of drinks."

"Always glad to serve," said Tony. "I know how you feel. Must be nice to have a visitor in this God-forsaken place."

"Makes me want to celebrate," said Kaggs, glancing out the window. "I'd like my friend to have a real party. Crab, invite those fellows in. We'll set 'em up for everybody."

"You can't do that," said Tony hastily. "It's against the law to likker up the brown people."

"The law!" scoffed Kaggs. He produced a wad of paper money and waved it in Tony's face. "Here's the law. Invite 'em in, Crab."

Crab had no interest in entertaining Ponapeans, but if Kaggs wanted to pay for it, why not? He stepped out of the door and motioned to the men. He raised an imaginary glass to his lips. The fishermen were not slow in crowding into the shop.

Liquor is like dynamite to a Ponapean. Even without it he is one of the most warlike of Pacific islanders. With it, he goes wild. Because of this fact the sale or gift of liquor to natives was strictly forbidden.

"There's only one way I can do this," said Tony to Kaggs. "I can sell the liquor to you – and you'll have to take the responsibility of giving it to the Ponapeans."

"Sure," said Kaggs heartily. "Say twenty dollars' worth of your hottest stuff. Here, Crab, it's your party," and he pressed a twenty-dollar bill into the seaman's hand. Crab passed it over to Tony.

"Okay," said Tony. "Now if you'll just sign this receipt."

"For what?" grumbled Crab.

"For the liquor – just to show I sold it to you. That puts me in the clear."

Crab, anxious to get on with the real business of drinking, signed the receipt. He looked around for Kaggs, but the gentleman had disappeared.

★　★　★

105

Two hours later Hal and Roger were distracted from their contemplation of the beauties of nature by wild shouts on the other side of the house.

Captain Ike had gone back to the ship. Omo was in the kitchen exercising his skill as a cook.

"Omo," called Hal. "Go out and see what's doing."

Omo went out. He came back in a moment to announce breathlessly, "A riot. Crab. He's been arrested."

Hal and Roger tumbled out into the road. A dozen drunken Ponapeans milled about. Two were bleeding from knife wounds. Far down the road they saw Crab reeling in the firm grip of two naval police.

At one side of the road stood a tall man with a slight hunch in his back. He held a black book in his hand.

He strolled over to join Hal. "Very unfortunate incident," he said. "Very unfortunate." His pitying gaze embraced the group of befuddled Ponapeans.

"What happened?" asked Hal.

"That seaman plied them with liquor. A violation of the laws of God and man. Only another of the many afflictions that have been visited upon the innocent folk of these lovely islands!"

Hal looked after the retreating form of Crab. "Who notified the police?" he asked.

"I did," said the stranger. "I considered it my duty as a citizen and as a missionary."

Hal noticed that the small black book in the man's hand was a Bible. How fortunate that the Ponapeans had a man of this sort to defend their interests.

"What will he get for it?" he asked.

"Too little," sighed the missionary. "Perhaps sixty days in jail – then possibly deportation to the States."

Hal's impulse was to go to Crab's aid. Then he reflected that nothing better than this could possibly have happened. Crab was his enemy. He was in the plot against him and Professor Stuyvesant. So long as he was on the loose he was dangerous. In jail he could do no more harm. This was a stroke of luck.

"I hope it's a good jail," he said.

"None better. He'll get a good bed and good food. It's more than he deserves."

Hal extended his hand. "I'm Hal Hunt. We just got in today on the *Lively Lady*. Pretty badly banged up by the hurricane."

"Indeed!" said the stranger sympathetically as he took Hal's hand. "My name is Jones. Reverend Archibald Jones."

"You have a church in Ponape?"

"No – I too have just recently arrived. My ministry

will not be in this island. There are already ministers and churches here. I feel that my call is to the small outer islands where the people have never had the opportunity to hear the Word. I am just now trying to arrange for transportation."

"You expect to charter a boat?"

"Not exactly. My society would not wish to incur that expense. My hope is to find someone else who is making such a trip and go along as a passenger."

"Which direction do you want to go?"

"North, south, east, west, it makes no difference. Wherever there are islands, there are people who need our message. But enough about me. Tell me of yourself – will you be staying in Ponape?"

"No," said Hal. "I'm planning a trip too," and felt like a heel because he did not go on at once to invite this kindly missionary to be his passenger. Caution held his tongue.

The Reverend Mr Jones did not press the matter. In fact Hal thought he showed rare delicacy. He said, "I hope you will have a pleasant visit in Ponape, and a good trip. And now I must go. I am expected at the sick-bed of one of my native friends." He shook hands again and was off.

A pretty good fellow, thought Hal. Decent of him not

to try to worm his way into my party when he learned we were going to the islands. Evidently a man of some education. And he talked just like a missionary, thought Hal, who had rarely heard a missionary talk. What a big, powerful fellow – but I suppose a missionary has to be pretty strong to stand that sort of life. And pretty smart too. This fellow looked smart – almost shrewd. Well, I suppose a missionary has to be shrewd to get the natives to do what is good for them. I've heard that a missionary down here has to be able to do almost anything – build a house, plant a farm, give people business advice, repair a motor, heal the sick. This man seemed equal to all that and more. He looks as if it would take a lot to stop him. I wish I could help him. But I can't – at least not until I know more about him.

And Kaggs' mind also was busy as he trudged off to the supposed bedside of his supposed sick friend: He's a fine young man. But the finer they are the harder they fall. I can twist him around my finger like a string. And Crab – ha! ha! – what a fool! I've put him where he can't make any trouble. Now I'll let nature take its course. In a few days this good-hearted young fellow is going to invite me to take a trip with him to the islands.

His mind ranged far ahead. He would learn the location

of the pearl island by going there. Then he would somehow get Hal and his brother out of the way. Something would happen to them. He would fix it so that it would look like an accident. No one would ever be able to pin anything on him. He'd go back to the island with a pearling lugger, clean out the bed, dispose of the shell locally, and take the pearls to New York and London. Every year he made it a practice to visit both cities to sell the pearls he had bought in the South Seas. He knew all the important jewellers. Nothing happened in the pearling industry, either in the South Seas or in the cities, that he did not learn about. He had known of Stuyvesant's project very early – when he had been in Celebes and the ship bearing the professor's Persian Gulf specimens had stopped there for supplies on its way to Ponape. He needed only one detail more – the position of the island.

Now he settled down comfortably to wait for Hal Hunt to present him with this information. Surely the young man would not refuse a helping hand to a poor faithful old missionary!

11
The Mysterious Passenger

"We have a boat for you," announced Commander Tom Brady, calling upon the Hunts the next morning. With him he brought two smartly uniformed young men whom he introduced as Lieutenants Rose and Connor. "It's not a very big boat – a thirty-footer."

"That's big enough," Hal said. "How about the motor?"

"A good Hakata motor – made in Japan. You see, the boat is one of a fleet the Japs brought down for bonito fishing. Now it belongs to a native fishing guild – they'll let you use it for a modest fee."

"What accommodation?"

"A cabin with four bunks. A galley. And a fishy smell."

"It's a deal," grinned Hal.

"I suppose," said Brady to Captain Ike, "you'll be going along as navigator."

"No. I'll stay here to put the *Lively Lady* in shape. Hal will do his own navigating."

Brady looked at Hal with new admiration. "Explorer – scientist – and now navigator. You're doing pretty well for a young fellow."

Hal reddened. Praise embarrassed him. And he didn't quite like being referred to as a young fellow. What if he was a bit younger than Brady, he was bigger and stronger and learning as fast as he could. "I'm afraid I'm still pretty green on navigation," he admitted. "But perhaps I have enough of it for a short trip."

"I'm sure you have," said Brady cordially. "It's too bad our police had to deprive you of one of your crew."

Hal understood that he was speaking of Crab. "I wouldn't have taken him anyhow," he said.

"And he'd be no use to me," said Captain Ike vigorously. "I don't know why I ever took him on in San Francisco.

He came highly recommended. But he was as lazy as a sea slug, as sour as a crab-apple, and always making trouble."

"Well then," said Brady, "he ran true to form when he likkered up our natives. Our regulations are very strict on that point. So when the missionary notified us . . ."

Hal saw a chance to learn more about the mysterious missionary.

"How about this Mr Jones?" he asked. "Do you have any information on him?"

"I'm afraid we haven't," Brady said. "He flew here from San Francisco a week ago. He represents some mission organization in California. He seems to know other parts of the South Seas very well. I believe he's hoping to get a ride out to some of the islands. Apparently he's quite devoted to the welfare of the natives."

"What he did yesterday proves that," granted Captain Ike.

"Ponape isn't tough enough for him," said Rose admiringly. "He wants to go out and help the natives on some little island where life is really rugged. I'd say he's okay."

"We need more like him," added Connor.

Hal reflected that if he had been fooled by the Reverend Archibald Jones, he was not the only one. The man was either extraordinarily clever – so clever that he could bluff these four very able and intelligent men – or else he was on the level. Hal was ashamed that he had had any doubts of the missionary's integrity. He was ashamed too that he had not generously offered to take him as a passenger.

Brady was saying, "You see how Rose and Connor feel about anyone who lends a hand to the natives. These two men may look to you like plain Navy – but Rose is a schoolteacher and Connor is a doctor. They're trying to see to it that the new generation of Ponapeans will grow up wise and healthy."

"They eat it up," Rose said. "Education, I mean. You never saw kids so anxious to learn."

"Is there much sickness?" Hal asked Dr Connor.

"A lot of it. Mostly diseases brought in by the white man."

"I'm afraid," said Hal, "the white man has given these people a pretty raw deal."

The doctor nodded. "Spanish sailors brought tuberculosis to the islands about a hundred years ago. Forty years ago a German radio operator brought leprosy to Yap. English traders brought dysentery to Palau. Americans brought measles and other diseases far more serious. These people weren't used to such diseases. They died like flies. The population of Yap went down from 13,000 to 4,000. Kusaie had 2,000 natives before American whalers came roistering ashore – they were reduced to 200. The hundred thousand of the Mariana Islands were cut down to 3,000."

"How many people are there in all your islands?"

"If you mean the 2,500 islands governed by the Navy as Trust Territory – the group called Micronesia – there are about 60,000 people. There used to be 400,000."

"Are they still dying off?"

"No. The Japanese checked the decline. We have to give them credit. They had good doctors and hospitals. But I think we are doing even better. Because the population is increasing now on nearly all of the islands."

"It must give you a great lift," Hal said, "to feel that you're helping these people to get a new start."

And he wished he were doing something like that. The collection and study of animals might be important, but it was cold business compared with helping your fellow man. What could he do for these islanders?"

Of course the first and easiest thing he could do would be to take the missionary wherever he wanted to go. He would do that.

12
To the Secret Atoll

Far behind lay Ponape, its lofty Totolom Peak wrapped in a thunder cloud.

Everywhere else the sky was blue. The sea was calm and the motor-boat made good time. Dolphins played alongside. Flying-fish reflected the sunlight on their outspread fins.

The name of the boat, *Kiku*, was lettered on the bow in Japanese characters. Kiku meant chrysanthemum.

Perhaps when the boat had been built in Japan it had been as beautiful as a flower and may even have smelled as sweet. But not now. It had a strong odour of dead-and-gone fish. Its decks and gunwales were scratched by the fins of countless bonito, the daggers of swordfish and barracuda, and the sandpaper-rough skins of sharks.

But everyone aboard was happy. Omo in the galley hummed a Polynesian chant. Roger at the tip of the bow tried to catch flying-fish in his hands. Hal at the wheel basked in the tropical sunshine tempered by the cool ocean breeze.

But happiest of all hands was the Reverend Archibald Jones. Every few moments without any apparent reason he would break into a hearty roar of laughter.

"You're feeling pretty good," commented Hal.

The missionary laughed until the tears came to his eyes. "Oh, it's rich, it's rich! Imagine! *You* taking me right where I want to go . . ." He checked himself. "I mean, my boy, it does my soul good. Your generosity has restored my faith in human nature. Yes, in the words of Holy Writ, it 'hath put a new song in my mouth'."

"It's nothing," Hal said.

"Oh yes it is. You have no idea what it means to me. No idea. Ha ha! Ahem! To think of being on my way at last to — to my chosen work among brown sheep that have gone astray. No wonder I feel like making a joyful noise unto the Lord."

Strange talk, Hal thought. Somehow the Scriptures seemed dragged in by the heels. And the joyful noise of his curious passenger seemed to have more of the devil than the Lord in it.

But Hal did not consider himself a judge of such matters. His acquaintance with clergymen had been limited. Perhaps they all acted this way, he did not know.

What of it? How Mr Jones chose to talk was no business of his. His good deed was to land the holy man on some inhabited island where he could help the natives. The chart showed two such islands on the way to Pearl Lagoon.

By noon all of Ponape, including its cap of thunder, had sunk below the horizon. There was not a scrap of land to be seen anywhere. There was not a sail, not a wisp of steamer smoke. There was nothing to show where they had come from or where they were going – nothing but the compass and Hal's calculations.

"I hope you're a good navigator," Roger said.

Hal got out the sextant and chronometer he had borrowed from the ship and took an observation. He entered the reading in the logbook. He set his course north by north-west. That ought to head him straight for Pearl Lagoon.

But he knew it would not be as simple as that. Winds would throw the *Kiku* off her course. Besides, they were now getting into the fringe of the North Equatorial Current. They had no way of judging its strength or exact direction. Its main trend was westward.

And to hit a tiny pinpoint of an island on the nose in this vast expanse of waters was a task that made Hal feel weak in the joints. The boat seemed so small and lost in this mightiest of oceans with the limitless sky above and, according to the chart, three miles of water between the keel and the hills and valleys of the sea bottom.

Hal checked his observations frequently, entering each new reading in the logbook. When night came the skies luckily remained clear and it was possible to steer by the stars. Omo and Roger relieved him at the wheel. Mr Jones was quite evidently not a sailor and spent the night comfortable in his bunk.

At sunrise the sea had humped itself a bit and the boat was rolling. Omo prepared a good breakfast and they sat down on the deck to eat it. Mr Jones finished first and with the plea that he was feeling a little seasick retired to the cabin.

A few moments later Hal went to the cabin to get the logbook. He found Mr Jones leaning over the open book and copying the readings on a slip of paper.

His back was partly toward Hal. It was curved like a barrel. Suddenly aware that someone was behind him, he hunched his back still more to cover his action and slipped the piece of paper into an inner pocket of his jacket.

Then he said cheerfully, "I was just glancing over your log. Very interesting. I hope you don't mind."

"Not at all," said Hal, but he was staring. Staring at that back. It was still hunched as if concealing something. Where had he seen a back like that? A back with a secret. A back hiding a sneak.

Then he remembered. A back hunched just like this one, hunched as if over a secret. The back of the man who had come furtively from the house next to Professor Stuyvesant's. The man who had stepped into the black car. The car that Hal had suspected of following his into the country.

It was not much to go on, a slight hunch in a back. But now, with this copying of the log and quick concealment of the slip of paper, things began to add up. The professor had feared that his room was wired and their conversation overheard. So he had not breathed aloud the bearings of the island. That was the one bit of information the enemy must get. And so this "missionary", who was probably not a missionary at all, had cleverly arranged to be taken straight to the secret island. And by the bearings in the log he would know exactly where it was and how to get there whenever he wished to come again.

Hal went back on deck, took the wheel from Roger, and began to think his way out of this one. He felt like kicking himself for having been so easy. Welfare of the natives indeed!

He knew he was up against a master, perhaps a murderer, a man who would stop at nothing in his ambition to acquire a fortune in pearls.

"What are you sweating about?" asked Roger, seeing the beads of perspiration pouring down Hal's face. "I'm as cool as a cucumber."

He would let Roger stay as cool as a cucumber for a while. No need to worry him yet. Perhaps, thought Hal, his own fears were groundless and the man was exactly what he claimed to be.

And if he were not, he must not be allowed to know that he was suspected. In that case he might take violent measures. It was better to let him think that his scheme was succeeding. If Roger and Omo shared Hal's fears they might by a word or a look tip off the passenger to the fact that he was under suspicion.

"I'll have to watch myself," Hal thought. He must give no hint that he smelled a rat. He must appear to be on the best of terms with his now unwelcome guest. At the same time, he must find a way to outwit him.

He puzzled and sweated over this problem for hours. But when he took his next reading an answer suddenly came to him.

He calculated the boat's position at 158° 15' east by 8° 40' north. But in entering the position in the log he subtracted 10° from each bearing. Thus according to the log the reading was 158° 5' east by 8° 30' north.

At the next observation he subtracted twenty minutes from each bearing, at the next thirty, at the next forty, and so on. Thus the error on the page of the log grew rapidly worse. But Hal, by simply adding the tens he had subtracted, always knew his true position.

He was not content with a noon sight, but took observations half a dozen times a day, because the chart indicated the prevalence of hidden reefs.

He left the logbook in the cabin and gave Mr Jones plenty of opportunity to consult it and copy the readings.

One minute of latitude was equal to a nautical mile, a bit more than six thousand feet. So an error of ten minutes meant the bearing was ten miles off. It would take only a few such errors to put an island so far off course that it could not be seen even from the masthead of a pearling lugger.

If this man were a pearl thief, his plan doubtless was, after learning the bearings of the island, to come back to it with a pearling lugger and divers and help himself. Hal was trying to make sure that he would never again find the island. With such inaccurate bearings there was as much chance of locating it as of finding a needle in a haystack.

The next day a few palms poked their heads over the

horizon and an island climbed up after them. Hal knew from his readings that it could not be Pearl Lagoon but the big passenger's eyes glowed with anticipation.

"This is perhaps your destination?" he asked.

"No," said Hal. "But perhaps you would like to be landed here. Judging from the number of canoes along the shore, there are plenty of natives here for you to minister to."

But Mr Jones was not interested. "I think I shall go a little farther afield. Probably this island is served from Ponape. My call is to virgin territory where the Bread of Life has never been broken."

Another island was sighted during the afternoon. But Mr Jones, learning that this too was not the goal of the *Kiku*, decided to continue.

Hal noticed that as they got farther from Ponape the chart grew less accurate. Some islands were marked with a P.D., meaning Position Doubtful. Islets appeared in the sea that were not on the chart and some on the chart were not to be found on the sea. Evidently the chartmakers were forced to indulge in a great deal of guess-work in regard to this almost unknown part of the Pacific.

It was a good place to get lost, Hal reflected. His head

buzzed with the mathematical difficulties of computing his observations, allowing for semi-diameter, parallax, refraction, dip of the horizon, and all that. He felt very green. If he managed to compute his way to that pinpoint called Pearl Lagoon, it would be a miracle.

Always the bearings of Pearl Lagoon drummed in his mind – bearings he had never written down – 158° 12' east by 11° 34' north.

It went through his mind so automatically that he feared he would repeat it aloud in his sleep. If Mr Jones in his bunk only four feet from Hal should hear it, the jig would be up.

Another night of sailing under the bright stars. A little after sunrise Roger at the wheel shouted, "Land-ho!"

"This is it," thought Hal, tumbling out of his bunk. He came out on deck. The missionary lost no time in joining him.

Ahead lay a ring of reef enclosing a green lagoon. At two places the reef broadened to make islands but there was not much growing on them. Signs of the hurricane had been seen on some of the other islands the day before. This place had evidently been hit hard. Palm trees had been snapped off within ten feet of the ground. Only the stumps remained.

Hal excitedly took an observation. What if he had missed the right island entirely? But the reading when he worked it out was the same as the singsong that kept going through his brain – 158° 12' east by 11° 34' north.

This was Pearl Lagoon!

He sliced off ninety minutes from each bearing and wrote in the logbook: "Sighted Pearl Lagoon at 156° 42' east by 10° 4' north."

Let him copy that, he grinned. If his enemy ever chose to sail to that spot, he would find no island or, if he did, it would not be this one. He would be ninety miles west of the correct position and about the same distance south. That would put him more than a hundred miles from Pearl Lagoon.

Hal was thankful that Mr Jones was no sailor. The way he walked about the deck showed that. He lost his appetite when the sea was rough. He had occasionally operated the engine controls and held the wheel, but any amateur could do that. The only time he had tried the sextant he had held it upside down and he had never made any attempt to compute position by the *Nautical Almanac*. He was entirely at the mercy of Hal's figures.

All right, let him take a good look at Pearl Lagoon. He would never see it again.

"Let's circle it," Hal said to Roger who was still at the wheel. "Don't go too close to the reef."

The atoll was less than a mile around. On the west side there was a good passage into the lagoon. Roger sped the boat through it upon the breast of an ocean swell. The water shoaled to a depth of only a fathom or two. The lagoon bottom seen through the clear green water was a paradise of coral castles of all the colours of the rainbow.

It was pitiful, the contrast between the beauty of the landscape underneath and the desolation of the hurricane-swept reef and its two battered islets.

"Certainly wouldn't like to be cast away here," shivered Roger. "Looks as if that storm didn't leave a thing alive. I'll bet it even killed the rats. Pearl Lagoon, eh? It ought to be called Starvation Island."

At a sign from Hal, Omo dropped anchor. Hal had selected the spot with some care. It was behind a high shoulder of reef which cut off the view of the northern part of the lagoon. The boat drifted to within a few feet of the reef where it was checked by the anchor chain.

"We're going ashore for a little while," Hal said to Mr Jones. "You probably won't be interested in this island because it's uninhabited. Perhaps you'll prefer to stay on board."

Mr Jones pretended to welcome the suggestion. "Yes, yes," he said. "I'll stay here. The place means nothing to me since there is no flock awaiting a shepherd."

Hal, Roger, and Omo went over the side into water less than a foot deep and waded ashore. They clambered through humps of coral to the top of the reef and trudged northward. A shoulder of the reef soon cut them off from the view of the man in the boat.

13
Pearl Lagoon

Up the west reef they walked to where it broadened into an island at the north-west corner of the lagoon. Then there was a narrow neck of reef to another island at the north-east corner.

"It must be here somewhere," said Hal. "Professor Stuyvesant said the north-east corner."

The island was only a few hundred yards across. The shrubbery, if there had ever been any, had been ripped away by the storm. Probably the whole island had been under water. The forlorn stumps of palm trees looked like monuments in a cemetery. A few palm logs remained – the rest had evidently been swept away.

It was hard going. The storm had left the surface a litter of coral blocks in piles sometimes ten feet high. If you stumbled and put out a hand it was cut by the sharp coral.

On the lagoon side of the island was a deep bay. It was not possible to see the bottom clearly for it was some ten fathoms down. The bay was a hundred yards across. The boys gazed down into its mysterious depths.

"Lucky we brought Omo," Roger said. "I could never get down that deep. How about you, Hal?"

"I wouldn't want to try it," Hal said.

Omo made ready to slip off his dungarees but Hal stopped him. "Wait a minute. Let's sit down and talk things over. Sort of a council of war."

He told them his suspicions regarding the missionary.

"Perhaps you're right," Omo said. "I've known a lot of missionaries. He doesn't quite ring true."

"I think he's a phony," Roger said. "Let's tell him so to his face."

"Not unless we have to," Hal warned. "He's probably armed and we're not."

"But he wouldn't kill us – just for some pearls."

"Don't be too sure. There may be a fortune in this bay. I don't think he would stop at killing to get his hands on it. Remember, this isn't home – with a police station every few blocks. Here the law is whatever a man chooses to make it. Unless he forces our hand, let's just go along as usual. But I thought you ought to know so that if anything breaks we'll be prepared to act fast. Okay, Omo. Suppose you take a look at the bottom of this bay."

Omo slid out of his clothes. Straight and strong and brown as the trunk of a coconut tree he stood poised on a rock overhanging the bay. His bathing-suit consisted solely of a pair of gloves. They would protect his hands when he seized the rough coral at the bottom to hold himself down or gripped the thorny oyster shells.

He began to go through the process that skin divers call "taking the wind". He breathed heavily, each breath deeper than the last, groaning and straining to force the air down. He pressed his diaphragm downward with both hands to increase his capacity. He pumped the air into his lungs as if they were a compressor, and held it.

Then he dropped into the water. He did not dive but went straight down feet first without a splash.

The momentum took him to a depth of about ten feet. Then he turned end for end and swam downward with powerful pulls of his arms and thrusts of his legs.

Hal and Roger had seen exhibitions of underwater swimming and had taken part in some of them. But they had never seen anything like this. Any American or European swimmer who could plough his way down to a depth of thirty feet was a champion. At that depth the pressure was tremendous. The water beneath seemed to be trying to throw you up like a cork exploding from a bottle.

But Omo went on down, to forty feet, fifty feet, sixty feet.

"And I'll bet he could go twice as deep as that if he had to," Hal said. "These fellows really know how to swim. They learn before they are two years old. Lots of Polynesian babies can swim before they can walk. They're as much at home in water as on land – amphibians like the seals, turtles, frogs, and beavers."

Now the boys could dimly see that Omo had stopped swimming. He was clinging to the coral bottom, his feet floating upward. He pulled himself down, let go, and took another hold a little farther on. He did this several times. He looked as if he were walking about the ocean floor on his hands.

Then he gripped something black and round and shot to the surface. He bobbed up out of the water waist high, sank back, came up again until his head was free, and clung to the rocks.

The compressed air came out of his lungs with a noise like the hiss of a piston. He breathed great gulps of pure air. His face was agonized and he did not seem to hear what the boys were saying.

Gradually his features relaxed. He looked up and smiled. The boys lent a hand as he clambered out of the water. He laid the black round thing on the rocks.

It was an enormous oyster fully fifteen inches across.

Roger shouted with glee. Hal silently thanked his lucky stars that he had found the right island, found the right bay, found the professor's oyster bed. This must be it, for the few oysters that grew wild in Micronesian waters were seldom more than six or eight inches in diameter.

"Are there many more like this?" Hal asked.

Omo nodded solemnly. "That's why the bottom looks black. It's covered solid with shells. Hundreds of them."

Roger danced with excitement. "That means hundreds of pearls."

"No," Omo said quietly. "Not every oyster produces a pearl. In fact we may have to open hundreds to get one."

"That's usually the way of it," Hal agreed. "But here the average may be higher because the professor has taken special pains to make favourable conditions."

"There might be a pearl in this one." Roger took out his sheath knife and tried to prise open the bivalve. He strained and sweated but it defied all his efforts.

"There's a little knack to it," Omo said, and took the knife. Instead of prising, he thrust the knife between the lips of the shell, deep into the central closing muscle. With the muscle cut, the shell sprang open.

Then he let Roger take over. "If there's a pearl," he

said, "you'll probably find it by running your finger along the inside of the lip."

Roger feverishly explored the inner edge of each shell. There was no pearl. Roger looked crestfallen. But he would not give up yet. "There might be one inside." He opened the shell completely and probed about in the oozy, sticky mass. He found nothing.

"What a mess!" he said disgustedly, and flung it behind him over a pile of coral blocks. It came down on the other side and hit something with a splash – and what sounded like a grunt. Roger darted behind the pile and encountered the Reverend Mr Jones wiping oyster out of his eyes, nose, and mouth.

He began to growl some remarks that did not sound well coming from a missionary. Then he remembered himself and tried to smile.

"What are you doing here?" demanded Roger.

The missionary did not deign to reply to this juvenile impertinence, but came around the pile to greet Hal and Omo. Oyster juice dripped from his ears.

"I was a little anxious about you," he said, "so I came to see if all was well."

"You were spying on us!" Roger said hotly.

Mr Jones looked tolerantly at Roger. "My boy, you must

try to remember that good manners are next to godliness."

"It's cleanliness that's next to godliness," Roger corrected. "And you'd better wash the oyster off your face."

Mr Jones turned to Hal with a grieved air.

"Do you stand idly by while your brother flings insults as the gamin of an earlier day hurled stones at St Stephen? Is it not your duty as elder brother . . ."

"My duty as his elder brother," Hal said, "is to protect him from such scum as you. He was right – you were spying on us."

"My son, you are overwrought. Your words are the hot irresponsible words of youth, but I would be a poor missionary indeed if I could not find it in my heart to forgive you," and he put his hand on Hal's shoulder.

Hal shook it off. "Can that high-toned talk. You're no more a missionary than I am. You're a dirty two-faced crook."

"Now, now," said the missionary patiently, "let's try to control ourselves. Tell me quietly what has given rise to this unfortunate misunderstanding."

Hal was seized by doubt. Was he wrong after all? Certainly this man was showing a patience and forbearance worthy of any missionary.

He tried a new tack. "Can you stand there and tell me you never heard of Professor Richard Stuyvesant?"

Mr Jones seemed to search his memory. "Stuyvesant, Stuyvesant," he mused. "No, I can't say that the name is familiar to me."

"And you didn't wire his laboratory?" persisted Hal. "You didn't listen in on his conversations? You didn't overhear when he commissioned us to come to this island? You didn't come out of the next house and get into a black sedan? You didn't follow us to the Hunt Animal Farm?"

"I don't know what you are talking about," said Mr Jones, but his voice had lost some of its assurance. A gob of oyster pulp dripped from the end of his long nose.

"And I suppose you didn't put Crab on the *Lively Lady* to get the bearings? He didn't go through my papers? You didn't wangle this trip with us so you could get our secret? Haven't you been copying the log? Did you get off on an island where you could preach to the natives? Not you. You don't care a hoot about the natives. You're interested in pearls."

Mr Jones sat down heavily upon a palm log. He spread out his hands. His big shoulders were hunched forward. His face was dark with anger but he controlled himself.

"Well," he said, "I see the game is up. You've got it pretty well figured out, haven't you? I'm afraid you're too smart for me."

Hal eyed him suspiciously. Was the fellow soft-soaping him to throw him off his guard?

"Yes," went on Mr Jones, "I see it's no use trying to pull the wool over your eyes. I should work with you, not against you."

"There's no way you can work with us."

"I'm not so sure of that, my friend. It's true I am not a missionary. That was just a playful deceit. I meant no harm."

"You meant only to steal this pearl bed."

"Don't say steal." The big fellow brushed away the unpleasant word. "I don't understand that this pearl bed belongs to anyone. This island isn't the professor's property. It doesn't even belong to the United States Government. It's part of a trusteeship under the United Nations – but even the United Nations doesn't claim to own it. It's nobody's – it's everybody's. And I'm part of everybody. So are you. This lagoon and anything that happens to be in it is common property. You and I have a right to it."

"You mean to say that after all the trouble and expense the professor went to to plant this bed . . ."

"The professor was a fool. He had too much faith in human nature. Well, it's human nature to look after

137

yourself, and that's just what I'm doing. Now I'll be frank with you. My name is Merlin Kaggs. I'm a pearl trader. I buy pearls from the diving outfits in the South Seas and take them to New York and London and Paris and sell them. I know pearls. You could do worse than to go in with me. I can get prices for pearls that an amateur in the business couldn't possibly match. And I'm willing to share with you fifty-fifty. How does that sound?"

"If you will stand up," Hal said evenly, "I'll tell you how it sounds."

The big man rose. Although Hal was six feet tall, Kaggs loomed over him like a Kodiak bear standing on its hind feet. Hal swung his right fist with all his might into the oyster-slippery face above him.

Kaggs staggered backward a few steps. He did not return the blow. His right hand crept upward under his jacket to his left shoulder and came out holding a gun.

"You know so much about me," Kaggs said thickly. "Perhaps you don't know I've killed a man for less than that."

"There's nothing to stop you from repeating the performance."

Kaggs' eyes blazed. "Any more lip from you and I will.

138

Sit down with your back to that palm log. Be quick about it! And your brother beside you. Snap into it!"

Roger looked doubtfully at his brother. Hal did not move. But both of them came suddenly to life when the gun roared. Kaggs fired two shots, one of them barely missing Hal and the other coming within a few inches of Roger. The bullets ricocheted on the rocks and went spinning off toward the ocean. The report echoed back from the reef across the lagoon. A lone gull rose from a palm stump and flew off.

The two boys thought it best to sit where they were told.

"You wouldn't consider putting down that gun and fighting this out man to man?" Hal suggested.

"Man to boy," sneered Kaggs. "I could break you apart with my two hands. But why take the trouble? I use my brains, not my muscles. If you had sense enough to do the same you'd come in with me on this deal. But since you won't, I know who will. Omo, come over here."

"You won't make any deal with Omo," Hal said.

Kaggs laughed harshly. "I never knew a native yet who couldn't be bought. Omo, I want you to dive for me. Right now. I'll pay you better than you were ever paid in your life. All right, get moving! Into the water!"

A slow smile came over Omo's handsome face. "You are making a mistake, Mr Kaggs," he said politely. "Perhaps your New Guinea savages can be bought, but not a man of Raiatea."

"You'll do what this gun tells you to do. Get going or I'll smear you all over the rocks."

Omo glanced at Hal, then back at Kaggs.

"How much will you pay me?"

"Now you're talking sense. I'll pay you a fifth of all you bring up, shell or pearls."

Omo nodded thoughtfully. "My gloves," he said. "They're on that rock behind you, Mr Kaggs."

Kaggs turned to get the gloves and Hal half-rose. Kaggs swung back to cover him with the gun.

"Get them yourself," he told Omo.

Omo passed behind him. Kaggs turned sidewise and kept a watchful eye on all three of his antagonists.

Hal made a quick move that attracted Kaggs' attention and at the same instant Omo bounded like a tiger upon the big man's shoulders. He locked an arm about his neck. As Kaggs' gun hand came up Omo seized the wrist and tried to squeeze the gun loose. Hal and Roger were attacking from in front.

Kaggs, straining every nerve, kept his grip on the gun

and turned its muzzle to bear upon Hal.

"Look out! The gun!" Omo cried. He vainly struggled to twist the arm that held it. The gun blazed. The pearl trader's previous shots had been warnings only, but this time he meant business. Only the Polynesian's tugging on his wrist prevented the shot from reaching its mark.

Again he brought the gun to bear on Hal whose fists were methodically crashing into his face.

Omo despaired of controlling that powerful arm. But there was one thing left that he could do. He swung around his opponent's shoulder so that he came between the gun and Hal. There was a shot and Omo fell to the ground.

Hal immediately dropped beside his friend. Vividly he remembered the night on the beach at Bikini when they had sworn loyalty to each other and had exchanged names. Omo had been true to his pledge.

Roger quit his pummelling of the giant's solar plexus to see what had happened to Omo. Kaggs promptly disappeared.

"Let him go," Hal said. He wouldn't leave Omo now. "We'll deal with him later."

Omo lay with eyes closed. Hal felt his pulse. It was still beating. Blood trickled from his right leg some ten inches above the knee.

Hal examined the wound. There were two holes, one where the bullet had gone in, one where it had come out. The skin about the first hole was scorched with powder burns because of the close range of the firing.

The bullet had probably gone through a muscle. Luckily it had missed the artery. The wound was bleeding, but not profusely.

Hal stripped off his shirt, soaked it in the lagoon, and bathed the wound.

"Wish we had some penicillin," he said, "or some sulfa powder."

"We've got both on the boat," Roger said. "Shall I go and get them?"

"We could take care of him better on board. Put him in his bunk. But it would be pretty hard to carry him over this rough ground. Suppose you run the boat over here. No, wait a minute. I think I hear the motor now."

Sure enough, across the lagoon came the gug-gug-gug of the *Kiku's* engine.

"Kaggs is bringing it. The fellow must have a white streak in him after all."

Out from behind an elbow of the reef came the *Kiku* and plodded its way across the lagoon and into the bay of pearls. Hal in the meantime had turned his shirt into a tourniquet and applied it just above the wound. He must remember to loosen it every fifteen minutes.

He could almost forgive Kaggs. Evidently the big fellow was sorry for what he had done.

"Show him where to bring the boat up against the rocks," Hall called to Roger.

Then he looked up, surprised, for the motor had quit. The boat was still a hundred feet away from shore. She had almost lost momentum.

"You'll have to give her a little more to bring her up," Hal called.

Kaggs' reply was a lazy laugh. He spun the wheel. The boat slowly turned and came to a standstill with her bow headed out toward the lagoon.

"You're making a slight mistake," Kaggs chuckled. "I wasn't planning to come ashore. Just wanted to exchange a few compliments with you before I leave."

Hal and Roger stared, unbelieving.

"What do you mean, leave?" demanded Hal, uneasiness crawling like a snake along his backbone.

"Just what I say. You won't take me up on my proposition, so I'll have to go alone. I'll toddle down to Ponape and get a pearling lugger and divers. Then I'll be back."

"You can't do it," Hal said. "You know you can't navigate."

"What of it? Ponape is a big island. If I keep her headed south I'm pretty sure to strike it."

"But Omo should be taken to a doctor. He may die here. Doesn't that concern you?"

"Why should it?"

"And this place . . ." Hal looked about him at the hurricane-ruined island and panic shook him. "You can't leave us here. We couldn't last until you got back. There's no food. I haven't even seen a crab. There's no shade, nothing to make a hut out of. There's no water. We'd die of thirst. And you'll go to prison."

"I've been to prison," Kaggs said. "I don't plan to go again. That's why I didn't shoot all three of you dead. If anybody asks me – and I don't suppose anybody will – I'll just say you decided to stay on the island till I come back. If you can't stick it out it'll be no hair off my hide."

His hand reached for the throttle.

"Wait!" called Hal. "At least you can do this. Reach into the first-aid kit and fling us that tube of penicillin and the can of sulfa."

Kaggs laughed. "Might need them myself, old man. No telling what might happen on the perilous deep you know."

The light breeze had been drifting the boat a little closer to shore. Suddenly Roger made a running dive into the cove and swam for the boat with swift powerful strokes. In a flash Hal was after him. If the motor failed to start at the first touch they might just make it. Exactly what they could do against an armed man when they got there they did not stop to consider.

Kaggs slipped the throttle. The engine roared into life. The propeller churned. The heavy boat got under way slowly and it seemed for a moment that the boys would overtake it. Then it began to pull away faster than they could swim.

They stopped swimming and, treading water, watched the boat chug away across the lagoon. Just before it rounded the spur of rock that hid the channel to the ocean, Kaggs waved his hand.

Then there was nothing to be seen but the wake of the boat across the lagoon. And nothing to be heard but the cry of the lone gull left by the hurricane.

"That's that," said Hal, thus mildly expressing the despair that iced his heart. They wearily swam back to the shore, crawled out onto the hot rocks, and dropped beside Omo.

Hal and Roger stared at each other in silence. It was still hard to realize what had happened to them. Their eyes travelled over the bare piles of coral blocks.

Roger began to laugh weakly. "I've always wanted to be cast away on a desert island. But I never meant it to be quite as much of a desert as this!"

14
Desert Island

Omo stirred and groaned. A wrinkle of pain went across his forehead. He opened his eyes. He looked up at Hal and Roger. Slowly he remembered what had happened.

"Sorry I passed out on you." He tried to get up but sank back, making a wry face.

"Better lie still," Hal said. Omo managed a grin. "What's been going on while I've been snoozing? Have I missed something?"

"Not much. We've just been saying good-bye to Kaggs."

"Good-bye?"

"He's gone — with the boat. To Ponape to get a lugger and divers."

Now Omo's eyes opened wide. "No! He must be bluffing — just trying to scare you into making a deal with him. He'll be back before night. He wouldn't leave us on this reef."

"Wish I could think so."

"But it would take him at least three days to get to Ponape. He might have to stay there a week or even two before he could get a lugger and divers — they're hard to come by. Then three or four days to come back. Does he realize what could happen to us in three weeks?"

"I think he does. But that doesn't worry him."

"Or even one week," said Omo, looking about at the desolation of white rocks under the blinding sun. "Do you know why this island is uninhabited?"

"No – why?"

"Because men can't live here. Or, at least, none have been willing to try. There could never have been enough to support life here – and what little there was was smashed by the hurricane. Even the birds have no use for the place. I haven't seen any fish in the lagoon. Roger called it Starvation Island. That's a good name for it. Or Dead Man's Reef."

He closed his eyes and wrestled for a while with pain. Then he looked up and smiled.

"I shouldn't talk that way. Guess it was just because I felt weak. Of course we can make a go of it – somehow. But there's a lot to do. I can't lie here taking my ease." He struggled to a sitting position.

"You lie down!" said Hal sharply. "Now see what you've done – started it bleeding again. And we have no medicine."

"Luckily that's where you're wrong," Omo said weakly.

"This is a medicine chest that I have my head on." His head rested on a palm log.

"What can we do with that?"

"Take your knife, Hal, and scrape the bark. Scrape it fine so as to make a powder. Then put it on. It's astringent. It will stop the bleeding."

"But is it antiseptic?"

"Oh yes. The sun has sterilized it."

Hal had often heard of the skilful use the Polynesians make of herbs, grasses, roots and trees for medical purposes, but had not expected to find a medicine chest under his patient's head.

He scraped until he had a plentiful supply of the powdered bark of the coconut palm and then applied it to the wound, binding it in place with a strip torn from his shirt which was serving as a tourniquet.

Hal put his hand on Omo's forehead. It was hot. Omo was tossing feverishly.

"We've got to get him into the shade," Hal told Roger. Squinting to protect their eyes from the glare they scanned the island. The blazing rocks laughed back at them.

There was a band of shade cast by a palm stump. They laid Omo in it. It was better than nothing, although as the sun travelled across the sky they would have to keep shifting the patient.

"Somehow we'll have to build a shelter," Hal said.

Roger laughed bitterly. "Fat chance!" But he got up at once and began to search the island for building materials.

Omo was muttering and Hal bent down to hear what he was saying.

"I hope that what I said didn't worry you, Hal. We can manage all right. After all, it won't be long. A week or two, or three, and he'll be back. He can find it okay – he's got the log to go by. It isn't as if he weren't coming back. That would be tough. No ships ever come by here. We could rot. But there's no need to worry about that – he'll be back."

"Yes, Omo," Hal said. "Now see if you can snatch some sleep."

A terrible chill settled upon Hal's heart. He alone knew that Kaggs would never come back.

Kaggs had the log to go by. What a bitter joke that was! Hal had intended it to be a joke on Kaggs. It had turned into a joke on himself and his two companions. A joke that might cost them their lives.

The bearings in the log were a hundred miles off. Finding no island there, Kaggs would not have the slightest idea in what direction to sail. The chances would be a thousand to one, perhaps a million to one, against his finding Pearl Lagoon. He might hunt for it for months, or years, without success. He could come within a few miles of it without seeing it. Nowhere did the reef rise more than ten feet above sea level and there was not a tree left standing. At a short distance the white reef might be mistaken for a wind ripple on the ocean's surface.

And even if Kaggs did by a miracle come upon the island after perhaps a year of search, what good would it do them? He would find their white bones among the rocks.

Perhaps Kaggs had not actually meant them to die here. Perhaps he had intended to get back before they perished. But Hal had fixed it so that he would not get back.

Would Roger and Omo blame him when they knew that he had signed their death warrants? They would try not to, but could they help it as they lay dying of starvation and thirst on this horrible white skeleton of coral rock?

At least he could not tell them yet. It might snuff out what little hope they had and endanger Omo's recovery.

Hal dismissed his gloomy thoughts and devoted himself to Omo. The wound had stopped bleeding. The native remedy had worked. He cautiously removed the tourniquet – it would be well to get it off to avoid any chance of gangrene. Still the wound did not bleed. Hal developed high respect for the astringent qualities of powdered coconut bark.

He took the torn shirt to the edge of the cove, soaked it, waved it in the air so that evaporation might cool the water in it, and laid it across Omo's hot forehead. Omo hardly seemed to know what was going on.

Roger was not having much luck. The natural material to make a roof would be palm leaves. There were numerous palm stumps, but most of the fallen trees had been washed away by the waves which had evidently rolled high across the reef during the storm.

A few of the logs had been pinned fast between the rocks. He examined them hopefully but their leaves had been stripped from them before they fell.

Well, it didn't have to be palm leaves. He shut his eyes, for the light was blinding, and tried to think what else he could use. Pandanus leaves would do, or taro leaves, or banana leaves. On a proper desert island there would be all of these and more. He had read many stories of castaways on desert islands. He knew just what a desert island ought to be.

It should be a jungle as full of food as a refrigerator. You had only to reach up and pluck a banana or a breadfruit or a wild orange or a lime or a mango or a papaya or a custard apple or a durian or a persimmon or a mamey or a guava or some wild grapes. The lagoon was full of fish, you could dig up any quantity of clams and mussels from the beaches, the birds were so plentiful you could catch them by hand, there were nests full of eggs in the cliffs on the seaward side, you could trap a great sea turtle when it comes ashore at night to deposit its eggs, you could drink pure water of mountain streams and bathe in woodland pools – and you could make a house of bamboo poles and palm thatch in no time.

He opened his eyes and the glare on the white rocks hit him so hard that he blinked with pain.

Then he saw something lying among the rocks just above the reach of the surf. It looked like a boat upside down. Perhaps it *was* a boat tossed ashore by the storm.

His heart began to thud with excitement. If it was a boat they could escape from Starvation Island. He ran toward it, stumbling over the rough coral.

It was not a boat, but a great fish. It lay belly upward and was quite dead. It was fully thirty feet long and as big around as an elephant.

Its body was brownish and covered with white spots. Its face was the ugliest Roger had ever seen. It looked like the face of a very unhappy bullfrog enlarged many hundreds of times. Far out at each corner popped out a small eye.

But the most terrific feature was the mouth. It was four feet wide. Long fringes drooped from its corners.

One would think that such a huge and hideous creature would be a cannibal and a man-eater, but Roger had already had some acquaintance with fish of this sort. He knew it to be a whale shark, the largest of all living fish, sometimes twice as long as this specimen. Although a shark, it was harmless and lived on very small creatures, some of them so small that they could be seen only with a microscope.

"But this isn't getting us a roof," Roger reminded himself, and started away. Then a thought struck him and he turned back. He tried to remember pictures he had once seen of the houses of tribes living along the Amur River in Siberia. In that region there were no trees to use as building materials, so the men made their houses of – fishskins!

What was the matter with building a shanty out of sharkskin?

He ran back to tell Hal. He expected his brother to

laugh at his idea but Hal said, "Why not? I think you've got something there."

They went back to the sea monster.

"That surely must be the plainest face in the whole Pacific Ocean," Hal said. He touched the hard sand-papery skin. "It's not going to be easy to cut that. But we have good knives. We'll slit him down the belly and then cut just behind the head and in front of the tail fin."

The skin was as tough as emery cloth. Sometimes the knife could not be forced into it unless pounded in with a coral block.

Hal, sweating and straining, said, "There's one good thing about it. Once we get it up it will be more durable than any roof of palm thatch. It ought to last as long as asbestos shingles!"

"And all we ask," Roger put in, "is for it to last a couple of weeks until Kaggs gets here."

Hal felt his heart sink. He was not ready to tell Roger yet, but shouldn't he begin to prepare his mind for the bad news that Kaggs would not return?"

"Of course," and he tried to speak lightly, "there's always a chance that we won't see him again."

Roger stopped and looked at him.

"Then what will happen to us?"

157

"Oh, we'll make out. We'll have to. Now then, let's try to flay the skin up at this corner. Boy, isn't it thick!"

After two hours of hard work they stopped for breath. The skin was not more than half off. The smell of the dead fish was overpowering. The sun beat down like hammers on their heads. Their eyes were narrowed to slits to avoid the glare. Roger wiped his perspiring face with his sleeve. Hal, having made a tourniquet, bandages, and a wet compress out of his own shirt, dried his face on his brother's shirt-tail.

"I could do with a drink of water," Roger said.

Hal looked serious. "What have I been thinking of? Water! That's more important than shelter – more important even than food. Let's leave the rest of this job until tomorrow. I'll see how Omo is – then we'll go on the trail after water."

Omo was asleep. The shadow of the stump had left him. Hal and Roger moved him into the shade and Hal soaked the compress and replaced it on the patient's forehead.

The quest for water began. The boys started out in apparently good spirits but secretly each had little hope. How could one expect to find fresh water on this sun-burnt reef?

"It must have rained a lot here during the hurricane,"

158

Hal said. "There may be some of it left in the hollows of the rocks."

Close to the shore a rock hollowed out like a bowl held a little water. Roger eagerly ran to it, scooped up a little of the water in his hand, and tasted it. He spat it out.

"Salty!"

"It must have been left there by the surf at high tide," Hal guessed. "Let's look farther away from the shore."

They found plenty of hollowed rocks but no water in them. In some were lines showing that they had contained water but it had long since soaked away through the porous coral.

Roger surveyed the coconut stumps.

"There must have been nuts on these trees."

If they could find them they would not lack for drink nor for food. How refreshing the sweet, cool, milky water of the coconut would be! And the soft white meat!

A diligent search failed to discover any coconuts.

"The trouble with coconuts," Hal said, "is that they float. When the sea swept over the land it must have carried them all off."

"What do we do next?" inquired Roger.

"Dig," suggested Hal. He led the way to the lagoon beach. "They say you can sometimes find fresh water if you dig a hole in the beach at low tide. How about this spot – just below the high-tide mark?"

"It sounds crazy to me," Roger said, "but mine not to question why, mine but to do or die," and he picked up a flat piece of coral to use as a shovel and began to dig.

At a depth of about three feet Hal stopped. "Quit digging. Let's see what happens now."

Water began to ooze into the hole. Presently it was four or five inches deep.

"But what makes you think this will be fresh water?"

"I don't think so," Hal said. "I only hope so. It has happened on other atolls. Shipwrecked sailors have escaped dying of thirst by drinking the water from holes like this one."

"But why would it be fresh?"

"The sea water filtering through the sand loses some of its salt. And then there's the rainwater that filters down through the rocks. Suppose you try it now. But be careful to skim off just the surface. The fresh water is lighter than sea water and lies on top."

Roger scooped off a little of the surface water and tasted it. Then he gulped down a couple of handfuls. "Salty," he said, "but not as bad as sea water."

Hal tasted the warm brackish water. He was disappointed. "It wouldn't take much of that to make you sick."

160

Roger was gagging and holding his forehead. Presently he lost his breakfast.

He turned upon his brother angrily. "You and your fresh water! What you don't know about how to survive on a desert island would fill a book."

"I'm afraid you're right," Hal admitted. "All I know is that the U.S. Navy instructs survivors to do just what we have done."

"They why didn't it work?"

"Perhaps because the sand is too coarse here to filter out the salt. Or perhaps there wasn't enough rain, or it sank away through the rocks."

"All right, don't stand there giving me perhapses. Find me some water."

"Sometimes," Hal said, "I think you're a spoiled brat. Do you suppose you are the only thirsty person on this reef?"

Roger was silent. They resumed their dreary search. They walked across the narrow part of the reef where it stretched like a bridge from one island to the other. On one side the ocean surf splashed among the rocks. On the other side a white beach sloped to the blue lagoon. The lagoon was as smooth as glass. It was not more than a dozen feet deep here and the bottom was a fairy city of pink palaces, towers, pagodas, and minarets, all built by the tiny coral insects.

It was very lovely if you could just forget being hot, tired, sore-eyed, and thirsty. But you couldn't forget.

The reef broadened to form the other island. They spent an hour or more exploring it. There was no water, except surf water, in the cups of the rocks. There were coconut stumps and logs but no leaves. They looked hopefully in the tops of the stumps for pockets of rainwater, but it had dried away.

Then they found a coconut! It was pinned under a rock where the waves that had buried the island had failed to dislodge it.

Trembling with excitement, they slashed away the husk. The nut inside was cracked. Inserting his knife in the crack, Hal prised off the cap of the nut. Both boys groaned when they saw the contents.

"Suffering cats!" Roger mourned. "It's rotten!"

Salt water entering through the crack had spoiled both the meat and the liquid.

Hal scraped out the inside of the nut. "At least we have a cup now."

"What's the use of a cup with nothing to put in it?"

"We'll find something."

They searched until the sun was low in the west. Their stomachs were now reminding them of the need of food as well as of water.

"Here's water!" exclaimed Hal. Roger came to see what he had found. It was nothing but a low flat weed rooted in a little soil between the rocks.

"So that's water!" sneered Roger.

Hal paid no attention to his sarcasm. He broke off one of the small pulpy leaves and chewed it. The leaf was full of a cool juice. It was wonderfully refreshing to the dry mouth and parched tongue. A grin of contentment spread over Hal's face.

Roger bit into a leaf. "Boy, does that taste good!" But he did not take any more. The two boys, with a single thought, dug up the plant and trudged with it to their own island. If they were thirsty, their feverish patient would be much more so.

Omo was tossing restlessly. He opened his eyes. They were bright with fever.

"We brought you some water, Omo. But it's water you have to chew. I don't know what your island name for it is – we call it pigweed or purslane."

Omo took the plant eagerly. He chewed the leaves, stems, and roots, extracting and swallowing the juice.

163

"It's wonderful," he said gratefully. "I hope you got plenty more for yourselves." His eyes questioned Roger.

"Take it all," Roger said. "We're okay."

"Sorry we can't offer you any dinner," Hal said.

Omo smiled. "Water was all I wanted. Now I can sleep," and he closed his eyes.

Hal looked for more pigweed but found none. The drop or two of water he had pressed out of the leaf seemed only to have increased his thirst. He was glad to see the killer sun sink below the horizon. The coral rocks quickly lost their heat. Thank heaven for the night! He dreaded the thought that another blazing day must come, and another, and another, until they died in this infernal sea-trap.

How to get water! It was still the number one problem. He sat down to think. His hand rested upon a rock. Suddenly he realized that the rock was damp.

The dew! The dew was falling. In the darkening shadows a mist drifted over the lagoon. If he could find a way to catch the dew . . .

The Polynesians had a way of doing that. If he could just remember how it went. He would like to ask Omo – but Omo must be allowed to sleep.

He went to the lagoon beach and dug a shallow hole in the sand about two feet wide. He placed the cup of the coconut shell at the bottom. He covered the hole with Roger's shirt taken from Omo's forehead. Omo would not need it now that the air was cool. He pierced an opening in the shirt just over the cup. Then he piled a pyramid of stones about three feet high over the shirt.

The principle of the thing was that dew would collect in the chinks between the stones, trickle through them to the shirt, and run down into the cup. In the morning there might be a cupful of fresh water.

Hal went back to find Roger stretched out on the rocks near Omo fast asleep. Hal tried to make himself comfortable on the lumpy coral.

But he could not sleep. The three words that separate life from death kept going through his brain – water, food, shelter.

He thought of the soft life at home. Where you slept in a smooth bed under a good roof. Where you had only to turn a tap to get water. Where you were called three times a day to a table groaning with food.

Life was so easy at home that a fellow got out of the habit of appreciating it. You took it for granted. Hal was certain he would never take it for granted again.

His throat was as dry as sandpaper and his stomach felt as hollow as a drum. He dozed off and dreamed of rain. He woke up with a start and looked at the sky.

There was not a cloud as big as his hand. The stars blazed like the hot merciless suns they were. The Milky Way looked like a path of powdered glass.

That other night on the island at Bikini he had heard small animals moving through the brush. Here on Dead Man's Reef, as Omo had called it, there was no sound but the sob and suck of the surf. There was even the smell of death, drifting across the island from the body of the rotting shark.

Hal fell into a troubled sleep.

15
The Sharkskin House

The light of early dawn woke him. There were kinks and quirks in his back where the rocks had jabbed him with their sharp elbows. But the air was cool and fresh. Hal did not feel quite as hungry and thirsty as he had the night before. He knew that was not a good sign – his system was becoming numb.

The brisk invigorating air put new ambition into him. Somehow they were going to beat this reef, and Kaggs too.

He tried to remember how it went in the poem – the morning's dew-pearled, all's right with the world. He rose cheerfully and went to see what he had caught in his dew-trap.

The coconut shell was nearly half-full of water. He had hoped for more but evidently the dew had been light. He took the precious liquid to camp.

Omo was stirring but seemed to be in a sort of stupor. Hal raised his head and poured half of the water down his throat.

"You drink the rest," he told Roger who was sitting up yawning, rubbing some of the creases out of his hide. Hal put the cup in Roger's hands and went off to renew his attack upon the sharkskin. That terrific sun would be rising soon and it was essential that they should have some protection against it.

Roger sat looking at the water in the bottom of the shell. If he had been offered a choice between the water and a hundred dollars at that moment he would have said, "Me for the water!" But shucks! – camels could go a week without water. And his brother had called him a spoiled brat. Omo was groaning softly. He was muttering, "It's so hot – so hot – so hot!" Perspiration ran down his face. If he was so hot before sunrise, how would he feel later?

Roger parted Omo's lips and emptied the cup into the brown boy's dry mouth.

Then, feeling pretty noble, he went to join Hal. He wanted to tell Hal what he had done so that his brother wouldn't think him a spoiled brat. But he decided to hold his tongue.

The red-hot devil of a sun rose before they finished flensing off the skin. It was a magnificent sheet nearly twenty feet long and eight wide. They scraped the fat off the inner surface. Then they stood back and admired their work.

"That was a good idea of yours," Hal said.

"Well, I remembered your telling me that somewhere they build houses of fishskin. Isn't it in Siberia?"

"Yes. The people called the Fishskin Tartars. Their food is fish, they make their clothes and shoes out of fish-skin, and their huts are built of poles with fishskin stretched over them. And you can always tell when you come near a fishskin village by the smell!"

"I know what you mean," said Roger, turning up his nose.

"The sharkskin won't smell so bad after the sun has cured it. But we ought to get rid of the carcass. Let's try to roll it down where high tide will take it."

By dint of hard labour they inched the monster's body down close to the water's edge.

"There's a lot of meat here," Roger said. "It's a shame we can't eat it."

"It's too badly decayed. Better eat nothing than that."

So, turning their backs upon the poisonous breakfast that the sea had offered them, they returned to camp, dragging the sharkskin behind them.

Now they launched into building operations in earnest. Having no nails, screws, or bolts, no beams, joists, or planks, nothing that a house-builder would ordinarily think necessary, they had to use considerable ingenuity.

"We have only enough skin for the roof," Roger said. "How about piling up rocks to make the walls?"

"Sure! But we'll need a ridgepole. And a couple of posts to hold it up. That palm log might do for a ridgepole. It's slender – I think we can lift it."

"And if we could find a couple of stumps the right distance apart they would do for posts."

There were plenty of palm stumps left standing. They found two that stood about eight feet high and a dozen feet apart. With their knives they cut notches in the tops of the stumps and hoisted the palm log in place so that it lay in the notches and stretched from one stump to the other. Now they had their ridgepole.

"Funny to start with the roof," Roger said.

170

"Not so funny. The Polynesians often do that, and the Japanese always do. Build the roof first, hoist it up on stilts, hold a celebration, and then build the house under the roof."

They stretched the twenty-foot skin over the ridgepole so that it was ten feet long on each side. Then they proceeded to build the walls. They piled coral blocks up to a height of about four feet. They fitted them together as well as possible so that the inside surface would be nearly vertical. On the outside the wall was solidly buttressed with more rocks. They left four gaps to serve as doors for getting in and out, and for ventilation.

Then they stretched the sharkskin out until it went smooth and straight from the ridgepole in both directions down to the tops of the walls. There they pinned it fast with lumps of coral.

The house was finished – and surely no stranger one had ever been seen, even in the land of the Fishskin Tartars!

They brought Omo in and laid him down on the least rough portion of the coral floor. He breathed a sigh of contentment for the place was dark and cool. The three-foot-thick rock walls defied the sun. The sharkskin, although not as heatproof as palm thatch, was thicker than shingles. The roof was a bit low, but it was better to have it low and snug in case of a windstorm.

171

The room measured only eight feet in the direction of the ridgepole, but nearly twenty feet the other way – quite big enough for three persons.

"There's even room enough to do our cooking inside on rainy days," Hal said.

"*If* there is any rain. And *if* we have anything to cook. And *if* we can make a fire without matches."

Hal gritted his teeth. "We've got to lick those ifs. We can't make it rain, but there must be some way to find fresh water. Let me think. You can get water from the *guiji* vine but none of it grows here. There's water in the barrel cactus but there's no barrel cactus. How about pandanus? It often grows even in as bad a spot as this. Those little air roots that look like leaves contain water. Let's go."

They went out with pretended enthusiasm but no real expectation of finding pandanus.

Hal picked up a pebble and gave it to Roger. "Chew on that," he suggested. "It makes the saliva flow and you'll almost think you're getting a drink."

They searched diligently the rest of the day. They found no pandanus nor anything else that yielded moisture. This reef seemed as dead and dry as the moon.

At night Hal again built a cairn of stones to collect dew. But a wind came up and dew did not form. In the

172

morning the cup was empty. Even the patient had to go without water.

Omo was conscious now. His leg gave him great pain and he suffered from thirst that had been made more intense by his fever. But the heat had gone from his forehead and cheeks. Hal consulted him on the problem of water. He told him what they had done to find it. "You probably would have had better ideas."

"No, I would have done just what you have done. You were pretty smart – that pigweed and then catching the dew."

"I never felt so stupid in my life," Hal grumbled.

Omo looked at his friend's haggard and troubled face. "You're letting worry get you down. Will you do me a favour?"

"Sure. Anything."

"You and Roger go in for a swim. Our people believe that when things get very bad it helps to turn your back on them and go and play for a while. It will relax you. You'll be able to think better."

"Very well, Dr Omo, if you insist," Hal said. "But it seems an awful waste of time."

"Boy, it sounds good to me," Roger said. "Let's go in on the ocean side – it will be cooler."

They plunged into the surf. The bottom did not slope gradually away but dropped abruptly to great depths. They performed like two playful seals, diving, swimming, splashing, and their cares flowed away like raindrops from a duck's back.

"You can't catch me," shouted Roger.

"What'll you bet?"

"I'll betcha this island."

"I don't want your blasted island, but I'll catch you," and Hal burrowed deep down after the disappearing form of Roger.

At a depth of twenty feet or more, Roger began following the shore. Hal was close behind. Where the bridge of reef widened into the second island Roger suddenly felt the water go very cold.

It seemed to be a submarine current coming from the land. In a moment he was out of it. Now Hal felt it. Astonished, both boys popped to the surface.

Roger shook the water from his face. "What do you make of that?"

"It comes from a cave in the land. Do you know what that means?"

"Can't say that I do."

"It means it's fresh water, or I'm a donkey's breakfast."

"You're probably a donkey's breakfast," agreed Roger.

"Wish we had a bottle. Well, let's go down and fill our mouths."

Hal dived. When his head came into the cold stream he opened his mouth and let the water crowd in. It was fresh and sweet! He swallowed it, gulped another mouthful, and came up. Roger emerged beside him.

"It's the real thing," he marvelled.

Hal was beaming. "Things are looking up," he exulted. "Stay here and mark the place while I get the cup."

In ten minutes he was back with the coconut shell.

"But it ought to have a lid or a cork," Roger said. "How can you keep it empty until you get down there?"

"I don't think it needs to be empty," and Hal dived with the shell which promptly filled with sea water. When he reached the cold stream he held the cup in it and turned it upside down. He pushed his hand into it a few times to change the water. The salt water, being heavier, should fall out of the cup and be replaced by fresh.

He turned the shell right side up and rose to the surface. He joined Roger on the rocks.

"Try it." He offered the cup to Roger who warily tasted the liquid. Then he began to gulp it down greedily.

"Go easy!" warned Hal. "You're as dry as a bone inside.

You'll have trouble if you take on too much all at once."

Refilling the cup at the submarine spring, they carried the precious liquid to Omo. When the fever-worn patient saw the cup full of water, tears came to his eyes. He took one sip, then put the cup aside.

"I've never tasted anything so good in all my life."

"Won't you have more?" Hal asked.

"Later. My stomach isn't used to such luxury."

"Now we have two of the necessities of life," Hal said, "shelter and water. But my insides tell me that we can't keep going much longer without food."

Omo groaned. "I ought to be helping you. And here I am lying flat on my back as useless as a log."

Hal looked affectionately at his brown companion. "You were mighty useful to me when you stopped that bullet."

"Forget it."

"I'll never forget it. Perhaps I can pay you back some day. Just at the moment the best thing I can do for you is to get you something to eat. Come on, Roger."

Roger hated to leave the cool shade of the sharkskin cave.

"I don't believe there's a mouthful of food on this infernal reef," he grumbled.

"There's one good sign," Omo said, "that gull that you

176

say is staying on the island. He wouldn't stay if there weren't anything to eat."

"I'm sorry to report," Hal said, "that he's gone. He flew away last night."

For a moment no one spoke. In spite of the water, despair lay heavy upon their spirits. Hunger made them feel weak and hopeless. Hal roused himself. He sprang up, not very briskly for his legs felt uncertain, and started out of the hut.

"Come on, old man," he called back to Roger. "We're going to show that gull he made a mistake!"

16
The Castaways Eat

Hunger sharpened their eyes. They went over the reef with a fine-tooth comb. Nothing was too small to escape their attention.

They turned over rocks and looked beneath. They moved logs. They burrowed in the sand of the beach.

It was most disappointing.

After three hours of it, Roger dropped wearily to the ground with his head against a log. He felt as if he never wanted to move again.

Gradually he became aware of a scratching sound. It seemed to be inside the log. He called Hal.

"Put your ear against this log. Do you hear anything?"

Hal listened. "There's something alive in there. Perhaps we can get at it with our knives."

They cut into the log which proved to be decayed. Presently Roger gave a grunt of disgust. He had uncovered something that looked like a fat caterpillar.

"It's a grub!" exclaimed Hal. "Later on it changes into the white beetle. Put it in your pocket and let's see if there're any more of them."

"You don't mean to say we're going to eat them!"

"Of course we are! Beggars can't be choosers."

They found fourteen of the grubs and took them to show to Omo.

"Aren't they poison?" Roger asked doubtfully.

"No indeed," Omo said. "Full of vitamins!"

"Won't we have to cook them?"

"Yes, but the sun will do that for you. They aren't used to the sun. Lay them out on a hot rock and they'll soon be roasted."

The roasted grubs were not half bad. In fact, with appetites made keen by two days of hunger, everyone voted them to be delicious.

"Where you found them there ought to be termites," Omo said. "They like rotten wood too."

Omo's guess proved to be correct. In another part of the log the boys came upon a nest of termites, the so-called "white ants". They were big and plump. Hating the sun, they tried to escape into their tunnels in the wood. Hal and Roger scooped them out and placed them on a hot rock, in the blazing sun. They curled up, died, and fried.

Again the boys dined. They became almost merry.

Roger smacked his lips. "I won't know what to do when I get home if I don't have my grubs and termites," he said.

Further search revealed nothing. Just before the sun sank in the west Hal dived to bring up more drinking water. It seemed to him that the submarine stream was not quite as strong as it had been. It was perhaps caused by the rain that had fallen upon the island a few days before. This water filtering down through the rocks was coming out below. But it would not keep coming if there were no more rain. Rather anxiously, Hal returned to camp, but said nothing about his fears.

"Surely there must be some fish in these waters," he said. "How can we catch them?"

They debated the possibilities. It was a real problem since they had no fishline, no hook, no rod, no bait, no net, no spear.

Omo, if he had been his usual self, probably would have come up with the answer. But he was very tired and presently went to sleep. Hal and Roger continued to wrestle with the problem, but the younger brother was getting drowsy.

"We might make a trap," Hal said, "if we had a crate or a box or a basket."

"But we haven't," yawned Roger, "so we don't make a trap."

"Yes, we do!" cried Hal, and was out of the hut before

he had finished the words. Roger sleepily followed, wondering what crazy idea possessed his brother now.

Though the sun had gone there was still some light in the sky. Hal trudged to the ocean shore where he began to fling rocks about.

"Will you tell me what you are up to?"

"We'll build a fish-trap of stone. Now's a good time – at low tide. We make a circular wall. When the tide rises it will fill with water and perhaps some fish will swim into it. When the tide goes down some of them may be left there, trapped."

"Pretty neat, if it works," agreed Roger, and they began to build the wall. They extended it a few feet into the sea so that even at low tide there would be a little water in the trap.

When it was finished the weir stood three feet high and was about twenty feet across.

Hal calculated that the tide would be high a little after midnight and low again at sunrise.

When the first rays of the sun felt their way into the sharkskin hut the next morning they found Roger awake and thinking about breakfast. His repast of grubs and termites had been long since digested and he was ready for something more substantial.

"Wake up, you dope! Let's see what's in our trap."

In the shallow water at the bottom of the trap several finny creatures were dashing about seeking a way of escape. One of them was a gorgeous fish in a coat of green and gold with fine stripes of blue and red. Hal identified it as an angel fish. There were two other fish that were less beautiful but better eating – a young barracuda and a mullet. Also there was a poisonous scorpion fish which they left in the pool hoping that the next tide would take it away.

Roger was about to lay hand on a cone-shaped starfish but Hal stopped him.

"There's poison in those barbs," he said. "If you puncture your hand on them your arm swells up and then your body and pretty soon your heart stops beating."

Roger gave it a wide berth. They caught the fish with their hands and took them to camp. Omo was delighted.

"Of course we could eat them raw," he said, "but they'd taste a lot better cooked. If I had any strength in these arms I'd make a fire."

"Let me try it," Hal said, not too confidently for he remembered his troubles in producing a fire on the floating island in the Amazon.

First he must get tinder. That at least was easy. From

the rotten log he scraped up a quantity of wood dust and split off chips and slivers. Then he and Roger accumulated a pile of bark and sticks cut from this and other logs.

"Now to find a firestick," Hal said. "It must be very white and dry."

"How will this do?" Roger brought up a piece of driftwood from the shore. It was extremely light and dry as a bone.

"Just the thing!" said Hal.

He split off a little of it and whittled it to a sharp point. Then he braced the larger piece against a stone and began to rub it up and down with the point of the small stick.

His hands moved faster and faster. Only strength and great speed would bring success. Perspiration dripped from his face. The point was wearing a groove. The wood dust scraped off by it fell to the end of the groove.

Faster went the point. The groove began to smoke. Then a wisp of flame rose from the dust.

Roger, lying on his stomach, encouraged the flame by gently blowing upon it. It was now burning brightly. Hal stopped scraping to lay slivers of wood across the dust. These caught fire. Larger pieces were added. The fire was burning well.

"Phew!" exclaimed Hal, wiping his forehead. "I think I prefer matches!"

The boys hurriedly and not too carefully cleaned the fish, then speared them on the ends of sticks and held them over the fire.

Breakfast that morning was a grand occasion. The merry castaways ate every scrap of the fish and washed it down with sparkling spring water. It was a delicious meal. Now they could forget the horrors of the first three days. They had conquered the desert island.

"At least we know now that we can hold out until Kaggs gets back," Roger said, picking up a stick in which he had already made three notches. He began on a fourth notch.

"What's that for?" Hal inquired.

"Just to keep track of the days," Roger said. "You see, the stick is just long enough for fourteen notches. That's when I expect to see that old motor-boat chugging into this lagoon. Boy, won't that be a happy day!"

"It's time I told you a few things," Hal said. "I haven't told you before because we were pretty low and I didn't want to make you feel worse. We'll have to forget about Kaggs. We'd better start building a raft."

Roger and Omo stared at him. "A raft!" Roger protested. "What's the use of that when there's a motorboat?"

"The boat won't come back," Hal said. He went on to tell them how he had altered the bearings so that Kaggs would not be able to find the island. "So I'm afraid I gummed things up pretty badly."

"You sure did!" agreed his younger brother indignantly.

"No, no," Omo said gently. "You did just what you had to do. It was the best thing to do. It means that Kaggs can't steal this pearl bed. You've saved the professor's experiment and perhaps some very valuable treasure. That was your duty to the man who employed you. As for us – we're not all that important. And anyhow, we'll get out of this. Luckily we have plenty of logs for building a raft."

"But we have to have more than logs," said Roger practically. "How are we going to fasten them together without any nails, bolts, screws, or rope? And have you forgotten the job we were supposed to do for the professor? We were to get him some specimens of his pearls so that he could see how they were doing. And Omo is the only one of us who can dive that deep. And I'll bet a plugged nickel that Omo won't be doing any diving with that hole in his leg!"

"Then we'll have to do the diving," Hal said.

Roger's jaw dropped. "Sixty feet? When we've never done more than thirty? You're crazy!"

Hal grinned and said nothing. He knew his kid brother. After Roger finished saying that the thing was impossible, he would probably be the very one to do it.

Presently Roger slipped out. After a time, Hal followed. Sure enough, Roger was practising diving in the bay of pearls.

Roger came up, puffing and blowing.

When he was able to speak he said,

"I can't get below thirty. I wish I had a pair of lead boots to pull me down."

"I'll run over to the store and get a pair for you. In the meantime you might use a rock."

"That's right, so I could."

Roger seized a rock twice as big as his head and slipped into the water. He went down rapidly at first, then more slowly, and finally reached the bottom. He held the rock under one arm and with the other pulled loose an oyster. Then he dropped the rock and rose to the surface. He laid the big brown shell on the shore.

Since he had not been down more than twenty seconds the changes in pressure had not greatly affected him.

"That was swell!" he chortled after he had caught his breath. "But it will take a year if we can only bring up one shell at a time."

187

"If we could make a basket . . ."

"Out of what?"

"I don't know. Let's ask Omo."

Omo, when consulted, sent them out to look at the heads of the fallen palm trees. He said they would find cloth and out of it they could make a bag.

"I think he's spoofing us," Roger said.

But they found the "cloth". It was like a mat, a brown criss-cross of fibres formerly wrapped around the bases of the leaves.

It was a simple matter to cut out a sheet of it with their knives. They laced the edges together with some of the fibres so that the sheet was turned into a bag.

"And why can't we make shirts out of this stuff?" Hal wondered.

Roger's shirt had been used to collect the water and Hal's had been ripped up for use as bandages and tourniquet. The tropical sun reflecting on the white rocks had badly burned their skin.

They made shirts. They were not quite of the latest fashionable cut but they served to filter the sun.

"And I want a pair of dark glasses," Roger said. The eyes of both boys were bloodshot, thanks to the merciless glare. Hal had been worrying about this. Castaways on such unshaded reefs sometimes went blind. So he welcomed his brother's suggestion.

They made masks of the matting long enough to go around and tie behind the head. They could see through the weave as through coarse cheesecloth. Most of the sun glare was cut off.

"That feels a lot better," Hal sighed.

"But I hope I don't look as funny as you do," Roger laughed, inspecting his brother in his brown mask and the shirt that resembled a shaggy doormat. With no razor to keep them down, bristling black whiskers had sprouted on his cheeks and chin. "You sure look like Blackbeard the Pirate."

"Let's surprise Omo."

The two masked bandits crept back to the hut and prowled into the dark interior. Omo who had been dozing looked up with a start and gave a cry of alarm – then he recognized his strange visitors. He admired the shirts, masks, and bag.

"I think you must be half Polynesian," he said, "you make such good use of what you find here."

The two boys returned to the cove in high spirits. Omo's approval meant a good deal to them.

"I only hope we're good enough Polynesians to bring up some pearls," Hal said.

But it was not too easy. Hal, after shedding his clothes, stepped in with the bag and a stone to carry him down. Reaching the bottom he quickly filled the bag with shell. But when he tried to rise with the bag he found it to be too heavy. He had to take out all but three shells before he could come up with it.

"What we need is rope," he said. "We'd tie it to the bag. The man on the bottom could fill the bag and the man on top could haul it up. I think we'd better suspend operations until we can find some rope."

"Guess you're right," Roger agreed. "We need it for the raft too — to fasten the logs together. But what chance have we got of finding rope on these rocks!"

They spent most of the day in the search. They learned from Omo that the Polynesians make rope from the husk of the coconut. But they had found only one nut and its husk wasn't enough to make even a ball of string.

A liana would do as a rope — but such stout vines did not grow on reefs.

On their Amazon journey, they had seen jungle Indians use strips of the skin of the boa-constrictor and of the anaconda as rope. But there were no snakes, large or small, on coral atolls. There were sometimes sea snakes in the lagoons. They could find none in this one.

But they did discover some much-needed food. They returned to camp in the evening with a cucumber, a cabbage, and a pint of milk!

"Won't Omo be surprised?" Roger chuckled. "Who'd ever have thought that we'd find a vegetable garden and a cow on a coral reef!"

Omo gratefully drank some of the rich milk. He knew that the cow from which it had come was the coconut tree – not from a nut but from a flower stem. And the cabbage was palm cabbage, the coconut bud resembling a head of cabbage or lettuce, but much better tasting.

The cucumber never grew in a vegetable garden. It was the sea cucumber or sea slug or bêche-de-mer, highly prized as a table delicacy by the Chinese.

They had found it on a coral shelf in the lagoon. It was shaped like a huge cucumber and had the same sort of a grooved or warty skin. It was a foot long but when they took it out it shrank to half that length.

Hal recognized it as the variety that is able to sting the flesh with its feelers and eject a poison that will cause blindness. So he did not touch it with his fingers but only with the point of his knife. He left it to die and dry in the sun while they went about their other errands.

After bringing it to camp, they cut it open under Omo's

direction and stripped out the five long white muscles. These they broiled over a fire. They made a surprisingly good meal.

17

The Giant with Ten Arms

The strange food gave Roger a nightmare. He squirmed and tossed, then woke with a start.

"The sea slug!" he screamed. "My eyes! I'm blind! I'm blind!"

"Aw, shut up and go to sleep!" growled Hal.

But Roger was too disturbed to sleep. He crawled out of the hut. He was relieved to find that he was not blind.

The tree stumps rose around him like black statues.

The clock of the stars told him that it was about 3 a.m. The Southern Cross was reflected in the lagoon.

He walked along the beach of the lagoon, trying to calm himself. He was still all stirred up inside. He crossed to the ocean shore. The sea was silent. There was not a ripple. The tide was going down.

He idly wondered what had been caught in the trap. He walked to its edge and looked in.

Then he got the start of his life. Two great eyes looked back at him.

They were as big as dinner plates. Surely no living thing could have such great eyes. He must still be dreaming. This must be another nightmare.

The eyes glowed with a ghostly green light. They seemed to have lamps behind them. They looked like green traffic signals, but of enormous size. They said, "Go!" and Roger felt like going, but his legs were so weak that he could scarcely move.

Suddenly the water in the pool shook as if agitated by some tremendous creature and the two circles of green flame came closer to Roger.

He let out a terrified yell, but still could not run. He was glued to the spot as if hypnotized. That was the way it was in a dream. He must be dreaming.

Hal came tumbling to his side. "What's all the hollering about?" he demanded angrily. "Why can't you let a fellow sleep?"

Then he saw what Roger saw. Like Roger, he could hardly believe that it was real.

"They look like eyes," he said. "They can't be. No eyes ever came that big. They must be little schools of phosphorescent plankton – little creatures that float on the surface."

"You're nuts!" Roger blurted. "Plankton don't swim in a circle. They're eyes, and nothing else. Gosh, they look as big as manholes." He drew back as if afraid he would fall into the great green pools. "Look out! It's coming!"

The Thing lurched toward them a foot or two, sending them back in a panic. Its movements splashed tons of water out of the pool. Great black twisting things like enormous snakes went up into the air and then fell back.

"A giant squid!" cried Hal. He approached to get a better look. Suddenly a great arm snaked out toward him. He jumped back just in time to escape it – but both he and Roger were soaked with spray.

"He's splashing sea water," Roger said.

"No, he's squirting ink. We're covered with the stuff. Don't let it get into your eyes."

195

They moved out of range.

Roger said, "No wonder they call him the pen-and-ink fish!"

"Yes, and it's good ink. You can write with it. It's like Indian ink. I remember something about an explorer who wrote a page in his logbook with squid ink."

"See him thrash about. Won't he come after us?"

"I don't think he'll come ashore."

"But can't he escape into the sea?"

"He could easily enough if he knew how. But he's as stupid as he is big. I don't suppose he's ever been in a spot like that before and he doesn't know what to make of it."

"I wish we could take him alive. Mr Bassin wanted one of these."

"He won't get this one. We can only hope we'll come up with another after we get back to our schooner. There are lots of them in the Humboldt Current."

"That's the current that flows up the coast of South America and then out toward these islands?"

"Right. You remember that book we read about six young scientists on a balsa raft? They sailed from Peru to the islands on that current. They saw dozens of these things. They rise and float on the surface at night and sink down to great depths in the daytime."

The huge green eyes burned now bright and now dim as if someone inside were turning the lights up and down. Roger shivered.

"Gosh, doesn't he ever wink?" He thought of the eight-armed monster he had wrestled with in the cave. Its eyes had been evil too, but small, and almost like human eyes. And they had not been phosphorescent like these. "Now I begin to see the difference between a squid and an octopus. I've always wondered."

"It's more than the difference between eyes like plates and eyes like thimbles. The body of the octopus is a bag; the squid is shaped like a torpedo. He looks something like a giant fountain pen, and acts like one. And he has ten tentacles instead of eight. Two of the tentacles are extra long. And the cups that line the tentacles are not suction cups. They are edged with sharp teeth and very dangerous. They can actually cut wire."

"Aren't you putting it a little strong?"

"Not a bit of it. On an expedition of the American Museum of Natural History scientists had the light steel wire cables used as fish-line leaders cut in two by these tentacle teeth. So look out for them – unless you're made of something tougher than wire."

As dawn came on and the darkness dissolved into grey

light they could see the monster clearly. It completely filled the walled pool. In fact there was not room for its mighty arms, which lay sprawled over the rocks of the shore.

Its torpedo-shaped body kept changing colour – from black to brown, from brown to tan, from tan to a sickly white.

The eyes were more than a foot across. They were even more terrifying than they had been at night. The green phosphorescence had faded out of them and they were now a deadly black like two dark caves out of which any horror might come. They were fixed upon Hal and Roger with savage hatred. The boys felt very small under that relentless unblinking gaze.

"Nightmare of the Pacific!" breathed Hal. "He deserves his name!"

The tide had not entirely ebbed. But it had gone down enough so that there was very little water left in the rock-rimmed pool. The squid could easily have escaped while the tide was high. But, unaware of its danger, it had sunk as the tide ebbed until now it was locked between the rock walls.

The water was black with ink expelled by the angry prisoner. Now and then it filled its body with water and ejected it like a rocket, but only succeeded in ramming its rear against the wall.

"Look at the size of it!" marvelled Roger. "It's twenty

feet if it's an inch — just the body — and those longest tentacles make another twenty feet."

"But it's really small as squids go. Specimens have been found with tentacles forty-two feet long. The fellows on one scientific expedition were lucky enough to see a battle between a giant squid and a sperm whale. The squid won. It was seventy-five feet long."

"Well," said Roger, "this dainty little forty-foot item is plenty big enough for my money! Too bad we can't use him. I suppose he'll escape when the tide rises."

"Perhaps we can use him!" exclaimed Hal. "Didn't we need rope?"

"Rope! How can you get rope out of a squid?"

"Those tentacles. I'll bet they could be cut into strips that would be as tough as leather."

Roger grunted his disbelief.

"Well, why not?" went on Hal. "If they can do it with boa-constrictor or anaconda hide, why not with this? Down in Malaya they use python skin. It's so durable they cover furniture with it and sell it in London shops. It's almost impossible to wear it out. And one of these tentacles is just as strong as any python or anaconda."

"Perhaps so," admitted Roger. "I know I'd hate to be hugged by one. But you can't just walk up and help yourself to a tentacle – his honour might object."

The sun had risen and its heat roused the monster to fury. The giant squid prefers the chill waters of the Arctic or Antarctic. It does not mind being carried from the Antarctic up into tropical seas by the Humboldt Current because that current is very cold. The squid stays in the chill depths of the current during the day. When the sun has gone it floats up to the surface but sinks when the sun returns. It is a rabid sun-hater.

The giant squid, trapped in the blazing heat, began to thrash about violently. Its tentacles flailed the rocks and their sharp teeth made deep scratches in the coral.

Suddenly with a mighty heave it lurched forward six feet and at the same time flung out one of its long tentacles. Roger fled to safety. Hal, trying to escape, stumbled and fell.

At once the great arm slipped around his waist. It tightened upon him. He could feel the teeth biting into him through his palm-cloth shirt.

Roger was beating the tentacle with a piece of coral and shouting, "Omo! Omo!"

The tentacle began to draw Hal toward the monster's beak. The huge eagle-like beak opened, revealing a jagged row of teeth. Hal clung to the rocks with all his might but it was no use. The tentacle, as powerful as a python, pulled him loose. He clutched other rocks and again was pulled away.

Omo came hobbling on his two hands and his one good leg, dragging the other after him.

"Hurry, Omo!" yelled Roger. Somehow he had faith that the Polynesian would know what to do. Roger flung away his rock. It had made no impression upon the tentacle. Now he caught his brother's foot in both hands, braced himself behind a boulder, and held on like grim death.

But two boys and a boulder were no match for the giant. It dragged both of them and the stone as well. Now Hal was within a few feet of the waiting beak.

"Look out!" he gasped. Another tentacle was feeling for Roger, who squirmed to one side to avoid it.

Omo, arriving at last, picked up a large rock. Then he stood up, balancing himself on his good leg, and hurled the rock. Long training had made him as accurate with a stone as with a spear or a bow and arrow. Though he was weak from his illness, new strength came to him at this moment when he needed it most.

The rock flew straight into the monster's jaws where it jammed so tightly that the creature could not get rid of it.

With a mouthful of rock, the giant must abandon its notion of making a meal out of the castaways. But it could still punish with its tentacles and it proceeded to do so.

"Quick! Help me with this log!" Omo called. Roger dropped Hal's foot and gave Omo a hand in lifting a coconut log.

"Now! Ram it between the eyes."

They ran forward with the log, Omo ignoring the excruciating pain in his leg, and crashed the end of the log into the monster's brain.

The squid threw up its arms in a violent spasm. Hal was lifted ten feet into the air, then dropped free upon the rocks.

The ten tentacles writhed and twisted as a snake does when in its death throes. Then the life went out of them and they lay still.

Roger and Omo turned to help Hal. But he was already on his feet. He was very unsteady. Where he had lain the coral was stained red. Blood flowed from the many cuts around his body.

"I'm okay," he said. "They're just scratches. Come on, Roger, let's give Omo a lift."

They acted as two crutches, one under each arm, and got Omo back to the hut. There the Polynesian boy collapsed in pain and for the rest of that day had a pretty bad time of it.

Hal and Roger went back to the dead giant. The rock that Omo had thrown was still locked in the great beak. Hal shivered as he looked at the serpent-like tentacle that had held him in its crushing embrace. He still felt dazed by the shock and terror of those moments.

"I'm sorry we had to kill the beast," he said. He had the naturalist's dislike for taking lives.

"It was either His Nibs or you," Roger reminded him. "Besides, we need his rope if we're going to get off this reef alive."

"That's right. And we'd better get busy before the tide comes along and carries him off."

The hide was like tough leather. It took many hours of hard work before the ten tentacles could be severed and laid out on the rocks to dry in the sun. "Tomorrow we'll cut them into strips," Hal said.

The tide had risen and was tugging at the body. "Say good-bye to the carcass," said Roger. "Or would you like to have some of it for dinner?"

"I think I'll pass that up. The Orientals eat the young squids and find them very tasty, but I'd hate to tackle this old granddad. However, there's one more thing we need from it before we let the sea take it."

With a block of coral he pounded the razor-sharp beak

203

until a part of it broke off. It was like the blade of an axe. Then he cut out a stick from the flank of a coconut log. With a narrow strap cut from a tentacle he bound the blade to the handle.

"It may not be beautiful," he said, swinging the jerry-built axe, "but it will come in handy when we build that raft."

18
The Pearl Divers

The next day narrow straps were cut from the tentacles of the giant squid. All flesh was scraped away from the inside surface. The straps quickly dried in the sun.

"Don't we need to tan them?" asked Roger.

"If we wanted them to last for years we would have to tan them. But it isn't necessary for our purposes. They will stand up all right for a few weeks."

"It seems funny to be making leather out of squid tentacles."

"Why so? They make leather out of other things just as strange – kangaroo, wallaby, buffalo, ostrich, deer, lizard, alligator, shark, seal, and walrus. Cannibals have even made leather out of human skin."

By tying together the ends of the four straps they had cut from one of the twenty-foot tentacles they were able to get a line more than long enough to reach to the bottom of the cove. They fastened it to the palm-cloth bag and were ready for diving operations.

"Let me go first," demanded Roger.

He tucked a rock under one arm, gripped the bag with

205

his other hand, and dropped into the lagoon. The ripples he left on the surface gave Hal a wobbly vision of his brother as he descended to the floor of the bay.

Roger had difficulty in keeping his feet under him. They insisted upon floating upward. He stopped this by gripping the rock between his feet. That brought his feet down and head up.

The pressure upon his body was tremendous. He felt as if he were being hugged by a monster. It was all he could do to prevent the stored breath from popping out of his lungs.

He began tearing loose the big bivalves and putting them in the bag. The shells were rough and sometimes thorny. He was sorry he had not worn Omo's gloves. Bloody scratches appeared on his hand. If a shark got a whiff of that blood — but there were not likely to be sharks inside the lagoon. He hoped not anyhow.

It took about fifteen shells to fill the bag. He stuck it out until the job was finished. How long had he been in this terrific compression chamber? It seemed like half an hour.

He left the full bag on the bottom and rose to the surface. Hal gave him a hand and pulled him out onto the rocks. He breathed with sharp whistling gasps. He writhed in agony, cramps convulsing his body. His features were contorted with pain and the veins stood out on his face and arms. He shook in the hot sunshine as if he had the ague. He felt cold and weak.

Hal was anxiously scolding him.

"You stayed down too long. You were down two minutes. Even the Polynesians can't do more than three."

Roger managed to sit up. "I'm all right," he said dizzily. "Pull up the bag. Let's see what we got."

Hal laid hold of the line and drew the bag to the surface. Before he took it out of the water he placed his arms beneath it lest the weight of the shell might break the palm cloth. He emptied the bag on the beach. Fifteen huge shells looking like so many black turtles lay before them.

They could not wait to see what they contained. They opened them one after another and explored for pearls. There were none.

Roger gazed into the depths of the cove with dismay.

"Don't tell me we have to go through that again!"

"Many times, I'm afraid. Now it's my turn."

"Wear the gloves," Roger advised him, looking at his own red hand. "It will save you some blood."

Hal put on the gloves, provided himself with a rock and the bag, and went down. He spent no time trying to bring his feet under him but let them float upward like sea fans while he hastily filled the bag.

Then he came up, trying to make the ascent as slow as possible. But when Roger had helped him out he lay on the shelf of rock completely exhausted, with drops of blood trickling from his ears, nose, and mouth. His chest rose and fell like a bellows as he breathed in great gulps of the good air.

"I'm afraid I'm no – amphibian," he panted.

Roger hauled up the bag and they eagerly opened the shells.

They worked alternately, Roger opening the first shell, Hal the second, and so on. Twelve shells were opened without result. The next one fell to Roger.

"Thirteen!" he grumbled. "There can't be any good luck in that one!"

He thrust his knife into the muscle, twisted it, and the lips of the shell eased apart. He ran his finger along the inside rim of the lower lip.

He stopped half-way. He looked up at Hal and his eyes became round and his mouth dropped open. He began to breathe fast.

"Golly, I believe this is it!"

His fingers closed upon it. He brought it out. For a

moment neither could speak. They sat stunned, gazing at it.

Then Hal whispered, "Holy Moses! It's as big as a barn!"

It was not as big as a barn, but it *was* as big as a marble. It was the largest pearl the boys had ever laid eyes upon. It was a perfect sphere. Held in one position it seemed white, in another its opalescent depths reflected all the colours of lagoon and sky. It seemed alive.

Roger dropped it in Hal's hand. Hal was surprised to find it so heavy. That meant it was a good pearl. He turned it slowly in his fingers. It did not have a single flaw or blemish. It was so unreal, so full of a mysterious light, that it seemed to be part of the sunshine or of the atmosphere.

When he cupped his other hand over it to shade it from the sun, it still glowed, but now like a moon.

Roger, a dazed expression on his face, murmured, "Boy! Wait till the prof sees that!"

"I think he'll decide that his experiment has been a success!"

"A success, and how! But it's a long way from here to the professor. Suppose we lose it. Or have it stolen. That Kaggs will be watching for us when we get back to Ponape – if we ever get there."

"Quit worrying!" laughed Hal. But it was plain he also felt the great responsibility that had been suddenly thrust

209

upon them. "That's the trouble with treasure," he said. "Once you get it, you have to start worrying about keeping it. Let's show it to Omo."

Inside the dark cave the pearl still gleamed as if it had a fire of its own. Hal held it before Omo's eyes. Omo whistled softly.

"It's the finest pearl I've ever seen," he said. "We never get them that big in these waters. Your professor has certainly proved how a Persian Gulf oyster can make itself at home in the Pacific! Hand me that cup of water."

He dropped the pearl into the coconut shell full of water. It sank swiftly to the bottom. "That shows its weight is excellent."

"Keep it for us," Hal said. "I'm scared to death for fear I might drop it. It will be safe with you. You take care of it."

"Not on your life!" exclaimed Omo. "It would keep me awake nights. I'm afraid you're stuck with it."

Hal reluctantly took the pearl, wrapped it in palm fibre to increase its bulk so that it would be less likely to be dropped unnoticed, and put it in the pocket of his dungarees. He felt as if it at once began burning a hole. Now he had something to be anxious about, day and night.

"Well," he sighed, "we may as well get back to work. The professor will want more than one specimen to judge by."

Before the day ended two more pearls had been wrapped in with the first. The second was a shade smaller, the third a bit larger. Together they represented what Omo called "a comfortable fortune".

"*Un*comfortable, I'd say!" snorted Hal. "I know I won't be comfortable until I deliver these dratted things to Professor Richard Stuyvesant!"

And in a troubled sleep he dreamed that the raft upset, and sank deep into the ocean, and a shark pulled off his dungarees. Then he saw that the shark was really Kaggs with an evil grin on his face and three pearls in his hand.

He woke in a sweat and clutched his pocket. The precious package was still there.

19
The Raft

The raft was built on a sand beach sloping down toward the lagoon.

Impulsive Roger began to haul logs at once. But cautious Hal, with his habit of looking ahead, foresaw that the raft when built would be too heavy for two boys to carry to the water's edge.

He placed one log near the shore and parallel to it, and another a little farther back. These were not to be part of the raft but would serve as rollers. The raft would be built on top of them and, when finished, could be easily rolled into the lagoon.

Seven logs fifteen to twenty feet long were laid side by side upon the rollers. The longest ones were placed in the middle to make a sort of bow. Logs that were too long had to be reduced to the right length. It could not have been done without the help of the beak-bladed axe.

The seven logs were lashed together with squid-hide straps.

The boys stood back and inspected their work.

"It begins to look shipshape," Hal said. "But we ought to have a cabin to protect us from the sun. And we should have a sail."

Roger laughed mirthlessly and looked about him at the coral rocks. "Not much material for either one," he remarked. "But wait a minute. How about that roof?" He was looking at the hut. "We could get a cabin roof out of that."

"And a sail too!" exclaimed Hal. Then his face fell. "But what do we do for a mast? A palm log would be too big."

The answer to this problem meant more hard work. With stone wedges hammered into a log by means of coral blocks, they split the log in two. After splitting again, and once again, they had a stake about eighteen feet long and four inches through. With their knives they shaped it until it was nearly round.

It was rough and crooked and would have brought shame to any shipyard, but the boys were proud of it.

They whittled and hacked until they had made a hole in the raft near the bow, and in this hole they stepped their mast.

The cabin and sails must wait until they had no more need for their hut.

The building of the raft took the best part of three days. More days were consumed in gathering supplies for the voyage.

The most important supply was water. They must get it at once or there would be none to be had, for the undersea spring was failing steadily. Several times a day they had been diving for water, bringing up each time a coconut shell full. And every time the stream was weaker and the water more brackish.

Hal consulted Omo.

"How are we going to carry water on the raft? One shellful would be no use, and we can't find any more coconuts."

Omo knit his brows. "That's a hard one. On our island

we had goats and we could make a water bag out of goatskin. Perhaps if a dolphin stumbled into your trap you could use its skin."

"But we can't wait for perhapses. We've got to store some water now before it stops flowing."

Omo returned to his whittling. He was skilful with a knife and had already made himself a pair of crutches out of coconut wood. Now, from thin slabs of wood that the others had split from a coconut log, he was fashioning paddles for use on the raft. He looked at the half-shaped paddle before him.

"We do almost everything with coconut. It feeds, shelters, and clothes us. I suppose you could even make a water cask out of a section of it, but it would be hard. You would have to hollow it out . . ."

"Hold on!" cried Hal. "How about using something that is already hollowed out?"

Omo looked at him with a puzzled air.

"On the other island," went on Hal, "we found a clump of bamboo. Of course it had been blown down by the storm, but——"

"Just the thing! Cut it into lengths about six feet long."

But when this had been done there was a new difficulty.

Three bamboo logs were cut, each about five inches

in diameter. They were hollow – but not quite!

At every joint the hollow chamber was closed by a stout partition.

How could these be broken down? Only the first one could be reached with the knife.

A swordfish came to the rescue. It had been caught in the trap two days before, and its excellent meat had provided many fine meals.

It was Roger who thought of calling upon the swordfish for help in the present emergency. He slipped away to the shore near the trap where the skeleton lay.

Dropping upon it a huge block of coral almost as heavy as himself, he broke off the sword. It was three feet long and came to a hard sharp point. He increased its length by lashing it to a stick.

Now he had a formidable spear. He knew that this spear would break much more than a bamboo partition. The swordfish has been known to ram its sword through the stout hulls of boats. One in Palau lagoon pierced not only the hull of a motor-boat but the metal petrol tank, letting out the petrol and setting the boat adrift.

Hal was delighted with his brother's ingenuity. Both gripping the spear, they rammed it down into one of the bamboo tubes. They broke one partition after another until all were gone except the one that closed the bottom end of the tube.

When the three tubes had all been treated in this way they carried them to the shore just above the submarine spring. They took turns in diving with the coconut shell, bringing up water and emptying it into the tubes. It was an all-day job. When the tubes were full they corked them with plugs of coconut wood. They carried them to the raft, laid them in the dips between the logs, and lashed them in place.

"Now whatever else happens, we won't go thirsty," Hal rejoiced.

The bamboo clump yielded some very useful byproducts. Bamboo shoots were growing up from the roots. They had evidently begun since the storm. Omo explained that this was not surprising – bamboo grows very rapidly, sometimes as much as a foot a day. The shoots added a much-needed vegetable to the diet of the castaways.

Also the bamboo gave them sugar! A sweet juice coming from the joints hardened into a white substance that Omo called Indian honey. It was almost like toffee and made a very pleasant dessert.

"Imagine finding candy on a desert island!" mumbled Roger, with his mouth full of the sweet gum.

The bamboo also gave them a cooking-pot. A single

section of bamboo was used for this purpose. Water could be boiled in it without any fear of burning the pot.

Another bamboo trunk was prepared for the storage of food.

They cut fish into strips and dried it in the sun. (How it smelled while drying!) It should be salted too, but they were at a loss to know how to get salt until Omo told them how it was done in the islands. Sea water placed in a hollowed rock was allowed to evaporate. When it was gone a thin film of salt was left.

As for the oysters they had brought up from the cove of pearls, they ate as many as they could, but had little luck in preserving them for future use. However, they packed a few untasty morsels of oyster into the bamboo tube along with the sun-dried salted fish.

Into the bamboo went also some dried seaweed of the sort considered good food by the Orientals. Roger was not enthusiastic about it.

"Looks like spinach to me," he grumbled. "And tastes worse."

A few birds had returned to the island, among them that comic creature known as a megapode. It flew as sluggishly as a cargo plane and waddled when it walked over the rocks. Evidently it had not learned to be afraid of human beings. It came running when Omo knocked two stones together. For some strange reason this sound had an irresistible attraction for the comedian.

Omo caught it easily and after it was dressed and cooked it was added to the store.

Sea urchins containing masses of eggs went into the tube. The eggs were edible but one had to be careful not to be stuck by the spines which, in this variety, carried a poison like a cobra's.

One night Roger was awakened by scratching on the beach. He crawled out of the hut in time to see what looked like a round dark boulder crawling toward the water's edge. It was a sea turtle, two hundred pounds of fine food. It had probably come ashore to lay its eggs in the sand, and that explained the scratching Roger had heard.

He could not allow it to escape into the lagoon. He ran after it and fell upon its back. It did not seem to mind and continued its march. Roger dug his feet into the sand, but was dragged loose.

He jumped off the back, seized the edge of the shell, and tried to turn the big fellow over. It was too much for him. He called for help.

Before Hal and Omo could get the sleep out of their eyes, the turtle had reached the lagoon and plunged in.

But Roger was not ready to quit. He swung himself on board the turtle's back as on a horse. He knew how Polynesian boys ride turtles, though he had never tried it himself.

He gripped the front of the shell just back of the leathery neck. Then he threw his weight backward and pulled up.

That prevented the turtle from diving. It was forced to swim on the surface.

But it kept straight on going out into the lagoon, headed for the pass and the ocean. Roger tried to remember what he should do next. Oh yes, he must get hold of one of those hind flippers.

He reached back with one hand and got the right hind flipper. He held it tightly so that it could not paddle.

With the other three flippers going and this one quiet, the turtle could not help going around to the right. Roger held on until it headed back toward the beach, then let go.

He could dimly see Hal and Omo on the beach.

"I'm bringing home the bacon," he called to them.

But the turtle had ideas of its own. It began to swing one way and then the other and Roger was kept busy seizing the right or the left hind flipper to keep his course straight for the beach. When he forgot to hold back on the front edge of the shell the creature promptly sounded and Roger was carried a fathom or so under water before he could collect his wits and bring his submarine back to the surface.

Hal and Omo waded into the water and helped him get his mount ashore. The big turtle snapped its jaws together and nearly nipped a piece out of Hal's leg.

"We'll soon stop that," said Hal, and took out his knife.

The turtle raised its head menacingly. Its leathery skin and appearance of great age made it look like an angry old man.

"Don't murder granpa!" cried Roger. "I've a better idea. Let's take him along with us on the raft – alive. Then we'll have fresh food when we need it."

"Good idea," said Omo. He was digging in the sand with a stick. "But it's grandma, not grandpa. Here are the eggs she was laying."

In a pit a foot deep the turtle had buried more than a hundred eggs.

Roger was surprised, upon picking one up, to find that it was soft like a rubber ball. It did not have a brittle shell like a hen's egg.

"How do you eat it?"

"You bite a hole in the skin, then squeeze the insides

into your mouth. They're good food. We'll boil them and take them along."

Grandma was tethered to a stump and the boys turned in. At dawn they were stirring.

They agreed that they had enough supplies. Today they would take off on their hazardous voyage.

They took down the sharkskin that had served them as a roof and cut it in two. It made two sections, each eight by ten feet. One would make the sail, the other the cabin.

A rough spar was lashed to the upper edge of the sail and it was then hoisted to the masthead by squid-leather halyards. To each of the lower corners of the sharkskin sail was attached a line by which it could be sheeted home.

The cabin was a simple affair. Three split bamboo canes were curved to form the framework, their ends fastened to the deck. Over them was laid the sharkskin with its two edges touching the deck and lashed fast to the logs.

The result was a shelter that looked something like half a barrel. It was precisely like the roof of a Chinese sampan except that it was made of sharkskin instead of matting.

"It's just like the *toldo* we had on our boat on the Amazon," Roger said.

It was, except that it was lower and snugger, which was a good thing in case of a Pacific storm. It was only three feet high and five feet wide. From front to back it measured eight feet. It was quite large enough to lie in and furnished protection from the tropical sun. Since the front and rear ends of it were open, the man at stern paddle could look straight through to the bow.

The turtle eggs were boiled and stored. Grandma was led on board and lashed to the mast.

Now that they were ready to go, they began to regret leaving the spot that had been home to them for two eventful weeks. They did not need to be told of the dangers of an ocean voyage on a raft.

They would be at the mercy of wind and wave. They would try to go south, but might just as easily be driven north, east, or west. Their paddles and crude sail would be of small consequence compared with the force of wind and current.

They tried to cover their fears by shouting and singing as they made preparations for casting off.

"Let me christen her," cried Roger. Lacking a bottle of champagne, he smashed a turtle egg on the bow log and proclaimed, "I christen thee the good ship *Hope!*"

Then the three mariners rolled the craft into the lagoon and hopped aboard.

The momentum of the launching carried the raft across

the bay of pearls. Hal and Omo studied its behaviour carefully.

"It floats high and dry," Omo said.

"And it holds its course well," Hal remarked. Thanks to the pointed bow, and the straightness and smoothness of the coconut logs, the vessel showed no tendency to yaw over to starboard or port. "How does she answer the helm?"

Omo at stern paddle put his weight on the blade and the vessel veered slowly to starboard.

"It does pretty well for a raft."

The wind was on the beam and Hal trimmed the great rectangle of sharkskin sail to take advantage of it.

But to get through the pass it was necessary to go straight into the wind's eye. Rather than trouble to lower the sail for the few moments necessary to make the passage, Roger sheeted it so that it was edge on into the wind.

Then the boys took to their paddles. It was a stiff job, but Hal had estimated correctly that the ebbing tide would help them escape from the lagoon in spite of the wind. After fifteen sweating minutes they were in the clear, and the home-made *Hope* rose and fell on the swells of the greatest of oceans.

20
Disaster in the Waterspout

The first two days of the voyage passed so smoothly that the mariners three almost forgot the anxiety with which they had begun the trip.

The wind held from the north-east and they sailed steadily south. If this kept up, they should reach Ponape, or, failing that, they would at least get into the shipping lane that runs from the Marshall Islands to Kusaie, Ponape, Truk, and Yap. There they might hail some schooner that would pick them up.

By day the sun was their compass and by night the stars. They roughly divided the twenty-four hours into twelve watches so that no man had to stick at the steering paddle for more than two hours at a time. Although they had no chronometer, they could compute time with a fair degree of accuracy by the angle of the sun or a star above the horizon.

Water sloshing up through the cracks between the logs kept them a bit wet all the time, but the dampness was cool and pleasant. When one began to suffer from the blows of the equatorial sun he had only to crawl into the cabin and lie in the cool shade of the sharkskin roof.

The bamboo tubes of drinking water nesting between the logs were kept cool by the water that splashed up from beneath. Hal was a trifle worried because the food seemed to be disappearing rather fast, but he hoped they would be able to catch some fish.

Brilliantly coloured dolphins played alongside. They were usually bright blue and green and their fins were golden yellow. But they could change colour like a chameleon and sometimes they shone like burnished copper. One flopped on board and as it died it lost its colour and became silver grey with black spots.

On the third day a big whale investigated the *Hope*. It came straight for the raft, blowing and puffing each time its great head reared up out of the water. It seemed strange to hear heavy breathing in these fishy wastes where breathing was not the fashion – except for the boys on the raft; and they almost stopped breathing at the thought of what a sixty-foot monster could do to a few logs.

"Just one flick of that tail," worried Roger, "and we'd be in the drink."

The whale circled the raft twice. Then he dived and up-ended his tail twenty feet into the air, carrying with it a huge quantity of water that fell like a heavy shower upon the voyagers.

The tail went down with a violent twist that sent a great wave of water across the raft from stem to stern, drenching its occupants.

"Ring up the plumber!" cried Roger, standing in water up to his knees.

But the raft had one great advantage over a boat. The water simply ran out through the floor.

The whale went under the raft and came up on the other side so close that another wave was rolled over the vessel. The beast's shoulder crashed into the starboard logs and it seemed for a moment that the good ship *Hope* would be turned into kindling wood.

As if satisfied with the scare he had given these intruders in his domain, the whale sounded and was seen no more.

The outside log with its lashings torn loose was about to float away. The boys recovered it just in time and tied it fast.

During the morning the wind failed and the heavy sharkskin sail thudded idly against the mast. The swells lost their rough finish and became as smooth as oil. Without a breeze, the sun seemed ten times as hot.

Omo looked about. "I don't like it," he said. "A sudden calm like this may mean trouble."

But there was no cloud in the sky. The only thing visible was a dark column like a pillar far to the east.

Presently, a few miles farther north, another appeared.

"Waterspouts," Omo said. "There are more of them in this part of the Pacific than anywhere else in the world."

"Are they dangerous?"

"Some are, some aren't. Those two aren't. They're something like the dust whirls on land – you've seen them. They carry papers and leaves several hundred feet high. 'Dust devils', you call them. But—" and he scanned the horizon anxiously, "those little fellows are often just a sign that a big one is coming. And a big one is like a tornado. In fact, that's just what it is, a sea tornado."

"But a land tornado can carry off houses!" said Hal.

"Exactly," replied Omo. "And I am afraid you are soon going to find out what a sea tornado can do." He was looking up at a point a little north-east of the zenith.

The others followed his gaze.

A cloud formed before their eyes. It seemed to be about three thousand feet up. It became rapidly blacker and blacker and squirmed violently so that it looked like a living monster. A long tail dangled from it.

No wonder, thought Hal, that the Polynesians call it a sky beast and have many superstitions about it.

Greenish lights that one might imagine were eyes gleamed in the writing blackness.

"It can't be as bad as the hurricane we had," Roger said.

"It can be worse," Omo replied. "Of course it won't last as long. And it isn't as big. A hurricane can be six hundred miles across but these things are never more than two or three thousand feet. But it makes up in violence what it lacks in size. I'd choose a hurricane any day."

Hal was itching to do something. "Can't we get out of here? Do we just sit here and wait for it to grab us?" He dug his paddle into the water.

"You may as well save your strength," Omo said. "You can never tell which way the thing will go. We might paddle straight into it. The only thing we can do is to hold on and hope."

The tail of the monster grew longer every moment. Now it looked like a long black tentacle groping toward the sea like the arm of an octopus.

The air had been breathlessly quiet, and still was around the raft. But from the cloud came a roaring or a rushing sound such as you hear when you paddle down a river toward a waterfall.

Now something was happening to the sea beneath that groping tentacle. The oily surface broke up into sharp ridges. Spurts of spray began to race round and round like elves in a wild dance.

The spinning became more intense. Now masses of water were joining the mad whirl, carried around by a screaming wind.

And yet there was not the breath of a breeze on the raft.

Hal knew that the land tornado acts in the same way. It may pick up one house and carry it away and not disturb another ten feet off. He had heard of a tornado that tore the roof from a house and yet did not budge a tin top resting on a churn outside the back door.

"It may skip us," he said.

"Perhaps." But Omo did not sound too hopeful.

"Shall we take down the sail?"

"If it wants the sail it will take it, no matter whether it is down or up."

It was agonizing to know that you were completely at the mercy of the monster and there was not a thing you could do about it.

The spinning water had now become a great whirlpool. But instead of a hole in the centre of the whirlpool, there was a hill. There the sea was bulging upward. It climbed higher and higher as if drawn from above. Now it rose to a conical point higher than the *Hope*'s masthead.

The whirling cone threw off spray and loose water that acted most strangely. Instead of falling to the sea it climbed into the sky, turning into a rapidly revolving ghost of mist.

The tentacle reached lower, the arm of the sea reached higher. They met and joined with a loud hiss.

Now it was truly something to see, that great spinning pillar three thousand feet high. At the top it spread out into the black cloud and at the bottom it spread again to take in the whirlpool. The whirlpool was a frightful thing to behold, a crazy merry-go-round of wild horses racing to the shrill organ music of the wind. The swirling maelstrom covered more and more of the sea. Now the storm circle was two thousand feet across.

Within the circle the waves rose to points and crashed together as if determined to beat each other's brains out.

"Bet that wind is travelling two hundred miles an hour," shouted Hal. But the roar of wind and water was so great that he could not be heard.

The lofty column began to lean as if the upper end were being pushed. Hal breathed a sigh of relief as he saw that it was leaning away from the raft. Those upper winds were carrying the sky beast southward and the *Hope* would escape its fury.

But the waterspout is a fickle giant and loves to tantalize its victims. The leaning tower changed direction, swayed one way and then another, writhed and twisted like a fabulous boa-constrictor hanging from a branch of heaven.

A seagull drifting placidly through the quiet sunny air was suddenly snatched by the whirlwind and tossed upward, spinning round and round, its wings beating helplessly, until it was swallowed by the sky beast above.

What made everything go up? Even at a moment of peril such as this, Hal's scientific mind asked questions and figured out the answers.

The air rushed upward to fill a low-pressure area above. It whirled, for the same reason that hurricanes whirl, for the same reason that ordinary winds are inclined to travel in circles, because of the rotation of the earth. The centrifugal force of this whirling made almost a vacuum inside the column and therefore the sea was sucked up. In a land tornado that vacuum around a house made the walls burst out because the air pressure was so much greater inside the house than outside. Corks pop out of bottles during a tornado for the same reason. And it suddenly occurred to him that if the storm caught the raft the plugs would pop out of the bamboo tubes and the water would be lost.

He had no time to consider this problem, much less do anything to solve it. Suddenly a giant finger of wind slipped under the cabin roof and carried it up and away. The boys threw themselves flat on the deck and held on.

The sail went next. It spun away like a crazy thing around the great circle of the whirlwind, rose to a height of a hundred feet or more, and then was tossed out to fall in the sea.

Daylight faded. The air seemed full of water. Omo shouted something but his voice was inaudible. There was a deafening roar and Roger would have clapped his palms over his ears if he had not needed both hands to hold himself to the logs.

Now the raft was caught in the frantic circle. The waves stood up in spear points, then crashed their tons of water down upon the raft and its passengers. At times the *Hope* was completely buried. Then it would leap up into the air through a smother of foam. The boys held on as if to the backs of bucking broncos.

Grandma was the first to go. A wave flicked her off and broke her leash. She was tossed a dozen yards, whirling like a top, before she disappeared into the flank of another wave.

Hal could look into the side of the wave as into a

store window. He saw grandma turn tail up and swim straight down to the depths where all would be calm and peaceful.

You could do worse than copy a wise old turtle. He resolved to do the same thing if the raft broke up.

The hill of water at the heart of the waterspout crept now closer, now farther away, keeping the sailors trembling between hope and despair.

The boys could not look steadily at anything. Their eyes were beaten shut by the wind.

With so much air flying past them, still it was difficult to get enough to breathe. You dared not face the wind – it would ram its way down your nose and throat and fill you like a balloon. If you turned your head away you were in a vacuum where there was no air to be had. You must bury your face between the logs, or protect your nose and mouth with your hand, in order to slow up the air long enough to get some of it into the lungs.

And just when you had found a way to do it, you would be buried under tons of water. Sometimes it seemed that you would never come up.

As the raft rose to the surface after one of these plunges, Hal saw that the whirling hill was bearing down upon them. It looked like a moving volcano, the black column rising from it resembling smoke. The entire column was leaning now, with its top passing over the raft. Hal thought it was like a tree – but ten times as high as the loftiest giant sequoia in California.

As the spinning hill approached, the wind changed its tactics. Instead of blowing sideways, it blew up. Now they were coming into the heart of the updraught.

On land, it was strong enough to carry up roofs and heavy timbers. Would it lift the raft, crew and all, and carry them high into the sky like Arabian Nights' passengers on a magic carpet?

More likely it would break up the raft and beat them to death with the thrashing logs. That was why they should swim down.

Hal put his mouth close to Roger's ear.

"Swim down!" he shouted.

The updraught was already tugging at their bodies. What was left of their palm-cloth shirts was now ripped loose and carried up the black pipe as through a pneumatic tube in a department store until it reached the cloud above.

If the hill would only stop coming, the centrifugal force might throw the raft away from it. Hal tried to believe that this would happen. If faith could move mountains, perhaps faith could stop a mountain from moving.

But the gods of the winds far above were deciding where the hill should go. They took a malicious delight in carrying it down upon the raft.

Suddenly the forlorn *Hope* faced a solid wall of green water. High up in this glassy wall, far above the raft, Hal was horrified to see a large shark. There it was like a stuffed specimen in a glass case.

He had only a glimpse of it before the raft upended on the flank of the hill and the tumultuous waters writhing under the suck of the tornado wrenched the logs apart as if they had been matches tied with find thread.

A moment more and those tossing logs might brain them. Hal knew that Omo would know what to do – but he clung to his log until he was sure of Roger. When he saw that both boys had dived straight down, he did the same.

It was not easy to swim down for the water was running uphill, twisting and tossing him, pushing him back where the sky beast might suck him up through its trunk as a butterfly sucks a drop of honey from a flower.

He put all his power into his stroke. Now the pressure upward was less and he could begin to swim out.

He stayed beneath the surface turmoil. It did not matter what direction he took so long as he swam straight. Any direction would take him to the edge of the circle.

The eternal quiet below was very soothing. After the frenzied tumult above he could almost rest as he swam. He was conscious of some current even at a depth of a couple of fathoms but he knew that this current was centrifugal and would help carry him out. This whirlpool, unlike most, whirled out instead of in.

When his wind was spent he surfaced, only to find himself still within the whirl. He submerged and swam on.

When he came up again he found himself among small choppy waves beyond the reach of the tornado.

The column was leaning more than ever and the entire spout was travelling toward the south-west. The circle of clashing waves, with the Tower of Babel in the centre, slid away across the sea and the scream of the winds diminished.

The air around Hal was now as quiet as it had been before the sky monster's arrival. The clashing waves gradually settled down.

It was not until then that Hal thought of the shark. He wondered if it also had been terrified by the commotion.

Now that the commotion was over, would it begin to take an interest in him and his companions?

He saw a brown head break surface a hundred feet away.

"Hi there, Omo!" he called. "How's tricks?"

"Glad you're okay, Hal," shouted Omo. "Have you seen Roger?"

"No. Suppose you circle around one way and I'll go the other."

They swam in opposite directions around the recently troubled area. Hal wondered how the younger boy had stood the experience. Would the kid be so scared stiff that he couldn't swim? Had he lost his head, come to the surface, and been bashed to death by flying logs?

He did not need to worry. When he found Roger, the boy was not only safe, but busy. He had discovered two logs and had towed one alongside the other. Now he was trying to lash them together with the broken pieces of squidskin strap that hung from the logs.

"Good work!" shouted Hal. "I'll see if I can find some more logs."

Omo joined the search. They swam back and forth across the circle where the raft had broken up and as far out into the sea in all directions as they dared, but found no more logs. They must be somewhere, but lay so low that it was difficult to spot them from any distance.

There was a blast of thunder. Lightning blazed in the black cloud that topped the waterspout. Thunder rolled again.

Then the great squirming hose that connected sky and sea broke in the middle. The lower part collapsed, causing gigantic waves. The higher portion coiled up into the cloud.

Bombs seemed to be exploding in the cloud. Then a heavy rain fell from it. The upper winds quickened and the thundercloud, with the rainstorm that hung from it like a trailing dress, travelled swiftly toward the horizon.

The sky monster was gone, but it left three badly discouraged boys behind it. Hal and Omo searched in vain for more fragments of the lost *Hope*.

Wearily, they returned to the two logs. They crawled aboard and lay down. Three men were too much for the slender raft and it began to sink.

Roger slid off into the water and held on by one hand. The raft rose until the top was about level with the surface. Every wave rolled over it and over the bodies that lay upon it.

The bamboo tubes of food and water were gone. The mariners were without sail or paddles, without shelter, without even palm-cloth shirts and eye-masks to protect them from the whipping sun, without enough of a craft to support all three of them at one time, without weapons except their knives in case of attack from below.

Roger, submerged up to his neck, kept glancing furtively about, expecting the dorsal fin of a shark to break surface at any moment.

"I don't know about you guys," he said, "but I'm a-feelin' mighty low!"

Omo, whose face had been twisted with pain by too vigorous use of his lame leg, raised his head and smiled.

"I'm rested now," he said. "Let's change."

He slipped into the water and Roger took his place on the logs.

"It's not so bad," Omo said softly. "We're all alive. We've got two logs, three pairs of dungarees, and three knives. And we still have some pearls to deliver – or have we?"

Hal clapped his hand to his pocket. "We have!"

"Good. So we'd better get about delivering them."

He slipped around to the end of the logs and began to swim, pushing the raft before him. He headed it south. Slowly it ploughed through the ripples.

Perhaps it didn't help much, but it was a lot better

than doing nothing. Hal's heart was filled with deep affection for his Polynesian friend. So long as there was such courage and patience aboard, the *Hope* was not lost after all.

21
The Wreck of the Hope

They took turns overboard. After lying on the hard logs for an hour or so with the waves breaking in your face, it was a relief to swim and push for a while and get the kinks out of your muscles.

And after swimming a while it was a relief to climb aboard and stretch out.

But as time went on each relief grew less and there was nothing but continual discomfort.

Night was especially hard to bear. It was impossible to sleep. You must be continually awake and alert, ready to hold your breath when a wave swept over. You no sooner dozed than you awoke half-strangled by water pouring into nose and mouth.

Dozens of strange and somewhat terrifying creatures came up to investigate this floating thing. The boys had never seen the ocean so full of life.

It is always full of life but the passenger on schooner or steamer sees little of it. A few dolphins and flying-fish may come near, but most denizens of the deep are afraid to approach the monstrous moving thing with smoke billowing from its funnels or sails beating the sky.

Even seven logs with cabin and sail are much more frightening than two logs, mostly submerged. This little floating affair might be just a strange fish, and the other fish came to call.

The depths below were full of travelling lights like a city at night seen from the sky. Roger looked down over the edge of the raft.

"There goes a lantern fish. And there's a star-eater. Gosh, what's that?"

Two enormous eyes were lazily following the raft. They

were more than a foot wide and they shone with a yellow-green light.

"That's your old friend, the giant squid," Hal said.

Roger shivered. "He's no friend of mine! Couldn't he reach up and grab us?"

"He could. But it isn't a pleasant thought, so let's not entertain it."

And Hal who was serving as the ship's engine at the moment put some extra power into his stroke and the two eyes were left behind.

But something far more startling now appeared. It seemed like another eye, but huge, not an inch less than eight feet across. It glowed with a silvery light. It came up on the starboard bow and moved slowly along with the raft about a fathom down. It looked like the full moon.

Roger was speechless. It wasn't often that Roger could find nothing to say. Omo put his hand on the boy's arm and found that he was trembling.

And who would not tremble when followed by a monster big enough to have an eye of such a size!

"It's not an eye this time," Omo said. "It's a moonfish – called that because it shines like the moon and it's round."

"A round fish? Are you kidding me?"

"No. What you're looking at is its head."

"Then where's the rest of it?"

"There isn't any rest. It's nothing but head. So some people call it the headfish. And it has one more name. Sunfish – because it lies asleep on the surface in the daytime and basks in the sun."

"Doesn't it ever have anything more than a head?"

"When it's young, yes. But it loses its tail, the way a tadpole does. Of course the head is really something more than a head because it has a stomach in it and other organs. And those little fluttering things on the edge are fins."

The fins seemed very small to propel such a big hulk.

"It must weigh close to a ton," Roger marvelled.

"They do. Sometimes we amuse ourselves by stepping out of our canoes upon a sleeping sunfish, pretending it's an island."

The underwater moon travelled along with the raft for several minutes. Then Roger's blood chilled as four great snakelike creatures swam over the light. They had no phosphorescence of their own and their twisting bodies were blackly silhouetted against the glow of the moonfish. They were from eight to ten feet long and as thick as a man's leg.

"Are they snakes?"

"Morays," Omo said, and he drew his knife. "A kind of

247

eel. Watch out for them. They will eat anything – including us."

"Mean customers!" Hal said, splashing to keep off attackers. "Who was that old Roman we read about in school who kept a tankful of pet morays? He used to feed them by tossing in a slave every morning."

Omo was peering intently into the water, knife in hand. "We call this kind *Kamichic*, the Terrible One. It's amphibious. It can even climb a mangrove tree and wait to pounce upon any prey passing below. While we were in Ponape a man was bitten by one and taken to the hospital. He died after two days."

The serpentine forms passed back and forth beneath the raft. Roger too had his knife ready.

"But would they come aboard the raft?"

"They might. Sometimes one of them boards a boat. It gets a grip on the gunwale with its tail, then flips its body in. Most animals won't attack unless they're bothered, but the moray is always spoiling for a fight. It has teeth an inch long and as sharp as the point of this knife."

Roger gripped his knife. "The first one that shows itself will get its head lopped off."

"That would be the worst thing you could do," Omo warned him. "The blood would bring the sharks. Besides, their heads and necks are very tough – but their tails are tender. They can't stand being rapped on the tail."

Roger, lying on his side and looking down, felt a touch on his back.

Before he could turn Omo reached forward and brought the heavy handle of his knife down hard.

"That one won't bother us any more!"

Almost in Roger's face a black tail slipped over the log, gripped fast, and powerful muscles flung a writhing figure up out of the sea. Against the stars Roger had a glimpse of an evil head and open jaws coming his way. But at the same instant his knife handle was thudding down upon the tail. A contortion twisted the eel's body and it fell into the water.

There were no more snaky forms to be seen against the submarine moon.

Roger felt dizzy and weak. He had as much spunk as any boy of his age, but this night was a bit too thick for him. He immediately fell asleep, but was as promptly aroused when water buried his face.

Omo saw that if the boy did not get some sleep he would crack.

"Sit up, Roger." The boy obeyed. "Now turn around with your back to me. All right – now just relax and go to sleep."

249

Roger was too weary to argue. Supported in a sitting position by Omo he let his head drop upon the Polynesian's shoulder and was instantly asleep. Now the waves rarely reached high enough to touch his face. When they did, Omo put his hand over the boy's nose and mouth. When it was Omo's turn to go overboard, Hal took his place. The change did not wake Roger.

The rising wind chilled the wet bodies of the castaways. They were glad to see the sun rise. But it had not been up for an hour before they began to long for the cool of the night.

Roger woke, refreshed by his sleep, but hungry and thirsty. He was indignant because he had been the only one to get any sleep.

"What the heck!" he fumed. "If you guys can take it, I can. I don't need a baby-sitter."

He looked at his companions' hands and then at his own. They were shrivelled and wrinkled by the salt water.

"We look like a pack o' mummies! Pass the cold cream."

There being no cold cream available, he slipped over the side and took Hal's place as motor of the not very good ship *Hope*.

Thirst and hunger became more acute as the day wore on. Constant immersion in the water had one good feature

— moisture was absorbed through the pores, and the moisture of the body could not be so rapidly evaporated, so that thirst crawled up on them more slowly than on land. But by night they would have given one of the pearls, if it had been theirs to give, for a long drink of fresh water.

During this night Roger insisted upon being baby-sitter for his companions, taking them alternately. He could hardly keep his eyes open. Once he did drop off and he and Hal, whom he was supporting, both rolled over into the sea. The cold plunge brought them smartly back to their senses.

The next morning found a school of bonito swimming about the raft. The boys repeatedly plunged their hands into the sea but failed to catch any of them.

"Wonder if we could make a fishline?" Omo was examining the bark on the logs. "We usually make it from the husk of the nut. But bark might do."

They spent most of the day picking out fibres from the bark, twisting and braiding them into a line. It was only five feet long when finished, but fairly strong. Omo gouged a splinter from a log and carved a hook. There was nothing to put on it for bait.

They dangled the hook in the water and hoped. Would any fish be fool enough to swallow a bare hook?

The school of bonito had disappeared. There were other fish, but they paid no attention to the hook.

Another night and another day. Sores began to appear on the boys' bodies due to salt water and chafing of the skin against the logs. Their feet were swollen and tingling and spotted with blotchy red areas and blisters.

"It's 'immersion foot'," Hal said, and added gloomily, "Salt-water boils will come next."

Their skins, constantly wet and salted, were being severely burned by the sun. Their eyes were bloodshot, inflamed, and painful.

Thirst cracked the lips. The tongue swelled until it seemed that there was hardly room for it inside the mouth. It kept trying to push its way out between the lips, like the end of a wedge. The whole inside of the mouth felt as if smeared with glue. Roger rinsed his mouth with sea water, and swallowed a little.

"Go easy with that," Hal warned him. "A very little won't hurt. But it's hard to stop with a little."

"Everybody needs salt," objected Roger. "What could it do to you?"

"Too much will put you in a coma. Then you have two chances. You may come out of it crazy, or not come out at all."

"What's the difference?" Roger said bitterly. "We'll get the purple moo-moo whether we drink sea water or not." He passed his hand over his forehead. "I'm beginning to see things already – things that aren't there."

"Such as what?"

"Such as a rainstorm. Cool, sweet rain falling! Over there." He pointed to the south-east. "I know it can't be, but . . ."

"But it is!" cried Hal. Not half a mile away a small shower was streaking down and spattering the sea. "Let's go!"

They tumbled overboard and joined Omo behind the raft. All three pushing, they propelled the logs rapidly toward the spot.

But before they could reach it they were sorely disappointed to see the rain fade into mist and the mist dissolve in sunshine.

"Look! There's another one!" This time it was only a quarter-mile west. Surely they could reach it in time. The water fell from a small black cloud that was being carried west by a light breeze.

They swam with all their strength. They soon saw that it was hopeless. They tired, but the breeze did not tire. The harder they swam, the farther away the shower seemed to be.

253

Presently the little cloud rained itself out and there was no sign that there had ever been a shower.

"Do you think we just imagined it?" Roger said doubtfully.

"Of course not. We all saw it, didn't we?" No one answered. "Well, didn't we? Didn't you see it, Omo?"

"I think so," Omo hesitated. "I – I'm not sure of anything any more."

"Well, here's something we can be sure of!" cried Roger. "Because I've got my hands on it. An albacore has swallowed our hook." He lifted the fish for them to see. It was black and glossy, not more than a foot and a half long, but plump with good meat.

They attacked it at once with their knives and devoured everything but the bones – and one scrap which they saved to bait the hook.

They felt better – and not so thirsty. The flesh of a fish, specially a juicy one like the albacore, contains moisture – and it is fresh water, not salt. But it was not enough. It hardly amounted to a tablespoonful for each man.

The baited hook worked better than the bare one and soon attracted a young sawfish. It was hauled aboard and quickly eaten, saving only enough for bait.

Where there are young sawfish there are apt to be large

ones and Hal was not surprised to see sudden turmoil in the water.

"Look out!" he cried to Omo who was swimming. A huge sawfish was wildly dashing about attacking small fish with its great saw. After slashing them to bits it would feed upon the torn flesh. The sawfish was sixteen feet long and could cut a man in two as easily as a fish. Many a whale has been attacked by a sawfish, and the whale has not always been the winner.

Omo did his best to keep out of the way of the great blade. The mangled bodies of the small fish rose to the surface and Hal and Roger seized as many of them as they could get their hands on.

Attracted by the blood, a huge tiger shark hove in view. It darted at some of the torn fish and gulped them down.

This annoyed the sawfish, which came at once to the attack. It did not plunge its weapon straight into the shark as a swordfish would have done. It came within six feet, then swung its saw with a sidelong movement and slashed deep into the body of the shark. Blood poured out.

"There'll be a hundred sharks here in ten minutes," Hal cried. "This is no place for us."

He slid overboard and Roger followed suit. Their legs tingled with dread of the savage saw.

They joined Omo and quickly pushed the raft away from the scene of slaughter. Looking back, they saw the sea boil with the thrashing of many sharks and turn red with their blood.

They munched tattered shreds of fish.

"That sawfish did us a good turn," said Hal. "You see, not *all* the luck is against us."

But on the following day the luck ran pretty thin. The only fish that came near were jellyfish. They covered the sea thickly for miles. The man behind swam through them and the two on deck were washed by them every time a wave went over. The stinging tentacles of the jellyfish, which are powerful enough to paralyse fishes, were like nettles on the boys' skins.

The worst of the jellyfish was the "sea blubber", a red jellyfish that reaches a breadth of seven feet and has tentacles a hundred feet long. When the swimmer became tangled in the tentacles of one of these he had to call upon his companions to help unwind the stinging threads from his body.

Even after the *Hope* had made its way out of the sea of jellyfish, the logs were still covered with a slippery stinging coat of jelly.

On the next day the first birds were seen. Noddies and

boobies sailed inquisitively around the raft.

"It means that land isn't far away," Omo said.

Sore eyes followed the horizon around but could not discover a single palm.

All three of the boys were now "raft happy". Or, as Roger had put it, they had "the purple moo-moo". They were sick of everything, even of each other.

Hal announced that he was tired of having Roger on the same raft with him. Roger retorted that he suffered most from not having anything to throw at Hal.

Each began to think the others were losing their minds. They said strange things. Omo began to talk in his island language. He talked on and on. Roger said, "I'm going up the beach". He rose and started to walk off into the sea. Hal caught him by the ankle and brought him down with a thump.

Hal saw rainstorms – rainstorms that weren't there – and islands with palm trees and waterfalls tumbling from high cliffs through tropical forests soaked with spray.

So they hardly knew it when the wind quickened, the sky darkened, and the sea rose. Rain fell. They had barely enough wit left to raise their mouths to it.

An angry sea flung the raft south-westward. By a sort of desperate instinct, they clung to the logs.

The darkness of the storm merged into the darkness of night. Hal was vaguely conscious of the screaming wind and the sickening lift and drop of the raft over steep waves.

Then there was a roar that was not exactly the roar of the sea. It was the roar of a shore.

It must be another of his crazy fancies. It sounded like surf pounding upon land but it might be only the hammers in his aching head.

The raft was speeding forward dizzily now, only to be sucked back, then driven forward again. There was another surge, and a grinding sound underneath. Then another lift, and a crash.

The logs broke apart. There was no more motion. Hal felt hard sand under his body.

He reached for Roger. The boy had been thrown free of the surf.

But how about Omo? Omo had been in the water with his wrist secured under the lashing of the raft so that if he became unconscious he would not be lost. The lashing must now be broken, for the logs had parted.

Hal explored. The stars were blotted out by the storm and he could see nothing.

He groped all about the logs, then ventured back into the surf. His foot struck something and he reached down.

It was Omo. Hal pulled him out of the surf and ten feet up onto the beach.

Omo was as heavy as a sack of meal. He must be half-drowned.

Hal knew what he had to do. Take the pulse. Get the water out. Apply artificial respiration.

Hal dreamed he was doing all these things. But he had dropped upon the sand and was sound asleep.

22
Rescue and Rest

Hal woke in heaven. A golden-brown angel with red hibiscus flowers in her dark hair was holding a coconut shell full of cool sweet water to his lips.

It was hard to get any of it past his great tongue but he managed to swallow a little.

The sun had risen but was not beating upon him. He lay in the shade of stately coconut palms richly loaded with fruit. A soft breeze brought him the scent of flowers. There was music somewhere.

Roger and Omo lay beside him. Other golden-brown angels were ministering to them. Handsome young men came through the grove.

But he was very weak and closed his eyes. Now he was back in the storm and the night, clinging to the logs. He was conscious of being carried, but whether it was the waves that were carrying him he did not know.

Very gently he was laid down. There were many voices. He smelled wood smoke and the heavenly odour of cooking food.

He opened his eyes. He and his companions lay on

clean mats in a sort of lanai or veranda in a village of thatch houses. Flowering vines clambered over the roofs. Above the houses stretched the protective arms of magnificent mango trees from which hung ripe orange-coloured fruits like ornaments on a Christmas tree.

At the edge of the veranda brown faces were peering in — gentle, friendly faces — not the faces of night and storm.

Someone was bending over him. It was his angel again. He smiled up at her. She fed him something from a wooden bowl with a wooden spoon. It was a sort of mush made of breadfruit, bananas, and coconut milk and he thought it the most divine food that had ever passed his lips.

When he choked she drew back, thinking she was feeding him too fast. But it was gratitude, not his thick tongue, that choked him.

An old man seated himself on the mat beside him. To Hal's surprise, he spoke English.

"Garapan is my name. I am chief of this village. You have had much suffering. Now you are among friends. You will eat, drink, and rest."

Hal tried to say something but sleep closed over him like a cloud.

★   ★   ★

When he woke the shadows were long. It must be late afternoon. His eyes roved over the peaceful village. There was no street; the houses were scattered among the trees.

And what trees! He had noticed the mango trees before. Now he picked out breadfruit, banana, orange, lemon, coconut, fig, papaya, and mulberry trees. All of them were heavy with fruit.

Orchids of many colours clung to the trunks and branches. Bougainvillaea, hibiscus, and convolvulus were in bloom.

There were moving colours too – the red-and-green of flitting parakeets, the rose-grey of doves, the metallic blue of kingfishers. And there were tame little birds that fluttered around doorways as if they were the familiar friends of the people inside. On their tiny coats nature had found room for six colours – red, green, black, white, blue, and yellow.

The whole wood gave out a contented chuckle of bird sounds. Mingled with this music was the soft murmur of voices in the thatch houses, and, from somewhere, singing to the accompaniment of guitars.

He turned toward Roger and Omo. They were awake and sitting up, entranced as he was by sight and sound. Roger expressed it as usual in noble prose.

"Boy oh boy!" he murmured. "Isn't this the cat's!"

"Let's not pinch ourselves," Hal said. "We might wake up and find it isn't true."

There was a chatter of voices inside the house. Then several girls and women came out with shells of water and bowls of food which they placed before the castaways – baked fish and yams, roast pigeon, creamy poi, and a great basket of fruit of more than a dozen varieties.

The chief came to sit with them as they ate. His kindly old face beamed.

"Where are we?" asked Hal.

"This is Ruac. One of the islands of Truk."

Truk, the paradise of the South Seas! Hal had heard much about it. It was a vast lagoon surrounded by a reef one hundred and forty miles long. Within the lagoon were two hundred and forty-five islands.

"Is this island inside the lagoon?"

"No, it is on the reef. The ocean is yonder, and the lagoon is on the other side."

"Are there any navy men here?"

"On the main island, yes. I went there this morning to report. They wished to come to see you at once. But I asked permission to care for you until tomorrow morning. They said you were reported missing from Ponape. If you

wish, they will put you aboard the U.S.S. *Whidbey* which leaves tomorrow for Ponape and the Marshalls. It is a hospital ship – you will have good care." He smiled. "I have said what I was told to say. Now I shall speak for myself. We wish you to stay with us for many, many days and let us be your father and mother, your brothers and sisters."

Hal could hardly keep back the tears.

"We can never forget your kindness," he said. "But we must go. We have much important business in Ponape."

The next morning an outrigger canoe bore the derelicts across the fabulous lagoon of Truk. The lagoon was circular and forty miles across. Upon every side rose lovely islands, dozens upon dozens of them. Some of them stood up like towers and minarets, clothed from sea to summit with breadfruit and banana trees, coconut palms, scarlet bougainvillaea and crimson hibiscus, brilliant against the deep blue South Sea sky.

Some islands sloped up gently from sand beaches. Others rose abruptly in steep cliffs. Five of the islands climbed to peaks more than a thousand feet high.

Some islands were large. Tol was ten miles long, Moen five miles. Dublon, headquarters for the navy, was three miles across. There were islands of all sizes, down to half an acre or less.

And below, what a pageant! The lagoon floor was a garden of coral and algae, of sea fan and oarweed, of bright blue sea moss and red sea cucumbers, of ultramarine starfish and of swimming fish in all the colours of the rainbow. There were corals like sponges and sponges like corals. There were green sponges, geranium-scarlet sponges, marigold-yellow sponges.

"It wouldn't annoy me to stay around here and sail on this lagoon for ever," Hal remarked.

But an hour later on the U.S.S. *Whidbey* they sailed out of the lagoon through North-east Pass and looked back regretfully to the lovely island of Ruac. They could see their friends on the beach waving to the departing steamer.

Hal climbed to the bridge and spoke to Commander Bob Terence.

"Would you mind whistling good-bye to those people?"

The commander grinned and opened the whistle valve in three long blasts of farewell.

The *Whidbey* was a floating hospital. It was equipped with an X-ray, a fluoroscope, a pharmacy, and laboratory. Its business was to cruise from island to island, healing the sick and training native nurses.

Of most interest to the boys were cool clean beds with white sheets. They did little but rest and eat. A skilful naval doctor treated their salt-water sores and sunburn. He pronounced Omo's wound to be nearly healed.

When Hal thought of Kaggs whose bullet had caused Omo so much suffering and who had left them all to live or die on a barren reef, his blood boiled and he could hardly wait to get his hands on the murderous pearl trader.

"I'll thrash him to within an inch of his life!" he vowed.

The commander radioed Ponape that the boys had been found and were coming on the *Whidbey*.

After three days of peaceful sailing the great Rock of Chokach was sighted and the *Whidbey* steamed into the island-studded harbour of Ponape. No sooner had the anchor been dropped than a launch came alongside and Commander Tom Brady and other officers climbed aboard.

Brady searched out Hal at once and began to ply him with questions.

"Where were you? What happened? What made you stay on the reef? Why didn't you come back in the boat?"

Hal laughed. "One thing at a time. In the first place – did Kaggs come back?"

"Kaggs? Who's Kaggs?"

"Oh, I forgot. You know him as the Reverend Archibald Jones."

"Jones was picked up by a fishing boat. He was stark

staring mad. He had lost his way. His provisions and water had run out and he had been drinking sea water. It made him as crazy as a loon. It was days before we could get any sense out of him. We asked him about you. He said you had decided to stay on the island until he got back."

"That wasn't quite the way of it," Hal put in. "He shot Omo, then abandoned us without provisions and skipped off in the boat. We could die there for all he cared. He wasn't a missionary – he's a pearl trader and his name is Merlin Kaggs. There's a bed of pearls up there and he's out to steal it."

Brady stared. "I always thought there was something screwy about his missionary talk."

"Is he here now?"

"No. He got a larger boat and some men and sailed again. We thought he was going to get you. So imagine our surprise when we got word you were wrecked on Truk."

"How long has he been gone?"

"About a week. He wouldn't say when he was coming back. He talked wild – claimed he was going to dig up the pot of gold at the end of the rainbow. He was still ninety per cent nuts. The men were almost afraid to go with him, he acted so strangely. He went about with a logbook clutched to his chest and wouldn't let anybody look in it. Began to foam at the mouth if anyone so much as touched it. He wouldn't tell us where he was going. Said it was a secret island and he had the bearings. He took along a native who has had training in navigation. So he'll get there all right."

"He'll never get there," Hal said. Brady looked at him inquiringly but Hal did not explain his remark. "I hope he comes back soon. He'll find me waiting for him with a meat axe."

Brady grinned. "I know how you feel, but go easy with the meat axe. There's a prison sentence waiting for the Reverend Archibald Jones."

But both Hal and Brady were wrong. Kaggs would escape the meat axe and he was not to go to prison. Something rather worse had already happened to him.

23
Toward New Adventures

The boys moved in with Captain Ike in the same house to which they had been assigned when they had first come to Ponape. The captain reported that the repairs on the *Lively Lady* had been completed.

"She's shipshape and rarin' to go."

"And how are the animals?"

"All in fine fettle. In fact, the octopus was feeling a bit too frisky. He got out of his tank and climbed the rigging.

I had to call in a gang of natives to help me get him back in his tank."

Hal sent a long radiogram to his father. And on the first plane flying east he dispatched a small but heavily insured package addressed to Professor Richard Stuyvesant.

He breathed more easily when the pearls were at last out of his hands.

Hal inquired about Crab, the young sailor who had tried to steal his secret and who had been clapped in jail for likkering up the natives. Crab was still in jail. Hal thought that he had been punished enough. He went to see Brady who, as deputy governor of the island, had authority to release the prisoner.

Crab was set free. He did not bother to thank Hal or Brady, but lost no time in signing on as a sailor on the next ship out.

Hal waited anxiously for some word of Kaggs. Since the pearl trader had the wrong bearings it should be impossible for him to find Pearl Lagoon. Should be. But suppose he had found it in spite of all! Suppose his men were even now at work diving in the bay of pearls. Suppose Kaggs wiped the bay clean of all its precious store. Then he would sail away with the treasure. He would not come back to Ponape.

Not finding the boys on the reef, nor their skeletons, he would guess that they had escaped and might have returned to Ponape. So he would give Ponape a wide berth. He would sail away with his fortune to parts unknown.

And then what could Hal say to Professor Richard Stuyvesant? He would have to admit that it was his fault. He had been fooled by the crook, had even taken him along as a passenger to the secret island! Imagine taking in a thief and showing him just where your money was hidden!

"What a dope I was!" The words drummed in Hal's mind over and over as he tossed sleeplessly on the Japanese mats of the house above the harbour.

When the sun rose he went down to the docks. A strange craft was just dropping anchor a hundred yards out. Several brown men and one white stepped into a dinghy and rowed toward shore.

Hal strained his eyes. Was he only hoping it, or was it true? The white man was Kaggs!

Hal's heart began to beat like a trip-hammer. Now would come the reckoning. Kaggs must answer now for his evil tricks.

The pearl trader doubtless toted a gun. Hal had no gun.

He did wear a knife, but had no intention of using it. His fists would have to do. He was seventy pounds lighter than the trader and several inches shorter. Never mind – a tiger is smaller than an elephant, but the tiger wins. He felt the muscles tensing like steel wires in his arms.

Kaggs stepped out on the dock. He walked unsteadily. His mouth hung open and his eyes stared. His unshaved black beard increased his wild appearance. His uncombed hair hung like a mat around his ears. The hunch in his back was more pronounced. He looked like a deformed giant. His great arms hung like cargo booms from his forward-thrust shoulders.

Hal stood in his way. Kaggs stopped.

"Hello, Kaggs," Hal said. "Remember me?"

Hal expected to see a hand slip up to the shoulder holster where he knew Kaggs carried his gun. Before it got half-way Hal would strike first. He would land a crashing blow on that wobbly jaw and another in the solar plexus.

But the big fellow's arms continued to hang. He stared vacantly at Hal. Failing to recognize him, he turned out of his way and staggered off along the dock, muttering meaningless words as he went.

One of the men from the boat had stopped beside Hal.

He held a sextant in his hand. He must be the navigator.

"Completely out of his head," he said, looking after Kaggs.

"What happened?" Hal asked.

"The crazy fool had some bearings in a logbook. He said they were the bearings of an island where there was a fortune in pearls. When we got to the position there was no island there at all. He was already badly touched in the head, but that made it worse. He just cracked to pieces. He wanted to hunt for the island but we had had enough of sailing around with a raving maniac hunting for islands that don't exist. We brought him back."

There was a commotion at the shore end of the dock and Hal turned to see the cause of it. Kaggs was roaring and struggling in the grip of two military police. He was led away, babbling vacantly. Hal could almost feet sorry for the devil who had left him and his companions to die on a Pacific reef.

Kaggs was taken not to jail, but to the hospital. On an early plane he would be deported to San Francisco, there to be consigned to a mental institution.

Hal told himself that he should be happy over the way things had worked out. He had a good collection of specimens to take home, the pearling venture had been successful, their lives had been saved, and their enemy defeated.

But he felt strangely let down. He had not had the pleasure of punching Kaggs in the jaw. He could not take any delight in the terrible punishment the sea had meted out to his enemy. He shuddered to think how near he and Roger and Omo had come to losing their minds during the drift of the ill-fated raft. He would not wish such a fate upon anybody.

But he had another reason for low spirits. The great adventure was over. When he was on the island or on the raft he would have given anything to be done with it all. But now that it was all done, he was lost. He felt like an employee who has just been fired from his job. Nobody needed him any more. He was being laid on the shelf.

It was too bad that he must turn his back upon the South Seas. He had seen just enough of its wonders to want to see more.

And what gave him most pain was that he would have to part with Omo. Omo had already been looking about for a schooner headed for his home island of Raiatea.

Hal knew that Omo was as sad as he himself was over the coming separation. Roger, Omo, Hal, they were three brothers, and it was a pity to have to break up their alliance.

Gloomily, he walked up into the town. He stopped at the radio station. There was a radiogram for him. He opened it eagerly. It was from his father.

He read it with growing excitement. Then he broke out of the office and ran all the way to the house.

He found Roger, Omo, and Captain Ike each sitting in his own corner, moping. No one was saying anything. The place was as sad as a tomb.

"Great news, boys!" Hal shouted. "I got a radiogram from Dad."

"I'll bet I know what's in it," Roger said. "He tells us to toddle straight home."

Hal did not answer. He began to read the message:

You have done a great job. Animal collection sounds fine. Ship it home on cargo steamer. Stuyvesant pronounces pearls superb and has warmest praise for your work. Come home if you have had enough.

"What did I tell you?" Roger interjected. "We nearly break ourselves apart doing their job for them and then, just when we can begin to enjoy things, we have to quit!"

"Wait a minute," Hal said. "There's more to it." And he read on:

If you wish to stay there is an opening for you and your ship with expedition of Scripps Oceanographic Institution now sailing from San Diego. Could meet you at Honolulu. They would outfit *Lively Lady* with diving-bell, diving-suits, nets, submarine cameras, etc., for deep-sea diving operations to study habits of great fish and capture specimens. If interested let me know and will air-mail you all particulars. Your mother sends love to you and most affectionate gratitude to your friend Omo.

Omo looked up and his eyes were filled with a warm happy light. He tried to speak but his voice choked.

"Golly, boys!" cried Captain Ike gleefully. "That means we hang together!"

Roger began to leap about the room to the great peril of the Japanese paper doors.

"Whee! Whoopee! Meet the deep-sea divers! I'm going to be the first one down in the diving-bell!"

Hal smiled. "It seems to be unanimously agreed that our answer is yes. I'll get a message off to Dad at once."

VOLCANO
ADVENTURE

Contents

Contents

Author's Note

The chief characters in this book are fictional, but the volcanic events described actually happened. A bell containing observers did descend 1,250 feet into the boiling crater of Mihara, the *Kaiyo Maru* was sunk by a submarine explosion, divers discovered Falcon Island fifty feet below the surface, Tin Can's thirty craters erupted so savagely that the entire population had to be removed, Mauna Loa has frequently sent rivers of lava to the sea, and Hilo was saved by bombing.

The author has personally visited all the scenes described. In his pursuit of information on the habits of volcanoes, he has climbed Asama, Aso, Mihara, Kilauea, Mauna Loa, Paricutin and Vesuvius, and has flown over Popocatepetl, Pelée, Momotombo, Izalco, Misti, Stromboli, Etna, Uracas and Apo.

1
Volcano in the Night

It was very dark. A heavy blanket of fog hid the stars. The fog was so thick that the three mountain climbers could hardly see each other even with the help of their electric torches.

The fog was cold, the wind was cold, every bone in Hal's body was cold. It was necessary to climb the volcano at night, for it would have been too hot a trip under the broiling sun. But Hal, shivering, thought he would almost rather be too hot than too cold. He had given his sweater to his younger brother, Roger, but he still had his trench coat and this he zipped up to the chin.

Roger puffed and panted along beside him. The boy was usually merry and mischievous, but after three hours of stiff climbing he had very little fun left in him.

"This old volcano must be as high as the moon," he complained. "Aren't we nearly at the top?"

"Afraid not," Hal replied. "We may be half way there."

Roger groaned.

"Save your breath, boys," said the third member of the party, "you'll need it. The hardest part is ahead." And Dr

Dan Adams, volcanologist, scrambled up the face of a cliff as easily as if it had been a flight of stairs.

Ignoring his own advice to save breath, he burst into song. The song rose over the shriek of the wind and the rumbling of the volcano.

Hal wished he wouldn't sing. There was something wild about it, something not quite right. Perhaps it was meant to be a cheerful song, but it made a chill run down Hal's spine. The night suddenly seemed full of strange, terrible faces swimming by in the flying fog.

"Snap out of it," said Hal, but he said it only to himself. He must keep a grip on his nerves. There was nothing the matter with the song. Why shouldn't the man sing if he wanted to?

It would sound all right in the daytime. Perhaps it was just weird because of the night, the fog, the screaming wind, the muttering mountain, the quaking of the earth beneath, the fall of ash and cinders upon steel helmets, the occasional flash of light far above when the crater threw up its column of fire . . . the unreality of the whole thing.

That must be why the song seemed so strange, more like the cry of a wild loon than the voice of a man.

The doctor was no wild loon. He was a sober scientist. He was the American Museum's expert on volcanoes. He had studied volcanoes all over the world. He had gone down into the craters, analysed the gases, measured the lava flow, charted the eruptions, written learned reports.

Volcanoes to him were just figures and facts. He was cool, mathematical, scientific, a brilliant scholar.

Hal thought how lucky he and Roger were to be chosen as his assistants. They knew nothing about volcanoes – but they had powerful young bodies and they had already had a few months' experience on expeditions in the Amazon valley and among Pacific islands.* Now summer vacation was almost over and they would ordinarily have been thinking about getting back to school. But since they were both below the average age of their classes their father, John Hunt, the famous naturalist and animal collector, had allowed them a year off from their studies to get a practical education on expeditions for him and his scientific friends.

So here they were, half way up an exploding Japanese volcano in the dead of night with a man singing like a wild loon.

Whang! A cinder the size of a hen's egg struck Hal's helmet and bounced away.

* For the story of these experiences see the books *Amazon Adventure*, *South Sea Adventure* and *Underwater Adventure* by Willard Price.

Luckily these cinders, which had been white-hot when thrown up by the volcano, were cold after they had fallen through a mile of chill fog. Hal almost wished they were hot.

The cold wind blew the damp fog straight through his clothes; he could wring the water out of his coat.

Now and then they climbed out of the fog into clear air. But their torches showed another fog bank above them and presently they were in it. So they climbed from cloud to cloud.

And all this time there was a nice warm fire near by. Inside the mountain. Hal put his hand on the ground. He could feel the warmth. A terrific fire with a temperature ten times the boiling point of water was burning under his feet while he shivered and shook with the cold. He couldn't wait to get to the edge of the crater where he could enjoy the heat from this gigantic furnace.

Suddenly the mountain shook itself like a wet dog and sent up a spout of flame.

Then a new shower of cinders fell. Falling on steel helmets they were harmless enough, but when they struck shoulders or backs they bruised the flesh. And one never knew when something bigger might fall. Mt Asama had been known to throw out rocks as big as motor cars.

That wasn't likely to happen just now. Asama was not in violent eruption. If she had been, they wouldn't be climbing her. She was just in one of her muttering moods.

That didn't mean that she was quite safe. In fact, only a few days earlier two climbers had been killed by a shower of rocks, and a month ago a man was trapped between two streams of lava and burned to death. Ashes and cinders were pouring down upon roofs twenty miles away and earthquakes had tumbled several houses in the near-by town of Karuizawa.

But this was not much compared with what Asama could do when she really got angry. In one eruption she had buried forty-eight villages a hundred feet deep under a river of boiling lava. That is twice as deep as Pompeii was buried. But then, Asama is twice the height of Vesuvius and can be twice as violent.

Now she seemed to be slowly building up in preparation for another terrific eruption. It might come in a year, a month, a day. Who could tell?

If anybody could tell, a trained volcanologist could. Perhaps Dr Dan Adams could solve the mystery of Asama.

Suddenly Roger stopped dead in his tracks.

"Ghosts!" he cried.

Hal and the doctor stopped and looked at Roger. Was

the kid cracking up? Both of them had some advice ready for him, but before they could speak Roger said:

"Up there," and pointed up the steep slope.

They looked but could see nothing. The fog closed in around them like a gigantic mosquito net. It swept swiftly across the ground, not in a solid mass, but in ripples or shivers before the wind. The doctor's wild singing had stopped but the wind was singing just as wild a tune and the roar of the volcano, the flashes of fire, the rain of rocks, the atmosphere of suspense and danger, were hard on the nerves. The boy couldn't be blamed for beginning to imagine things.

"What's the matter with you blokes?" Roger said disrespectfully. "Up there!"

They looked again. Now they saw what Roger's keen eyes had picked out in the fog. Far up the slope, three lights seemed to be doing a ghostly dance.

Were they fireballs from the volcano? Were they the glowing parts of a stream of lava that was sweeping down upon them and would soon bury them in its blazing depths?

"Evidently we're not alone on the mountain," said the doctor. He cupped his hands around his mouth and yelled, "Hello-o-o-o!"

The lights above stopped moving. The three climbers listened. But no human voice rose over the scream of the wind and roar of the volcano.

The doctor called again. This time there was an answering cry from above.

"Come on," said the doctor, "we're going to have company." And they lost no time climbing up around the lava boulders and over slippery ash until they came to the three lights, which they found were held by three young Japanese climbers.

"*Komban wa*," said the oldest of the three, and ran on in Japanese. Then, as his torch caught the faces of the newcomers, he said,

"Ah, I think you speak English. I too speak English. I teacher of English in Nagoya Middle School. These are two of our students, Kobo and Machida. They no speak good like me. My name Toguri."

The doctor introduced himself and his two companions and everyone shook hands, all equally delighted to have company on the climb to the crater's mouth. Now the night and the mystery, the fog and the cold, the wailing wind and thundering mountain, did not seem quite so nerve-racking.

And what made Hal and Roger especially happy was

that the doctor did not sing any more in that weird, blood-curdling way of his but talked reasonably and cheerfully as the six climbed on up the shaking mountain.

2
Fog and Fire

The darkness was turning from black to grey. Day was coming. Presently there was enough light to see by and they could turn off their torches.

And what a dreary waste they saw! Great black blocks of lava, streams of ashes, not a tree, not a bush, not a blade of grass. The moon itself could not be any more bare and bald. This was a place where nothing dared to grow and it seemed as if man himself had no right to be here.

Only the fog was perfectly at home, rushing and rippling over the wet black rocks. It came in bursts and billows. One moment you could see twenty feet ahead, the next moment you could hardly see your hand before your face.

In the darkness and fog they had lost what little trail there had been. Now they simply blundered upward, slipping in the ashes, scratched by the sharp, glassy ridges of lava, clambering up cliffs like mountain goats, trying to keep their balance when the ground shook. Suddenly a violent quake made the rocks bounce. There was a sliding, ripping sound above them.

"Look out!" cried the doctor. "Under this ledge – quick!"

The six huddled in the shallow cave under the projecting ledge as tons of rock, ash and cinder thundered down like a deadly waterfall within a few feet of their faces. While it passed their hiding place it completely blocked out the light. Then it rampaged down the mountainside, its roar becoming fainter and fainter as it was swallowed up in the fog.

"Stay where you are for a minute." A few rocks that had been too slow to keep up with the avalanche now came tumbling down. Some of them were quite big enough to kill a man. When all seemed quiet again, the climb was resumed.

At last the ground began to level out and the six weary volcanologists found themselves upon what appeared to be the top of the mountain. But where was the crater?

This was no simple volcano. It did not rise to a point. The top of the mountain consisted of mile upon mile of hilly country. Somewhere there was a crater. But, without a trail to follow, who could tell where it might be? In clear weather the rising smoke could be seen. In this dense fog, the six explorers could only see each other.

It was bitterly cold, for they were now more than eight

thousand feet above sea level. The sweeping fog seemed to go straight through them. They huddled behind a great rock and held a council of war. The great rock split the fog as if it had been a river and it rolled by on either side.

"We make fire," said Toguri, trying to speak cheerfully. He looked about for wood. There was not a twig, not a leaf, to be seen anywhere.

The six ransacked their pockets and brought out various small pieces of paper. When they were all put together they made a pile a few inches high. The doctor set it alight and they all warmed their hands over the tiny blaze. In less than five minutes it was out.

"I hungry," said Toguri. "You hungry?" He produced a small wooden box and opened it to reveal some fish and rice. "We call this *bento*. You like?"

"Yes, indeed," replied Dr Adams. "And perhaps you would like some of this." And he produced a few chocolate bars. So they shared each other's small provisions.

Roger, dipping into the bento box, got hold of something that looked like a white worm. He held it up and examined it doubtfully.

"Octopus tentacle," said the cheerful Toguri. "Very good. You like?"

"I like," said Roger, and gulped it down.

Only one of the six did not eat. That was Kobo. He sat on a block of lava a little apart from the rest. His face was pale and drawn and he seemed to be sunk in painful thought.

The doctor stood up. "Now, Toguri-san, how are we going to find that crater?"

The teacher of English waved his hands and grinned. Nothing seemed to bother him.

"Perhaps we no find. I think we lost. Perhaps fog go away, then we find. Perhaps fog no go away. Many miles of hills on top of this mountain. Sometimes people wander about in the fog here for days. We just stay here. Nothing we can do."

Dr Adams did not say what he thought. He thought that Toguri must be a pretty poor teacher of English, and a pretty poor teacher of courage.

"I think there *is* something we can do," he said. "Somewhere there's a trail leading to that crater. If we can find the trail we're all right. Now, I have a plan. We'll make a human wheel. You, Toguri-san, stay here. We five will go out as far as we can still hear your shout. That won't be very far because this fog deadens sound – perhaps about five hundred yards. We'll leave Machida there, then go five hundred yards farther, then leave Kobo, and go on out, posting Roger, and then Hal, and I'll be at the end. That will make a line nearly a mile and a half long. Then, while Toguri-san stays here at the rock, the rest of the wheel will begin revolving clockwise. If that trail is within a mile and a half of this rock in any direction, we'll find it."

"Isn't someone likely to get lost?" asked Hal.

"Not if each man keeps within call of the next man at all times. Let's start. Keep shouting, Toguri-san."

While Toguri settled back against the rock, well satisfied with his part of the plan, the five struck out into the fog.

"*Yoi!*" shouted Toguri, in Japanese fashion. They went on. "*Yoi . . . yoi . . . yoi . . .*" The shout was becoming faint now as they stopped and left Machida, then went on.

So the men were posted, calling back and forth to each other, until the line ended with the doctor.

"March!" he shouted. The command was passed down the line, and the big wheel began to move. It had not made more than a quarter turn when the doctor shouted, "Here it is. The trail. Join me here."

The word was passed down the line and within twenty minutes all stood together on the trail. But which way to the crater?

They listened to the volcano's roar. Because of the fog, it seemed to come from all around them, and from beneath, and from above.

"I think it may be this way," said the volcano man, and struck off along the trail, the others following.

Kobo brought up the rear. Hal, glancing back, saw that the young student's face was very sad and his eyes were cast down. He dragged his feet. You would have thought he was going to his own funeral. What was the matter with Kobo?

Hal dropped back beside him and tried to start a conversation. But he knew no Japanese and Kobo was too shy to attempt to use the little English he had learned. He gave Hal a sad smile and they trudged on in silence.

If Kobo seemed unhappy, Dr Dan seemed a little too happy. Hal had come to think of him as Dr Dan. "Just call me Dan," Dr Adams had told him. "After all, I'm only about ten years older than you, and you're a bigger man than I am."

It was true that Hal, though only in his late teens, was a mite taller than the doctor, broader of shoulder and more powerful of body. But the doctor was wiry and strong, and very clever, Hal thought. Hal felt he owed the scientist some respect and could not quite bring himself to address him as Dan, but compromised on Dr Dan.

A shower of stones fell but Dr Dan did not seem to notice them. With his head up he marched on so fast that the others had difficulty in keeping up with him. The roar of the volcano grew louder. The sun had risen but was unable to get through the fog. The fog was more dense than ever because evil gases and smoke had joined it. Toguri was choking and coughing.

But in spite of the fumes and the falling stones and the quaking of the ground and the increasing thunder of the monster, Dr Dan strode along boldly, almost too boldly – as if he were afraid to show fear. And again he broke into the wild song of the night. It sounded as weird by daylight as it had in the darkness.

Suddenly he came to an abrupt halt.

"We have arrived!" he cried.

The others came up beside him. A few feet ahead the ground dropped away to nothing. Great billows of smoke rose to mingle with the flying fog.

Their eyes could make out nothing but their ears told them that they were standing at the edge of the crater.

3
Crater's Edge

A noise like the roar of ten thousand angry lions came up from the pit.

Beneath that noise there was another like the rumble of freight trains over a bridge. Then there was a higher note, the sound of escaping steam, like the hiss of a great serpent. And there were sudden explosions as if charges of dynamite were being set off.

The din became so terrific that when Dr Dan spoke again no one could hear him.

Hal remembered what he had read in *Terry's Guide*: "Mt Asama is the largest, angriest and most treacherous volcano in Japan. The dangers at the summit are manifold and should not be regarded lightly."

It was terrifying – and yet pleasant, because the heat rising from the fires beneath felt very good after a night in the chill fog. Each one of the visitors revolved like a chicken on a spit in order to warm himself all over.

From a bag that Hal carried, Dr Dan produced various instruments, a thermometer, a pyroscope, a small spectroscope. He began to take readings and jot down the results in his notebook. He captured some of the rising gas in a test tube and put it away for later study.

He spoke again, but although the boys could see his lips move they could not hear a word. Dr Dan signalled to the boys to follow him and set off along the edge of the crater.

Hal, looking back, saw a strange sight. The three Japanese had lined up in a row and were bowing deeply to the smoking crater.

Hal had read about this – the way the Japanese worship their volcanoes. Their religion, Shinto, makes every volcano a shrine or holy place. The god of the volcano must be treated with deep respect or he will become angry and destroy the villages in the country below.

The god is a terrible god and nothing pleases him so much as human sacrifice. In the old days human victims were thrown into his hungry mouth. Anyone selected to be given to the god was supposed to regard it as an honour.

Nowadays no one is thrown to the god, but many persons still give themselves to him of their own free will. In this way they think they are performing a holy act, and at the same time they are escaping their own troubles. The man who has lost his job may jump into a volcano. The woman whose children misbehave may end her life in the crater.

The young lovers whose parents will not let them marry may leap together into the flames. The student who has failed in his examination may choose to die here.

In Europe and America such an escape from duty would be considered cowardly. The Japanese do not think of it in that way and every year hundreds of disappointed people go to the arms of the fire god in any of the fifty-eight active volcanoes of Japan.

Hal looked back again. Toguri and Machida were wandering off along the edge of the pit. But Kobo still stood where he had been, gazing into the crater. Then he sat down on a rock and buried his head in his hand.

Hal wanted to go back to him. But what could he do? Perhaps there was nothing wrong. If there was, Kobo's Japanese friends could look after him. Dr Dan was already fifty feet ahead and signalling impatiently for Hal to come along. Hal hurried to catch up.

It was an exciting walk along the crater's edge. One side of your body was chilled by the fog, the other side baked by the fire-breathing monster. The ground was very hot underfoot. Hal found himself walking on the edges of his shoes to avoid the heat.

Here and there steam spurted up between the rocks. If you didn't watch where you were stepping and one of these steam jets shot up inside your trousers it was like being boiled alive.

The falling stones had been cold far down the mountainside. Here they were hot, and if one fell on your shoulder and stayed there for a moment it burned the cloth. Every boy likes to throw stones down a precipice. When Roger picked up a pebble to throw into the volcano he dropped it with a howl and sucked a burned hand.

The doctor was making a topographical survey of the crater's edge. Every hump and hollow, every fissure and steam jet, was carefully examined. Figures and facts went down in the notebook.

The noise was ear-splitting. Compared with that uproar, a steel mill would be as quiet as a cemetery. The fire god was gritting and grinding his teeth, then spitting them out in sky-rockets that flamed up through the gloom to a great height, changed as they fell from white-hot to red-hot, and slapped down on the rocks. There they lay, pasty plops of liquid rock slowly congealing into a sort of dough, still glaring red, and sending out a terrific heat.

The doctor rushed over to one and took a reading with his electric pyrometer. He showed the reading to the boys, 1100 degrees Centigrade.

Dr Dan shook his head gravely and pointed up. They understood his warning. These falling puddings were dangerous. They must keep watch above and not get struck by one of them. It was easy to imagine what would happen. One touch of this blazing lava, eleven times as hot as boiling, would set your clothes afire and you would go up in flame like a Roman candle.

But it was hard to watch both the sky and the ground at the same time. Roger got cross-eyed trying to do it. He wished he were a bird which can look in one direction with one eye and in the opposite direction with the other.

Suddenly the fog blew away and the sun lit up the dreary waste of grey ash and black lava and made a rainbow in the rising steam. The last ribbons of fog went up like writhing ghosts.

The volcano men stopped to look at the view. Thousands of feet below lay Japanese villages under thatched roofs, rice paddies like squares on a checkerboard, Shinto temples and pagodas on small hilltops, sparkling streams. Beyond the valleys rose ranges of mountains, blue in the distance. Far to the south was the perfect cone of Fuji. Away to the west gleamed the Japan Sea.

Splat! A blazing pudding of lava fell within ten feet of them. This was no time to be looking at the view and they went on warily, watching the sky and the ragged ground underfoot.

The gases made the eyes run with tears and irritated the nose and throat. Sometimes the fumes were suffocating and you just had to stop breathing for a moment and wait for the changeable wind to bring a gust of fresh air.

Then the breeze carried the gases away and pushed the column of smoke and fire to one side so that they could see down into the crater for the first time. The sight was terrible – and Hal, happening to glance at Dr Dan, saw that his face had changed.

He was no longer the cool scientist. His jaw was tight, his eyes were staring, as he looked into that awful pit. A terrible fear seemed to be stamped on his face, but still it was not quite like fear. It was a blank expression, a frozen look.

Hal wondered if the man had lost his senses. He was afraid he might step off into space, and put a hand on his arm. He found the body as rigid as a marble statue.

The doctor did not look at him, did not seem to know that he existed. He did not move a muscle.

Hal tried to shake him, but he seemed to have turned into stone. The cheekbones stood out, the neck muscles were tight, the hands were clenched.

So he stood for two long minutes.

Then a little colour crept back into the pale cheeks, the arm that Hal was holding relaxed, and the doctor's eyes moved. He glanced at the hand that gripped his arm and then at Hal and smiled doubtfully, as if wondering why Hal was holding on to him. Hal released his hold. The doctor pointed to a lava fountain at the bottom of the pit and once more he was the calm and interested man of science. He evidently had no memory whatever of those two terrible minutes.

Asama means Without Bottom, and for centuries the Japanese believed that the volcano had no bottom. But during recent years the bottom has been steadily rising and could now be plainly seen about six hundred feet down.

There, fountains of white-hot lava shot up into the air. Some rose as high as the crater's edge, then fell back. Others kept on climbing thousands of feet into the sky and fell on the mountaintop, with great danger to the volcanologists.

Below the fountains was a boiling white lake of liquid stone. It churned and rolled like the rapids of a great river. Pockets of gas exploded and burst into flame. Huge rocks were hurled up against the sides of the crater and fell back only to be hurled up again. Small stones by the thousand leaped up half a mile into the sky as if shot from a gun. Everywhere steam spurted out of cracks like smoke from the nostrils of a dragon. The din was terrific. The boys put their hands over their ears.

But the doctor did not seem to mind. He focused his pyrometer on the crater floor. Its temperature was 2500 degrees Centigrade. He made notes. Then he pointed to a patch of yellow and orange on the inside slope of the crater about fifty feet down. The noise slackened for a moment and he was able to say,

"I'm going down to take a look at that."

He unslung the coil of line that he carried on his shoulder. Although small, light rope, it was nylon and very strong. He looped one end of the rope around him under his arms and gave the rest of the coil to the boys.

"Just let me down easily," he said.

He stepped over the edge and down the steep slope, the hot ashes sliding under his feet. The boys paid out the line. When he slipped they braced themselves and checked his fall.

He reached the colourful deposit of minerals and studied it with his spectroscope. The boys held the line taut. Hal couldn't help thinking, what would happen if a blob of sizzling lava should fall on the line and burn it in two?

The doctor looked up and signalled that he was ready to come back. He scrambled up through the sliding ashes while the boys hauled in on the line.

When he stood beside them again they were breathless from exertion and excitement, but he seemed quite unaffected by his descent into a blazing volcano.

It was about a mile around the crater's edge and finally they came near the spot from which they had started. They looked for the three Japanese but the smoke from the volcano now drifting around them cut down visibility.

Suddenly, through the smoke two figures came running after them. They recognized Toguri and Machida. Both were greatly excited.

"You come," Toguri called. "You come – quick – see."

They turned and ran back into the smoke, Dr Dan and the boys following them. They stopped beside something blue that lay in a heap on the ground.

4
The Discouraged Student

It was a coat. The blue coat of a school uniform. Hal picked it up. He guessed at once what had happened.

"Was Kobo in trouble?" he asked Toguri. "He seemed very unhappy."

"Kobo take English examination," said Toguri. "He fail – no good."

Hal wondered how anybody could pass an English examination with such a teacher as Toguri.

They all went to the edge of the crater and looked down. It was impossible to see anything, the smoke was in the way.

"We go," Toguri said. "We go – tell his mother."

"Wait," said Dr Dan. "He may still be alive. I'll go down and see."

The Japanese stared in disbelief.

"Go in crater?" exclaimed Toguri. "No can do."

"He may not have fallen all the way down. Perhaps he landed on a ledge." Dr Dan uncoiled his line and began to knot the end about him.

Hal looked again into the pit. The sun was well up now

and already very hot, but still it did not penetrate that pall of smoke. The thought of going blindly into that crater made Hal sweat. But if Kobo was down there, it was Hal's fault – or so he felt. He blamed himself because he had not gone back to Kobo when he saw that something was wrong.

"Give me that rope," he said to Dr Dan. "It's my turn to go down."

The doctor protested. But when he saw that Hal was determined, he looped the rope about his chest.

Hal wiped the sweat from his face. The heat from the crater with the heat from the sun made him a little sick. The gases from below smothered him.

"Here we go!" he said. "Hold tight!"

He backed gingerly over the rim. At once he began to slip in the ashes, but the others braced themselves against the pull of the rope and held him up.

He raised his eyes for the last time to the faces of his brother, the doctor, and the two Japanese, all at the rope. Would he ever see them again – these four?

Four? There seemed to be five. He counted again. The gases made his eyes smart and the smoke made it hard to see. But there were certainly five. Four at the rope, and one standing behind them looking over their shoulders, an expression of great curiosity on his face. The fifth man said in halting English,

"What you do?"

The four turned to face him. They were so startled that they almost dropped Hal into the crater. Hal scrambled up to safe ground.

"Kobo!" he exclaimed. "You're all right!"

Kobo looked blank.

"You had us worried," Dr Dan said. "We thought you were down there."

"Very sorry," Kobo struggled in English, and then explained in rapid Japanese to Toguri. Toguri passed on his explanation.

"He say too hot here so he go back there – sit – think. He pretty sad."

"Why does it hit him so hard?" Hal wanted to know. "In our country lots of boys fail and it doesn't worry them too much. They just try again."

"Ah, you no understand," said Toguri, and he went on to tell Kobo's story. Kobo's father had died in the war. His mother and sister were working very hard to put Kobo through school. The least he could do was to succeed in his studies. When he failed he was very much ashamed. He had let his mother and sister down. All the neighbours would have contempt for him. He couldn't bear to go home. He didn't know what to do.

Hal looked into the face of the young student. Something there appealed to him very strongly. This was a fine boy. He loved his mother and sister and felt deeply disgraced because he had not been able to do his part. He looked bright enough – he would probably pick up English very quickly if he were with people who spoke it well.

Hal took the doctor and Roger aside.

"Listen," he said: "I have an idea. How long are we going to be in Japan?"

"About a week," said Dr Dan.

"That's not very long. But still I think it might be enough. He's eager to learn."

"What do you have on your mind?"

"If we can take Kobo along with us and talk English with him sixteen hours a day every day, I believe we could teach him more in a week than Toguri could in a year. Then if the school could give him another chance at the examination, he ought to be able to pass it."

Dr Dan thought for a moment, then smiled. "You're a good lad, Hal, and I think your plan might work. It all depends on whether the exam can be repeated. Let's ask the teacher. Toguri-san, could you step over here for a moment?"

Toguri, when told of the plan, was delighted. Yes, he was sure that the school would allow Kobo another examination. "School know I am very bad English teacher," he said humbly. "*I* know I very bad English teacher. But school no can afford good English teacher. Englishman or American cost too much. We do best we can. One week with you – I think Kobo pass examination."

"How about Machida?" Hal asked.

"Oh, Machida science student. He no study English."

They went back to Kobo and Toguri told him of Hal's plan. Kobo could not believe it. Why should strangers and foreigners do this for him? He stood looking at Hal and his thanks were in his eyes but he could not think of the right words. Two large tears ran down his cheeks. He smiled through his tears and managed to say:

"I very thank."

"He go home with me," said Toguri, "tell his mother – then come meet you in Tokyo. Yes?"

It was so agreed.

"Now that that's settled," said Dr Dan, "let's get out of here. I don't trust this volcano. It's been too quiet for the last half-hour. I think it's getting ready to give us a bath of hot lava!"

They started down the mountain, but by a different

route, because Dr Dan wanted to visit the place where lava had buried forty-eight villages.

As they went, the volcano god began to roar again as if angry that these six juicy morsels of food were escaping him. The doctor stopped every once in a while to plunge the spike of his thermometer into a bed of hot ashes. The top layer was only uncomfortably warm, but three inches below the surface the bed was twice boiling hot.

"We could fry eggs here," said the doctor, "if we had any to fry."

Which reminded them that they were hungry again and they stopped to consume the rest of the chocolate bars, rice and fish. While having their lunch they did not sit down, nor even stand, but kept dancing about so that their feet would not be burned.

Then the doctor hurried them on. The growls of Asama were growing louder.

5
The Strong Man

Although down hill, it was hard going. The heat beat down from the sun and up from the ground. It was necessary to climb over large blocks of lava. Most of them were solid and probably weighed many tons, but Roger was astonished when he bumped against one as big as a horse and it moved. It seemed to be riddled with small holes like a honeycomb.

A mischievous idea came into Roger's head. He liked to play tricks upon his older brother who was so much stronger and wiser than he.

They stopped to rest for a moment. Roger said,

"Hal, are you all right?"

Hal stared. "What do you mean – all right?"

"Aren't you sick or something?"

"Of course not. Why?"

"Well, you just look so pale and weak. I'm afraid this trip has been too much for your delicate constitution. You look tired out."

"Me tired? You're crazy. If anybody gets tired it will be you, you little shrimp. We'll probably have to carry you home on a stretcher."

"Well," said Roger, "we can easily find out who's tired. How big a rock can you pick up and throw down the hill?"

Hal looked about him. He selected a lava block as big as his head. He got his hands under it, hoisted it with some difficulty, and threw it down the slope.

"There," he said. "If you can lift anything half as big as that I'll crown you king of the May."

"I think I'll try this one," Roger said, and put his arms around the block as big as a horse.

Hal was much amused. "Don't make me laugh, kid. You couldn't even budge that, let alone lift it."

Roger braced his back, tensed his sturdy young muscles and straightened up with the great block in his arms. Then he threw it down the mountainside.

Hal was speechless. He stared at Roger, then at Dr Dan who was laughing.

"Impossible," muttered Hal. "Impossible."

"A very good demonstration, Roger," Dr Dan said, still laughing. "Let's go down and take a look at that boulder."

When they reached it, Dr Dan put his hand on it and rocked it back and forth as easily as if he had been rocking a cradle. It was as light as if it had been made of paper instead of stone.

"Pumice," Dr Dan said. "The rock that floats. Yes, it will actually float on the water. The lightest rock in the world."

"Does it come from the volcano?"

"Yes. It's really just lava — lava turned into foam. You know how light water is when it is turned into foam. That is because it is full of bubbles each containing air. Well, this is rock foam. It also is made up of bubbles, each containing air or other gases, some of them lighter than air. Some of the bubbles have burst and that's what makes all those holes."

"But does it really float on the water, like a raft?" Roger wanted to know.

"It does. When the volcano Krakatoa erupted, so much pumice was thrown out on the sea that it made a great floating island three miles across. Some people thought it was a solid island and built their houses on it. One morning they woke to find that a storm during the night had carried their island away over the sea far out of sight of any land. After eighteen days they were rescued by a passing ship."

"I'd like to take a ride on a pumice raft."

"You may have a chance when we get to studying the submarine volcanoes. Just now I think we'd better walk rather than talk. I don't like the sounds coming from that volcano."

They scrambled on down the mountainside. But the boys were too much interested in the stories the volcano man could tell them to allow him to walk in silence.

"What makes a volcano, anyhow?" Roger asked.

Dr Dan smiled. "Well, that's a pretty big question. Have you ever gone down in a mine?"

"Yes, we went down in a coal mine in Pennsylvania."

"Was it warm or cold?"

"It was hot. The deeper we went the hotter it got. We nearly melted."

"Exactly. Now if you had been able to go on down, say twenty miles, you certainly would have melted, and you would find everything around you melted too. The rocks would all be turned into hot soup with a temperature of several thousand degrees. The same thing happens in a steel mill where iron ore is heated until it melts and flows like water. Now then, if you step on an orange what will happen?"

"It will crack and the juice will squirt out."

"Just so. Think of the millions of tons of earth pressing down upon that rock soup. Naturally, if it can find a crack it will squirt out. And that's just what a crater is. A crater is a crack in the earth's surface. The rock soup sees its chance to escape and up it comes. That rock soup is what we call molten lava. Lava is just rock in a liquid state. It may be any kind of rock, or many kinds together – no matter, it is still called lava.

"Of course, when the lava spurts up through the crack it tears away dirt and rocks and stones and sends them flying up into the air along with the lava. If rain water seeps down through the crack it is turned into steam by the terrific heat. And you know how strong steam is – in a locomotive, for instance. The steam in the volcano may cause terrific explosions that kill thousands of people. The explosions may split the crater so that the molten lava flows out in a great river and covers dozens of towns and villages. And that's just what happened here. You are walking right now on the surface of a river of lava a hundred feet deep. Under it are thousands of Japanese houses. And in them are men, women and children, ten thousand people buried for ever."

"Why for ever?" asked Hal. "Vesuvius buried Pompeii, but now they have excavated the city."

"That's true. But Pompeii was buried under ashes, not lava. It was easy to shovel away the ashes. But these forty-eight Japanese villages lie under a hundred feet of solid rock."

"Is it likely to happen again?"

"I'm afraid it is. Japanese volcanologists believe that

Asama is preparing for another great eruption. After my observations today I am inclined to agree with them. The lava lake in the crater is rising at the rate of fifteen feet a year. No one can say with certainty, but it is quite probable that within the next ten years Asama will put on another big show. But before that it will put on plenty of little shows and a little show would be enough to kill the lot of us, so let's hurry along."

Asama was now roaring like a wild bull and sending up a tongue of yellow flame thousands of feet into the blue sky. Clots of half-solid lava spattered down on the rocks. Each man kept watch above, and dodged when he saw something coming for him.

And even so, a sticky chunk of red-hot paste struck the sleeve of Machida's coat and stuck there in spite of all his efforts to shake it off. The coat burst into flame. Machida whipped it off and beat it against the rocks to put out the fire. He finally succeeded, but there was nothing left of the coat but a black, charred mass. He threw it away.

The six pressed on more anxiously than ever.

"There's an inn at the foot of the old lava flow," Dr Dan said. "If we get to it, we'll be all right."

Great quantities of ashes were now rising from the volcano. They formed a black cloud in the sky. The sun was blotted out. It grew as dark as if it had been late evening instead of noon. Sudden flashes of light stabbed through the darkness.

"Is that lightning?" asked Hal.

"Yes. Lightning and thunder are very common over volcanoes, because the rising heat disturbs the electrical balance of the atmosphere. I wouldn't be surprised if we have rain too."

Presently it came: a deluge of rain, but not clean and pure as rain should be. It was a mud rain. The ashes in the sky mixed with water came down as mud.

"That volcano god finds plenty of things to do!" complained Roger. "But I never thought he'd begin throwing mud pies at us."

Within ten minutes they were plastered with mud from head to foot. They looked more like clay statues than men. They had trouble keeping the stuff out of eyes and mouths. It covered their ears so they could hardly hear each other. It piled up on their feet and made them heavy. It covered the ground like glue and made walking difficult.

The six mud-men staggered on through the unnatural night. What if they should lose their way? Hal looked anxiously at Dr Dan. He hoped that the doctor wouldn't begin to sing and that the strange attack that had turned him to stone at the edge of the crater would not be repeated. They depended upon the doctor to guide them to safety.

But the doctor seemed calm enough as he clambered over the rocks as nimbly as the heavy caking of mud on his body would let him. Toguri also seemed to know the way.

Gradually a light became visible ahead. It turned out to be a lamp in the entrance to a Japanese inn.

What a relief to step under the projecting roof and be sheltered from that crazy shower of mud! They tried to clap their hands to call the maid. But no sound came from those mittens of mud.

They shouted, "*Ohaiyo!*" There was a pattering of sandals in the corridor and a maid appeared. She cried out when she saw six mud statues standing in the vestibule. More maids appeared and the proprietor, all with cries of concern and sympathetic laughter.

Muddy shoes were removed, feet were tucked into sandals called *zori*, and the six mud-men were hurried straight to the bath. They were shivering with cold, for the heat of the day had vanished when the darkness and rain began.

Off came the mud-plastered clothes and were taken away at once to be washed and ironed.

Then six dirty men poured buckets of hot water over

themselves, applied soap generously, and rinsed themselves clean under more bucketfuls of hot water.

Then they stepped down into the bath. There is nothing in the world quite like a Japanese bath. It is a tub of very hot water three feet deep. This one was large, about fifteen feet square, more like a miniature swimming pool than a tub.

You don't go into a Japanese tub to get clean. You get clean first, then you enter the tub and squat in it so that only your head is above water. And there you soak for a half-hour or more, enjoying the warmth that seems to relax every muscle and nerve in your body, smoothes away your troubles, and leaves you perfectly content with the world and hungry for dinner.

So they happily soaked and relaxed. Then they stepped out to dry themselves and each slipped on a *yukata* provided by the inn, a sort of light-weight kimono, and they were led to the room that had been assigned to them.

Here they sat down on the soft mat-covered floor before an ankle-high table and were soon manipulating chopsticks over a delicious dinner of hot rice, baked fish, fried prawns, wafers of seaweed, a steamed custard of eggs, mushrooms and chicken, and a dessert made of beans in a syrup of sugar and honey.

Dinner over, the maids carried away the tables and the six were left to themselves.

The Japanese felt perfectly at home, but the others found the room a bit strange. It was nothing like the sort of hotel room they were used to. There was not one stick of furniture in it – no chairs, no bed, no table, no telephone stand, no writing desk, no chest of drawers, no dressing table, no carpet, no curtains.

There was also no dirt. The room was spotlessly clean. Even the floor was as clean as a dinner plate for no one ever came into the room with shoes on. The sandal-like zori were left outside in the corridor. The room was floored with straw mats called *tatami*, three inches thick, soft and springy, and as clean as a whistle.

The three Japanese lazily stretched themselves out on the floor, and the others followed their example. They were surprised to find how good it felt.

"Not bad at all!" exclaimed Roger. "A lot better than sitting up in a chair when you're tired."

They talked over the events of the day. Hal drew Kobo into the conversation and painstakingly corrected his faulty English.

6
Stories of the Volcanoes

The mud rain thudded on the tile roof. Already there must be a heavy blanket of mud on the roof. Roger looked up.

"I've always wondered what it would feel like to be buried alive," he said. "Perhaps we'll find out."

Dr Dan laughed. "I think the rain will finally conquer the mud and wash it away. But of course there's always the chance that it won't. This was the way Vesuvius buried Herculaneum – under a sea of mud."

"Have you climbed Vesuvius?" Hal asked.

"Yes. It's easy compared with Asama. It's only four thousand feet high. From the top you get a marvellous view of Naples and the bay and the Isle of Capri. And you can look down into a very angry crater. Vesuvius has blown her top many times, and will probably do it again. But the worst was when she buried Pompeii and Herculaneum."

"What year was that?"

"Only seventy-nine years after the birth of Christ. What a day that must have been! When people came out of their houses that morning they saw a great black cloud over Vesuvius. Flashes of lightning shot through it and the sound of thunder rolled down the slope of the mountain.

"Then there was a violent earthquake. The ground danced, people lost their footing and fell. Great cracks opened up in the streets, so wide that chariot horses could not jump over them.

"The mountain began to shake with explosions. The black cloud rolled down over the city. It became so dark that no one could see more than a few feet away except when a flash of lightning lit up the scene.

"Lava puddings like those we saw today began to fall and burned many people to death. Small bits of pumice showered down. Sulphurous vapours made people choke. Then the shower of ashes began. Tons and tons and tons of ashes. At first people didn't mind them too much. They just waded through them and laughed. The children had great fun playing in them and throwing them about. The ashes were only ankle-deep.

"But they kept on falling. Soon the people were up to to their knees in ashes. They went inside their houses. But the earthquakes began to shake the houses down upon their heads. So they went out into the street again.

"The ashes were up to their chests. Now they really became frightened. They began to leave the city. Some escaped, others were not able to battle their way through the ashes which were now over their heads. They were buried alive.

"Still the ashes came. They covered the houses, and then the theatres, and then the great public buildings. At last there was nothing but a smooth plain of ashes with the city completely buried far beneath.

"That was what happened to Pompeii. What happened to Herculaneum was a bit different, and more terrible. Over this city rain began to come down in torrents. It turned the ashes into mud.

"Here too the people were afraid to stay indoors because the earthquakes were tumbling the houses down around their ears. They went out into the streets and tried to wade their way out of the city. But they could not wade through the mud. It was up to their knees and it was a very sticky kind of mud, like glue or cement.

"It held them fast. They could not move. They cried out for help but no one could help them. The mud rose to their waists, to their necks. It crawled up over mouth and nose, over the eyes, over the top of the head. On, up over the tops of the highest buildings. Still the mud came until it was one hundred and thirty feet deep.

"Then the shower stopped. The mud began to dry into a hard, stony substance, very much like cement. So the people of Herculaneum stood in the streets in their great cement coffin for eighteen hundred years. People forgot that they had ever existed and new towns were built above their heads.

"Now an attempt is being made to excavate these cities. Much of Pompeii has been uncovered, but the cement coffin defies the diggers. They cannot disturb the new towns so they bore tunnels beneath them. They have reached the theatre and several beautiful temples. It is a hard job, and perhaps most of the city will remain sealed for ever."

"All the things a volcano can do!" marvelled Roger. "It buries these forty-eight villages under lava, Pompeii under ashes, Herculaneum under mud."

"But that's not all," said Dr Dan. "It can destroy a city without using lava or ashes or mud. Remember how Mt Pelée killed forty thousand people in five minutes?"

"Tell us about it," prompted Hal.

"It won't take long to tell because it didn't take long to happen. Mt Pelée – you know where it is, on the beautiful island of Martinique in the West Indies – had been growling for days. The people of the city of St Pierre at the foot of the mountain paid little attention to it. They weren't as wise as the animals.

"The wild creatures left the mountain. Even the snakes

crawled away. The birds stopped singing and flew to other islands.

"One morning at seven-thirty the volcano stopped growling. There was complete silence. 'Ah,' said one man to another, 'you see we were sensible not to run away. Pelée has quieted down.'

"The silence lasted for fifteen minutes. Suddenly there was a deafening explosion like the roar of thousands of cannon. The whole side of the mountain was blown to pieces. Out came a huge purple cloud that rolled down with the speed of a hurricane upon the city.

"Lightning zigzagged through it and besides the lightning there were brilliant fireworks in the form of serpents and circles. The cloud was made up of burning gases, terrifically hot.

"The people barely had time to speak before the burning cloud was upon them.

"I said that forty thousand people died in five minutes. It really took less time than that. The effect of the blast was almost instantaneous.

"The wall of fire swept out into the harbour and sank sixteen ships. The water of the harbour was heated almost to boiling point. Only two ships managed to limp away to safety after most of their crew had been killed. The fire hurricane burned the others and hot whirlpools sucked them down.

"Some of the ships were set on fire by rum – can you imagine that? Thousands of casks of rum stored in the city were exploded by the terrific heat. The blazing rum ran in rivers down the streets and out to sea, setting fire to the ships.

"Sailors on the two ships that got away looked back upon a frightful scene. The city was blazing. Houses lay in heaps, great trees had been torn up by the roots. Not a human being moved. Not a human voice was heard. The sailors believed that every last person had perished.

"They were wrong. One man, just one, still lived. He was discovered four days later by rescue parties. He was a prisoner in the city jail. He was locked in a cell so far underground that the gases and flames did not reach him.

"He saw nothing – his cell had no window. But he knew from the noise and heat that something terrible was going on. Then all became quiet.

"For four days he was without food and water, almost without air. He shouted for help. He tried to break the lock of his cell, but it was no use. He counted himself the unluckiest man in St Pierre.

"Then he discovered that he was the luckiest. He was

found and brought out into the light and saw the ruins of the city. It was one of the strangest twists of fate in all history – this man who had committed murder and had been condemned to die, was the only one in the whole city to live."

So the volcano stories continued through the afternoon and evening as they rested in the snug, dry little inn, mighty thankful to be there.

After supper, the maids brought *futons*, thick, heavy quilts, and spread them on the floor. They made a great bed twenty feet wide. Six small, round pillows were placed on the bed and six men crawled in between the quilts.

This all seemed quite natural to the Japanese. But the visitors, who were taller, found the quilts a bit short and their feet stuck out. However, they curled them up as best they could and were soon asleep.

For some hours there was no sound but the muffled pat-pat of mud on the roof.

It must have been about two o'clock in the morning when a sharp earthquake shook the house with a clattering, crashing sound and a scream split the air – the scream not of a woman but of a man. Hal felt a sudden commotion in the covers and then someone ran over him, still screaming.

Hal groped for the light and switched it on.

Dr Dan, looking very odd in his yukata which was too short for him so that his bare legs projected beneath it, was frantically beating upon the walls with his fists. Then he smashed the wood-and-paper door that led to the garden and was about to step out when he suddenly stopped screaming, turned slowly, and blinked at the light. Five astonished men sat up in their beds and watched him.

A puzzled look passed over the doctor's face. He seemed surprised to find himself out of bed and standing. He turned out the light and crawled in.

"What goes on?" came the half-asleep voice of Roger.

"Pipe down," warned Hal.

The others were soon asleep again but Hal lay staring up into the darkness, wondering and worrying about the doctor's strange behaviour.

Why should the man be so terrified by an earthquake? Earthquakes were common in Japan. An average of four a day were reported, though most of them were too faint to be felt except by the seismograph. Especially a man who made a business of volcanoes should be used to such things.

The doctor was no coward – Hall thought of how readily Dr Dan had faced danger during that exciting day. And yet, how about those two awful minutes at the edge of the crater when the doctor had frozen stiff as he looked down into the pit? When it was over he did not seem to remember what had happened but calmly descended into the crater at the end of a rope.

It was all very puzzling. Could it be that at some time in the past the doctor had had a terrible experience in a volcano, had perhaps suffered mental shock or injury to his head or nervous system – something that would explain these moments when he seemed to lose all control of his actions?

To Hal it seemed a dangerous situation – dangerous for the doctor and for Roger and himself. Were they going to explore fire-breathing volcanoes in the company of a half-crazy scientist? If he could just remain himself, there was no finer companion or abler volcano man. But suppose he lost his grip just at some critical moment? A bad accident might result.

Hal wondered if he should talk to Dr Dan about it. But Dr Dan probably didn't realize anything was wrong. If he had had a frightful experience, he would probably rather not talk about it.

It might be better to say nothing to him. You could hardly step up to a man and say, "You're crazy." Perhaps this shock, whatever it was, would wear off. In the meantime, thought Hal, he would just have to keep watch over the doctor day and night to prevent him from hurting himself or others.

Anxiously pondering these problems, Hal lay awake the rest of the night.

7
The Diving Bell

Perched on camels, the volcano explorers jiggled and jounced their way up to the edge of another angry crater.

The camel is not native to Japan; these animals had been brought from the Gobi Desert and for years had been used to carry visitors to the top of Mt Mihara.

"What a view!" cried Hal, scanning the sea below, dotted with steamers and sailing ships. Mihara stands on an island at the mouth of Tokyo Bay. At the north end of the bay lay the great city of Tokyo; to the west, blue mountain ranges; to the southwest, the beautiful cone of Mt Fuji. South and east stretched the mighty Pacific, speckled with islands.

But Roger wasn't looking at the view.

"I wish this camel would stop trying to sharpen his teeth on me," he complained.

The camel was continually turning its head to bite at Roger's legs.

"Don't let him bite you," warned Dr Dan. "Camels don't brush their teeth and their bite is poisonous."

Toguri and Machida had gone home, but Kobo, after a visit to his mother, had returned to spend a week with

337

the volcano men. He was as happy now as he had been blue before. He kept chattering with anyone who would talk with him and was absorbing English as a sponge soaks up water.

"How about that big surprise you promised us?" Hal asked Dr Dan. "When are you going to tell us about it?"

Dr Dan laughed. "Pretty soon you'll see for yourself. But I can tell you a little now. You boys have been down in the sea in a diving bell. What would you think of going down into a burning crater in a diving bell?"

The boys could only stare at Dr Dan. The question took their breath away.

"When I was in Japan a year ago," went on Dr Dan, "I was talking with a Japanese friend of mine who is editor of a great newspaper, *Yomiuri*. He was asking about my volcano plans. I told him that I hoped some day to go down into Mihara crater. I would need something like the diving bells that are used at sea. Just as the diving bell is watertight so that it keeps out the sea, this would need to be airtight to keep out the poisonous gases.

"The editor was much interested in my plan. He said his paper would like to work with me to carry it out. The *Yomiuri* would be glad to pay the cost of the experiment because it would make a big story for the paper. If I would tell them just how to do it they would construct the diving bell and have it ready for me on my return to Japan.

"Now they have done as they promised and the bell is waiting at the edge of the crater."

"Has this sort of thing ever been done before?" Hal inquired.

"A few times. A man named Kerner went down 805 feet into the crater of Stromboli. Another explorer named Richard went down in a sort of wickerwork gondola into the crater of Raoung in Java – but he had a bad accident. The trouble was with his gondola. I think our diving bell will work very much better."

Hal could only hope fervently that the doctor was right. At least no one could say that Dr Dan lacked courage.

Now the rim of the crater could be seen, a great column of smoke thundering up out of it.

"There it is!" cried Roger. At the edge of the crater a large object of steel and glass glittered in the sun and beside it was the crane that would lower it into the pit and bring it up again. A number of Japanese men were examining the steel-and-glass diving bell. The boys dug their heels into their camels' sides and hurried to the scene.

There they slid to the ground and were introduced by

Dr Dan to Mr Sanada, editor of the *Yomiuri*, and his friends.

Dr Dan and the boys examined the diving bell. It was round, stood about seven feet high and was six feet in diameter. The lower part was of steel, the upper part of glass with steel supports. The steel was in two layers with an air chamber between. The glass also consisted of two panes with space between them, the purpose being to keep out the heat. The top was of steel and in the middle of the top was a large iron ring to which the cable was attached.

Dr Dan opened the tightly-fitting steel door and went inside. A heavy asbestos mat covered the floor, and the walls and ceiling were also insulated.

"I think you will find everything in order," the editor said. "You see we have put in a telephone so that you can keep in touch with us. If you get into any trouble just tell us and we will draw you up at once. And here is the dog."

At the end of a leash a small dog whined uneasily as the ground trembled under its feet and the explosions in the crater sent up clouds of smoke.

"What's the dog for?" Hal asked.

"The dog is a surprise to me," admitted Dr Dan. "But I think I know why Mr Sanada brought it. I had told him that when the man went down into Raoung he took a dog with him. A dog would warn him if there was any carbon monoxide gas. You see, this very deadly gas has no smell. It is heavier than air and therefore lies low. If any of this gas seeps into the bell it will lie near the floor and the dog will be affected first. When the man sees this happen he can signal to be hauled up before the gas rises in the bell high enough to kill him. It's a good plan – except that it's hard on the dog."

The little dog looked up at Dr Dan with pleading brown eyes and whined.

"I think I'll take my chances without the dog," Dr Dan said. "Now if you'll give me that bag of instruments, Hal, I'll get going."

"But you're not going alone," objected Hal.

"Why not?"

Hal could not tell him why not. But the reason why not was very clear in his mind. Suppose the doctor should have one of his strange moments while in the depths of the volcano. Somebody must go with him.

"You might need some help," Hal said. "I'll go along."

"Me too," chimed in Roger.

Dr Dan smiled at them both. "I'll make good volcano men of you yet," he said. "But you don't seem to realize that this is a dangerous experiment. The bell will go down all right but whether it will come up is another question.

Any one of a number of things might happen. If you are still determined to go, Hal, I'll take you. But there will be room for only two – Roger will have to stay topside."

Roger looked both relieved and disappointed. He was glad not to go down, yet sorry to miss the adventure.

Hal and the doctor took their places inside the bell. The editor shook hands with them as if he expected never to see them again. The door was closed and locked. First Dr Dan tested the telephone.

"Can you hear me, Sanada-san?"

Mr Sanada, with earphones clamped to his head, replied, "I hear you perfectly."

"Very well. We're ready to go."

The crane's motor whirred. The slack of the cable was taken up and the hook came tight on the ring with a clanking sound. The bell wobbled. The two men inside gripped a handrail on the wall to keep their footing.

The bell left the ground and went straight up about ten feet, then it swung out over the crater. There it rested for a moment as if to give its occupants a last chance to change their minds.

Hal had a heavy feeling in the pit of his stomach. He suddenly hated to leave this beautiful upper world and go down into, who could tell what? He looked out to the white sails on the sea, the sweep of the Japanese mainland, and tranquil Mt Fuji in the distance.

The Japanese were looking up from the crater's edge. A little farther along, other visitors were reciting Buddhist prayers and throwing lighted incense sticks into the crater. They were worshipping the gods, gods very much like devils, that lurked at the bottom of the pit.

Hal looked down through a small glass window in the floor of the bell. The sight made him a little dizzy. Red cliffs dropped away to unknown depths. As the swirls of smoke parted he could see hundreds and hundreds of feet down, and still no bottom. He felt as he had in dreams when he had stepped off a high precipice into space. This was almost the same, except that now he was not dreaming. Fire flashed far below, an explosion shook the mountain and the bell swayed. The thought of going down into that awful pit . . .

But the doctor was calling over the telephone, "Lower away!"

The bell began to descend. The doctor was already busy with his observations. He was looking at his pocket altimeter.

"We are now 2512 feet above sea level," he said.

The far view disappeared. They were now below the edge of the crater. Down they went past the blood-coloured walls. Here and there were patches of bright green or deep blue. Everything went down in Dr Dan's notebook.

Now and then he called for a halt so that he could study the deposits more carefully. He made readings with his spectroscope. Then he looked again at the altimeter.

"We're one hundred feet down." On down. "Two hundred feet." Down, down. "Three hundred feet."

Hal was looking through the floor window. "There's a ledge of rock projecting from the wall. I'm afraid we're going to strike it."

"We may just be able to clear it." Dr Dan phoned to the men above, "Slowly, please. Very slowly."

But the bell could not quite get by the ledge. One edge settled on it and the rest of the bell began to tip over into empty space.

"Stop!" called Dr Dan. "Stop lowering."

The order was not obeyed quickly enough. The bell tipped farther, suddenly slipped off the ledge and swung out into space. It swung back and crashed into the wall with a shock that jarred and bruised the men and nearly smashed the thick glass. Out it swung again and in for another crash, but not so severe as the first. Three more bangs, and the bell swung without touching the wall.

Hal, clinging to the handrail, forgot his own terror when

he looked at Dr Dan's face. It was very pale and the eyes began to stand out strangely.

Hal put a hand on his arm. "Dr Dan, look! That geyser of hot water shooting out of the cliff. That's something for your notebook."

The volcano man seemed to come to himself. He turned to look at the geyser and out came his little book. Then he grinned at Hal.

"Ready to go on down?"

"Ready if you are."

Four hundred feet down. Five hundred feet. Six hundred. Seven hundred. Still no bottom to be seen. Nothing below but the orange of the flames seen through coils of rose and blue smoke.

Eight hundred feet. Nine hundred feet.

As they neared the hidden lake of fire the bell was shaken more and more by the explosions. It was repeatedly thrown against the wall. Hal was thankful that the volcano was really not in violent eruption. If it had been it could have tossed this little steel-and-glass thing half a mile into the air. Hal spoke his thoughts to Dr Dan.

"Half a mile?" said the doctor. "That would be easy. Mihara could do better than that if she really got down to business. In one eruption she threw rocks bigger than this bell three miles out to sea. Now there's a strange deposit."

He was looking at some white object on a flat ledge.

"Skeletons!" exclaimed Dr Dan. "There must be three or four of them. It must have happened recently Even the bones will crumble away quickly in this heat."

Hal wiped the sweat out of his eyes. In spite of the insulation, the heat inside the bell was becoming intense. The flames below were getting much too close. He had been sorry for the people who had fallen or jumped in – now he was beginning to be sorry for himself.

The bell was not descending smoothly, but in jerks. Dr Dan spoke through the telephone.

"Go easy, boys. No jerks. It's not comfortable – besides it might break the telephone wires."

"The motor is giving us a little trouble," came the answer.

Hal, in spite of the heat, felt a cold prickle in his backbone. What if the motor should conk out entirely and leave them down in the pit!

Another hard jerk, and a snapping sound above. Dr Dan looked up anxiously. He spoke into the telephone.

"Hello! We've descended far enough. Haul us up now! Hello! Hello!"

There was no answer. The wires had snapped. It was easy to understand what had happened. The cable supporting the bell could stand the jerks, but the telephone wires which ran up alongside the cable had not been able to bear the strain.

Did the men above realize that the wires were broken? If so, they would immediately haul up the bell.

But the bell kept going down. It went more smoothly now and the men were probably congratulating themselves on having fixed the motor.

A thousand feet down and still descending. The heat was suffocating. White-hot lava bubbled out of cracks in the cliff. Eleven hundred feet down. Impossible to signal for a stop.

"Our only chance is that they'll try to use the phone and find it doesn't work."

Twelve hundred feet. Now they could plainly see the lava lake close below. It was a raging sea of orange and vermilion lava, boiling, rolling over upon itself, leaping up in bloody fountains. Mammoth bubbles threw up fireworks around the bell. The explosions were deafening.

Hal felt as if he must cry out. He must scream as the doctor had in the night. He looked at the doctor, expecting to see terror in his face. But the doctor was too busy to be frightened just now. He was making notes. He would probably keep on making notes until the bell sank into the blazing lake.

The bell jerked to a stop. Perhaps the men at the crane had tried to use the telephone and found no connection. The bell wavered and waited for what seemed a long time. Then it began to rise.

Dr Dan pulled out his altimeter, and made a note in his book. He showed the note to Hal.

"Total descent, 1250 feet."

He grinned with the happiness of a scientist who has done his job well. Whether they would get back safely to the top did not seem to worry him.

It worried Hal a lot. The bell jumped like a scared cat when explosions went off beneath it. The sudden blasts sent it bouncing against the cliff, then spinning and swinging in space. He noticed that at one point the outer layer of glass was broken. If the inner layer also was smashed, the poisonous gases would pour in.

Sky-rockets soared up through the smoke and a volley of rocks struck the bottom of the bell. There was a long rumbling and then a terrific crash as if a hundred locomotives were meeting head-on. The crater god lifted the bell as easily as if it had been a baseball and hurled it against the cliff. Broken glass tumbled into the bell. Smoke and gas flooded in through the gaping hole.

Hal stuffed his shirt into the hole. It was not a very

good cork. Some gas would come through it and around it. But if the crane motor didn't fail and if there was nothing to interrupt their ascent they might reach the top in time.

The light was changing from firelight to daylight. Now and then they could catch a glimpse of the sky through the smoke. But Hal's rising hope was checked when Dr Dan reminded him of the ledge on which they had stuck during the descent.

"We'll strike it again on the way up," said Dr Dan. "If we hit it too hard we might break the cable. Too bad I can't telephone those fellows to slow down."

He had hardly finished speaking when the roof of the cage struck the ledge with a jarring bump and the bell's ascent was checked. Fortunately the cable still held. But the margin of the rocky shelf firmly pressed down upon the roof of the bell so that further ascent was impossible.

"I was hoping we could slide by," said the volcano man. "But it doesn't seem to be on the cards. There's not very much that we can do. If we had a boat hook we could push ourselves off. But this tub doesn't seem to be equipped with boat hooks. Perhaps the chaps upstairs will have an idea."

He tucked the shirt more tightly into the hole.

"Breathe as lightly as you can so that we don't use up the good air any faster than necessary."

The men above did realize what had happened for they could see the bell clearly when the smoke parted. They tried lowering it a few feet and then raising it. This was done repeatedly, but every time the steel roof caught under the ledge and refused to slip by.

Roger looked anxious, forgetting his own hurt feelings. He had been pretty sore at not being allowed to go down in the bell. He felt that the Japanese regarded him as only a youngster and of no real importance to the expedition.

"How did they happen to bring you along?" Mr Sanada had said. "You can't be more than fifteen years old."

Roger, big for his age, actually had a year to go yet before he would be fifteen, but he wasn't going to admit it.

"Well," he said, "I guess age doesn't matter so much as experience."

"Oh, so you've had a lot of experience with volcanoes?"

"Quite a bit." He wouldn't tell the man that this was only the second volcano he had ever seen in his life.

"I suppose it takes a lot of study to become a volcanologist."

"Yes, it does."

Mr Sanada was looking at him with new respect. "I'm afraid I under-rated you. I thought you were just a kid who had come along for the ride. Now I see you're a trained scientist — quite remarkable in one so young."

Roger turned away to hide a laugh. It was fun bluffing this fellow. But somehow he wasn't quite happy about it. Truth to tell, he was a little ashamed. Oh well, now that he had made the bluff, he would have to live up to it. He tried to look important, and to make scientific remarks about the crater and its boiling contents.

But when he saw the bell in great danger he dropped his pretence and was just an anxious boy worrying about his brother.

After all attempts to get the bell past the ledge had failed, the man at the crane stopped trying. He turned off his motor. The Japanese gazed blankly at each other. Mr Sanada turned to Roger.

"You're a trained volcano man," he said. "What do you think we should do?"

Roger felt very small. It there had been a hole as big as a mousehole he would have crawled through it.

"I . . . don't . . . know," he admitted.

"What do you do in similar cases?"

"Well," stumbled Roger, "we . . . usually send a man down. He could push the bell out a couple of inches — then it would get by the rock."

"Of course!" exclaimed Mr Sanada. "Why didn't we

think of that? We have plenty of rope here and we can let you right down to the ledge."

"Me!" cried Roger.

"Yes – not that any one of us wouldn't be willing to go. But this is obviously a job for a man who knows volcanoes."

Roger gulped. He looked down to the ledge. The stinging smoke and suffocating gases flooded up into his face. He stood up, feeling green and cold. The Japanese were waiting, and Mr Sanada was looking at him curiously.

"Where's the rope?" said Roger.

It was brought and he had it looped about his chest just as he had seen Dr Dan put it on.

Then he stepped to the edge of the crater. He did not look down into it again – he didn't dare. He turned his back to it and, while the men held the line taut, he let himself down over the edge.

Now he was dangling in space like a spider at the end of a thread. Down he went, rather jerkily, past the red wall. The explosions from below terrified him. He thought at that moment that if there was anything he would never want to do it was to be a volcanologist.

The fumes were stifling. If he only had a gas mask! He was being cooked by the rising heat. Luckily there were strong air currents so that occasionally the heat and gas and smoke were carried away from him and then he could take in deep breaths of almost pure air. He made a practice of holding his breath until these moments came.

His feet struck the ledge. Now he was standing on the rocky shelf. He got down on his hands and knees and crept to the edge. The roof of the bell was caught firmly under the rim.

Roger looked up. He could see the Japanese peering down. He signalled for the bell to be lowered. There was a moment's delay, then the bell eased down an inch or two.

Roger lay flat on the shelf, his head and shoulders over the edge. He could reach the roof of the bell. He signalled for the bell to be raised. Up it came, slowly. Roger, with his hands on the rim of the roof, pushed with all his strength. The bell cleared the ledge with an inch to spare and continued its ascent. As it went by, two grinning faces looked out to the boy on the ledge.

Roger was hauled up and arrived at the top a moment after the bell had landed. Dr Dan and Hal were released from their gassy prison. They were very happy, though dizzy and faint from the effects of the gas.

Hal looked proudly at his younger brother. "Good work," he said, and put his arm about the boy's shoulders.

Mr Sanada burst in with:

"How fortunate we had a good man to send down after you! Remarkable — so young, and yet he's made such a study of volcanology, visited so many craters — he was telling us about it."

Dr Dan looked at Roger and chuckled. Roger blushed to the roots of his hair. What would the doctor think of him? He waited for Dr Dan to tell Sanada just how much he really knew about craters.

He glanced up. But there was no sarcasm on the doctor's face, only a friendly smile, and all he told Mr Sanada was:

"Roger is a good volcano man."

8
The Boiling Lakes

The good ship *Lively Lady* sailed west.

Behind loomed a volcano sending up a mile-high column of rose-and-blue smoke. It was Mihara, into which Dr Dan and Hal had descended in the diving bell.

Ahead lay more volcanoes. Hal and Roger were not anxious to get to them too soon.

Their adventures on and in Mihara had tired them and they were glad to lie on the deck in the sun. They felt at home. How good it was to be in the arms of the *Lively Lady* once more.

It seemed a long time since they had set out from San Francisco in this gallant little sixty-foot, Marconi-rigged sailing schooner to capture creatures of the deep sea for their animal-collector father.

They had learned much about the Pacific and what goes on beneath its waves. They had found Captain Ike Flint a fine captain and a good friend. Now the ship had been chartered by the American Museum of Natural History for its study of Pacific volcanoes. But Captain Ike remained as master while Hal, Roger and their Polynesian

356

friend, Omo, had been kept along with the ship. Dr Dan Adams believed that though they knew nothing about volcanoes they were strong in body and brain and would be quick to learn.

Hal, as he stretched out wearily in the soft sunlight, hoped the doctor had not been disappointed.

He would have been encouraged if he could have heard the conversation up forward between Dr Dan and Captain Ike.

"They're tough," the doctor was saying. "Hal insisted on going down in the bell with me. When we got stuck, the kid came down at the end of a rope and pushed us off."

Leather-faced little old Captain Ike chewed the stem of his pipe. "I'm not surprised," he said. "After the things I've seen them do, diving for shark and octopus and such, I wouldn't expect them to be scared by a bit o' smoke and gas."

Dr Dan smiled. "Captain, have you ever looked down into a crater?"

"Can't rightly say I have."

"Well, let me tell you it's more than a bit of smoke and gas. The thundering racket, the heat, the earthquakes, the fountains of fire, the explosions, the flying rocks, the fumes – well, it's hell let loose. And to go down into a crater –

357

it can be pretty terrifying. I once had an experience . . ."

Captain Ike waited for him to continue, but the doctor's face had become as still as marble and the eyes were fixed and staring as if made of glass.

"You were saying . . ." the captain prompted. But there was not the slightest movement in the scientist's face or body. For a full minute he remained so. Then his features melted, his eyes moved, and life seemed to flow through him once more.

"Let's see," he said, "where were we? Oh, I was telling you about the boys . . ."

But Captain Ike was thinking to himself: "This poor fellow remembers something that he might better forget."

Kobo, the Japanese student in search of English, sat beside Hal and Roger and kept them talking in that language. He was learning fast.

Handsome, brown Omo in his perch in the crow's-nest listened to the deck talk as he scanned the shore of Japan, looking for the passage that would take them to their next Japanese volcano.

"Bungo!" he cried at last. "Three points to starboard." The little ship swung to the right to brave the tide rips and whirlpools of the Bungo Channel.

Then Japan's inland sea, probably the most beautiful sea

in the world, with its three thousand fantastic islands and its surrounding mountains crowned with old castles and temples, opened up before them.

The ship rounded to port, and ahead lay one of the strangest sights of the world – a whole mountainside bristling with geysers of steam. Among the geysers were houses, for this was the city of Beppu. Beyond rose a column of smoke from Aso volcano.

"I suppose this is the only city on earth," Dr Dan told the boys, "where hot water doesn't cost a penny. Poke a hole in the earth anywhere and up comes hot water or steam or both. Every house gets its hot water from underground. The water never stops coming up – taps can be left running all the time, it doesn't matter. No wood or coal is needed in the kitchen stoves. Meals are cooked by steam from below. Factories run by steam. Powerhouses use steam to make electricity to light the city. Beppu is sitting on a red-hot boiler. Some day the boiler may burst, but until it does the people cheerfully use its power to run their city."

"Judging from those geysers," said Hal, "there's more power than they can use."

"Yes, most of the steam just shoots up into the air and goes to waste. Most of the hot water runs down into the bay. There's enough power here to run all of Japan, if it could be harnessed."

The ship anchored in the bay close to the beach. Roger rubbed his eyes.

"These people must be headhunters!"

His brother laughed. "What makes you think that?"

"Look at all those heads lying on the beach."

Sure enough, a row of human heads lay on the sand. They were all Japanese. Some were the heads of men, some of women. There were children's heads, too. In some cases the eyes were closed; in others, they were open, as if the heads were still alive. Roger's eyes nearly popped out when he saw some of the heads move and begin to talk to each other.

"Come ashore," said Dr Dan. "When we get close to them you'll see what it's all about."

They stepped out on to the dock and down on to the beach. Now Roger could see that the heads had bodies attached to them, but the bodies were buried in sand. Steam rose from the sand.

"Beppu is famous for its sand bathing," said Dr Dan. "How would you like to try it?"

It seemed a curious way to take a bath, but the boys were willing to try anything. In the nearby bathhouse they paid a small fee, removed their clothes, put on trunks, then came out on to the beach.

Roger was the first to be buried. An old woman with a shovel dug a grave for him in the steaming sand, then told him to lie in it. He lay down, but immediately jumped out with a howl of pain for the wet sand was almost boiling hot.

All the Japanese heads laughed at him and chattered to each other. He could imagine what they were saying, "These foreigners – they can't stand much."

The old woman cried shame upon him. She took him by the arm and pulled and pushed him down into the steaming grave and before he could leap out again she began to shovel sand over him. When a neat burial mound had been raised, and nothing remained visible but his red-hot face, she knocked the breath out of him by giving the mound a final whack with the flat of her shovel.

Roger was quite sure he could not stand the sizzling heat for more than five minutes. But by the time the others were buried his pain had merged into blissful comfort, he felt his muscles and nerves untying their knots and time became of no importance. For an hour they all lay stewing happily and were sorry at the end of that time to see the old woman coming with her shovel to dig them out.

"And now to see the boiling lakes," said Dr Dan. "Beppu has a dozen of them. The Japanese call them *jigoku*, which means hell. And when you see them you'll think the name fits."

The first was Blood Hell and it was something to remember. A small lake of blood-red water boiled and rolled, let out great gusts of steam, and threw up jets of red liquid to a great height. "Iron sulphide," explained Dr Dan. "Sometimes it spouts three hundred feet high. And, believe it or not, this bit of a lake is five hundred feet deep." He busied himself with his instruments and notes.

Then came Thunder Hell. This was a noisy one. It growled, grumbled, hissed and screamed. Sometimes in the past it had overflowed to bury people and houses under a scalding flood. To prevent it from doing this again, the Japanese had brought in two gods to watch it. On one side of it stood a statue of the Fire God, and on the other, the Wind God.

White Pond Hell was a vivid blue pool six hundred feet deep, continually bubbling with what Dr Dan said was natrium chloride.

A statue of a great dragon stood guard over Gold Dragon Hell. As if this were not enough to keep the waters under control, statues of Buddhist saints had been placed around the pool. The caretaker of the pool took the boys into his house where they saw his wife cooking by steam straight out of the earth.

The snouts of alligators and crocodiles poked up out of Devil's Hell. The great reptiles were kept in this hot water to speed their growth. When they reached full size they would be shot and their skins used to make shoes and jackets.

In Sea Hell picnickers had let down a basket of eggs to boil them in the bubbling water.

Most curious of all was a boiling waterfall. Bathers stood under it with pained expressions on their faces and let the scalding water beat upon their shoulders and backs. This was believed to be a cure for rheumatism.

Not only humans liked the hot water, but animals as well. The boys were constantly tripping over snakes and toads that lived along the edges of the lakes, and monkeys swarmed on nearby Monkey Mountain. These monkeys were smart. They would come down to the bay, dive in, and catch fish in their hands. One had been taught to operate a small train that ran around a circular track. Dr Dan and the boys took a ride behind the monkey motorman.

It was nearly dark. "How about spending the night ashore?" Dr Dan proposed. "Captain Ike and Omo will take care of the ship. Here's an inn that looks attractive. Kobo, what does it say on that sign?"

The sign was in Japanese. "It says the name of this place is The-Inn-by-the-Well-by-the-Cedar-Tree."

Here they spent the night. The rooms were clean, the food good, and the chief attraction was the great tiled bath full of crystal-clear hot water welling up out of the earth and continually running over.

9
The Avalanche

The next day they went to the crater of Aso – a long distance, so the trip had to be made by train. Then a stiff clamber up through lava boulders. At last they stood looking down into a boiling pot half a mile wide.

Hundreds of feet down were thunderous tumbling pools of sulphurous mud sending up geysers of fire. They were like red clutching fingers that barely reached those who stood peering over the edge. Some of the rising clouds were of snow-white steam, others were pitch-black smoke.

The gases were stifling. Everyone got out his handkerchief and tied it across his nose to keep out the stench of brimstone. An icy wind pulled and pushed as if determined to throw them in. Their backs ached with cold while the cooking heat struck them in the face. The doctor made his usual observations and records and the boys helped him whenever they could.

They were glad to get down from the biting cold of this mile-high mountain to a tea house on the slope, where they drank hot tea and ate curious little cakes filled with sweet bean paste.

Again the *Lively Lady* put to sea, and again she put in to a Japanese port, this time to visit the monster volcano called Sakura-jima.

"*Sakura* means cherry," said Dr Dan, "and *jima* means island. Cherry is all right — it describes the colour of the red-hot lava — but island is all wrong. It used to be an island until 1914 when a terrific eruption threw up so much lava that the sea was filled between the volcano and the mainland and the island was turned into a peninsula. The city on the mainland was shaken to bits and one village near the volcano was buried under 150 feet of lava. Ninety-five thousand people lost their homes."

"Is that the only time she erupted?" Hal asked.

"By no means. Old Cherry has blown up twenty-seven times in the past five centuries."

"Well, I hope she'll all done now."

"I'm afraid not. They say she's getting ready to stage a new act. Let's go up and see for ourselves."

The way led at first through orange groves and vegetable gardens. Everything was growing lushly in the soil kept warm by the fires underneath. Farther up the trees and fields disappeared and there was nothing but savage black rocks. Every once in a while the shaking of the mountain

would dislodge a rock and it would come tumbling down, a great danger to climbers.

At last they reached the dropping-off place and looked down into their fourth crater. Old Cherry deserved her name – the waves and fountains of liquid lava were cherry-red. They looked very angry and it was easy to believe that they were planning mischief.

The doctor went to work with his instruments, and by now Hal and Roger were able to be of real help to him.

"Let's go around the crater," suggested Dr Dan. "There won't be time for us all to make the complete circuit. Suppose we split up – two will go one way and two the other and we'll meet at the far side. Roger will go with me."

The doctor and Roger struck off while Hal and Kobo went in the opposite direction. There was no path along the edge of the crater and the way was very rough. The lava here had been exploded by gases into glassy fragments as sharp as needles and pins, and when Hal stumbled and fell he came up with his hands full of slivers.

"Not the nicest place in the world to go for a walk!" he said as he picked the sharp points from his hands.

"Not the nicest place to go for a walk," repeated Kobo, practising his English.

At every step they crushed through a bed of black lava

glass a foot deep. Their socks were soon cut to ribbons and their legs bled. The blades of glassy rock were as sharp as razors.

"Obsidian," Hal said. "In ancient times before iron was discovered people used to make knives out of this stuff."

Hal stopped to jot down in his notebook items that he knew the doctor would want to have. He stood still only a moment, but the scorching heat from below came up through the soles of his boots and made him move on in a hurry.

They clambered over ridges twenty feet high that looked like great waves of the ocean suddenly turned to stone. They were panting and puffing now, and sweating at every pore.

"I think we stop little time now, rest," suggested Kobo, and sat down heavily on a rock. He leaped up at once for the rock was as hot as a stove. They stumbled on along the crater's edge.

Hal suddenly stopped. He was looking down the steep slope into the crater. About thirty feet down gleamed some peculiar blue stones.

"That's something the doctor will want," said Hal, "a sample of that rock."

"But you cannot," objected Kobo. "It is too – up and down."

"You mean too steep? Oh, I don't think so – if I take it slowly."

"But we have no rope."

"I think I can manage without one."

He turned his back on the crater and lay down on his stomach, his feet over the edge. Then he eased himself gradually down the slope, using his hands and feet as brakes. Fortunately the volcanic glass had given way to a sort of gravel that was not so hard on the hands.

He was to learn in a moment, however, that even gravel can be dangerous. Stones that he dislodged with his fingers or feet tumbled down the slope, and kept on tumbling until they splashed into the fiery red lake far below.

Hal had nearly reached his goal when he was suddenly terrified by a new sensation. The whole gravel bed on which he lay had started to slip. If this was a real landslide it would carry him straight to his death in the lake of fire.

He tried to keep his nerve. He knew that if he scrambled upwards he would only make the slide move faster.

He lay perfectly still while his body slipped inch by inch and the stones tumbled past him.

Then the slipping stopped. He did not move. What to do now? If he tried to climb he would start the landslide.

He could do nothing but stay where he was. Even that was dangerous, for his weight might start the gravel moving. He was in a pretty fix. Looking up, he saw that Kobo was starting down towards him.

"Stay where you are," he cried. "You'll only make it worse. Go and get Dr Dan."

He knew as he said it that it was a foolish suggestion. It would take an hour to fetch Dr Dan and this was a matter of minutes. At any second the slide might begin.

"No time get doctor," called Kobo, and kept on coming.

"Go back," demanded Hal. "You can't do a thing. No use two of us getting bopped off."

He found himself thinking a crazy thought: if Kobo was "bopped off" then all the time he had spent teaching the boy English would be wasted.

Kobo was creeping lower. The idiot – he would start everything going and they would both slide down.

But Kobo stopped on a solid flat rock about ten feet above his friend. He called down to Hal.

"Take off your . . ." His English failed him. He slapped his legs. "Take off – the word, I do not know."

"What are you talking about?"

"These," he slapped his legs again. "Take off."

"You mean my trousers?"

"Ah, yes – trousers! Take off. Do same like me." He undid his own trousers and began to slip them off.

He'd gone plumb crazy, thought Hal. Gone clean out of his head.

Suddenly he understood Kobo's plan. Yes, it might work. Very carefully he moved his hands down to his belt. He loosened the belt and the waistband. The stones started moving and he lay still. When they stopped he began inching off his trousers. He took his time about it. Better go slow with this than fast with the avalanche.

At last they were off. He tossed them up to Kobo. He did this as lightly as he could, yet it started a slipping of gravel. Hal slid three inches nearer the hungry fire – then the movement stopped.

Kobo fastened the two pairs of trousers together with his belt. Then he lay flat on the rock and threw Hal one end of the crude lifeline. Hal caught it.

But would Kobo be able to draw him up? Hal was much larger and heavier than the Japanese.

Hal did not expect much. Probably Kobo could not lift him. Or the trousers would split, or pull apart. Then he would start sliding and wouldn't stop until he plopped into a bath twenty times as hot as boiling water. And with his trousers off! Well, he wouldn't suffer long.

The heat, the noise, the danger – they made odd notions race through his brain. He didn't want to die with his trousers off. He had heard an old soldier say, "I want to die with my boots on." That was the way he would like to die, too, if he had to die – in full uniform, fighting a glorious fight. But to pass out by slipping and sliding half-dressed into a pot hole – that was no way to die. That was something to make anybody laugh. He could laugh at it himself, and he did. Kobo was astonished to see him laughing.

Another fancy struck him: if he turned up at the pearly gates without his trousers would St Peter let him in?

All this fled through his half-dizzy mind in a moment. Then he heard Kobo calling:

"You big boy. I no can bring up unless you help. I count to three. Then you come like everything and I pull like so. Are you ready?"

"Ready!" replied Hal. His day dreams were gone now and he tensed himself for the big effort.

"*Ichi!*" began Kobo. Hal knew that ichi meant one. In his excitement Kobo had forgotten his English and was counting in his own language.

"*Ni!*" Hal gathered up all his strength. "*SAN!*" yelled Kobo, and pulled.

Hal leaped upward at the same instant. The stones flew

375

out from under his feet. There was a muttering growl and the whole gravel bed upon which he had been lying began to slide. A ripping sound told him that the trousers were coming apart at the seams.

But by now he had his hands over the edge of the solid rock occupied by Kobo.

There he dangled as everything went out from under him. Every stone that slid started another stone sliding. The landslide spread left and right until it seemed that the whole slope was roaring downwards. It thundered like the hooves of a thousand wild horses and clouds of dust rose from it.

The avalanche crashed down into the lava lake making a sound like heavy surf on an ocean beach.

Helped by Kobo, Hal scrambled up on to the rock. Then they turned and climbed on firmer ground to the edge of the crater. Here they looked back on a terrifying sight as the avalanche carried billions upon billions of tons of rock down into a blazing lake so hot that it would almost immediately turn the hard rock into flowing liquid.

Half dazed by their experience they trudged on along the edge of the crater until they met Dr Dan and Roger. As soon as they saw them these two gentlemen began to laugh.

Hal thought, they wouldn't laugh if they knew what we have been through. Then his mind cleared a bit and he realized that something was missing. They had forgotten to put on their trousers. Kobo was still carrying them in his hand. He began to untie them from each other.

The doctor was no longer amused. He could see by the bedraggled and weary appearance of the two boys that something pretty bad had happened. They were bruised and battered and covered with dust.

"We heard an avalanche," Dr Dan said. "Were you mixed up in it?"

"We certainly were," said Hal. "And I'd be at the bottom right now if it hadn't been for Kobo. Kobo and two pairs of trousers."

He and Kobo pulled on their badly ripped trousers.

Dr Dan was looking at them thoughtfully. Then he turned and started down the mountain with Roger. For a while they walked in silence, each too full of his own thoughts to speak. Then Dr Dan said:

"Well, Roger, I think Kobo has paid for his lessons."

"I'll say he has!" agreed Roger.

10
The Sinking Ship

Again the *Lively Lady* sailed, this time due south. Japan was left behind.

Left behind also was Kobo who had returned to his school for another examination. Hal anxiously wondered what the result would be. He was to get word later that Kobo had passed with flying colours.

Dr Dan came running up the companionway to the deck.

"Captain! Crowd on every inch of sail. Use the auxiliary too."

"What's the rush?"

"I've just had a radio call from the Hydrographic Office. They report an eruption about two hundred miles south."

Captain Ike called to Omo to loose the staysails and start the engine.

"What course?" he asked Dr Dan.

"Set your course for Myojin Island."

Captain Ike scanned his chart.

"There's no such place. It says here Myojin sank out of sight forty years ago."

"She's just popped up again."

Hal and Roger, who had been loafing on the deck, suddenly came to life.

"Are we going to see a big eruption?" inquired Roger.

"According to the seismographs it's so big that if it exploded in the middle of New York, there would be no New York."

"Who reported it to Tokyo?" Hal asked.

"The captain of a fishing schooner. His ship was nearly buried under ashes. He escaped just in time."

"Did they tell you anything more?"

"They're sending their own exploration ship to have a look at it. Her name is the *Kaiyo Maru*. She's already on the way with nine scientists and a crew of twenty-two. If we're lucky we may catch up with her."

"Did you say that the volcano is making an island?"

"Yes. There used to be an island there years ago, then it disappeared. Now a new island is being thrown up."

"Isn't that unusual – for a submarine volcano to make an island?"

"Not at all. Most of the islands in the Pacific were thrown up by submarine volcanoes. Even the coral islands rest on the rims of old volcanoes."

"And new ones are coming up all the time?"

"Exactly. There are more than twenty islands in the

Pacific now that did not exist fifty years ago. The Pacific, you know, is the most volcanic part of the globe. There are about three hundred active volcanoes in the world, and seven-eighths of them are in or around the Pacific. Probably there are a great many volcanoes beneath the sea that we don't know about and every now and then one of them tosses up an island. Sometimes the island doesn't last. It may disappear again."

"What makes it disappear?"

"It may be made up mostly of volcanic ash, and in that case the waves will gradually wash it away. If it is made of solid lava it is more likely to stay. But even a solid island isn't safe if there's a volcano under it. The terrific forces in the volcano may push the island higher, or they may shrink and let the island drop beneath the waves."

Dr Dan picked up the binoculars and scanned the horizon ahead.

"I see it!" he exclaimed. "The column of smoke."

Roger grinned. "I think you're kidding us, Dr Dan. You said it was two hundred miles away. Nobody can see two hundred miles."

"That's where you're wrong. You can see a million miles."

"A million miles!"

"Of course. How about the sun and the stars? They are

millions of miles away but you can see them very plainly."

That gave Roger something to think about.

"Now I suppose you'll be asking me another question," said Dr Dan. "If we can see the smoke two hundred miles away, why can't we see the *Kaiyo Maru* which is fifty miles or so ahead of us?"

"Oh, I know the answer to that one," said Roger. "The ship is too low – the curve of the earth hides it. The smoke cloud is very high."

"Right. At least two miles high."

"When do we get there?"

"Perhaps early tomorrow morning. What speed are we making, Captain?"

"Seventeen knots."

"A wonderful little ship!" said Dr Dan.

The *Lively Lady* trembled as if with pleasure at this compliment. She vibrated like a harp with the pull of the wind on the sails. She flew over the waves like a flying fish.

She was no ordinary fishing schooner. She did not carry the usual gaff mainsail. She was equipped with the fastest sail in the world, the triangular Marconi. There was no foresail. Instead, between the two masts, billowed two great staysails. A big jibsail bulged over her bow. She was built for speed and had won several cup races.

They overhauled the *Kaiyo Maru* just before dark. The steam-driven vessel was plodding along at about ten knots. The *Lively Lady* skimmed past her like a bird. The boys were very proud of their swift ship.

True, if the wind failed she would stand still, while the steamer would keep plodding along. But with the right wind the sailing ship was hard to beat.

Passing close to the other ship, the boys lined the rail and waved. At the rail of the steamer stood the nine scientists and some of the crew. Compared with the *Lively Lady*, the steamer seemed so slow that Roger couldn't help calling, "Get a horse!"

If he had known that every man on that ship would be drowned before another day passed he would not have felt like joking.

The Japanese at the steamer's rail grinned back and shouted admiring comments on the appearance of the *Lively Lady* and its speed. Then their ship was left behind and the growing darkness slowly blotted it out.

"We'll be the first to get there!" exulted Roger.

There was little sleeping done that night. Every hour or so the boys came on deck to look ahead to the pillar of cloud and fire.

As they drew nearer it seemed to grow larger and taller.

It threw out arms and the top was shaped like a head, so that you could imagine it was a great giant breathing fire and fumes and getting ready to pounce upon the little sailing ship. The *Lively Lady* seemed very much alone now in this great black sea with the evil giant as high as the sky looming over it.

Roger was no longer sure that he wanted to get there first. He wished now that the *Lively Lady* had slowed down so that they might have had the other ship for company.

Blinding flashes of lightning ripped through the cloud and shot down into the sea. Suppose one of them should strike the *Lively Lady*? Thunder came in sudden smacks and whacks as if a dozen giants were clapping their hands. Along with this come-and-go thunder, caused by electrical discharges in the cloud, there was the steady thunder of the submarine volcano itself as it sent millions of tons of boiling lava and white-hot rocks spurting up into the sky.

"How deep is that volcano under the sea?" Roger asked Dr Dan.

"We don't know yet. From the way it's behaving, I'd guess it to be perhaps three hundred feet down."

"So all that hot stuff has to shoot up through water three hundred feet deep?"

"That's right."

"Why doesn't the water put out the fire?" Roger grinned to himself. Now he thought he had asked one the doctor couldn't answer.

"That's a good question," Dr Dan said. "Ordinarily water does put out fire. And it doesn't take three hundred feet of water either. Just a spray of water may put out the fire in a burning house. But that's because the fire isn't very hot. It's hot enough to burn wood, yes, but not hot enough to turn metal into liquid. The heat in the earth is at least ten times as great. It turns solid rock into liquid. When that blazing liquid shoots up through the water it changes every drop of water it touches into steam. So you see, instead of the water cooling the fire, the fire boils the water. Most of that great cloud is steam."

A zigzag dagger of lightning split the sky and struck the water within a few hundred yards of the *Lively Lady*.

"I think we're close enough," suggested Captain Ike. "How about heaving to until daylight?"

Dr Dan agreed.

The *Lively Lady* came up into the wind. The staysails and jib were lowered and the mainsail flapped idly.

It was a terrible two hours until daylight, the roaring and gigantic bubbling of the submarine volcano and the crash of thunder in the towering cloud made sleep impossible. The flashes of lightning in the cloud were like sudden fireworks. For an instant they lit up the sea for miles. Then the sea went black again. But the two-mile-high column always glowed with the light given off by the streams of white-hot lava shooting up into it.

The *Lively Lady* was no longer moving forward, but she was not lying still. She hopped and leaped like a frightened deer. Every explosion of the volcano sent tidal waves rushing over the sea. They picked up the ship and tossed it into the air, then let it fall deep into a trough. They collided with the ocean's own waves and sent up great jets of spray.

Crash! The worst explosion yet shook the sea.

"I'm afraid that will start a big roller," said Dr Dan "Better lash yourselves to the rail or the rigging."

They made themselves fast and waited. Several minutes passed.

"Guess it was a false alarm," said Hal.

"Don't be too sure. It takes a little time for it to get here."

"Look!" cried Roger. "What's that coming?"

It was like a moving wall. It towered black against the coloumn of fire. It seemed as high as the masts. It was bending over the ship.

The men curled themselves into balls to withstand the

shock. The wall of water broke over them. Hal's lashings were torn apart and he was swept across the deck to the rail. There he clung desperately. The ship lay over on her beam ends. Would she completely turn turtle?

She would not. The brave little ship righted herself and the water drained away from her deck.

"Boy, was that hot!" cried Roger, when he could get his breath. "I feel like a boiled eel."

He got no answer through the dark from his brother. He called anxiously.

"Hal, are you there?"

Hal, who had been bruised when flung against the gunwales, replied rather weakly, "Yes, I'm here. But I came near leaving you for good."

"Tie up again," warned Dr Dan. "There's more to come."

The following waves were smaller but just as hot. They scalded the skin and made the men choke and gasp for breath.

Then something solid struck Roger in the face. He grabbed it. It lay limp in his hands.

"Now they're throwing fishes at us," he called.

"Yes," answered Dr Dan. "I've had several of them. Hang on to them. We'll cook them for breakfast."

"But why are they coming aboard?"

"They're paralysed by the heat. It makes them float to the surface. This would be a wonderful place for a fleet of fishing schooners just now. They could get thousands of tons of fish with no trouble at all. Do you hear the birds?"

The air was full of the scream of gulls and terns as they wheeled about over the dark waters.

"They've come to pick up the fish. But it's a dangerous place for birds, too. I think they are going to be sorry that they were so greedy."

The sky was turning from black to blue. As the dawn came a strange scene was revealed to the men on the *Lively Lady*.

The giant of steam, gas, smoke and flying lava towered to the sky. It was made up of rolling billows and puffy pillows like a thunder cloud, but whoever saw a thunder cloud standing on the water and rising two miles high? Its hair was braided with snaky shafts of lightning and thunder rolled down its sides.

The sea was not made of waves as the sea should be. It was humping and jumping, sending up hills of water with sharp peaks. Steam drifted from the peaks. The whole sea was bubbling with the escape of gases from beneath. Geysers of gas and steam shot up here and there.

Not far away a big whirlpool swept round and round.

A wall of water circled it and at its centre was a deep hole. If a ship as small as the *Lively Lady* got caught in that whirl it would go straight down to Davy Jones' Locker.

"I never saw so many fish in my life," exclaimed Roger. On every side were the upturned white bellies of fish that had given up their fight for life in the scalding water. Most of them were small, a foot or two in length.

"The small ones feel it first," said Dr Dan. "The big fellows can stand it a while longer. There's one now."

A great shark that must have been twenty feet long raced through the water gulping down dozens of fish. Presently the boys sighted another shark, and then another. Their huge jaws opened and their teeth as big as spearheads crunched a dozen fish at a time. Blood stained the water, attracting more sharks.

"I hope we don't get dumped into that sea," said Hal fervently. "I'm willing to let the sharks have it all to themselves."

But the sharks were not left to enjoy their breakfast alone. Thousands of birds sought to seize the fish before the sharks could get them. Petrels, terns, gannets, gulls, kittiwakes, wheeled and screamed and boldly plucked their breakfast, even from the open jaws of sharks. They were all wildly excited.

Very calm by contrast was a great albatross with a wing span of seven feet that glided smoothly down, plucked up a fish in its great curved beak, and soared up again without bothering to flap its wings. The smaller birds scattered quickly out of its way.

"And what's that big black one?" Roger asked.

"A man-of-war bird," said Dr Dan. "Isn't he a whopper? He must be ten feet across. See what he's doing!"

The man-of-war bird did not bother to go to the sea for his breakfast. He snatched it from the beaks of the smaller birds. He went around like a tax collector demanding payment from every bird that came near him with a fish in its mouth. The gulls scolded and the petrels whined, but it did no good.

One saucy tern hung on to its fish tightly when the man-of-war tried to tear it from its beak. The big bird had an answer for that one and calmly gulped down both the fish and the tern.

The man-of-war had another strange trick. He seized a gannet that had already swallowed its fish and squeezed the smaller bird so hard that the fish popped out. Then he made a swift lunge and caught the fish before it reached the water.

Then with a flirt of his tail he pursued a petrel. But it was a thin petrel and the big bird evidently decided that it contained no fish; he turned away and chased a plump kittiwake, caught and squeezed it, and got another fish.

"How mean can you get!" said Roger.

The sun came up like a read ball of fire in the smoky sky. Dr Dan was using his binoculars.

"The *Kaiyo Maru!*" he said.

Within an hour the Japanese ship had arrived. She did not draw close to the *Lively Lady*, for the tossing sea might have crashed the two ships together. But there were friendly waves and shouts between the two vessels, then the *Kaiyo Maru* steamed closer to the eruption.

"What are they going to do?" asked Roger.

"Make a survey. You see, that ship belongs to the Hydrographic Office in Tokyo. You understand what that means?"

"Not quite," admitted Roger.

"'Hydro' means water and 'graphic' means to write. It's the business of a hydrographic office to write down information concerning the waters – oceans, lakes, rivers. The charts Captain Ike is using were made by the U.S. Hydrographic Office. The Japanese make similar charts and when a new island appears they have to send out scientists to measure it. They find out how long it is, how wide it is, how high it is, how deep the sea is around it and so forth. All this information will appear on the next chart that is printed. Ships' captains wouldn't dare sail without these charts — so you see how important the work of the hydrographers is."

"I don't see any new island."

"It's hard to see because of the smoke. Take these binoculars and look just at the foot of the cloud. Now can you make it out?"

"Oh, that big black thing! I thought that was a cloud. Why, it must be a mile or two long. And a couple hundred feet high."

"And growing every minute," put in Dr Dan. "And a week ago there wasn't anything there but water. Captain, suppose we sail around the island."

"Okay," said Captain Ike, "provided we keep at a respectable distance. I'm not hankerin' to lose my ship."

It was a strange passage as the *Lively Lady* sailed through a sea of floating fish and the clouds of screaming birds.

Most spectacular were the leaps of the makos. The mako is the greatest jumper of all sharks. Catching sight of fish on the surface, they would come up from the deeps at terrific speed, snatch their food and, unable to stop, would shoot ten or fifteen feet into the air. Then they would come down with a heavy splash and disappear.

One shot up so close to the ship that when he fell he nearly struck Roger who was standing at the rail. Roger jumped back just in time. The big shark smashed the rail to smithereens, then fell into the sea.

Hundreds of birds, too full to swallow anything more, perched on the masts and rigging and on the upper edges of the sails and whined mournfully at the sight of so much food that they were unable to eat.

A changing wind made the gigantic column lean over the ship. Ashes and cinders began to shower down upon the deck. Many of them were burning hot and started small fires which the men quickly put out.

Captain Ike came back to speak to Dr Dan. The captain's face was drawn and anxious.

"Doc, how soon can we get out of here? I don't like this a bit."

Dr Dan looked up from his instruments and notes. "I'd like to watch this a while longer. It's very interesting."

"Interesting my hat!" grumbled Captain Ike as he went forward. He could not understand the scientific man's passion for acquiring knowledge about the strange forces of nature.

The wind carried the smoke over the ship and the sun was obscured. It grew as dark as evening although it was not yet noon. The gases that were mixed in with the smoke and steam made the men choke and cough. The birds flying above were overcome by the gas and began to fall in showers upon the deck.

Through the half-dark could be seen the *Kaiyo-Maru* sailing close to the volcanic island. Then a cloud of steam and smoke hid it from view.

Suddenly the sea began to shake violently and the ship trembled and bounced.

"Earthquake," said Dr Dan.

There was a rumbling sound that steadily grew louder. It was like the roll of drums in a great orchestra. It became deafening and Roger clapped his hands over his ears.

Up it seemed to come from the centre of the earth, up, up, rolling louder and louder, until it ended in a gigantic crash that seemed as if it must be enough to blow the world apart.

A monstrous fountain of fire burst up out of the sea and climbed up into the cloud. A blast of hot air struck the ship and heeled her so far over that her starboard rail was under water. The men clung like monkeys to the rigging. The ship righted herself with difficulty.

"Point her up!" Dr Dan shouted to the captain. "Tidal wave coming."

Such an eruption was bound to start a tremendous wave.

It would have to be faced head-on. The *Kaiyo Maru*, closer to the volcano, would feel it first.

Dr Dan strained his eyes to catch sight of the other ship. Billows of steam rolled aside and he saw it, wallowing in a bad sea. The ship was broadside to the volcano. She was evidently trying to come around to point in, but would she have time to make it before the big wave arrived?

"I'm afraid that ship is in for trouble," Dr Dan said. "There comes the wave."

Even without binoculars Hal and Roger could see it – a towering bank of solid water rushing from the eruption toward the *Kaiyo Maru*. It buried the ship completely out of sight, then came tearing on to do the same for the *Lively Lady*.

But by the time it arrived it had lost part of its power and the little ship had turned and was ready to take it head-on. The men had lashed themselves fast. They took a long breath as the water thundered down upon them, for it was the last breathing they would be able to do for a while.

They were under twenty feet of water. This was deep-sea diving without any of its pleasures. They felt the water tearing past them, trying to wrench them from their fastenings.

Dead birds that had been lying on the deck were picked up by the flood and flung in their faces.

It was the longest sixty seconds they had ever known before the little ship came up like a submarine and rode on the surface once more.

Dr Dan's first thought was for the *Kaiyo Maru*.

"There she is!" he cried. "Bottom up. Captain . . ."

But Captain Ike did not need to be told to go to the rescue. He had already had the *Lively Lady* moving towards the wreck. Only the upside-down keel of the *Kaiyo Maru* could be seen. As they came nearer they could see bits of wreckage floating in the water with a few men clinging to them.

But only a few. Where were all the rest? There had been a crew of twenty-two, and nine in the scientific staff. Most of them must be imprisoned inside the ship.

Another big wave, smaller than the first, rolled in. When it had gone by there were still fewer men clinging to wreckage. Would the *Lively Lady* be in time to save anyone?

The great blast of fire had started hurricane winds. They came straight for the *Lively Lady* as if determined to prevent her work of rescue.

The Japanese ship was settling lower and lower. Finally

it disappeared beneath the waves carrying its prisoners with it.

Now only one man could be seen, clinging to a spar. The tumbling waves dashed him here and there, but he hung on. The *Lively Lady* hauled in close to him. A line was flung, but failed to reach.

Before it could be thrown again, the wind picked up the *Lively Lady* and tossed her back on her haunches, then spun her round and carried her swiftly out to sea. So lightly did it spin her along that she might have been a chip instead of a ship. In vain did Captain Ike try to bring the helm around. Nothing that man could do was equal to the strength of the hurricane.

Not till they were far out to sea did the wind suddenly drop; then a dead calm succeeded it.

"Shall we go back after that man?" Hal asked.

"No use," said Dr Dan. "I saw him go under just as the wind struck."

The tragedy weighed heavily upon their hearts. How sadly the news would be received in Tokyo. But a message must be sent, and Dr Dan sent it.

From Tokyo it was relayed to the hydrographic offices of other nations. So it happened that some weeks later the following notice appeared in the U.S. Hydrographic Bulletin:

KAIYO MARU

The Hydrographer notes with deep regret the sinking of the Japanese Hydrographic Office survey vessel *Kaiyo Maru*, with the loss of all on board.

The *Kaiyo Maru* had been dispatched to survey the newly-discovered Myojin Reef which had appeared as a result of a volcanic explosion. In addition to her regular complement of twenty-two, under the command of Capt. Harukichi, she carried nine scientists, including Dr Risaburo Tayama, Chief of the Surveying Section; Mr Terutoshi Nakamiya, Chief of the Oceanographic Section; Mr Minoru Tsuchiya, Assistant Chief of the Surveying Section; and Dr Kiyosuke Kawada, Assistant Professor of Tokyo Education University. Aside from a few pieces of wreckage, no trace of the vessel has been found. It is presumed that volcanic action contributed to the loss of the ship.

The Hydrographer expresses the condolences of the United States Navy Hydrographic Office to the Japanese Hydrographic Office and the families of the men who gave their lives in the advancement of science and marine safety. In this disaster, the maritime world has suffered a severe loss.

The notice was boxed within a heavy black line. That black border meant sympathy, the sympathy one man has for another, no matter whether they be of the same nationality or the same race. For men of science the world around know only one race – the race to learn the facts of the universe, and they will let no danger stop them in their quest for truth.

11
Diving to the Lost Island

"Who would have thought there could be so many volcanoes under the ocean?"

Hal was perched in the crow's-nest with Dr Dan. From this point high up the foremast of the *Lively Lady* they could see spurts of steam rising from the sea. They looked like the spoutings of whales but really came from underwater craters. There was a constant rumbling sound and the smell of sulphur. Rocky islands dotted the ocean.

"They are called the Volcano Islands," Dr Dan said. "You can't see some of them because they are under the surface. We are sailing over an island right now."

"Sailing over an island!"

"Yes. It poked its head above the waves in November 1904. It was a rocky island with a circumference of two miles and had a fine pumice-stone beach. These islands were Japanese at that time and Japan was very proud of her new island. But it lasted for only two years, then sank out of sight."

"See that smoke on the horizon ahead? Perhaps it's a steamer."

"No, I think it's another volcano. It's name is Uracas. While some islands are sinking, that one is rising. It's already more than a thousand feet high and still growing."

They did not reach Uracas until late at night. The boys tumbled out of their bunks and came on deck to look at it.

Ashes were showering down on the deck. The ship was trembling from the shock of the explosions. Uracas was a thousand feet of fire, topped by a column of smoke that went up several thousand feet more.

The mountain wore a white-hot coat of flowing lava

that sizzled and roared as it struck the sea. The illuminated mountain lit up the sea for miles.

The volcano was shaped just as one would imagine a volcano should be, tapering steeply up to the crater. Its perfect toboggan-slopes were kept smooth and straight by the frequent flow of lava and ashes.

Roger was puzzled. "What's that at the top – snow?"

It did look as if the volcano were wearing a cap of snow. "White sulphur," said Dr Dan.

The streams of blazing lava ran down over the white cap and then over the coal-black cinder slopes to the sea. The steam that rose when the lava struck the water glowed with the light from the blazing stream so that the whole volcano seemed to be floating on a bed of fire.

The glowing column of smoke turned and twisted like the tongue of a great dragon licking the night sky. Every few minutes another explosion came, throwing up fiery gobs of lava and burning ashes into the cloud.

"Sea captains call it the lighthouse of the Pacific," Dr Dan said. "They use it to check their bearings. It can be seen more than a hundred miles away – its column of smoke by day and its pillar of fire by night. Have you ever heard of Stromboli? It's called the lighthouse of the Mediterranean. It stands in the sea near Naples and throws up blazing lava every ten minutes. Ships find it very useful to guide them to the port of Naples. Uracas is just like it."

Again, a few days later, Dr Dan announced that the ship was sailing over a sunken island.

"It was called Victoria Island," he said, "in honour of Queen Victoria. It became part of the British Empire. A man named Marsters landed on the island with a gang of men to gather guano, bird droppings, valuable as fertilizer. They went away with a heavily loaded ship. A year later they came back but they couldn't find their island. They sailed right over the position of the island as we are doing now. They thought something must be the matter with their reckoning, so they searched the sea in every direction for a hundred miles. It was no use. Mr Marsters was very sad about it because the guano on that island was worth thousands of pounds. Perhaps some day it will come up again and the first man to get there may make a fortune."

"I'd like to go down and take a look at a sunken island," said Hal.

"Well, that's just what we're going to do tomorrow morning, when we get to Jack-in-the-Box."

"Why do they call it Jack-in-the-Box?"

"Because it pops up and down. Its proper name is Falcon

Island because it was discovered by the British warship *Falcon* in 1865. A lively volcano kept spouting lava and rocks until it had formed an island three miles long. Since it was near the Tonga Islands the King of Tonga claimed it and the Tongans danced all night in honour of the new island that the god of the sea had given them. Soon after that it disappeared."

"That must have made the Tongans pretty sore."

"It did. They held a scolding party and they all scolded the sea god. That didn't bring back their island. So they made a doll to look like the sea god and they poked it with spears and burned its fingers and toes. They thought if they tortured the sea god enough he would give them back their island. It didn't work. Then they decided to be nice to the sea god and perhaps he would be nice to them. They went to the shore and sang songs telling the sea god what a good fellow he was. They threw their best food into the sea for the god.

"Perhaps the way to a god's heart is through his stomach. Anyway in 1928 the submarine volcano began to spout and up came the island again. Once more the Queen claimed it and the Tongans celebrated. The sea god was generous this time and kept piling up the island until it was six hundred feet high.

"But ten years later in spite of all the food they could throw into the sea and all their prayers and songs, the island disappeared.

"So you can see why ship captains call it Jack-in-the-Box."

"Do you think it's going to pop up again?" asked Hal.

"That's what I want to find out. Ships have been reporting disturbances in the sea at that point. Tomorrow we'll go down and take a look."

The prospect of exploring a submarine volcano was enough to get the boys up early the next morning. When they came on deck they found the ship had already heaved to. She lay softly rising and falling on a quiet sea.

"Jack-in-the-Box should be directly under us," said Dr Dan. "Listen."

A deep rumbling sound could be heard. Then a geyser of steam shot up from the sea not far from the ship.

An unnaturally bright look always came into Dr Dan's eyes when he was close to danger and he was in the habit of pressing his hand against his left temple, as if in sudden pain. Hal saw these signs now, and they worried him.

At some time in the past something had happened that had been a severe blow to this man's nervous system. For anyone in such a condition, diving was dangerous. Even for a normal person it was hard on the nerves. Hal thought back to his own exciting experiences underwater. How much did the doctor really know about diving?

"Have you done much diving, Dr Dan?" Hal asked.

"Some."

It wasn't a very satisfactory answer. Hal tried again. "Have you used the aqualung?"

"Yes."

"How often?"

Dr Dan showed some annoyance. "What is this – a cross-examination?"

"I'm sorry," Hal said. "I meant no offence. You see, we had some pretty stiff times when we were diving for the Oceanographic. I think it scared me a little."

"You don't need to go down if you don't want to."

"It's not that," Hal said. "I just wondered – about you."

"Well, for your information," Dr Dan said with some heat, "I've used an aqualung just once and that was in a swimming pool. My business has taken me up volcanoes, not down into the sea. But I understand that diving with an aqualung is very simple and I'm quite willing to try it. If you and Roger want to stay on deck, that's up to you."

The taunt made Hal flush. He struggled to keep his temper.

"I was hoping," he said, "you would let us go down and you stay on deck. You could tell us just what to look for. We would bring back a report."

"And just why should you go down and not I?" Dr Dan was becoming more and more angry.

"It's only that – that—" Hal stumbled. "Well – it takes a good deal out of you. It's hard on the nerves."

"But why should it be any harder on me than on you? What are you getting at?"

Hal had gone too far to be able to go back. "When we were at Asama," he said, "walking along the edge of the crater – you didn't seem quite well. I mean – you stopped and stood for a couple of minutes as if you didn't know what was going on."

Dr Dan laughed. "Your imagination is running away with you. I'm not surprised – a volcano often has that effect upon a person who has never seen one before. The sight of it and the sound of it are enough to make you think crazy things. That's what happened to you."

"Then," persisted Hal, "that night in the inn when the earthquake came you jumped up screaming, and beat on the wall like a madman."

Dr Dan stared and his breathing came quick and hard. "I don't know what's got into you, Hunt. Why you should make up these wild stories is beyond me. Next you'll be reporting to the American Museum that I'm not in my right mind and you'll try to take over my job. You have a lot of conceit. You've seen six volcanoes and already you think you know more about volcanoes than I do."

"Not about volcanoes," Hal said. "But about diving. Have you ever heard of drunkenness of the deeps?"

"No, I have not, and I don't see what that has to do with it."

"Divers sometimes get it. The pressure of the water packs too much nitrogen into the body tissues. I believe carbon dioxide has something to do with it, too. Anyhow, you get dreamy and woozy. You feel drunk. You forget where you are, you think you're in heaven, or walking on a cloud. You're apt to drop the air intake from your mouth and without any air you're done for."

"But thousands of aqualungers go down without getting this — drunkenness of the deeps."

"Yes, but it's always possible. It has a good deal to do with the nervous system. It's more likely to happen to a person if his nerves are — well — a bit on edge."

The angry doctor forced himself to smile. "Hal, the very fact that I haven't punched you on the nose for all this stuff and nonsense is sufficient evidence that my nerves are not on edge. Now, let's not waste any more time. Fetch up the aqualungs and let's get moving."

Hal shrugged his shoulders and went below. The doctor looked after him with a puzzled frown on his face.

The gear was brought up from the hold. Hal and Dr Dan checked the equipment. The aqualung tanks were tested to make sure that they were full of compressed air.

Hal, Roger and the doctor got into their swimming trunks. They slipped their feet into rubber fins that flapped like a duck's feet as they walked over the deck. They put on belts loaded with one-pound chunks of lead. These weights were to counteract the lift of the water. Without them they would not be able to sink. Each of the two older men belted himself with five pounds of lead, but Roger took only four – since, strangely enough, the lighter a man is the less it takes to make him sink.

Then each man spat into his mask, rubbed the spittle over the glass, and rinsed it off in sea water. This would prevent the glass from fogging. Then the mask was strapped to the head. It covered the eyes and nose. From now on all breathing would have to be done through the mouth.

Each aqualung was put in place on a man's back and strapped tight. Now they looked like men from Mars. The

410

short air-hose was looped over the head and the mouthpiece placed in the mouth.

They practised breathing. The air came hard at first and the doctor's face grew a bit purple. A few sharp breaths, and the air began to flow easily.

The young doctor led the way to the gunwale and climbed over. The three let themselves down into the sea. They sank a few feet, then hung suspended.

They were in a pale green world. The surface of the water above them looked like a silken veil being waved gently by the breeze. Down through it came dancing, wavering shafts of sunlight. At one side was the dark shape of the *Lively Lady's* hull.

Small fish swam up and looked them over curiously, opening and closing their mouths. They seemed to be saying, "Oh, Mabel, look at these funny things! This is something to write home about!"

One of them came close enough to nibble Roger's toe. He kicked and they all fled – but soon came back, ohing and ahing as before.

The water was quite warm. That would be because of the fires beneath. There was a constant rumbling and every once in a while came a sharp jolt that shook the sea and started queer currents coming and going.

The doctor seemed content to stay put for a moment, practising his breathing. Hal stayed near by. He was determined not to let the doctor out of his sight. Roger had already started swimming downwards. He was used to diving but, being adventurous, he was apt to take chances that might get him into trouble. Hal wondered how he was going to keep watch over both of his companions, the one too inexperienced, the other too venturesome.

At last Dr Dan began to swim down and Hal followed. Bubbles rose in streams from the exhaust valves of their aqualungs. Small fish rushed at the bubbles, thinking they were something to eat.

Hal began to feel the pressure on his eardrums. He remembered learning that water pressure is doubled at a depth of thirty-three feet. The mask began to press too tightly against his face. He exhaled a little through his nose into the mask. That was the way you increased the air pressure inside the mask against the water pressure outside. On the other hand, if the mask was a bit loose and began to leak, you inhaled through the nose in order to bring it more tightly against the face.

He wished that he had thought to tell Dr Dan about these tricks. But then the doctor might have thought he was just trying to show off his superior knowledge. It was hard to give advice to your boss.

Now it was possible to see the bottom. But it was the strangest sea bottom that Hal had ever looked upon.

It was a crater, very much like the craters he had seen on land, though smaller. He could not see clear to the other side of it but, from the curve, he judged it to be about five hundred yards in diameter. The inside slopes were very steep and descended to mysterious depths where the water became almost black, shot through with rays of firelight.

At every explosion the blackness would suddenly disappear in a blaze of lights that hurt the eyes and underwater billows would be set up that beat the bodies of the divers back and forth.

Hal, floating over the crater, felt like an aviator in a balloon or helicopter looking down into a live volcano. No burning breath came up from this volcano, but the water was quite hot. Large bubbles of gas rose. These did not bother the divers for they were breathing the pure air from their aqualungs. Yellow streaks in the water were probably sulphur.

Dr Dan deliberately swam down into the crater. Hal came close behind. He could not see Roger anywhere. Where was that young fool?

This was a new sensation, actually inside a crater, but floating just out of reach of its fiery claws. The only trouble was the heat – it was getting hard to bear. A little more of this and the fish would have boiled humans for supper.

Now the bottom of the crater could be seen. It was a bubbling pond of red lava, burning fiercely in spite of the chilling ocean, tumbling and leaping and sometimes exploding to throw up fountains of fire and rocks. This vision of a submarine volcano would remain with Hal all his life.

It was too hot for comfort. Hal was relieved to see Dr Dan turn and swim upwards. They reached the edge of the crater and stopped to rest. Still there was nothing to be seen of Roger, and Hal grew more anxious.

Suddenly a major explosion shook the volcano and up came a geyser of lava and stones, tearing along at great speed with a ripping, sizzling sound, and finally bursting into the air above and falling in a heavy shower. Hal was thankful that they had not been in its path. Down came the rocks and chunks of lava through the water to settle on the slopes of the volcano. They had lost their red heat but were still hot to the touch.

If this sort of thing continued – if more and more material were thrown up and deposited on the slopes of the volcano, the island of Jack-in-the-Box would rise again

from the sea. Then the Tongans could have another party; and the hydrographers would have to put the island back on their charts.

There was that young rascal at last. Hal could see Roger coming through the blue. Roger caught sight of him at the same instant and finned his way towards him, excitedly waving his hands and pointing down the outside slope of the volcano.

He landed between Hal and Dr Dan and tugged at their arms, then swam away, looking back to see if they were following.

Evidently the kid had found something. Hal and the doctor swam after him. The sea grew darker as they went deeper. Presently they made out through the gloom a mysterious form. It was not rock and it was not waving kelp.

It was a house. Near it were other houses. In fact, here was a whole village beneath the sea.

Dr Dan was delighted. Roger had put his time to good use and discovered something very interesting. The doctor walked about, each springy step taking him ten feet or more because of the buoyancy of the water.

The houses were built of lava blocks with wooden rafters so firmly embedded in the blocks that they had not floated away. The thatch that had once covered the rafters had disappeared.

Dr Dan was quite excited by this discovery and went from house to house examining the method of construction and picking up small articles that had been left by the people who had once lived here. He began to go into one house but leaped back when the arm of a large octopus licked out towards him.

He turned towards Hal and laughed excitedly, almost dropping the air intake from his mouth. Hal could see his eyes bright and hard within the mask. The doctor began to wave his hands about in happy fashion, like a child.

Hal's worst fears were realized. The doctor had that strange underwater malady that was variously called "drunkenness of the deeps", "sea intoxication", "rapture of the depths", "nitrogen narcosis", or "diver's sleep".

Whatever you chose to call it, it was bad. He must get the doctor to the surface at once.

Hal pointed upwards and began to swim. But the doctor did not follow. Hal went back and took his arm and tried to swim up with him. Dr Dan fought him off and his eyes blazed with indignation.

Hal beckoned to Roger. The boy was quick to realize

that something was wrong with the doctor. He took one arm and Hal the other and they started up.

Dr Dan furiously wrenched himself loose. Then he went dancing away among the houses. Each push on the ground sent him bounding up several feet high. This delighted him. He made higher and higher jumps.

A house barred his path. He made a mighty leap, soared twenty feet up into space and came down upon the ridge-pole. He laughed again but the air intake luckily remained in his mouth. He walked along the ridge-pole as if it were a tightrope. Reaching the end of it, he leaped to the roof of another house.

Hal signalled to Roger and they swam up to the depths-crazed doctor. Hal again pointed upwards, smiled at the doctor, tried to quieten him.

But when he ventured to put his hand on Dr Dan's arm a wild look came over the doctor's face and he swung out with both fists. Hal got one in the face and Roger one in the stomach. Fortunately the water cushioned the blows.

When they recovered from their surprise the doctor was gone. He went prancing off over the rooftops, as happy as a colt in a field of clover. Hal and Roger swam swiftly after him.

If the doctor should slip on a rafter and fall into a house he might very well drop into the arms of a hungry octopus. It was just such black holes as these that the octopus loved.

A shadow passed above and Hal looked up to see a lazy shark watching with great interest the antics of these strange humans. Then another shark moved in. Hal felt that he and his companions were becoming too popular.

Dr Dan came slowly walking towards Hal. He stopped and cupped his hand behind his ear as if he were listening. A dreamy smile lay on his face. It is common for one suffering from rapture of the depths to think that he hears lovely music, a great orchestra, or a heavenly choir.

Dr Dan raised his eyes and saw the sharks. They appeared to interest him but he did not seem to realize what they were. He swam up towards them and Hal was not quick enough to stop him.

The doctor came close under the bigger shark. Then with all his force he punched its white belly.

If he had done this to a tiger shark or a white shark he would not have lived to regret it. Luckily this was a sand shark and although he was huge he was also a bit timid. He contented himself with switching his tail and swimming off.

The swing of the big tail caught the doctor on the side

of the head, knocked off his mask and dislodged the air intake from his mouth. He began to sink slowly like a limp rag. Evidently the blow had knocked him unconscious. Without air, he would very quickly drown. Blood trickled from his forehead.

Hal and Roger already had him in their grip and were forcing him up towards the surface.

The other shark came nearer, attracted by the smell of blood. Hal could see it more clearly now and realized with a shock that this one was no sand shark. It was a mako, often called the man-eater because it does not hesitate to attack divers.

Hal and Roger thrashed the water in a vain attempt to frighten it away. At last they broke the surface and looked about for the ship. It lay a good five hundred yards distant. They could easily lose a leg or two to the mako if they tried to swim that far.

Hal dropped the intake from his mouth and shouted. The quick ear of Omo heard him and the Polynesian boy came running to the forepeak.

"Bring the boat," shouted Hal. "Shark!"

Omo flung off the painter of the boat that lay on the water alongside the ship, jumped in and rowed with all his might. Hal and Roger faced the shark and beat the water with the palms of their hands. They knew it was hard to scare a man-eater, but they could only try.

The shark edged closer. Its ugly face appeared above the surface, then sank again. The boys shouted and slapped and were glad that Omo's arms were strong.

The small boat came zipping over the water with the speed of a flying-fish. It seemed to worry the man-eater, and he hesitated to strike. He had just about made up his mind to it when the boat arrived and stopped with a savage back-churning of the oars.

"What happened to Dr Dan?" cried Omo as he hauled the limp form of the doctor into the boat. The others climbed in and they set out for the ship.

"He went drunk," said Hal. "Then he lost his air."

In a few moments the doctor was on the ship's deck and was being manipulated to get the sea water out of him. After this was done, he lay unconscious for a good five minutes.

"He'll come out of it," Hal said. "His pulse is all right."

At last the doctor's eyes fluttered open and he looked lazily about. He pressed his hand against his left temple. So he lay for several minutes, resting. Then he smiled at Hal, a rather bitter smile.

"Well, my boy, you see I didn't get the bends after all."

"The bends?" said Hal. "I said you might get drunkenness of the deeps."

"Oh, is that something different?"

"Quite different."

"Very well, then, I didn't get your drunkenness of the deeps."

Evidently the doctor remembered nothing of what had happened during the last dreadful half hour.

"That was an interesting village," he said. So he did remember the village.

"And an interesting shark," put in Roger.

Dr Dan looked up at him inquiringly. "There were no sharks, Roger. Perhaps you mistook some shadows for sharks."

"There were sharks, Dr Dan," Hal said. "And you had a run-in with them. But you didn't know about it. You were drunk."

Dr Dan looked at him a long time without answering. Then he sat up and began to unstrap the fins from his feet.

"Hal," he said slowly, "I don't know what your game is. Whatever it is, I don't like it. I thought you were a good sort. It seems I made a mistake."

Roger came to his brother's defence. "There really was a shark, Dr Dan."

"I saw it, too," Omo said.

Dr Dan looked up with a bitter smile. "So you are all in the plot against me. That amounts to mutiny, doesn't it? Well, you won't get away with it. I may have to put up with you until we reach Hawaii – then what a pleasure it will be to get rid of you and your ship."

12
The Eruption of Tin Can

The news came crackling over the air:

"Eruption at Niuafou."

The *Lively Lady* trimmed her sails for Niuafou.

"Sailors call it Tin Can Island," Captain Ike told the boys.

"Because the people get their food in tin cans?" guessed Roger.

"As a matter of fact, the people live on coconuts and fish. No, there's a stranger reason than that for calling it Tin Can Island. Ships carrying mail don't bother to go inshore. Natives swim out to get the mail. The ship's carpenter seals up all the mail in large biscuit tins. When these are thrown overboard they float because of the air in them and the swimmers push them ashore. Now they sometimes come out in a canoe because a shark got one of their swimmers."

"I think I have some stamps from Tin Can Island in my stamp collection," said Roger.

"Yes, stamp collectors are pretty keen to get them. They'd better get them while they can. Some day that old volcano is going to blow Tin Can Island right off the map."

It was only two hundred miles from Jack-in-the-Box to Tin Can, less than a day's run for the *Lively Lady*.

The first thing to be seen was a pillar of smoke. Gradually the island beneath it came into view.

"I've been looking it up in my geology manual," Dr Dan told Captain Ike, as the boys listened in. "This island is really one big volcano. It stands on the bottom of the ocean six thousand feet down. That means that the volcano is more than a mile high, but only the rim of the crater projects above the surface. Inside the crater is a lake three miles wide. There's supposed to be a break in the rim – if we can find it, we can sail into the lake. Let's try it."

"Doesn't sound too good to me," said Captain Ike doubtfully. "Don't like the idea of sailing my ship straight into an exploding crater."

"The lake isn't exploding. The eruption is coming from vents in the rim."

"But the lake could blow up any time couldn't it?"

"I suppose it could. We have to take that chance. We're here to study this thing, and how are we going to study it unless we get close to it?"

Captain Ike grumbled and chewed on the stem of his pipe. The boys had gone up to the crow's-nest to get a better look at the strange crater-island.

425

Captain Ike lowered his voice. "There's something I've been wanting to say to you, Dan Adams. If you know what's good for you, don't get yourself into tight spots. It makes your nerves go haywire."

"That's ridiculous!" exploded Dr Dan. "The boys have been filling your ears with wild stories. I must say I'm disappointed in those boys. They are tricky and underhanded, and the older one seems to have some idea of discrediting me so that I will be fired and he will get my job."

"Now be reasonable, Doc. How could he get your job knowing so little about volcanoes?"

"That's just the point," said Dr Dan. "He doesn't know so little. He's seen quite a number of volcanoes by this time and he's been studying every book I have on board. I hate to give him credit for it but he has a sharp mind – he learns fast."

"So you're afraid of him," Captain Ike taunted. "A boy not yet out of his teens!"

Dr Dan bristled. "I'm not afraid of anybody. But I don't trust him, nor his brother, nor that Omo."

"Do you trust me?"

Dr Dan shifted uneasily. "You talk like the rest of them."

Captain Ike chuckled. "Put your mind at rest," he said.

"Nobody wants to do you in. You've got the boys all wrong. I suppose you wouldn't believe me if I told you they saved your life when you went balmy during that dive."

Dr Dan's cheeks paled and his eyes fixed upon Captain Ike grew hard and bright. "That's their story," he said. "You weren't down there to see for yourself, were you? Yet you take the word of a couple of schoolboys against mine."

Captain Ike could see that the doctor was getting dangerously angry.

"Skip it," he said. "Forget it. Where did you say that channel was?"

"Somewhere on this side. Probably over there at that low point."

The doctor's guess proved to be correct. As they came closer, they could see the pass into the lake. It was a very narrow pass, not more than thirty feet wide, but the *Lively Lady* easily slipped through. Then the little ship found herself, for the first time in her life, actually inside a volcano.

All around rose the crater wall. In most places it was about six hundred feet high but on the northern side reached almost a thousand.

The boys had seen something like it before. It reminded

them of Crater Lake in Oregon. There, too, a crater was filled with water, but it was a dead crater.

This was a live one. Only a few jets of steam rose from the lake itself. But on the western shore a row of small craters like chimneys sent up clouds of smoke and steam. They were the children of the great crater. Dr Dan counted them.

"Thirty craters in action," he said.

That part of the rim was very savage and terrible. But the rest of the circular island was beautiful. It was heavily wooded with mangoes, coconuts, ironwood, pandanus and other tropical trees and shrubs. Peeping from the trees were native villages. The boys counted nine of them.

"It gets me," said Captain Ike. "All these people – living on the edge of a volcano."

"Thirteen hundred people live here," Dr Dan answered. "There have been five bad eruptions in the last century – still they hang on. Not that I blame them much." He looked about at the beautiful groves of trees and the cosy villages on top of the craterwall. "A nice place to live – so long as it doesn't blow up."

Only one man on board had been here before. That was the brown young sailor, Omo, who had been born in the South Seas and lived there all his life. He had once visited Tin Can in a trading schooner.

He pointed to a village perched on the highest point of the north rim. "That's the village of Angaha," he said. "The high chief of that village rules the whole island. Once some of his people rebelled and went to the south rim and built their own village. They refused to pay taxes to the high chief. Their headman declared he would rather have his village destroyed by the gods than pay taxes to the high chief. He had hardly said these words before the ground opened up under his own house and hot lava began to spurt out. It killed him and burned his house and flowed out through the village. It burned every house to the ground and killed sixty people."

"And that was blamed on the gods," Hal said.

"Yes. The gods get blamed for everything bad and thanked for everything good that happens. You see, the people don't understand the scientific reasons for these things. For instance, when there's an earthquake, they think it's caused by their god Maui. He is supposed to be sleeping far down in the earth and when he rolls over, that makes an earthquake."

"He's rolling over now," said Hal, as a violent shiver ran through the lake, making the *Lively Lady* dance. Landslides of rock and ash slid down the crater walls and splashed into the lake. Screams could be heard from the shore and Captain Ike, who was using the binoculars, reported, "That tumbled down several houses. The people are running around like frightened ants."

"I'm afraid they're in for a bad time," Dr Dan said. "Thirty craters all going at once can make a lot of trouble."

Ashes and cinders were raining down upon the deck. Now and then a larger chunk arrived. Hal picked one up – it was not very hot and it was extremely light.

"It's pumice," he said. "Just like that big rock we found on Mt Asama."

He tossed it into the water and it floated. Patches of pumice like little yellow islands bounced up and down on the ripples.

Another object struck the deck with a loud thud. Roger went to pick it up.

"Don't," warned Hal. "It's hot!"

"But the one you picked up wasn't hot."

"I know, but it was pumice, full of air holes. That's one of the blocks – I've been reading about them. And that's a bomb," he added as something burst with a loud report only ten feet above their heads and the fragments fell about them.

"Well, what's the difference between a block and a bomb?"

"A block is a piece of solid rock. A bomb is a block that is hollow inside and filled with gas. The gas explodes and blows the rock to bits."

The god Maui rolled over again in his sleep. Avalanches thundered down into the lake. In the village of Angaha a stone church on the heights suddenly swayed, then dissolved, and fell flat. Showers of bombs were exploding over the houses, setting many of them on fire. The people were in a panic. Where could they go to escape the thirty monsters?

"They ought to be evacuated," said Dr Dan. "But it would take a bigger ship than ours to carry them off. We'd better send for help."

He went below and dispatched a message summoning any ships within call to come at once to remove the inhabitants of Tin Can Island.

He got only one response. It was from a steamer by the name of *Matua*. Its captain reported that his ship's position was nearly two hundred miles from Tin Can and he could not promise to arrive before morning.

Blasts of fire shot up from the craters. At the same instant another violent earthquake shook the island and a great section of the ridge broke away and fell into the lake.

431

"I've had enough of this," said Captain Ike. "Like it or not, I'm taking the *Lady* out of this hell-hole." He gave orders to Omo and the ship was smartly brought about and headed for the pass.

An unhappy surprise awaited the little ship. She arrived at the rim only to find that there was no pass. The earthquakes had tumbled millions of tons of rock down into the thirty-foot channel, filling it completely from one side to the other. Where there had been clear water there was now a wall of rock twenty feet high.

13
The Ship in the Volcano

"Now you've done it," stormed Captain Ike, venting his anger on Dr Dan. "Got us trapped in a live volcano. What'll you do about that?"

"Your guess is as good as mine," admitted Dr Dan. "We probably can't do anything until morning. Then perhaps we can land and cross the island and escape on the *Matua*."

"And leave the *Lively Lady* here?" exclaimed Captain Ike. "Not on your life! I'm not going to abandon this ship to be burned and sunk. If she stays, I stay. You got her in here – you'd better stir your volcanic brains to get her out of here because I'm not leaving until she does."

The *Lively Lady* put about and sailed to the side of the lake farthest away from the thirty craters. Even here the shower of ashes, cinders, blocks and bombs was continuous and dangerous.

Terrified natives on top of the ridge signalled to the ship, but there was nothing the *Lively Lady* could do for them. Conversation was impossible at such a distance and the cliff was too steep at this point for anyone to climb up or down.

Every moment more houses burst into flame. Their thatch roofs and basket-like walls made them burn as easily as paper.

The sails of the *Lively Lady* were tight-furled and hoses were kept busy sprinkling her down and putting out the small fires that repeatedly burst forth in spite of all that could be done.

So far the great crater in which lay the lake had appeared to be dead, except for a few spurts of steam here and there. But now it began to show signs of fiery life. Three small islands in the lake, each with its own little crater, began to grumble and smoke.

They were little craters in comparison with the chief crater three miles wide, but Hal estimated that even the smallest of them was a thousand feet across. Soon the three island craters were bellowing like bulls and throwing up blazing volleys of blocks and bombs. The bombs exploded like cannon.

"Close your eyes," Roger said, "and you'd think it was a naval battle."

"But you'd better not close your eyes," said Hal, "or you'll get a whack on the head."

It was necessary to keep constant watch above to avoid the falling rocks. They could be seen long before they arrived. It was fairly easy to step out of their way at the last moment and let them whang into the deck.

Easy, unless they came a dozen or more close together and you couldn't get out of the way of one without getting into the way of another.

As night came on they glowed in the darkness and looked like fireballs dropping out of the sky. Hundreds of the bombs exploded in mid-air, flinging red-hot slivers in all directions. It was like a grand display of fireworks.

"Remember the fireworks we saw at the New York State Fair?" Roger said. "It cost them two million dollars. And we get this for nothing."

Hal laughed. "Just born lucky, I guess," and he jumped to dodge another block.

"You fellows had better get below," said Captain Ike briskly as he passed with a bucket of water to put out a fire.

The boys seized the deck hose and helped him. When the blaze was out Hal said:

"You need us up here. Besides, we wouldn't want to miss the fun."

Captain Ike growled. "What fools you young-uns can be! So this is fun! When you get as old as me and have a ship to look after you won't think it's fun to get caught in a blowing-up volcano."

"Guess you're right," said Hal and began industriously hosing off the heavy load of ashes that lay on the deck.

Roger seized a shovel and went about looking for heavy chunks. While he searched, he kept the shovel over his head like a steel helmet – blocks whanged down upon it and bounded away. When he found blocks, bombs, pumice stones, or pasty blobs of hot lava, he shovelled them off into the water. Where he saw fire starting he called his brother, and Hal came running with the hose.

So they kept working feverishly for two hours to save the ship. Then they breathed more easily as the three island craters quietened and the shower of fire ceased. They began to hope that the eruption was dying down.

But old Tin Can was only drawing in his breath and getting ready to burst out with a new performance. The god of the underworld had failed to wipe out these human ants with one trick, so he would try another.

With a deafening roar the cliff above their heads split open and a jet of flame shot out. With it came strange greenish clouds that rolled and tumbled and then sank towards the ship.

"Gas," said Dr Dan. "I wonder what kinds."

He began sniffing as eagerly as if he were smelling a fragrant rose. The gases had a very bad smell.

"Sulphur dioxide, ammonia, azote . . ." Dr Dan named them off. "But the worst are the ones you can't see or smell — carbon dioxide and carbon monoxide."

Everyone began to cough and choke. Soon they were gasping like fish out of water. It seemed to Hal as if a heavy blanket had been laid over his nose and mouth. He was suffocating.

At the same time a drowsy laziness was stealing through him. All he wanted to do was to lie down and sleep. It no longer seemed important to save the ship or to save himself. Nothing mattered any more.

He roused himself fiercely. He knew what was happening — the carbon gases were getting them down. But how could they escape them?

"Let's sail out into the lake," he suggested. "Perhaps it won't be so bad out there."

"There's no wind," objected Captain Ike. "But I can use the engine."

"Don't do that!" yelled Dr Dan, but he was too late. Omo, who was as quick as a cat, had already jumped to the motor and pressed the starter. At once there was a deafening explosion and a blaze of flame and Omo was thrown ten feet across the deck. The motor conked out.

"Lucky that was just a small pocket of gas," said Dr

Dan. "If it had been a big one it would have taken all of us and the ship too. Some of these gases are highly explosive. We can't use the motor."

"Then we're stuck," said Captain Ike, sitting down heavily on a hatch cover, pressing his hand against his dizzy head.

"Are there any gas masks on board?" Dr Dan asked.

Captain Ike snorted. "Gas masks! Whoever heard of a ship carrying gas masks?"

He relaxed and lay down on the hatch cover. That seemed a sensible thing to do. Everyone felt the same way – why not give up and relax?

"Gas masks," Hal mumbled dreamily. Then a sudden thought stirred him awake. "Gas masks! Why of course we have gas masks, or something just as good. The aqualungs!"

They stared at each other, trying to clear their brains. Along with the suffocating gas had come intense heat and the perspiration rolled down their faces. It was hard to think. The idea began to penetrate. The aqualungs – yes, why not?

They got unsteadily to their feet and hurried as fast as their wobbly legs would take them down the companionway to get the aqualungs. They brought them to the deck and put them on. When the mouthpieces were in place they began to breathe the sweet and blessed air from the tanks.

It was like gradually coming out of some horrible dream. The mists that had clouded their brains slowly cleared. In the light of the burning houses far above they could see each other's faces becoming less tight and drawn and the drooping eyes opening with new hope. Life began to seem rather important after all.

But were they to be free of the gas only to be baked in the heat? The sweat rolled down their bodies as the temperature steadily climbed higher and higher. Out of the vent in the cliff came the breath of fires twenty miles down, fires hot enough to make iron run like molasses.

Hal leaned heavily upon the rail and looked down into the black water. It had never looked more cool and inviting. If he could only bury himself in it! It was pretty sad to be so close to coolness and yet perish of the heat.

Bury himself in it – why not? Why hadn't he thought of it before?

The others were astonished to see him suddenly break into a laugh and beckon them to the rail and point downwards. Then, without bothering to undress, he climbed over the rail and let himself down into the water.

At any other time it would have seemed warm, for, although the fires were not directly beneath it, its temperature had been raised a little by the hot objects that had fallen into it. But to Hal in his superheated condition it seemed delightfully cool. He felt new life flowing through his parched body.

He waited anxiously for the others to join him, hoping they would not be overcome by the heat before they could enjoy this delicious relief. They were soon with him and floated about with their heads above water, broad smiles on their faces.

But the heat on their heads was still terrific and they presently sought refuge beneath the surface. Down they went, ten feet deep to escape the warmer surface water. There they hung, breathing easily, comfort and coolness stealing into their bones.

Above them was a red glow and at one side was the black shadow of the hull of the *Lively Lady*. Fish swam over their heads making black silhouettes against the gleam of the fires. They could only hope that the fish would all be small and friendly. Hal thought of the shark that had taken the mail swimmer.

Perhaps there were no sharks in the lagoon. On the other hand, there might be more sharks here than outside because the refuse from the villages was probably thrown into the lake.

But he felt it would be more pleasant to be nibbled by a shark than slowly roasted to death by volcanic heat.

A greater shadow now lay overhead, shutting out the glow. It was too broad to be a shark, and too still. What would be that broad? A moon fish would be only four or five feet wide – this was much wider.

It could be a sea bat or manta ray, that great pancake of a fish that measures ten feet or more across. Hal looked for the long whip tail that could cut like a knife, but could not see it.

Roger had also noticed the thing and decided to find out what it was. Before Hal could stop him he swam up and poked his fist into the black object. All he got for his pains were a few bruised knuckles but the black thing did not move.

Hal and Dr Dan joined in the investigation. Touching the bottom of the mass, they swam out until they reached its edge. Then they raised their heads above water and found that the thing was a small island of pumice, the rock that floats. The pumice blocks were piled almost three feet high.

Roger, who could never let well enough alone, gleefully clambered up on to the island.

441

"This is something to tell them when I get home," he crowed. "Afloat on a raft made of rock."

Then the raft suddenly gave way beneath him and he dropped through the hole into the water, scratching himself plentifully on the sharp-edged rocks as he passed.

Hal and Dr Dan also retreated again underwater, for the heat above was still intense.

How long would they have to stay below? The air in the aqualungs would last for only one hour. Then they would have no choice. They must come up, or drown.

Their watery prison seemed to be growing darker and darker. Hal hoped this meant that the fires above were dying down. But he was afraid that this explanation was too simple. He suspected a different reason for the growing darkness – more pumice was drifting in to cover the surface. A rock roof was forming over their heads that might become so thick and so broad that their escape would be cut off.

They would be like the divers he had heard of who had gone down in arctic waters to explore a wreck that lay on the bottom. The ice floes closed in over their heads and they never came up. This situation would be the same except that the roof would be rock instead of ice.

He could see Dr Dan looking up and knew that the

scientist was also aware of the growing danger. Would it excite him, cause him to do wild things, or freeze him in one of his strange trances? Then the air intake would drop from his mouth and he would be finished.

Hal thought of the bitter and untrue things the doctor had said of him. He had practically called him a coward and a sneak. If it had been anybody else, thought Hal, he would have given him a sound thrashing. But he couldn't thrash a sick man. There was nothing for Hal to do but to swallow his resentment and play nurse to this crackpot, and hope that some day whatever was wrong in that brilliant brain would be corrected.

When Hal judged that three-quarters of an hour had passed he went up to investigate. He had to search for several minutes before he could find a hole in the pumice. He thrust out his head.

The flame spouting from the fissure in the cliff was no longer white-hot, only red-hot. The heat that lay on the water was less terrific than before, but still too much for a human body to bear. Hal felt his head steaming as if it had been poked into an oven and his eyes began to ache.

He dropped again below the surface and saw the light above him fade as the pumice closed in and filled the hole.

He could not see a thing. He could only hope that the others were still near by. He groped about in the dark, hoping to lay his hands upon Roger, Dr Dan, anybody.

At last he got hold of something cool and smooth – but it jumped away from him with such speed that he concluded it must be a surprised fish.

Then his hand closed upon someone's wrist. It was a fairly small wrist and might be Roger's – he hoped so.

Keeping his grip, he continued the search with his free hand. Finally, he clutched a trembling something that might be the tentacle of a giant octopus – no, it was a human arm, and it would hardly be Captain Ike's or Omo's for he could not conceive of any power on earth making those hard-bitten sailors tremble. It must be Dr Dan, and his nerves had begun to slip. The arm jerked once or twice but Hal held on.

Just a few minutes now and everything would be decided, for better or worse.

It happened sooner than he expected. His air died down, failed completely, and he found himself sucking a vacuum. He took his hand way from Roger long enough to turn the little lever on his tank that switched on the five-minute reserve.

He felt for Roger's lever to see if the boy had turned

it on – he had. Then he explored to see if the doctor had done the same – he had not. Hal twisted the lever so that new air would rush into the scientist's lungs.

He felt other hands now, probably Omo's and Captain Ike's. It was good that they were all together. They must stand by each other. They had only five minutes now before the reserve air would fail – five minutes to escape from their underwater tomb.

Hal rose towards the surface, drawing the others with him. He had laid his plans. It would do no good to go hunting for holes. There might not be a hole for hundreds of yards and the chances of their finding it were very slim.

If they scattered and went in different directions one or two of them might find holes but the rest would perish. They must stay together and work together.

He rose until his head grazed the pumice roof.

He took the block his head had touched, drew it down into the water, and pressed it into Roger's hands. Then he gave Roger a push.

The boy guessed his brother's plan. The blocks were to be removed one by one to make a hole in the roof. Each block must be taken several yards away before it was released or it would simply pop back into the hole. Roger left his rock at a safe distance and came back for another. In the meantime Hal had been initiating the others. Dr Dan joined him in plucking chunks from overhead and passing them to Roger, Omo and Captain Ike who carried them away.

Presently a light broke through; after the removal of a few more blocks there was a man-sized hole.

Then Hal seized Roger and in spite of that young gentleman's efforts to make somebody else go first he was pushed up through the hole. He scrambled out on the roof. He reached down and helped the next man up – Dr Dan.

The doctor noticed that the hole was beginning to close again. He worked above to keep it open while the men below removed more blocks. Then up came Omo, Captain Ike and, finally, Hal. The last man was hardly out before the opening closed again.

The men breathed the last of the tank air, then dropped the intakes from their mouths. The evil gases had thinned and the heat was no longer intolerable.

The next thing was to get to the ship. It lay fifty yards away. That did not seem far; but moving over the roof was more of a job than it appeared to be. Although the blocks were wedged tightly together and, in some cases, lightly cemented to each other by the heat, it was unsafe to trust one's full weight on any one spot. Also the roof was thicker in some places than in others.

So they went along on all fours, sometimes even lying flat, the better to distribute their weight, and inching forward as if on thin ice. At one time Dr Dan's foot went through and he would have followed it if Captain Ike and Omo had not been close enough to pull him out. After this incident the doctor lay for a moment, breathing hard. But he pulled himself together and the crawl to the ship continued.

Only when they were all safely aboard did he let go completely. In the middle of a sentence he dropped to the deck and was at once sound asleep – or had he fainted? Hal could not be sure which.

Just to make certain that the man had not died of heart attack Hal felt for the pulse. The fact that it was going like a power hammer indicated that the doctor was far from dead.

"Let's get him into his bunk," Hal said.

Omo unstrapped the aqualung and he and Hal carried the limp figure down to the cabin. They stripped off the wet clothes, towelled down the body, and tucked the doctor still sound asleep into his bunk.

Hal and Roger were glad to crawl into their own bunks for a few hours' sleep. Omo curled up on the open deck for a nap, ready to jump into action at any moment.

14
Saint Elmo's Fire

Captain Ike was too anxious about his ship to take rest. He strode up and down the deck muttering and grumbling, watching the spurts of flame from the cliff, the firelight of burning villages, the blazing fountains that shot up irregularly from the thirty craters.

Above all he watched the weather. His seaman's nose told him that the huge cloud of steam, smoke and gas that shut out the sky was very much like the clouds that announce a hurricane. Not knowing much about volcanoes, he couldn't be sure, but he didn't trust those rolling, tumbling masses that seemed to be fighting battles with each other as they were carried here and there by contradictory air currents.

Forked lightning leaped back and forth, as if the giants of the upper air were making war upon each other with huge yellow spears. In other parts of the cloud there was a different kind of lightning that came in sudden sheets instead of spears. It was as if someone were hanging out washing on the clothes lines of heaven and then suddenly snatching it away again.

"I don't like it, I don't like it, I don't like it." Each time Captain Ike put his foot down he said, "I don't like it."

Then he stopped in amazement and looked up at the masts. They were glowing like the illuminated hands of a watch. A shimmering ghostly light bathed them from top to bottom. Even the rigging was all lined with light.

"A good sign!" cried Captain Ike.

Omo started up. "Did you call?"

"No, lad. But look what we got here. Ghosts have come aboard."

"That is very bad," said Omo. "Our people believe those are the spirits of the dead. Something very bad will happen."

"Nonsense. Don't you know what this is? It's St Elmo's Fire. St Elmo protects sailors. This is a sign he's looking after us. We're going to get out of here okay."

"Isn't that just a white man's superstition?"

"White men don't have superstitions. It's just you browns who have the superstitions."

But he had no sooner said it than doubt struck him. How could he say that the brown man's notions were any more foolish than the white man's? He had known some pretty silly whites and some very sensible Polynesians.

"Oh well, perhaps we're both wrong," he admitted. "The

science fellows say it ain't ghosts at all, just electricity. Look at that!"

An orange-coloured star glowed just above the point of the foremast. Captain Ike stared. "Spooky, ain't it? Some say it's the Star of Bethlehem that will lead us safe."

"But our people say . . ."

"There we go again," laughed Captain Ike. "It never happens except when there's lightning so it's probably electric, as they say. And there's a blue star perched on the mainmast. The orange, they tell me, is a positive discharge and the blue is negative. Listen to it!"

A distinct hissing or crackling sound came from the illuminated masts and rigging. It grew louder when lighting flashed overhead and died away whenever the sky went dark. For more than an hour the orange and blue blurs of light, vaguely star-shaped, burned above the mastheads. Then they disappeared as a heavy fall of rain hit the ship.

With the rain came wind, wild blundering wind that seemed to come in circles rather than in straight lines. The ship was anchored fore and aft but the anchors began to drag. Now it seemed that the *Lively Lady* would be carried against the rocky slope of one of the small islands, and now that she would be dashed into the cliff.

Hal and Roger came tumbling up, but there was little that anyone could do. Man was weak and small indeed in the grip of the volcanic storm. Dr Dan, if he had been awake, might have told the why of what was going on, but could have done nothing to prevent it.

The crater lake began to twist and bounce under the wind and the floating pumice scraped up and down on the ship's hull. At every grind and scratch, Captain Ike winced.

"Won't be a speck of paint left on her!" he lamented. "We'll be lucky if it doesn't scrape a hole in her hull."

The heat was now a thing of the past. The men, soaked to the skin, were chilled by the rain and wind.

And still there was heat, plenty of it, where the craters tossed up their fire into the face of the rain and the houses burned in spite of the downpour. Frequent earthquakes rumbled, starting avalanches on the cliffs and opening new cracks and fissures.

At dawn the storm abated but the earthquakes continued. After each one there could be heard several loud explosions that did not seem to come from the quakes themselves nor from the craters. Evidently they woke Dr Dan, who came on deck at sunrise.

"Those big bangs — what are they?" asked Captain Ike.

"Steam explosions," Dr Dan said. "Those quakes open

up big cracks in the earth. If the cracks are under water, the water rushes down into them and strikes the hot lava. There it is changed into steam and that makes an explosion."

Omo brought some hot food from the galley. The tropic sun began to dry out the wet clothes and warm the chilled bodies.

But there was small comfort in the fact that they were still trapped within a live volcano. They might save themselves by landing where the cliffs were low and crossing the island to the outer beach where they could be taken aboard the *Matua*.

But how about the *Lively Lady*? "I won't leave her," insisted Captain Ike. Nor did anyone else want to leave her. Their ship had become a trusted and loyal friend and they would not abandon her. But how could you ride a ship over a wall twenty feet high?

"Let's up anchor and take a look at that channel," said Captain Ike. "It may be open now."

There was no reason why it should be open and it wasn't. After the ship had ploughed slowly and heavily through the drifting pumice, the path that led to the ocean was found to be still choked with rock. They gazed at it helplessly.

"If we only had some dynamite," mourned the unhappy captain.

"Dynamite," repeated the others. At that moment dynamite seemed the most precious thing in the world. But there wasn't so much as a firecracker on board, let alone a stick of dynamite.

At one side of the pass a few feet above the water's edge was a crack in the rock. Smoke was coming from it.

"One of the quakes must have done that," the doctor said.

They all stared dully at the smoke rising from the crack.

Then Hal's weary mind began to turn over, very unwillingly, like a cat that doesn't want to be disturbed. A crack. Smoke. Smoke meant fire. It must be very hot down in there.

He turned to Dr Dan. "What were you saying about steam explosions?

"Just that when water gets into a crack and strikes hot lava it makes steam and you get an explosion."

"Enough of an explosion to blow that rock out of the pass?"

"It would probably do a lot more than that," said Dr Dan. "What are you getting at?"

Hal hesitated. "It's a crazy idea. Probably it wouldn't work."

Dr Dan said sarcastically, "Then why waste our time with it?"

But the others were not so easily satisfied. Captain Ike demanded:

"What's on your mind, lad?"

"Well, I was just thinking, if water down that crack would make an explosion, why don't we put water down the crack?"

"How could we do it?"

"With the deck hose."

Roger began to dance. "Oh boy! That would blow the rock out of the pass and we could get out. Let's go!"

"Hold on," said Hal. "It's not so simple. It might blow out the rock – but at the same time it would blow us to Kingdom Come."

Gloom settled once more upon the group. It had seemed a brilliant plan and for a moment they had imagined themselves safely outside the murderous volcano. Now once again they were hopeless prisoners.

Dr Dan's forehead was furrowed in thought. "I'm not so sure the plan wouldn't work," he said.

"But we have to bring the ship alongside to get the hose into the crack," said Hal. "An explosion would blast us to bits."

"Not necessarily. The explosion wouldn't be immediate. It takes a little time for steam to form. If you set a kettle of water on a hot fire does it begin to steam right away?"

"No, it may take ten or fifteen minutes."

"Exactly. Of course this fire is hotter than the fire in a stove. But we'll balance that by putting in a lot more water than you could get into a kettle, or a thousand kettles. If we pump a ton or two of water into that crack it ought to take ten or fifteen minutes for it to generate enough steam to make an explosion. We'll have time to haul off to a safe distance. I think you have something, Hunt," he acknowledged with a bitter smile. "I wish it had been my plan instead of yours, but I'm willing to go along with anything that will get us out of here."

But Hal had another objection to his own plan. "The crack," he said. "It will act like a safety valve. The steam will escape through the crack and there won't be any explosion."

"Oh yes there will. How do you suppose all these other explosions occur? An earthquake makes a crack, water rushes in and makes steam that causes an explosion, in spite of the fact that some of the steam escapes through the crack. The point is that the crack is too small — it lets out only a tiny fraction of the steam. Think of a steam locomotive — you may see steam escaping from the valves but still there is enough to drive the pistons and pull a train a mile long. You see, the magic of steam is expansion. When water turns into steam it expands and must have sixteen hundred times as much space as when it was in the form of water. That means that enough water to fill a box four feet wide would change into a mass of steam as big as a house. That little two-inch crack won't let out enough of it to matter. I think we'll have an explosion, and a good one. Let's try it."

15
Escape of the Lively Lady

It was amusing to see how the doctor went to work to carry out the plan of the man he disliked so heartily. Hal thought it showed that Dr Dan, though a bit sick in the head, was still a good sport.

With Omo at the engine and Captain Ike at the wheel the ship was brought close alongside the rocks. Hal and Dr Dan climbed ashore with the hose and Roger, determined not to miss anything, came after them.

The ground was hot underfoot. The crack was only a foot or so long and just wide enough to admit the nozzle of the two-inch hose.

The three men peered down into the fiery chamber. It opened out below into a cave that seemed to extend towards or beneath the pass and was brilliantly illuminated by the glow of white-hot lava.

They could look more than fifty feet down but still could not see the bottom. It was this tremendous chamber of fire that they were going to turn into a gigantic steam boiler. Fooling around on top of a steam boiler was nervous work. They could only hope the doctor was right and the thing would not pop as soon as the water struck the lava.

Hal signalled to Omo to start the pump. Water from the lake poured up through the hose and thundered down into the white cavern. It struck the blazing lava with the wild sizzling roar of cold against hot and immediately a cloud of steam rose. Was the thing going to blow up after all without giving them time to escape?

But as the deluge continued the pocket where the water landed turned from white to a dull red and the steam diminished. The cold water was being rapidly heated but more water kept tumbling in to delay the process. For five minutes the flood continued. Then Dr Dan shouted:

"That's enough!"

Omo turned off the pump. At the same moment he threw the idling engine into reverse. The ship was already moving backwards when the men scrambled aboard. The engine spluttered – everyone looked anxiously at Omo. It would be most unpleasant if the motor should fail now and leave them to be the victims of their own plans.

The engine coughed and spat, but it was only teasing. It did not really mean to let them down. Perhaps it loved the *Lively Lady* as much as they did. While threatening at any moment to go dead, it managed to keep turning and steadily drew the little ship back out of danger.

Dr Dan was not satisfied until they were half a mile away and close to one of the small islands. There the *Lively Lady* came to and the men gathered at the bow to await anxiously the result of their experiment.

The lazy plume of smoke issuing from the crack had been replaced by a strong, erect jet of steam. It was very slender but it shot up to a height of twenty or thirty feet.

"We could have plugged that hole," said Roger.

"It wouldn't have done any good," Dr Dan said. "The steam would have blown the plug out."

The hiss of the escaping steam could be plainly heard across the water. Then the column of steam suddenly enlarged to twice its former size.

"That means it has torn away some of the rock and made the hole bigger," said Hal. "If it keeps on doing that . . ."

But Dr Dan was not disturbed. He knew the mechanics of steam. "It's like this," he said. "Suppose there's a giant in that chamber. He gets one finger out through the crack. Does that mean he can escape through the crack? Of course not. He's too big. The only way he can get out is by breaking the chamber apart. That's what I think the steam giant is going to do any minute now."

461

They watched in silence, their nerves tight. Were they far enough away? Even the doctor could not tell how strong the explosion might be. At least they were sure no natives would be hurt – their villages were on the higher part of the ridge far from the pass.

By the way, where had the villagers gone? Hal scanned the heights but could see no one around the burning houses. Falling bombs were continually starting new fires but there was no one to put them out. Where had the people disappeared to?

He looked again towards the pass. The jet of steam was now so strong and high that it looked like Old Faithful of Yellowstone. The hissing had changed to a harsh sound that cut like a knife. The giant was becoming very angry.

Then with a roar and a blast of fire he broke out of his prison, flinging rocks in all directions, cold rocks and blazing rocks and liquid lava and billowing oceans of steam that cut off the view.

Now they could see nothing – except some whizzing fragments that fell towards the deck. They dodged these to the best of their ability and waited in suspense for the cloud to clear.

It thinned with tantalizing slowness. The men strained their eyes. Now they could see the ridge again but it had changed. There was still a heavy mist where the pass should be.

As it lifted they almost choked with relief for there, shining bright between the black rocks, an open channel led from the lake to the ocean.

"Glory be!" shouted Captain Ike. "She's all clear. Omo, engine!" He beamed at Dr Dan. "I forgive you," he said. "But it's the last time you'll ever get this ship into a volcano."

Dr Dan grinned. "That's all right with me," he said. "I didn't enjoy it too much myself."

Under power, the *Lively Lady* sailed to the pass.

"Slow," cautioned the captain. "May be rocks under the surface."

The ship crept out through the channel. Her keel felt no rocks – the explosion had done its work thoroughly. In a few moments the vessel was rising and falling in the free and open ocean with all the elbow room between American and Asia. Everybody was fairly intoxicated with this new freedom.

Their gaoler roared his anger at their escape. Earthquakes shook the island, sending waves in pursuit of the *Lively Lady*, and the craters tossed out fire and showers of rocks.

Through the rumbling and the roaring came another note, a long even note, the whistle of a steamer.

"Must be the *Matua*," said Dr Dan. "We ought to be able to see her when we get around this headland."

As they circled the point they could see it plainly – the approaching steamer under its plume of smoke. Hal understood now why the people had deserted the burning villages. They had seen the steamer long before and had gone down to the beach to await its coming. They stood on the shore, hundreds of brown men, women and children, and a few white men who might be Roman Catholic priests or Wesleyan missionaries. Some of the islanders had small bundles on their backs, but most had saved nothing. They stood there hopeless and homeless, their beautiful island ravaged by fire, their plantations buried under ashes and cinders, their lives endangered by the shower of death from thirty craters.

As the *Lively Lady* came near, a canoe put off from shore carrying several islanders and a white man. When it came alongside, the white man stood up in the boat and addressed Captain Ike, who was at the rail.

"My name is Kerr," he said. "Missionary here."

"I'm Captain Flint. Come aboard."

"We saw your little ship in the lake," said Kerr as he climbed up. "I'm afraid you had a bad night. Is there anything we could do for you now?"

Captain Ike was surprised. "It's not a question of what you can do for us, but what we can do for you. Good of you to think of us, but you must have had a lot tougher time than we did."

"Terrible," admitted the missionary. "This was one of the most beautiful islands in the South Seas. Now it's nothing but a smoking ruin. Thirteen hundred people have lost practically everything they owned. We don't know what to do – stay on the island or try to get away. It all depends on whether the eruption will die down or get worse."

"That's something I wouldn't know," said Captain Ike. "But we have a volcano man aboard – he might be able to tell you." He introduced Dr Dan.

"I wish I could give you some encouragement," the doctor told the missionary, "but frankly, I believe the eruption is just starting. The worst is yet to come."

"Then what a blessing it would be if your ship and the *Matua* could take us off. Do you think that would be possible."

"Not only possible," said Dr Dan, "but it's all arranged. The *Matua* is coming because I called her last night. I couldn't consult you first, and of course you don't have to leave, but I would strongly advise it. Your people have already lost what they owned – if they stay they will lose their lives as well."

"But we can't pay for our passage."

"That won't matter so far as the *Lively Lady* is concerned. Of course I can't speak for the skipper of the *Matua*." Dr Dan looked at the approaching ship. "He seems to be bearing down on us. In a few minutes he'll have a chance to speak for himself."

The *Matua* was a big inter-island trading steamer well known in the South Seas. She was sturdily built but so old that some people claimed she dated from the days when ships of this sort carried slaves to the plantations. But whether she had ever been a slaver or not, she had broad decks and a big hold large enough to carry hundreds of passengers, provided they were willing to sleep on deck and below without bunks.

With a jingling of bells and churning of reversed propellers the *Matua* came alongside the *Lively Lady*. There it lay like a whale beside a goldfish, its bridge as high as the little ship's masthead.

From the bridge peered down a face that looked none too pleasant where it could be seen at all between the clumps of scrubby whiskers.

"You called me," shouted the owner of the face. "Where are the passengers?"

"Yonder on the shore," Captain Ike replied.

466

"All those? Hell's bells! I've got something to do besides lug kanakas around the Pacific."

Mr Kerr came forward. "Captain, I'm one of the missionaries on this island. You can see what the eruption is doing to our island. The volcanologist here tells us it's going to get worse instead of better. We have to get away."

"Oh, you have to get away, do you? So you think we have to take you. You expect us to take you away because you don't like a little fire and brimstone. What'd you come here for in the first place? You knew it was a live volcano. This ship is a trader – I have to show a profit to the owners. Now, talk business. How many people are there?"

"Thirteen hundred."

Captain Ike said, "We can take a hundred on the *Lively Lady*."

"That leaves twelve hundred," said the captain of the *Matua*. "Where to?"

"Since the island belongs to the Queen of Tonga," said the missionary, "I suppose we should be taken to Tonga."

"Tonga!" grumbled the captain. "A good three hundred miles. Throw me two days off my schedule. Smell up my ship with twelve hundred sweating kanakas. Well, nobody can say I ain't good-hearted. I'll take the lot of you at a pound apiece."

"Twelve hundred pounds," muttered Hal. "The big pirate! That's more than thirty-three hundred dollars."

The missionary's face was flushed with anger but he kept his voice steady. "I know this is a great inconvenience to you, captain, but it is an emergency. You might say it's a matter of life and death. And as for your price, I have no doubt it would be fair enough under normal circumstances. But you must understand we are destitute. We would not be able to pay for our passage."

The captain's face purpled. "And you bring me a hundred miles off my course to tell me this? By the Holy Harry, if I had my way I'd dump you all into those craters. Goodbye – I'll see you in hell!"

He laid his hand on the telegraph to signal the engine-room.

"Wait a minute," called Dr Dan. "You've forgotten something. These people belong to Tonga. Perhaps the Tongan government would pay their passage."

"Perhaps the moon is made of green cheese," retorted the captain. "I can't waste time on perhapses."

"But you can easily find out," insisted Dr Dan. "Call Tonga and ask."

The captain grumpily clawed his beard. Then he

muttered an order to the mate who went back to the radio room.

Within twenty minutes a reply came from Tonga. Queen Salote of Tonga would personally stand responsible for the fares of the refugees.

"All right," barked the *Matua* captain, "let 'em come."

The missionary went ashore and the people could be seen gathering around him to hear his report. Then with happy shouts they rushed to the water's edge. A few of the old folks got into the one canoe but all the rest leaped into the sea and swam for the ships, regardless of sharks. Women perched their babies on their shoulders where they could hang on to their mother's hair. The tots were not frightened for they were well used to the water. Many a Polynesian baby learns to swim before he can walk.

Up the rope ladders of the *Lively Lady* and the *Matua* clambered the dripping swimmers. Soon both ships were packed to the gunwales. Crowded together like sardines, it would be an uncomfortable voyage, but the Polynesians, with their ability to be lighthearted even in the face of disaster, chattered and laughed and sang.

(So it was that Niuafou, more often called Tin Can Island, was evacuated. The island was burned to a crisp by the frightful eruption that followed. Months later a few hardy spirits returned. Now, as this book is written, nineteen people have rebuilt their homes among the blackened ruins. There they defy the volcano god who continually mutters through his thirty mouths, "I *told* them to keep off my island. Shall I have to tell them again?")

16
The Burning River

When the thirteen hundred refugees had been delivered to Her Majesty, Salote, Queen of the Tongas, the *Lively Lady* sailed for Hawaii.

All the Pacific had been talking about the eruption that for many weeks had been gathering strength on the southernmost island of the Hawaiian group.

The greatest volcano in the world, Mauna Loa, had sent lava snakes crawling down to destroy the lovely city of Hilo. Every day the fiery rivers came closer. How could they be stopped before they reached the city?

Dr Dan was anxious to study the new eruption, and to do what he could to help solve the problem. He had another reason for wishing to land at Hawaii. There he could get rid of the *Lively Lady* and her crew.

"She's a fine little ship," he admitted to Captain Ike as the schooner smartly tacked into the trade wind on the long "uphill" climb to Hawaii. "And that fellow Hal has his points – but I don't trust him."

"You've reached the point where you don't trust anybody," said Captain Ike. "If you ask me, I'd say there's something wrong in your noggin."

Dr Dan smiled in an attempt to be tolerant. "I'm not surprised that you talk that way. Hunt has poisoned your mind against me. He's made everybody on this ship think that I'm touched in the head. For all I know, he's reported me to my bosses. He wants my job."

"What makes you think so?"

"Why else would he invent such stories – that I lost consciousness on the edge of Asama crater – that I went wild when an earthquake struck the inn – that I got drunkenness of the deeps when we dived at Falcon? He wants to do me in. I'm sure of it."

"You'd have been done in several times if it hadn't been

for Hal," Captain Ike reminded him. "Who was it that thought of using aqualungs to escape the gas? Who was it took us down into the water when we would have died of the heat? Who was it figured a way to get out when the pumice roofed us over? Who was it got my ship out of Tin Can by blowing open the pass?"

Dr Dan said no more but he was not convinced. "Yes," he thought to himself – "I'm quite aware that Hunt did all those things. And that's just the trouble. I'm supposed to be the leader of this expedition – but half the time he's leading it. He's coming up with the ideas. He's as smart as he is crooked. He wants to make me look like a fool and build himself up at my expense. Well, he won't put it over. I'll fire him and all his gang the moment we set foot on Hawaii."

But he didn't.

He was on the point of acting when they stepped ashore at Hilo. Something held him back. In some strange way, he felt that he had need of Hal.

The fiery serpents were approaching the city of Hilo and the people were in a panic. It was a difficult and dangerous situation. Ideas were needed, and Hal had a way of coming up with ideas. He would not fire Hal just yet.

There was something of nobility in his decision. He

saw it to his own advantage to dismiss Hal – but to the advantage of Hilo to keep him. So he would keep him for the sake of thirty thousand terrified people who needed all the help they could find. Hal lacked technical knowledge of volcanic phenomena, but he had a way of getting people out of tight places.

So Hal and his friends could stay a little longer, just until this emergency was over. Then they must go.

Dr Dan was met on the dock by a brisk, intelligent-looking man, Dr Janno, volcanologist in charge of the volcano observatory on the slope of Mauna Loa.

"We were glad to hear you were coming," said Dr Janno. "Several villages have already been burned out. If something isn't done within the next two days this beautiful city will be destroyed. We need your advice."

Dr Dan introduced Hal and Roger. Captain Ike and Omo had remained on the *Lively Lady*.

"Well, now," said Dr Janno, "we won't waste any time. If you'll come back to my car I'll take you up the mountain."

Before them as they walked along the dock rose the city of Hilo in all its beauty, with its fine buildings and lovely gardens and palms. Behind it towered the giant that was threatening to stamp it out, the mighty volcano of Mauna Loa. It was so huge that it seemed about to topple over on to the city although the peak of it was really thirty-five miles away.

Roger was fascinated and a little frightened. "Is it true," he asked, "that Mauna Loa is the biggest volcano on earth?"

"Quite true," said Dr Janno. "Not only that, but it is probably the largest single mountain of any sort on the globe. It rises 13,700 feet above sea level and goes down 18,000 feet below, so its total height is 31,700 feet. Its volume is about ten thousand cubic miles. Compare that with eighty cubic miles for Mt Shasta. Vesuvius is a child's toy compared with Mauna Loa."

They stepped into the car, drove back through the city and up into the country. There was a continuous booming sound like the firing of heavy cannon. Frequent quakes shook the ground and opened up cracks in the road. Crews of men were working to fill the cracks so that cars could pass. But new cracks were continually opening.

One split the pavement directly ahead and the car came to a stop just in time. The crack was ten feet wide and all of fifty feet deep.

Dr Janno was not disturbed. "We can drive around through the field," he said, and they did so.

They were not more than half a mile out of Hilo when Dr Janno stopped the car. They got out and looked up at a huge black monster creeping along over the fields toward the city. It was thirty or forty feet high and perhaps an eighth of a mile wide. The front of it was steep like a cliff. But this was a moving cliff. It was a liquid cliff, made of yellow lava, blazing hot, steadily oozing forward towards the city.

The sides and top of the lava river were black where the lava had cooled somewhat and hardened. Every once in a while a burst of gas would explode through the black shell and break a hole through which the yellow lava could be seen. Geysers of steam shot up here and there. The whole river smoked. It made a grinding, crunching sound as it inched along.

"At the rate it is moving," said Dr Janno, "it will reach Hilo in two days."

The yellow front of the river touched a group of trees and they went up in flames as if they had been made of paper. Behind the trees was a house. Its family had deserted it and it stood there looking small and terrified in the path of the fiery colossus. A yellow finger reached out and touched the house. It seemed to explode rather than burn and in a few minutes it had completely disappeared in smoke.

"You can see what is going to happen when the lava flow reaches the city," Dr Janno said. "Well, come along. I have more to show you."

They drove on over broken and patched roads, steadily climbing the mountain slope. They stopped at last on the brink of a crater. They looked down into a pit six hundred feet deep to a lake of boiling lava.

"This is Kilauea," Dr Janno said. "Anywhere else on earth it would be called a great volcano. But here it plays second fiddle to Mauna Loa. See that hotel on the edge of the crater? It's entirely heated by steam from the volcano."

They drove several thousand feet higher, then left the car and walked. They came again to the river of lava. Here, too, it was more than thirty feet high but only about a hundred feet wide. And now they could see where it all came from. It did not issue from the crater of Mauna Loa but from a fissure on the slope. It came out in tremendous spurts and fountains, shooting five hundred feet high, a sight to take the breath away. The sound was like the roar of a great waterfall. The liquid rock fell all about the crack and then flowed down the mountainside. For several hundred yards it kept its yellow colour. Then it darkened as the outside was cooled by the mountain air. A little further down the outside crust was black and stiff. But the river of fire flowed on inside it.

"That is the way our lava tunnels are formed," Dr Janno said. "If the fountain should suddenly stop all the lava in

477

the tunnel would keep on flowing until it had come out the lower end. Then you would have a hollow tunnel. We have one twenty-seven miles long on this island, and another six miles long. People sometimes make their homes inside these tunnels, and thieves use them as their hide-out."

Roger was fascinated by the five-hundred foot geysers of fire.

"They look like devils dancing," he said.

Dr Janno laughed. "That's what the Hawaiians think, but they regard them as goddesses, not devils. Let me tell you a little of the story of this volcano – it's rather thrilling. The chief goddess in charge is Pele – when the craters erupt the natives say that Pele and her sisters are dancing, and they will dance down the mountainside and kill the people unless something is done to please them. Pele is supposed to be fond of pigs and ohelo berries, so these are tossed into the flames as offerings.

"Once, in the year 1790, an army camped near by and failed to make offerings to Pele. There was a frightful eruption and four hundred people were killed.

"When new eruptions came eleven years later the priests tried to satisfy the goddesses by throwing live hogs into the burning stream, but it did no good. Finally, the great King Kamehameha cut off his own hair and gave it as an offering. Pele was apparently satisfied and the lava ceased to flow.

"But a few years later Pele was once more making mischief. The people begged the royal lady Kapiolani to make offerings to the angry goddess. But she had been to school and had no use for the old superstitions. She walked to the edge of Kilauea crater, broke off a branch of berries from an ohelo tree and, instead of throwing half of them in to Pele as was the custom, she ate them all. The people trembled and waited for her to be struck down by a shaft of fire, but she was not harmed.

"You would have thought that that would kill the superstition for good and all. But it did not. In 1880 a great lava flow came dangerously close to Hilo and the people begged Princess Ruth to save them. She went to the river of fire, made a prayer to Pele, then tossed in a bottle of brandy and six red silk handkerchiefs. The flow stopped at the very edge of the town.

"Of course that revived the old superstition. When there was another eruption in 1887 the native priests said it could be satisfied only by the sacrifice of a victim of royal blood. The Princess Likelike starved herself to death to appease the anger of Pele. That time it didn't work – Pele went right on making trouble.

"You would think the Hawaiians would have grown out of such a notion by this time but, believe it or not, many of the natives are throwing pigs and ohelo berries into this river in an attempt to stop it before it reaches their homes. They pray to Pele – then they go to the churches and pray to the Christian God."

Dr Dan said, "With their homes in danger, they must feel desperate. You can hardly blame them for trying everything."

"It's human nature," agreed Dr Janno. "But if their prayers are going to be answered I'm afraid it is we volcano men who will have to do something about it. It's our job – but I've racked my brain and can't think of any way to stop that flow before it reaches Hilo."

It was a magnificent and terrible sight, the great river, yellow near its source, black lower down, zigzagging around hills and through ravines, down thirty-five miles of mountain slope to within half a mile of the city.

About a thousand feet below where they stood the river bent sharply to the right to get past a rocky knoll.

"Down there where it turns right," Hal said. "What would happen if it could be made to turn left instead?"

Dr Janno was amused. "That is what President Roosevelt used to call an iffy question," he said. "There's not much point in thinking about it since no power on earth could turn that river out of its course."

"But if it could be done . . ." persisted Hal.

"Oh, if it could be done, of course our problem would be solved. The flow would follow that ravine to the northeast."

"Would it strike any village or town?"

"No. There is nothing but wild country down that valley."

"So it could flow down and into the sea without doing any harm?"

"Yes. But as I said, it can't be done."

"Perhaps not," said Hal. "But I was just wondering – if the river could be dammed at that point so that it would flow the other way . . ."

"My dear young man," said Dr Janno impatiently, "how could you possibly dam that stream? It has about the volume of Niagara below the Falls. In fact, the Niagara River would be much easier to dam because it flows out in the open. This one is flowing inside a rock tunnel. How could you get at it to dam it?"

Dr Dan saw that Janno was irritated. "Forget it, Hal," he said. "We mustn't waste Dr Janno's time with impossible schemes. We've got to be practical."

But Hal was not willing to give up yet. "You said no power on earth could stop it," he said. "I believe you are right."

"Well, I'm glad you see that," said Dr Janno.

"Perhaps no power on earth could do it," went on Hal, "but how about sky power? Couldn't planes drop bombs? Or am I being too imaginative?"

"I think you are," said Dr Janno, and he turned to Dr Dan. "I wonder if we could continue our discussion without further interruptions from your young friend?"

Hal grinned. "Sorry, doctor. I know when I'm not wanted," and he wandered down the slope to take a closer look at the bend in the river.

17
Bombs to Save Lives

"A most persistent young man!" said Dr Janno.

But Dr Dan did not answer. He was gazing thoughtfully at the black river. "It's just possible," he mused.

"Now, doctor," said Janno, "you're not giving any serious thought . . ."

"Yes, I think it's worth considering. That crust over the lava flow – how thick do you suppose it is?"

"Oh, I don't know, perhaps six feet – perhaps ten."

"Would a demolition bomb break it up?"

"That's a question that only a bomb expert could answer. I suppose if they used enough bombs they could smash the roof."

"Then the broken pieces would fall into the stream. If there were enough of them they would dam it up and make it overflow in the other direction."

"Pretty theoretical," objected Dr Janno. "Besides, where would you get the bombers?"

"What's the matter with the U.S. Army? Isn't there a bombing squadron stationed at Luke Field?"

"I believe so. But they wouldn't touch it. Their job is

war, nor volcanoes. This would be an expensive operation. They wouldn't feel justified in spending military money on a civilian project."

"I seem to remember," said Dr Dan, "that army planes have sometimes been used during national disasters, such as fires and floods. As for expense, it wouldn't be as costly as the loss of the city of Hilo. What do you say we ask them?"

"I don't understand," said Dr Janno, "why you give so much weight to the wild suggestion of a boy who has been reading too much science fiction. He seems to have considerable influence over you."

Dr Dan reddened with anger and embarrassment. "I don't care to discuss that. My relations with Hunt are not as pleasant as you suppose. In fact, he's about to be dismissed. All the same, I feel this notion of his is worth looking into. After all, it won't do any harm to ask."

Dr Janno waved his hands in grudging consent. "Very well, we'll ask. We'll go down to the observatory and telephone."

They called Hal and returned to the car. They drove back to the edge of Kilauea crater and entered the Volcano Observatory. It was a stone building built to resist the falling fires of the volcano. It was full of fascinating machines, the magnetometer, seismograph, pyrometers, gravimeters, spectroscopes, and the walls were covered with charts and diagrams. Dr Janno took up the phone and called Major Hugh C. Gilchrist, commander of the Kilauea Military Camp. He explained Hal's proposal to the major.

"Please understand," he said, "that this is not my suggestion. Personally, I consider it totally impractical. I doubt that any bombing squadron could deliver enough power to turn the flow from its course."

The others could not hear the major's answer. Then Janno spoke again. "Oh, you misunderstood me. I didn't mean to imply that the Army can't do great things with its demolition bombs. But you must realize that you are dealing here with one of the greatest forces of nature."

Another pause. Then Janno again: "Well, I'm surprised that you take the suggestion seriously. Remember, I do not stand responsible for it. However, if you wish to call Honolulu . . ."

He put down the phone. His eyes were wide open with astonishment as he turned to face Dr Dan and the boys. "The major thinks it's worth a try," he said. "He's going to radio the Chief of Staff in Honolulu. We're to wait here for further word."

In half an hour the major called back to say that a plane with three officers of the bombing squadron on board was on the way to inspect the lava flow area. The volcanologists were requested to go back to the bend to mark by their presence the exact spot where the bombing should take place.

They returned at once to the right-angle kink in the tunnel of fire. The flight from Honolulu would take about an hour. While waiting, they carefully inspected the terrain. Dr Janno became more optimistic.

The plane came in over Hilo and followed the lava stream up the mountain to the point where the men stood. There it circled round and round while the bombing officers studied the situation, made measurements, and took photographs. Then the plane flew off in the direction of Honolulu.

The volcano men returned to the observatory and anxiously waited for a report. Hal could hardly bear the suspense. When he closed his eyes in an effort to keep calm, he could only see the fiery claws of the orange-and-black monster that, given two days more, would wipe out the homes of thirty thousand people.

The answer came at last, but not over the phone. Major Gilchrist arrived in person. He was fairly bursting with news.

"They are going to do it," he said. "The Army Transport *Royal T. Frank* is already on the way with twenty six-hundred-pound TNT bombs and twenty three-hundred-pound pointer bombs. The ship will get here early tomorrow morning. The bombing planes will be scheduled to arrive at the same time, ten of them. The Ordnance Department will supply several civilian employees to supervise unloading the bombs from the ship, fusing them, and loading them into the planes. Then we'll take a crack at your river."

Dr Janno warned him, "That may be all you can do – crack it."

"We'll do better than that. You'd be surprised to see what a mess a six-hundred-pounder can make. The bomb men tell me it will dig a hole twelve feet deep in solid rock. It ought to smash up the crust on top of that flow."

"I'm rather surprised," said Dr Janno, "that the Army is so much interested."

"Why shouldn't we be interested? Hilo is the second largest city in the Hawaiian Islands. Naturally we want to save it if we can. And it isn't only the city. Hilo Harbour is second only to Pearl Harbour and very important from the standpoint of defence. If this flow continues it will not only destroy the city but fill the harbour. So you see we have good military reasons, as well as humanitarian reasons, for doing what we can to stop it."

18
Forest Fire

Early the next morning the ship arrived and the bombs were transferred to the airfield where ten fighter-bombers, two observation planes and two amphibians were already waiting. They had come in at dawn from Luke Field, Honolulu, and were manned by twenty officers and thirty-seven men.

Each plane was loaded with two six-hundred-pound demolition bombs, armed with 0.1 second delayed action fuse, and two three-hundred-pound practice bombs for sighting shots. The first attack-bomber took off at 8.45 a.m. and was followed by the others at twenty-minute intervals.

The two observation planes flew to the point where the bombing was to take place and circled to watch the operation. The officers had invited Dr Janno and Dr Dan to accompany them in one observation plane, and Hal and Roger in the other. The boys looked down with the greatest interest at the bend in the black snake as the first bombing plane came over.

A black object dropped from the plane. It struck the

rock roof of the river just at the bend and sent up a grey ball of smoke. It did not seem to have damaged the roof.

"That was just one of the three-hundred-pound practice bombs," said the officer beside Hal. "It contains only black powder and sand so it will send up a cloud of smoke that can be plainly seen. Then the bombers can tell whether they are on the target."

The fighter-bomber circled and came back over the bend. It climbed high, poised, pitched forward, and dropped another black object, much larger this time. This was one of the six-hundred-pound TNT bombs.

It struck and exploded with a sound like a crash of thunder. The surface of the lava stream that had cooled and hardened into black rock was split into thousands of fragments that flew in all directions. The explosion had broken through the roof and a fountain of white-hot lava from the flowing river beneath shot up into the sky several hundred feet. There it turned to orange-red, glistened in the sun, spread out like a fan, and fell again. The black serpent had lost some of his life-blood. The officers were delighted with the result.

The plane came in again and dropped another big bomb. This one broke a hole twenty or thirty feet wide and the great broken chunks of black rock fell into the lava river, partially choking it. Lava began to overflow from the hole and run off to the left.

This was just what Hal had hoped for. He was greatly elated, but he reminded himself that there is many a slip, and something might go wrong yet. He waited eagerly for the next bomber.

This one dropped a practice bomb but it went sadly off target. It came in and dropped another exactly on the bend. It circled again and this time let go a big fellow. This one enlarged the hole in the roof by twenty feet, and the lava crust, broken up into boulders, tumbled into the stream. The dam was building up higher. The second bomb added to the obstruction and increased the overflow. This had now formed a definite stream of glowing lava, as yet only six or seven feet wide, running off in the opposite direction into the valley that would carry it harmless to the sea.

Every bomb continued the damage until the monster's back was completely broken and the opening filled with rock. The choked river, seeking a way of escape, poured out at the side and down in a mighty river through the uninhabited valley.

Hilo was saved. The liquid lava in the tube below the dam would continue for a while to ooze out at the lower end but would spread and harden before it could reach the town.

Hal's satisfaction was marred by a new anxiety. He noticed that the orange-red river in its new course down the wild valley was threatening at one point to climb over a ridge. On the other side of this ridge was a little settlement of a few houses that would be burned out if the river succeeded in reaching them.

When the bombing mission was completed and the observation planes had returned to the airfield, Hal mentioned what he had seen to Dr Janno and Dr Dan.

"Yes, I noticed that," said Dr Janno. "No use talking with the army men about it – it's not a job for bombing planes. But I do think we ought to drive up there and investigate it. Unfortunately I have to get back to the observatory."

"Then suppose we investigate for you," proposed Dr Dan.

"Good. But you'll need a car. I think I can borrow an army jeep for you."

In the borrowed jeep, Dr Dan, Hal and Roger drove northwest over a low range of hills, then west up the wild valley through which the new lava flow was crawling to meet them. The little-used road was really nothing more than a trail and made rough riding. Finally, they got to the ridge where they could see the settlement on one side and the lava river on the other.

"It doesn't look so bad from here," said Dr Dan. "The ridge is high enough to protect the village. I think we can report that all's well." He looked at the approaching river. "It's coming fast. Let's get out of here."

They backed the jeep around and drove down again into the wild valley. The air was very hot. Smoke and steam drifted overhead, and curious strings of glassy thread. These accumulated on the bushes until they were loaded with them like decorated Christmas trees.

"What are all those stringy things?" Roger wanted to know.

"It's lava," said Dr Dan. "The superstitious natives call it Pele's Hair. They say that the furious goddess is tearing her hair and casting it out on the winds. Actually it comes from the fountains of lava that spurt up from the river. The wind tears this sticky stuff apart and pulls it out into long threads and blows it all over the country to decorate the trees and bushes."

The forest was high around them now and they could see the molten river. They should be getting farther from it – but, strangely enough, the heat seemed to be increasing. There was the crackling sound of burning trees.

Then they came around a turn to find the road blocked by a stream of blazing lava ten feet high. They brought the jeep to a sudden halt.

"No chance of going that way," said Dr Dean. "We'll have to go back and see where this trail leads."

About they went and back up the trail.

The increasing smoke made them cough. The bushes were burning now at the side of the road. The heat was intense.

Suddenly the jeep again came to a halt, facing another yellow stream.

Evidently the river had divided into two flows and they were neatly caught between them. Every tree or bush the lava touched burst into flame. The fire was licking the wheels of the jeep.

"Let's get out of this thing before it blows up," said Hal, and they tumbled out.

They plunged into the woods with the fire close behind them. It was a tropical forest, full of logs and tangled with vines, and they had no machetes. They tore at the brambles and creepers and scratched their way through.

They gasped and panted and fought and moved forward – but the fire was coming forward, too, and its fiery breath scorched their backs. Side by side, tense, terrified, they slashed their way through the jungle. Their arms ached, their hands bled. The fire was gaining on them. The burning of their legs, backs and the nape of their necks was hard to bear and they could smell their own scorched hair.

Roger, the smallest, could wriggle through faster. He was some ten yards ahead. Hal came next with Dr Dan crashing along behind him. Suddenly this noise stopped and Hal looked around to see what had happened to Dr Dan.

The doctor was no longer fighting. He was standing as

494

rigid as a monument. Then his muscles suddenly let go and he crumpled in a heap on the ground.

"Roger!" Hal called. "The Doctor!"

They picked up the limp form of the scientist and struggled with it through the bush. Foot by foot they advanced and second by second the heat increased and all around them the leaves were shrivelling and crackling into fire.

At last they burst through jumbled-up branches into an open stretch of gravelled ground. Breathless and choking, drenched with sweat, they carried their burden on down the valley. Behind them the wall of forest they had just left went up in flames with a great crackling roar.

There was another sound now, the drone of a motor, and an army jeep came rattling up the valley to stop beside them.

"It looked pretty bad over here," said the driver. "We thought you might need help. Climb in."

Thankfully they loaded the still unconscious doctor into the car and got in after him.

"What happened to your buddy?" said the officer at the wheel.

"Went blank and won't come out of it," Hal said. "I'm afraid it's not just an ordinary faint. Something basic. I think we'd better get him to the hospital right away."

"There's a place in Hilo," said the officer. "But I think if it's anything serious we'd better get him to Queen's Hospital in Honolulu. It's only five minutes more to the airfield and we'll commandeer a plane for you. Within an hour he'll be in bed."

Grateful for an army that can do more than fight, Hal and Roger saw the doctor transferred to an army plane and they flew with him to Honolulu. The hospital, notified by radio telephone, had an ambulance at the airfield to meet them and soon the unconscious scientist was under a physician's care in the famous Queen's Hospital.

He lay with eyes wide open staring fixedly at the ceiling. His breathing was rapid and his pulse fast. He evidently knew nothing whatever of what was going on. Hal and Roger sat near while the physician, Dr James Clark, made his examination. Then the doctor sat down and faced Hal.

"Tell me, how did this happen?"

"We were working our way through the brush to escape a forest fire. Suddenly he went rigid and fell down."

"But if he had merely fainted he would have been out of it long before this. Was he subject to such seizures?"

"Sometimes he would freeze up and stand like a marble

statue for a minute or two. His eyes would be prominent and staring and his face would go pale and then blue. When I took hold of his arm I would find the muscles as hard as ropes."

"In what circumstances did this happen?"

"Well, the first time was when he looked down into the crater of Asama. He looked as if he recalled some horrible experience."

"After it was over, did he remember what he had done?"

"No, he didn't remember a thing."

"Did the attack ever take some other form?"

"Once when there was an earthquake during the night he jumped up screaming and beat the walls as if he had suddenly gone mad. Then there was the time he got deep-sea happy when we were diving at Falcon Island. And sometimes he would burst out singing in a wild way."

"Very interesting," said Dr Clark. "I'm beginning to see a pattern. How about his disposition – was he sometimes irritable?"

"He became very suspicious. He thought we were all conspiring against him."

"Exactly," said Dr Clark. "It sounds very much like *petit mal.*"

"What's that?" asked Roger curiously.

"Well, it's a mild form of epilepsy."

Hal was startled. "I never thought of that. I always supposed an epileptic was – well – weak in the head, a bit insane. But Dr Adams is a very intelligent man, even brilliant."

"My friend," said Dr Clark, "don't forget that we are all weak in the head and a bit insane. And as for epileptics, some of them have been men of unusual mental ability. Julius Cæsar, Petrarch, Peter the Great, Mohammed, Napoleon – every one of them an epileptic, and a genius. Some forms of epilepsy are very terrible. Since you don't say anything about convulsions, I assume that this is the mild form, *petit mal*. Don't be deceived by the word mild. It is mild compared with the extreme form called *grand mal*, but even *petit mal* can be fatal."

"But what could have been the cause of it?"

"There are many possible causes. Mental shock could do it, or a physical injury. In his line of work, I would guess that some time he might have had a nerve-racking experience, or an accident, or both."

"He once began to tell our captain about some terrible experience he had had, but then stopped. He evidently didn't want to talk about it."

"Did he ever complain of chronic pain in any part of his body?"

"Nothing but a headache in his left temple. He didn't seem to attach much importance to it."

"Ah, but it may be very important. I think we'll take an X-ray of that head."

The patient was still unconscious when brought back from the X-ray room. The physician closeted himself with two other doctors and together they went over the negatives. Then Dr Clark returned to Hal, still carrying the pictures. He held one up to the light.

"There's the cause of the trouble," he said. "That dark wedge – it's an internally broken piece of the skull and it presses upon a nerve centre. At some time or other he has suffered a blow on the head as well as severe psychological shock. That wedge must come out and it is important that the operation be performed at once or he may never regain consciousness. Can we get the consent of his nearest of kin?"

"I don't know anything about them," said Hal. "He's employed by the American Museum of Natural History in New York. They would know."

"We'll cable them at once. But there's no time to be lost. While we're waiting for a reply we'll go ahead with preparations just as if we were sure the answer would be yes."

Dr Dan was already on the operating table and the surgeon standing by when consent came from the scientist's father in New York. The operation proceeded at once.

In the corridor outside the operating room was a row of chairs for anxious friends – "worry row" as Roger called it. He and Hal waited there for word from within. They realized now how fond they had become of the young scientist, in spite of his sick suspicions. Brain surgery was a delicate and dangerous business. The patient, already weakened by shock, might pass out under the strain.

Half an hour, and still no word. Then a nurse came out of the operating room and scurried down the hall. Hal was after her in a flash. "How's it going?" The girl shook her head and hurried on.

Hal went back and sat down heavily in his chair. Now what did that shake of the head mean? That the nurse wasn't allowed to talk – or that the worst had happened?

A full hour went by. The boys were out of their chairs now and pacing up and down the corridor, as anxious as expectant fathers.

Then the operating room door opened and a body covered by a white sheet was wheeled out and down the hall. The boys waited impatiently for the doctors. At last

Dr Clark and the surgeon came out and hurried past.

"Wait a minute!" demanded Hal, and the physician turned back.

"Is he all right?"

"He'll do," the doctor said. "The operation was successful. We got the wedge out but of course the whole area is inflamed. Your friend will need a long rest – six months or so before he goes poking into any more volcanoes. Now, if you'll excuse me . . ." and he was off.

With mixed feelings Hal and Roger walked back to their patient's room. Their chief feeling was of relief that the operation had been a success. But they were unhappy to learn that their volcano expedition was ended.

Again they sat beside Dr Dan's bed. He was still unconscious, but it was different now, and better. The staring eyes had closed and the breathing was slower and relaxed.

"Just a good, normal sleep," the doctor said. "Why don't you boys go and get something to eat?"

Roger went out while Hal stayed beside the patient. When Roger returned Hal set forth, but as he passed the reception desk on the main floor he heard a man asking for Dr Dan Adams.

Hal stopped. "I heard you inquiring for Dr Adams," he said.

"Yes. I'm a reporter for the *Honolulu Advertiser*. I wanted to interview him about the bombing."

"Sorry, he's in no shape to be interviewed. He's just had an operation and now he's asleep."

"Could you be his assistant, Hal Hunt?"

"That's right."

"Then perhaps you could give me the story."

Hal hesitated. "I'd rather he'd do it — but I don't know when he'll be able to. Very well, I'll tell you what I can."

Hal had hardly finished with the reporter when two more men came inquiring for Dr Adams. The reception clerk told them he could not be seen and they were just turning away when Hal introduced himself.

"I'm Dr Adams's assistant," he said. "Can I do anything for you?"

"This is Mr Sinclair and my name is Scott. Like Dr Adams, we work for the American Museum. The museum has just cabled us that Adams is in this hospital and we came to see if there is anything we can do."

"That's very good of you," said Hal. "He's asleep now, and I was just going out to get a bite to eat. Perhaps you'll join me and we can talk about it in the restaurant."

Over pancakes and bacon with coconut cream and coffee, Hal told the scientists of the stirring events of that day — the bombing of the lava flow, the escape from the forest fire, the flight to Honolulu, and the operation. "The doctor says he'll have to take six months' rest."

"Where does that leave you?" said Sinclair.

"At a loose end, I guess," said Hal. "But it doesn't matter about us. The important thing is for him to get well. You haven't told me what sort of work you are doing for the museum."

"It's an interesting job," said Sinclair. "They are trying to collect some information about whales and whaling. It's easy enough to learn about modern whaling methods — what they want to know is how whaling was done in the exciting days of sailing ships and whaleboats. There are just a few of those famous old ships still on the seas. We've discovered one that still goes after whales and we're going to go with her."

Hal's eyes sparkled. "You are in for some fun," he said. "I'd like to hear more about that — but just now I want to get back to our patient. How about dropping around again tomorrow morning? He may be awake then and able to see you."

Dr Dan slept all the rest of the day and all night. The

boys would have liked to stay by him but hospital rules did not permit it. They went to a hotel and came back in the morning.

19
Understanding

Dr Clark met them in the lower hall. "Your man is awake," he said, "and anxious to see you. I think you will find him much changed."

The nurse let them into the room. Dr Dan lay with eyes closed and in his hand was a copy of the morning paper.

"You won't stay too long, please," the nurse warned. "He's still quite weak, you know."

"Weak, nothing," said Dr Dan, opening his eyes – and the boys noticed that there was none of that bright hardness in his look to which they had become so unpleasantly accustomed. "I feel like a new man. Everything looks different to me this morning. Boys, sit down, I have something to say to you. It's in the nature of an apology."

"That isn't necessary," Hal said. "Wouldn't you do better just to lie quietly and let us talk?"

"No, I must tell you this. I've been very unfair to both of you, and to Captain Ike and Omo, too. I wish they were here so I could tell them so."

"They'll be coming," said Hal. "I sent them a telegram last night."

"The doctor has been telling me a lot of things I didn't know," went on Dr Dan. "He says I haven't been normal for a long time. And I can see now that he is right. I've been a perfect stinker, but I hope you won't blame it on me but on that wedge in my head. He tells me I've been having lapses of memory and any one of them could have done me in if you hadn't been there to look after me." He reached out and gripped Hal's hand, and Roger's. "And all the time I thought . . . I'm very much ashamed of what I thought. Especially when I saw your interview. Of course you've seen it."

"No, we didn't stop to get a paper."

Hal took up the newspaper. The whole first page was devoted to the story of the bombing of the lava flow. There were pictures of the explosions, photographed from the observation planes. There was a statement by Dr Janno, and an expression of gratitude from the mayor of Hilo. There were reports by the bombardment officers and a general military report by the Chief of Staff who stated:

"The total cost to the army of this operation was $25,000. It saved from destruction buildings and property worth at least $51,000,000. Therefore from a purely

508

financial standpoint the operation appears to have been justified. More important was the saving of the lives and homes of thirty thousand people. Those who witnessed the bombing declare that the execution of the mission was superb and that the bombs were placed exactly where they should have been. This aerial bombing of a lava flow made history for science in performing a great geological experiment with success."

Then there was the interview with Hal, one paragraph of which ran as follows:

"In spite of Dr Janno's statement that the bombing was originally the idea of Mr Hal Hunt, Mr Hunt, when interviewed, refused to accept the credit. He attributed the success of the operation to the careful and brilliant plans laid by the visiting volcanologist, Dr Dan Adams."

"I felt pretty cheap when I read that," said Dr Dan. "And after all my crazy notions that you were out to discredit me and take my job. I can't understand now how I ever got such ideas. Of course the bombing plan was yours, and you're going to be stuck with it as soon as I'm able to talk to reporters. They're going to get the real story."

"Don't bother about that," said Hal. "Your job now is to take a good long rest and get well. Then there'll be some more volcanoes to be conquered."

"And I'll be ready for them! I won't be afraid any more. I'm not afraid now."

"Afraid!" said Roger. "I never noticed that you were afraid."

"I'm glad I was able to conceal it. Every time we came near an eruption I was all nerves, ready to jump out of my skin. It all began . . ."

He stopped, and smiled. "I never wanted to talk about it. It was one of those horrible things you want to forget. Now I don't care whether I remember it or not. It was at the volcano Paricutin in Mexico. I slipped and fell several hundred feet down the inside slope of the crater and gave my head an awful whack on a rock. It knocked me unconscious, and when I did come to I found the slope was too steep to climb. I was roasted by the heat from the boiling lava and weak and giddy from the blow on my head. I spent all night in that crater and every hour worse things happened in my head. It was like torture in the dungeons of the Inquisition. Every moment it seemed I couldn't stand it an instant longer. Then I had my first lapse of memory and during it I got out of there, I can never tell how. But ever since then I have had a deadly fear of volcanoes. Now, thanks to the operation, my fear is gone. After a few months I'll go back to volcanoes and they'll be just a job to me, like any other. But that's enough about me – how about you? I'm afraid I'm leaving you rather up in the air."

"Honolulu is a busy place," Hal said. "We'll probably find something to do here."

"Well, I have a suggestion. Before you came this morning I had a short call from two of my colleagues at the American Museum. I believe you met them yesterday – Sinclair and Scott."

"Yes, I talked with them," Hal said. "Their project sounds pretty exciting."

"They liked you," Dr Dan said. "And what I told them about you and Roger didn't make them like you any the less. They're looking for some young fellows to help them on their whaling expedition. How would it appeal to you?"

Roger's eyes began to pop with excitement.

"After all," went on Dr Dan, "you'd still be working for the American Museum. Just a change of bosses."

"We don't want a change of bosses," Hal said. "We'd rather go on with you. But since we can't – the whaling sounds great. We'll think about it. Now we're leaving so you can have some rest."

"Well, don't think about it too long. They're leaving in a few days."

The boys walked down the hall, strange emotions churning in their chests.

"What a chance!" exclaimed Roger. "A few days to decide! A few minutes is enough for me."

But Hal, as the older and wiser, felt that the matter must not be decided hastily. In fact, he did not make up his mind until they were out of the front door.

If you enjoyed this book, you might like to read
the other **Willard Price** books in the series:

ARCTIC & SAFARI

⇀ ADVENTURE DOUBLE ⇀

Dive into two action-packed adventures!

Hal and Roger Hunt face danger from all
sides among the ice floes of Greenland in
Arctic Adventure. But is it the killer whales,
the grizzly bears or an evil human who
will be the biggest threat?

And in *Safari Adventure* the boys fly
straight into the jaws of death when they
find themselves hot on the blood-stained
trail of a gang of poachers in Africa.

'Willard Price makes the pulse-rate soar'
INDEPENDENT ON SUNDAY

ISBN 0 099 48772 1

If you enjoyed this book, you might like to read
the other **Willard Price** books in the series:

DIVING & AMAZON
ADVENTURE DOUBLE

Dive into two action-packed adventures!

Hal and Roger Hunt are plunged into the
depths in *Diving Adventure* when their
specimen-collecting trip to the Undersea City
takes a deadly turn.

And in *Amazon Adventure* the brothers are
on a mission to explore uncharted territory
in the Amazon, but when they go off course
in the greatest jungle on earth, it's the
survival of the fittest.

'Willard Price makes the pulse-rate soar'
INDEPENDENT ON SUNDAY

ISBN 0 099 48773 X

ALPHA FORCE

Mission: Survival

SURVIVAL

Alex, Li, Paulo, Hex and Amber are five teenagers on
board a sailing ship crewed by young people from all
over the world. Together they are marooned on a desert
island. And together they must face the ultimate test –
survival! Battling against unbelievable dangers – from
killer komodo dragons to sharks and modern-day pirates
– the five must combine all their knowledge and skills if
they are to stay alive.

The team – Alpha Force – is born . . .

ISBN 0 099 43924 7

If you enjoyed this book, you might like
the Alpha Force series:

Target: Drug Rat

RAT-CATCHER

Alpha Force are an elite team of five highly-skilled
individuals brought together to battle injustice.
Together they join a covert SAS operation in South
America, fighting to catch an evil drugs baron. To gain
information, they infiltrate a tight-knit community of
street kids then head into the isolated mountains where
a terrifying and twisted hunt is to test their individual
skills to the max . . .

ISBN 0 099 43925 5

ALPHA FORCE

Target: Ivory Hunters

HUNTED

Alpha Force head to Namibia to compete in an extreme sports contest. When they discover a horrifying threat to the local wildlife, they snap into action, only to find themselves facing a desperate flight across the African plains, pursued by a group who are prepared to shoot to kill. The team freefall into danger . . .

ISBN 0 099 46425 X

ALPHA FORCE

Target: Toxic Waste

HOSTAGE

Alpha Force have flown to Northern Canada to
investigate reports of illegal dumping of toxic waste.
The team must dive into an icy river, cross the harsh
landscape on snowmobiles and mobilize their caving
skills to complete their mission. But they need all
their courage and determination when they come
face-to-face with a man who is ready to kill
– or take a hostage – to stop them.

The team face their toughest challenge yet . . .

ISBN 0 099 43927 1